Suzannah Dunn

was born in 1963 and lives in L novella and short stories published together under the title *Darker Days Than Usual*, and a highly acclaimed full-length novel, *Quite Contrary*, which was awarded a runner-up prize in the Betty Trask Awards.

SUZANNAH DUNN

Blood Sugar

Flamingo
An Imprint of HarperCollins*Publishers*

flamingo

ORIGINAL

The term 'Original' signifies publication direct into
paperback with no preceding British hardback edition.
The Flamingo Original series publishes fine writing at
an affordable price at the point of first publication.

Flamingo
An Imprint of HarperCollins*Publishers*
77–85 Fulham Palace Road,
Hammersmith, London W6 8JB

First published in Great Britain by Flamingo 1994
9 8 7 6 5 4 3 2 1

Author photograph by Claire McNamee

A catalogue record for this book
is available from the British Library

ISBN 0 00 654707 9

Set in Galliard

Printed in Great Britain by
HarperCollinsManufacturing Glasgow

Acknowledgements

Thanks to the friends who helped: Katie Stead, for the cappuccini and sympathy, and David Supple for the rioja routine; Nick Richmond, for stepping so patiently over and around the manuscript for so long; Chrissie Gittins, for trips and treats; Paul Tebble, for the phone calls; Lynne Sims, for a funny kind of inspiration, twenty years of laughs; and Steve Bryant, for easing me into thirty. Belated thanks for jobs, food and lodgings, and even for my desk, to Carol Painter and Jo Adams, and David and Diane Clark. Thanks to Jonathan Warner for his relentless enthusiasm, and Charlotte Windsor for making everything all right in the end.

1981

....

Beside me, Roz is craning towards a mirror, applying lipstick. The small swelling of her stomach, bound by the navy blue school skirt, presses against the rim of a washbasin. The red stub of lipstick melts onto her lips. I once read in one of the magazines sprouting from Roz's school bag that there is a right way and a wrong way to apply lipstick: *The secret of successful lips*. The article instructed readers to *imagine that you are painting a picture of a pair of lips*: in other words, don't dab. Watching the slow sweep of the lipstick around Roz's mouth, the spread of red to the corners, to the tips of her lips, I realize once again that I am in the presence of an expert.

Beside Roz, Ali is brushing her hair. Ali's hair is dark and sleek and smooth; it beats with each stroke like a silky wing in the heavy summer air. We are not supposed to brush our hair over the basins. We were informed of this during assembly one morning by Miss Killick, the Senior Mistress: 'This practice blocks the pipes and must cease.' The washbasins, like toilet bowls, are white and whispering water. The basin below me is drained but damp, retaining an icy film. The washbasins are made of enamel, the material of teeth. They are hung with plugs, small black amulets on chains; and they bear the words *Armitage Shanks*. It seems to me that *Shanks* is a mixture of *Shucks* and *Thanks*, an expression of resignation. The washroom is quiet. We are alone. When the bell rang a few minutes ago it brought a flurry of small girls from the row of navy blue cubicle doors behind us. They came to the basins, their eyes averted, and whisked their hands in trickles of lukewarm water before leaving.

Roz lowers the waxy red stub and presses her lips together, printing lower lip with top, and top with lower. Her scrutiny in

7

the mirror spins into anxiety, disappointment, submission. Turning away, she raises her chin so that the new red line is hard and shiny in the soft white skin of her face. She hands the lipstick wordlessly to Ali. Ali examines it briefly and returns it, shaking her head.

'Not your colour,' Roz admits, sympathetic.

She waves it at me, but I decline. It is too hot this afternoon for a fatty smear of lipstick. I leave the line of basins and lean against the icy white radiator. The washroom is the sole cool place in the school. There is a glimmer of daylight frozen above us in the long sliver of opaque glass, the narrow pane on the high sill. During the winter the washroom is warm and we collect around the radiator, slumped in our coats against the coiled pipes, each of us immobile and thickened like chrysalids.

Ali reaches into the bag at her feet. She lifts a make-up bag and takes a lipstick: her own, her own colour, a different colour. Somehow Ali is a different colour from Roz. During the summer, Ali is the colour of caramel. Her lips are full, unlike Roz's, and they are chocolate. Despite the identical shade of brown hair, Ali is dark whilst Roz is fair. During the summer, Ali darkens and Roz blushes. The milky skin on Roz's long thin nose bursts with freckles which she buries in snowy powder. She wants to be blonde. She has a blonde streak framing her face: the result of a spittle of dye from a bottle in her mother's bathroom cabinet.

You're blonder than me, I tell her.

But I am not blonde at all. My hair is the colour of sludge, but I am not dark like Ali because my skin is so fair and I am not fair like Roz because I have no freckles. I am pale-skinned and black-eyed.

Tubercular, says Mum.

Lipstuck, Ali pouts at the mirror. The dark pupils of her eyes loom between eyelids blackened with pencil. She looks like Cleopatra. She was plain, once, when she was younger, but not now. Roz's eyes are green. I had never seen green eyes before I met Roz; I had assumed that they existed solely as descriptions in books or untruths in passports. There is something creepy about green eyes: *the green-eyed monster*, unnatural, unpredictable. Roz's eyelashes, coated with mascara, protrude like tiny black hairy legs around the shiny shell of each eye.

I have known Roz and Ali for six years. I met them on our first day here: we were *new girls*. But Roz and Ali came here together from primary school, and have known each other since they were five. So, in a sense, I was the new girl. Our first lesson, on our first day, was Science.

'Groups of three, please,' our teacher said. Roz and Ali, standing together, were two. Our teacher wanted us to collect earthworms in buckets. He moved amongst us on the school field, striking our heads with his fingertips: *One, two, three*. Roz, Ali, me. We stood together, shivering in the wind.

'Come on,' said Roz eventually, reluctantly; dipping her fingertips into the bucket of water and sprinkling the ground as we had been instructed. Then she bent and peered into the grass. Suddenly she squealed. 'Hold the bucket closer,' she shouted to Ali.

In the old days, Ali was tubby. Or shapeless, perhaps. But not now, although she is a different shape from Roz and me. Somehow she is smooth; somehow, when she is dancing with us at parties, she ripples. She once told me that her mother had been a model.

'What kind of model?' I asked, surprised.

Ali stared at me with her round brown eyes.

'No, sorry,' I said, 'I didn't mean . . .'

What did I mean? I was thinking of the stories of the models in the sixties, of Twiggy and Jean Shrimpton, who became rich and famous. Ali's mum is not rich and famous. She works part-time in the Dressmaking Department at Hinton's Department Store. Often I go into Hinton's on Saturdays to escape the wind and rain on the High Street, and to be greeted by Ali's mum's grin of pins. It is not embarrassing for Ali's mum to brandish a tape measure because she is as slim as the pointed tips of her shoes. The shoes chirp on the floor when she crosses the Dressmaking Department to greet me. She is too nice for Hinton's.

9

Now Roz nudges me. 'What are you going to wear to the party?' she asks me, as I reach for my bag.

One of our classmates has been persuaded to have a party tomorrow night whilst his parents are away.

'I don't know.' As usual, I have nothing to wear.

'I need a new pair of trousers,' she muses.

So do I; but, unlike Roz, I will be told by Mum that I *Must do without*.

'I'm going shopping this weekend,' Roz adds.

Mothers are supposed to love their children; but my mum says that *Children should learn to fend for themselves*. She says that the maternal instinct is over-rated, although she likes small babies.

All that stuff about lifting cars off babies, she says: *well, it's true for babies, because babies are so vulnerable, but not for older children*.

So, in the unlikely event of such an accident, I will remain trapped beneath the car whilst I learn to fend for myself.

Roz's mum works as a nurse: Roz says that this is so that she can provide *The little extras*. The little extras, for Roz, are new clothes. Roz's dad pays maintenance. He is a policeman. He takes Roz and her little brother on holiday every summer to Tenerife.

Roz turns away from the mirrors. 'So, anyway, what shall we do now?'

She means, Shall we go home? We are supposed to go to the library for Free Study. Usually we go to Current-Affairs-And-General-Studies at the end of the afternoon but not on Fridays because our tutor – Mr Allan, the Headmaster – spends Friday afternoons arranging Saturday Morning Detention. (He spends the afternoon reviewing the worst offences of the week before summoning the offenders to his office, and informing their parents by telephone). There are no Current Affairs on Wednesdays, either, because on Wednesdays we have Games. Both Current Affairs and Games are under the same heading in the prospectus: *Extra-curricular Activities*. Mr Allan says that extra-curricular activities are *broadening*. I agree with him about the Current Affairs but disagree about the Games. Games means mini-skirts, cold winter winds, hard hockey sticks, and then mould on the shower curtains: in other words, degradation, intimidation, organized violence, injury, and hypothermia. I plan to take the Government to the European Court of Human Rights on the issue of compulsory physical education as soon as I find time.

Everyone, except me, hates Current Affairs: *A waste of time*, they say. In Current Affairs we discuss topics: euthanasia, or public funding for the arts. No one, except me, participates in these discussions, and I participate because I dislike silence. Mr Allan addresses me with enthusiasm, his gold-rimmed rectangular glasses winking at me in the afternoon sunlight.

'No Affairs today,' Roz confirms cheerfully, hugging her bag. 'No Affairs with gorgeous Mr Glinty-Glasses.'

Ali smirks. 'Mr Gorgeous *what?*' she murmurs, moving behind Roz towards the door.

'Mr Gorgeous *nothing*,' I insist as I join them. 'Gorgeous Mr Nothing.'

I do not like Mr Allan; I do not believe in Mr Allan. He implies to us in Current Affairs that if we *play fair*, if we *play by the book*, if we *pay our dues*, then our lives will be rewarding and successful; but I know that this is not true. Rewarded and successful, he is plagued by anxieties about the thin end of the wedge. And those wedges are fattening with each Current Affairs discussion. Yesterday afternoon, the problem was gay rights activism.

'Homosexuals,' he said, smiling his nervous smile; 'What if homosexuals wanted to visit this class to advocate their point of view?'

Advocate their point of view? I frowned into Mr Allan's glasses. He had informed us that the issue was theoretical: no gay rights activists had proposed a visit to our school. This did not surprise me: who would want to visit a school run by Mr Allan?

'But if they did,' Mr Allan said proudly, 'I would not allow it.'

'Why not?' I asked him.

The lenses switched on. He smiled at me. 'Because they might convert you,' he said, pleased.

11

'Convert me?' I peered at him. 'How? Will there be a slide show?' My classmates tittered appreciatively. Beside me, Roz's blonde streak flashed through her brown hair.

'That's enough,' said Mr Allan to the class. He was no longer smiling. There was the usual faint note of panic in his voice.

I shrugged: 'You let a marine come here last week to talk to us about joining the navy.'

Behind me, someone screamed with laughter: everyone knows that the marine, directed by the secretary to wait for Mr Allan in a reception room at the end of the corridor, had waited by mistake in the broom store. He was discovered by a Fifth Former who had been sent to fetch a dustpan and brush.

Mr Allan twitched in his chair, lenses glinting. Silence thumped through the room.

I shrugged again: 'I might have been converted into a member of the armed forces.'

Suddenly Mr Allan laughed, eager to joke, to present himself as a man with a sense of humour.

I sighed at him. 'No pasarán,' I said solemnly.

Now the washroom door explodes open as Roz reaches for the handle. It flies past her and crashes into the wall. Roz reels, her bag held tightly against her chest, and steps backwards onto Ali's toes. Lucy comes towards us through the doorway, smiling.

'Lucy,' says Roz faintly: a familiar mixture of surprise, disdain, resignation.

Lucy steps past us towards the row of mirrors. 'Hi,' she says, glancing at herself, and jabbing at her spiky gold crown of hair. 'How about a trip into town this evening to the Patisserie?'

Lucy has a car on permanent loan from her mother.

'Yes,' I agree quickly.

Ali's eyebrows flex upwards in delight.

'Good,' says Lucy. 'Chocks away, then. Eight o'clock.' And suddenly she is back at the door. Ankle socks are wriggling beneath her heels and disappearing into her shoes.

I confide, 'Lucy, we're going home.' Will she come, with the car?

'Just let me fetch my stuff from the art room,' she says. There are flecks of paint on her thin bare legs. She is a walking Jackson Pollock. Her hand, on the door, is dark with bruises of ink. She is encased in a long thin green cardigan which is disfigured by holes. How has the cardigan escaped detection by Miss Killick? The rules, rigorously enforced by Miss Killick, decree that the school colour is navy blue: *There must be no aquamarine*.

And Mr Allan classifies cardigans as *Leisure Wear*. He is keen to impress upon us that *There is a time and place for everything;* he reminds us during assemblies that *Leisure Wear will only be tolerated in the vicinity of the Games Department*. Sometimes he adds as an explanation that *We are not in America*. He is more tolerant of white lab coats: Sixth Form scientists can wear them everywhere in school except the dining hall; but in the dining hall they are *Off-putting*: Science at lunch time is *Inappropriate*. He is enthusiastic that clothes should be appropriate: *I wouldn't wear pyjamas to a Parents' Evening, would I?*

And we do not reply, but snigger behind his back, enthralled at the prospect.

'Before we all go rushing off into town tonight,' Roz says loudly, impatiently, 'do we know whether we have any money?'

When she says *we all* in a loud and impatient voice, she means Lucy. She is searching slowly through her bag for her purse.

'I have some,' I reply. 'For emergencies.' Mum insists each morning that I must take some money for emergencies.

Is cheesecake an emergency? Roz regards me dubiously.

I reassure her: 'Really, I have enough.'

'We'll survive,' offers Lucy, swooping towards us from the doorframe.

Roz glances at Ali.

'We'll survive,' murmurs Ali.

Roz scowls, pinching the rim of her purse until it yields. She peers inside. 'Good,' she pronounces, poking at banknotes. 'Money. So, eight o'clock.'

We follow Lucy through the doorway. 'My mum has Celebration

13

Cakes between six and half-seven,' she calls to us. *Celebration Cakes* is an evening class: Lucy's mum will need a baby-sitter for Lucy's brother.

Celebration Cakes: I wrinkle my nose. 'Tell your mum to go easy on the icing.'

Lucy laughs, her paint-stippled limbs spinning in the gloom. 'She doesn't go there for the icing. She goes there so that I have to stay at home with the baby. She suspects that, otherwise, I spend my spare time roaming Gloucester Avenue and vandalizing a selection of quality bus shelters.'

'A slight exaggeration, surely, Lucy,' I admonish: I am sure that Lucy's mum never suspects anyone of anything. I remember her enthusiasm when she told me about the Celebration Cakes: 'Some people are so very clever, aren't they? You should see some of the cakes. It's something that I've always wanted to be able to do.'

Lucy halts at the entrance to the Art and Craft corridor. 'Oh yes? And why else would my mum go to Celebration Cakes? What has she ever had to celebrate?'

Without Lucy, we continue on our way through the main corridor, heading for the car park. We hear the voice of a teacher in a classroom somewhere: loud, emphatic, grudging. Roz pushes against a door labelled *Emergency Exit*.

'Emergency-Exits-are-for-Emergencies,' I chant, quoting the rules, reaching forward to assist Roz with the handle.

'And for Exits, presumably,' she replies.

The door yields and the three of us step together from the corridor into the courtyard.

'Freedom,' sighs Roz, glancing at the sky.

'Nearly,' I correct, closing the door behind us. The courtyard is dense with buildings: Teaching Rooms, Science Labs, Language Labs. On the hot concrete walls there are bibs of dampness beneath gutters and sills. The huge windows bear dusty watermarks. The paving stones, like the flat roofs of the lower buildings, collect a scum of debris: exercise books, splayed in puddles after a feathery fall; small crouched crabs of orange peel; and sometimes, more spectacularly, an item of furniture, usually a chair, legless. Ten years ago, when this school was built, people said that it was *modern*.

Ten years ago, this was a grammar school, *the* grammar school.

'Escape,' lusts Roz.

We tip-toe across the courtyard, protected from view by the pampas grass that rears from the black water of the Biology Pond.

'I can hear footsteps,' warns Ali.

We pause, and peep. Deborah Steiner is walking across the courtyard towards the Language Labs.

'We're okay,' I confirm, unnecessarily, with relief.

In the distance, Deborah Steiner turns and smiles at us, and briefly raises a hand. We respond reluctantly, uncertainly, with tense smiles. She draws open the door to the Language Labs and drifts away across the threshold.

'Debbie Steiner,' mutters Roz, although nothing remains of Deborah Steiner except the slapping of the door into its steel frame. Roz is puzzled by Deborah Steiner: two years ago, Deborah Steiner was a new girl in our class, too old to be new. She was colourless, she wore no make-up, and she introduced herself as *Deborah*. Now, two years later, she is less new but still *Deborah*, still colourless, and still without make-up; but somehow it does not matter. Nowadays the pupils of her eyes are smooth stones in shallow water; and the pony-tail, the long cool fountain at the top of her head, has been untied and cut so that it swings and shines around her face. Contrary to the laws of nature, Deborah Steiner has *developed* a baby face. For Roz, I suspect, this is the-thin-end-of-the-wedge: for Roz, beauty necessitates black rakings of mascara and stumps of bleeding lipstick. For beauty, Roz pays dues.

At the end of each term, Deborah Steiner's report resembles the first page of the telephone directory: lots of As. Last year she received a prize at Speech Day for exam results.

'Well done,' Mr Allan said to her on the stage, sounding relieved rather than pleased: he had been unable to prevent the recent conversion of the school from grammar to comprehensive, and was

15

frantic to display *A continuing commitment to excellence*. He flapped the book token at Deborah, and peered off-stage.

In the audience, Mum shifted on the seat next to me. 'Who's that?' she asked.

'Mr Allan,' I replied. Deborah Steiner was stepping soundlessly from the stage after the twitch of applause.

Mum rattled with impatience. 'Don't be silly; who's the girl?' 'A new girl,' I replied.

Mum's tongue snapped with irritation. Later, when the orchestra players were fluttering in noisy preparation on the stage, she nudged me. 'There's that new girl again,' she said.

Deborah Steiner was solo violin.

'So, she's musical as well,' said Mum, delighted by the discovery. Mum describes people as *musical* as if they are clockwork.

'Some people have all the talent, don't they,' she said, implying that I have none.

Roz's green scrutiny is shimmering all over the distant door. 'Debbie Steiner,' she murmurs.

'Off to the Language Labs,' confirms Ali. Ali studies French. Deborah Steiner studies French, also German and Spanish. We all study English, and Deborah Steiner sits across the classroom from us, frowning over the texts. In the Language Labs, linguists sit alone in booths, remote in headphones, murmuring. I learned French for O level; but I remember nothing from a year of German lessons except how to ask for a kilo of potatoes, although I have no idea what a kilo looks like. Mum is dismayed that I plan to study English at university.

What's the use of all this English? she protests. *You already speak English.* Then she snorts, *Or, at best, a version.*

At Speech Day Mr Allan hailed Deborah Steiner as a *polyglot*; and, ignorant of the meaning of the word, Roz and I tittered because it did not sound like a compliment.

We resume our escape from the courtyard. To reach the car park we must pass through the Biology corridor. Roz walks ahead of us to the Science building and snatches at the door, hauling it

16

towards us. On the threshold the hairy mat is thick with strands of grass and soil snatched from rugby boots. As she turns to me from the sudden darkness of the corridor, Roz's small black pupils bloom inside her green irises. She is turning to warn me of the pulse of a pair of stubby stiletto heels in the distance. 'Miss Killick,' I conclude, my arm flailing behind me to prevent Ali from joining us.

'Girls!'

Too late. I freeze.

'Girls, stay there.'

Roz rotates towards the voice, the smooth soles of her shoes jammed and squealing on the tiles. I detect that she is eager for a confrontation. Miss Killick halts in the corridor, facing us, and erects a buffer of folded arms across her chest. 'The gruesome threesome,' she smiles the embittered Killick smile. She is wearing the Killick tweed twin-set. The skirt is distressingly short, and her knees in brown stockings look like walnuts. 'Where were you going, girls?'

I shrug.

Roz sighs. 'To the car park.'

Ali and I turn to Roz, incredulous: the car park is *out of bounds*; the penalty is litter duty on the school field each lunch time for a week. Roz glances at us, and shrugs, careless.

'Rozalyn Smith,' continues Miss Killick, 'you know very well that the presence of pupils is forbidden in the car park during the school day.'

The voice is thick with threat.

Roz looks at me; I look at Roz; we suppress laughter, clamping our lower lips with our front teeth. I know that we are laughing at the same notion: *presents* in the car park, brightly wrapped, tied with ribbons, piled around the cars.

'The car park is strictly out of bounds.'

Strictly out of bounds: surely somewhere is either out of bounds or it is not out of bounds? How can it be *strictly* out of bounds? It is Miss Killick who is strict; strictly Miss Killick. For generations she has been spitting strict rules into disinfected school corridors, and she has been more vigilant than usual since the conversion of our school from Grammar to Comprehensive. She tells us that we *Look like comprehensive girls* whenever we flout the rules regarding uniform. Perhaps comprehensives have a problem with car parks; or perhaps, for Miss Killick, car park means bike shed, and bike shed means cigarettes and sex. I cannot imagine that anyone would want to go to our draughty damp bike sheds for cigarettes or sex.

Roz turns cheerfully to Miss Killick. 'We needed some paper from Lucy's car.'

'Paper? Piffle.'

Roz bites hard into a smile.

Miss Killick's mottled grey perm jerks towards me. 'And what is so very amusing, Eulalia Blaney?'

No one calls me Eulalia, no one except Mum. Eulalia is my given name, given to me by Mum. Dad is baffled: one morning, when he left for work, I was a nameless baby; and when he returned in the evening I was Eulalia. He says that there had been talk of Jane but no mention of Eulalia. He had never heard of Eulalia. Mum says that men are no good with names. She says that she saw Eulalia in a book.

Yes, I protest, *But I've seen the name Genghis in a few books and I'm not planning to use it for my baby.*

She says that Eulalia is *unusual*.

Really? I reply sarcastically.

Sometimes she tries to blame me: *You looked like a Eulalia.*

At least I am not plain Jane Blaney like my sister.

Most people call me Lalie. My baby sister calls me Lala. Roz has been known to call me Eu: *Eu Blaney*; *You! Blaney!* Dad prefers *Eul*, which, unfortunately, to me, suggests *Yule log*. (I am pleased that although Mum is Margaret, Gran insists upon Daisy; or worse, and much more appropriately, *Daze*).

Miss Killick likes to call me Eulalia Blaney. And she likes *Rozalyn Smith,* and *Alison Mortimer*; and, worse still, *Lucy-Ann Evans*. I wonder about Miss Killick's own name: I suspect that she is an Agnes or a Hilary. I doubt that she is a Gladys or an Eileen. Looking

18

at the stiff tweed buffer of bosom, I wonder whether she is a Miranda or Dorinda or Colette: old-fashioned names but silk-stocking sensual. I smile to myself. I can be sure that she is not a Hayley.

Miss Killick turns around to investigate a clatter at the end of the corridor. Lucy is sauntering through the navy blue gloom towards us.

'Lucy-Ann Evans,' says Miss Killick.

Lucy is wearing a large straw hat. Her face is lit by a pale moon of brim. Her chin rests on a bouquet of pink satin ribbon.

'Lucy-Ann Evans, please remove that article from your head.' Miss Killick's rules stipulate that hats are an offence.

Lucy halts, and the brim wobbles. She is smiling. I expect a curtsy or a pirouette. 'I've tried wearing it everywhere else apart from my head but it doesn't look quite right,' she says lightly.

Miss Killick's lips sink over bony teeth. 'Remove it,' she barks. Lucy sighs noisily and pulls in exasperation at the bow.

Miss Killick is inflating herself. 'I am sick of this disregard for school rules.' The cry is for no one in particular. Tension scars her forehead. 'This wanton disregard.' Wanton? I hope that she will say *tawdry*: she said tawdry last year when Lucy wore a scarlet dress to a school performance of *Charley's Aunt*.

'And I suppose you all think this is highly amusing.'

It never crossed my mind. There is nothing amusing at school; and nothing amusing about Miss Killick except the Senior Citizen perm and the name: *Killit*. Even the name is less amusing for us now, after six years.

'Who do you think you are?' she barks at us.

Who does she think *she* is? She hobbles through these corridors, snapping at children. She is Senior Mistress in a local comprehensive: she is not Prime Minister; nor doctor, lawyer, bank manager; nor midwife, mechanic, potter, restaurateur. She is no one, nothing. Senior Mistress: Dominatrix. She is nothing; especially, in her own eyes, since the school has become comprehensive.

Nowadays no one becomes a teacher in a secondary school if there is an alternative. No one claims in Careers Guidance to want to be a teacher: tinker, tailor, soldier, teacher. No one wants to return to school after university. Each September the new recruits to the teaching staff are 2.2, grade C. They suffer colds throughout the first year, deserted by their antibodies; and in the second year, when the probationary year is over and there is nothing else to do, when the colds have improved, they marry. Sometimes they marry each other. When the women marry, they change their names, become lost in men's names. When teachers marry each other, they replicate: once there was Barstow and McGuire, now there is Barstow and Barstow. Barstow and Barstow sounds like an estate agency. When the men marry, they put on weight but lose it several years later during divorce.

Most of our teachers leave. The women leave after two years of marriage to have babies: Mr Allan eventually announces in Assembly that there has been *A happy event*, and we sing an appropriate hymn. Mr Allan organizes hymns for Assembly despite hinting to us during Current Affairs that he is a non-believer. Roz tells me that it is his job to maintain Christianity. According to Mr Allan, male teachers leave for industry. So there are no hymns. I imagine that our ex-teachers in industry are stoking boilers. Or I imagine the Chemists with test-tubes and the Physicists with cog-wheels. Our History teacher left last term for industry. Perhaps he is working in Personnel.

I should have left school last year for the local Sixth Form College. The college has no uniforms, no opinion on aquamarine. It has a canteen, silvery with steaming urns of tea; students do not queue in silence in the playground at lunch time, waiting for permission from a teacher to enter the dining hall for meatballs and sponge and beakers of water. The students attend college for lectures, not for Assemblies and Games. The Principal is a bureaucrat concerned with time-tables, with City and Guilds and work placements, not with moral character.

'It's two buses away,' said Mum. 'Think of winter evenings.'

The local college is on the one-way system, on the by-pass, beyond the industrial estate, far away from here.

There is nothing wrong with my moral character. I stare at Miss Killick, at the sharp edges of the small silver crucifix lodged on a bony collar below the pair of worm-pale lips. There is nothing wrong with me; there is everything wrong with Miss Killick. She works in Education but she dictates with *don't, can't, won't.*

Mum tells me to *Bear with her because she has been stuck in schools for a long time:* a rare moment of kindness from Mum, reserved by uncanny coincidence for my enemy.

I suggest that she should not be in a school if she does not like people. Mum insists that in the olden days there were few options for *A woman in her position*: when she says *Woman in her position,* she means spinster. She succeeds in making me feel guilty: it is said that Miss Killick's fiancé was killed during the war, in the last week of the war or perhaps on the last day. Was this the point at which Miss Killick became a spinster? When did she cease to be a normal woman and become a spinster?

Bear with her, says Mum, *because what else can she do for a living now?* I suggest that she retires.

There has been talk at school of early retirement. The early retirement of senior members of staff and the lack of new recruits will leave us with the recent ex-probationers: the women enormous with pregnancy and then suddenly gone, like burst balloons; and the men waxing and waning with marriage and divorce.

The car park is the-thin-end-of-the-wedge for Miss Killick; and there are no wedges allowed in Miss Killick's school. (No wedgies, either, because Miss Killick decreed several years ago that *There must be no wedge heels because they are dangerous on staircases and unseemly.* Miss Killick is dangerous on staircases and unseemly). Now she is staring at Lucy, who is picking at a glittery crust of paint on her hands. Ali's brown gaze bounces between them. Miss Killick's pupils, magnified by prescription lenses, are biting into ghostly grey haloes of iris.

Is she afraid of us? But why? Why are we such a threat? Why is it so important that we do not leave half an hour early on a midsummer Friday afternoon? Are the consequences so dire? She is trying to smile a superior smile, but the mouth is edging with difficulty across the face. Perhaps she is jealous of us: next year we will be leaving here. We will live away, in cities, despite her recommendations of colleges in the countryside in Wales or Lancaster or North Yorkshire where we can be free from distractions. She will remain here. She has been here since the day the Chairman of the Education Committee arrived from the Council Offices under a hail of popping flashbulbs to force a veil from the inauguration plaque in the lobby. The Chairman has gone to wherever Chairmen go, but a small gilt frame haunts the lobby with peace-in-our-time black and white. His fifteen minutes of fame has become ten years of obscurity. The framed photograph is almost indistinguishable from a light switch, and the underside is damp with mushrooms of chewing gum. But Miss Killick remains with us, flesh and blood. Very fleshy, very bloody.

'There can be no reason for this constant rebellion,' she says, staring hard at Lucy to imply that Lucy lacks the capacity to reason. 'If you continue in this manner you will all jeopardize your chances of becoming prefects next year. At four o'clock I shall be looking at the gate and I expect to see you all there, leaving school at the proper time. If not, you can expect an interview with Mr Allan on Monday morning. In the meantime, I am going to speak to Mr MacKenzie about you.' She turns and stalks away, the noise of each step rivalling the loud lamentations of a teacher in a nearby classroom.

Lucy sighs and the hat shoots on a spurt of pink ribbon towards the ceiling. 'What's wrong with a bit of colour in life?'

Roz flashes, 'Colour? Life? What about home?' She is eager to blame someone. Her eyes contract. 'And pink-and-green-should-not-be-seen.'

I like anything different but I admit to myself that I am not sure about pink-and-green.

'Well,' I say hastily, 'Mr MacKenzie will no doubt be worried

22

speechless by our misdemeanours.' Mr MacKenzie is Head of Sixth Form. Miss Killick implies a solidarity between them, but we know that they despise each other. They both teach English: Mr MacKenzie is Head of Department, and our teacher; Miss Killick teaches juniors, and concentrates on War Poetry. It is obvious that Miss Killick finds Mr MacKenzie distasteful, and we suspect that she blames him for everything: he is excitable, lax; and not even English, but Scottish. Mr Mac*Kinzie*, I call him, to accentuate the Scottish.

For Miss Killick, English is Jane Austen; for Mr MacKenzie, English includes Greek Tragedy and Magic Realism. They share Shakespeare, with Mr MacKenzie favouring the bawdy jokes. I watch Miss Killick disappear from the end of the corridor into the Administration Block, and it occurs to me that Mr MacKenzie's sole concern will be that he was not invited to leave with us.

·*Let's escape this bloody place*, he says, on hot afternoons; striding from the classroom, scooping his shirt sleeves from his wrists to his elbows and then beckoning to us with a wave of a short thick forearm. *What are we, monkeys in a cage?*

English requires no blackboards or bunsen burners: so, on summer afternoons we follow him from the classroom to the school field and sit around him on the grass, fingering dandelions and daisies.

On cold days we remain indoors with Mr MacKenzie, but we rarely sit at our desks. Mr MacKenzie says that it is inappropriate to sit behind a desk to discuss Catharsis. Sometimes we sit in the classroom in a circle, our desks pushed against the wall; and sometimes we sit outside the classroom on the floor in the corridor. We are not supposed to sit in the corridor: Miss Killick says that we are a fire hazard. We are not supposed to discuss Catharsis, either, but Miss Killick is oblivious; and, anyway, she is not Head of Department, so she has no say. Our set text is *A Midsummer Night's Dream*, but Mr MacKenzie prefers to discuss tragedy and tragic heroes.

The syllabus demands that we read Chaucer, but Mr MacKenzie

23

says that fiction is about possibilities. So, sometimes, he drags thick black curtains across the classroom windows and projects slides onto the dirty white walls: Rodin's smooth stone prayer, or the yellow clotted fields of Van Gogh. He talks above the noise of the projector about form and content, appearance and reality. *Possibilities* are different from *Opportunities*: Miss Killick is in charge of Opportunities, of Careers. She stocks her office with colourful leaflets entitled *Opportunities For Speech Therapists, Looking Forward To Accountancy,* and *Why Be A Cartographer?* Mr MacKenzie's classroom walls, by contrast, are dark with photographs of migrant workers starving in the dust of the American Mid-West. His office is often noisy with Jazz or Rock and Roll.

'Jazz and Rock and Roll were slang for sex,' he told us, once. I was unable to resist adding, 'Similarly, Dinner and Dance.'

After Miss Killick's departure, the corridor is quiet but not peaceful. Ali shudders. Roz stares at the floor; bitter eyes beneath plum eyelids. It occurs to me that Mr MacKenzie will envy us our trip to the Patisserie. He has a sweet tooth. He is never without a packet of jelly babies. He is an ex-smoker. *My lifesavers*, he says when he offers them to us, reaching towards us with a noisy fistful of membranous cellophane. We do not select the red babies because they are Mr MacKenzie's favourites. We know that they are his favourites because his teeth are red; no longer yellow with nicotine but red with babies.

Roz glances at her watch. 'I don't care what I do, but I'm *not* going to the library.' Each word was brief with panic.

'Roz,' I sigh regretfully, 'if we go out onto the field, the Jolly Jackboot will find us again.'

'I don't care. I can't face the library.'

The Library: the rows of low yellow bookcases, the cacti in yoghurt pots, and a Lowry print in a white wooden frame on the wall. This afternoon the windows will be levered outwards into the hot air of the courtyard.

'We can all sit behind the Atlas shelf and talk,' I suggest.

Roz shrinks against the wall.

'Roz . . .'

'You don't know how much I hate it here,' she wails.

As a reflex I check dates but conclude that hormones are not responsible. I lay my hand on Roz's shoulder. 'Of course I know,' I purr, close to an ear. 'You know I know.' I squeeze the shoulder, to soothe. 'I hate it here, too, remember?'

'But it's all right for you,' she wails.

What does she mean?

'It's all right for you,' she repeats, turning from the wall, anguished. 'Because there's Mr MacKenzie and everything.'

'What do you mean?'

'You understand it all, you like it all, it's what you want to do.'

'What?'

'Books. I hate books. I just want to get out of here and be a lawyer or something.'

'But you like *Catcher In The Rye*.'

'Everyone likes *Catcher In The Rye*.'

Affection trickles through me. 'Come on,' I coax with a smile, 'twenty-five minutes in the library – twenty minutes by the time we arrive – and then we can go home.'

She concedes with a petulant, resentful expression: a Roz expression. Lucy resumes the swinging of the hat.

'Lucy,' I enquire, 'are you coming to the library?'

The hat swoops towards our feet. 'No.'

'Oh.' The hat soars. 'Where are you going, then?'

'The Art Room, I suppose.'

Of course: the Art Room, Lucy's refuge. I do not understand the Art Room: the chaos of open cupboards; the persistent, staining dust; the gilt on paper and plaster, dried and shrunk; the alchemy worked in small pots with stiff brushes.

'Ali?'

Ali smiles politely. 'The Typing Room.'

The Typing Room?

'There's a Typing Room?' Roz is Roz again: indignant, intrigued, demanding an explanation.

25

Ali shrugs off our attention. 'Yes. With machines.'

'I never knew,' continues Roz, with gusto.

'Six machines, I think.'

'You *did* know,' I tell Roz. 'We were sent there once to look for some photocopying paper.'

Roz glares at me. 'Surely I know what I know.'

'Anyway,' says Ali, 'I could do some practice.'

I flick my gaze towards Ali. 'Nice.' I did not know that Ali could type.

Beside me, the green-eyed monster is puffing, 'I didn't know you could type.'

Ali shrugs again. 'I taught myself on my mum's typewriter.'

Roz and I would like to be able to type. Our mothers have told us that typing is something to fall back on. But Roz's mum trained as a nurse, and she falls back on nursing. What about my mum, a housewife? Does she fall back on husband and children? Roz and I could have learned to type in the Fifth Form but the course was reserved for those who were not taking many exams. Last year, in our year, there was a boy on the course who professed an interest in business and computers, but usually the class is full of girls who have been studying social biology and domestic science in order to learn about contraception and nutrition.

Roz teases her index finger between my ribs. 'So what are we going to do in the library? Practise reading?'

I twist away from the finger. Roz is right: going to the library now is a waste of time. And since when have I done what Miss Killick has told me to do? 'This is ridiculous,' I announce. 'I'm going home.'

'But what about Killick,' Roz says wearily, 'and High Noon at four o'clock?'

Stepping towards the door, I look back over my shoulder. 'She won't know. She'll forget. She'll be busy with someone else.'

The three of them are still standing together, surly and sceptical.

'What's the worst that she can do to you?' I plead, turning to face them.

26

Suddenly Lucy sniffs a little laugh. 'She can jeopardize our chances of becoming prefects,' she says, very carefully. The hat lurches on the ribbon.

'I wasn't ever going to be a prefect,' I agree as she joins me.

'Of course you'll be a prefect,' Roz calls indignantly, hurrying to us.

'No I won't.'

'Yes you will.'

'No I won't.'

Roz is laughing, her head tilted backwards on her shoulders so that a long pale skein of neck unfurls between chin and collar. 'Yes you will. We'll all be prefects. There aren't many of us in the Upper Sixth. No one fails to make the list.'

'But I'll refuse.'

Roz's reddened lips close softly. 'Oh yes?' She is twinkling with sarcasm.

'Seriously.'

'Seriously?' She halts; and everyone halts. 'Seriously?'

'Yes.'

'Why?' Her features glow with dismay.

'It's exploitative.' I stand in front of them, feeling conspicuous.

Roz deflates noisily with a sigh. 'Oh don't start, Lalie.' This is a familiar refrain.

'Seriously,' I counter: another familiar refrain. 'Think about it, Roz. They're only interested in us when it suits them: not only is it cheap labour, but it's a way of keeping all of us in line.'

'So?' Wearily, Roz resumes her pace towards me; and, in the corner of my eye, Ali and Lucy whirr with unspecific movement.

'So that's how the system perpetuates itself.' I am backing away from them. 'So I can't do it.'

Roz smiles. 'Think of England.'

'You'll be doing their dirty work for them,' I warn.

Roz sighs. 'But it'll be a laugh. Why do you have to be so serious? It's our one chance for a laugh in this place in seven long years. For once we can tell everyone else what to do.'

'Exactly.' I do not want to admit that I am tempted. I would love to send the pack of preening Third Formers from the washroom each lunch time.

Roz is pleading with me: 'It's for one year, one year, that's all. And of course it's bad, but it'll change eventually, like everything, given time.'

I do not reply. There is no reply that will not venture elsewhere and snipe at more of Roz than her hopes for prefectdom. I remain silent in the hope that this will communicate my disgust.

'And we can sit in the back row in assembly,' Roz continues frantically, 'and we can eat in the Staff Dining Room.'

Lucy begins to tap her lower lip with an inky tie-dyed fingertip. 'They'll go mad.'

She means that Mr Allan and Miss Killick will not be pleased when I refuse to be a prefect. Mr Allan and Miss Killick insist that it is a *duty and a privilege* to be a prefect: not sometimes a duty and sometimes a privilege; but both, simultaneously. How can a duty be a privilege? Surely it is a contradiction in terms. I used to hear *duty and privilege* at Guides, and in war films: words spoken around a flag. Duty and privilege, and Queen and country: whenever I hear *Queen*, I think of postage stamps; whenever I hear *country*, I think of weather maps and the weather man telling us with don't-shoot-the-messenger belligerence that there will be rain in most areas by six o'clock. Queen and country: post-boxes and rain.

Mr Allan will not go mad at me. I know that Mr Allan will appeal to my better nature. Which implies that I have a better nature, and that it is responsive to his appeals. I doubt him on both counts. He will invite me into his office, past the huge desk to the low table – a coffee table without coffee – and the low chairs: Casual Corner. I will drown in the cushions of a low chair and lose sight of him across the table, through the leaves of a begonia. Then he will loom through the leaves and ask for *A moment or two of your time*: a ploy, a plot, a technique perfected by Jehovah's Witnesses or Moonies or the Department Store woman on the wrong side of the perfume counter with a grenade of sample perfume. Crossing his legs, releasing pale shin between trouser and sock, he will explain that he has heard that I am having some difficulties with the idea of becoming a prefect.

'No difficulties,' I will reply: 'I don't want to be one.'

'May I ask why?' His chin will pivot on his fingertips, as if he is praying for my soul. The *may-I-ask?* is asked before I can refuse, out from behind the begonia before I can duck.

I will tell him that I do not believe in the system.

'System?' The tone will be polite, indulgent. 'System? There is no system. There is me, you, and the rest of us, teachers and pupils: no system.'

He will force a psychiatric smile: *System, what system? Footsteps, what footsteps?*

Does he believe this? *This won't hurt*: he is like a dentist drunk on his own gases.

But I *feel* a system. I am a cog, trapped, forced, wearing thin.

'The best prefects work on their own initiative, responding with sensitivity to each situation, solving problems without referral to any system; and I chose you because I value your judgement and your tact.' I know that this is what Mr Allan will say.

Lucy is gnawing at a fingernail. 'They'll go mad. It'll be worse than ever.' *It*: the persecution.

Roz is eager to agree. 'Yes, it'll cause so much hassle.' She means so much hassle *for them*.

Ali is frowning, deliberating. 'Perhaps it's important for our CVs.'

This is the first time that I have heard mention of CVs. Has typing gone to her head? Exasperated, I throw my hands into the air. I had not been expecting a boycott, but I had been hoping for support.

Roz reaches for my wrist. 'Yes, you'll not be Head Girl.' She squeezes with urgency. 'And you must be Head Girl. It'll be wonderful.' She means wonderful *for us*. She smiles. 'And you can lead the revolution from the lectern.'

I wriggle from her grasp. 'I won't be asked to be Head Girl.'

'You will, if you stop this business about the prefects.'

29

'No, I won't.'

'Yes, you will.' She laughs and pinches my cheek. 'It's obvious. Killit hates you, but she hates everyone. Allan will choose you because you're good at speeches.'

'Not *speeches*, Roz.' I blow a huge hot sigh. '*Discussions*. Anyway, no.'

'Who? Who, then? Who else? There's no one else.' Roz subsides with a deep red smirk.

'Deborah Steiner.'

'Debbie-Steiner, *who-she?*' She laughs. 'Debbie Steiner? You're joking.'

'No. Seriously. Deborah Steiner. She'll be Head Girl. You wait and see.'

'No, no, no,' Roz is tolling behind me, 'she's a mouse. A *sheer mouse*.'

At our secret door I turn and dump my bag into Ali's arms because I need my fingers free to fiddle with the latch. Ali's eyebrows rise as her arms sag: a pair of scales. 'What's in here?' she exclaims.

'Rivers,' I reply, meaning Geography: Geography books and folders. I am behind on rivers. My Geography folder contains one diagram of a river, in cross section: a leak sprung in a wall of rock, tumbling down the page, cutting through the land before sloughing across a plain towards a small blue basin of sea. The diagram insists that the leak is a youthful river; and the fat blue slug, ancient. Our Geography teacher taught us to trace rivers across maps on the journey from the hills to the sea.

We live in the Thames Valley but it does not seem like a valley: there are no rocks, no distant scarecrow trees, no echoes of birdcall, no sheep, no hikers, no soft sandy soil of an ancient plain, nor any sea. There is just Waltham Cross, Waltham Abbey, Walthamstow: Waltham, Waltham, Waltham, as far as the eye can see, as far as the bus will travel. There is no river except the Thames, twenty miles away, beached in the middle of London. Before Geography lessons, the sole occasions when I heard mention of a valley was on The News: *Thames Valley police*. Now our Geography teacher tells us that we live in a valley; that although I do not see it, it is all around me. *Watch out, watch out, there's a valley about.*

We hurry into the car park. On the horizon I can see the parade of shops: newsagent, launderette, chemist, bathroom fittings. Ali exhales with relief when I take the bag. 'I'm glad I don't do Geography.'

'I'm glad I don't do French. All that conjugating.'

She glances at me and we titter routinely. We are closer to the shops and I can see that the bin outside the newsagent is under a cloud of ice cream wrappers. The primary school children have come and gone. 'Conjugation's all right when you get used to it.'

'Like anything.'

'Like anything.'

Ali runs the palm of one hand very quickly down the back of her head. 'That prefect business . . .' she offers.

'It doesn't matter.' It matters to me, but not necessarily to anyone else.

'It *does* matter. And you're right.'

'I know I'm right.' I grin, although she is not looking at me. 'I didn't say I wasn't right.'

I hear the closing crack of Roz's compact, and glance involuntarily behind me, in her direction. There is a heap of powder on her nose. Lucy is nearer me, with a fistful of tinkling car keys. After a couple of long strides, she falls into step with me. 'That prefect business . . .' she says.

'Yes?'

'I've been thinking. You're right. But no meetings, okay?'

Would I expect Lucy to come to a meeting?

Ali severs herself from us with a nod. She lives nearby, behind the shops. It has always seemed strange to me that she lives so close to school. For some reason, this obvious nearness of Ali's home to school is rarely mentioned by any of us. Perhaps we flinch from the vague sense of Ali's helplessness; perhaps her misfortune is beyond a joke. I wonder how she feels to see school every day, at weekends and during holidays.

Now Lucy pipes, 'Are you not coming in the car?'

'Lucy.' Ali sighs. 'I live over there.' She waves a hand in the air.

'But are you sure?'

'Of course she's sure,' I tell Lucy. 'She has lived there all her life.'

'Ha, ha,' Lucy responds flatly, but barely distracted.

'Yes, I'm sure, thanks,' Ali replies politely but firmly. 'But come and fetch me at eight o'clock, eh?'

Ali's home is different from ours in another sense, too. She is the sole one among us with an older brother or sister. Her sister, Grace, is two years older than us; she left school two years ago and went to university. The rest of us live with babies: Roz's brother is eleven; Lucy's brother is three; and my youngest sister, the last in a long line, is not always out of nappies. Ali is the baby in her home. Presumably she has had a lifetime of borrowing Grace's clothes, make-up, records. What can I borrow from my sister? Nappies? Now I remember Mum musing on Grace, several years ago: 'Ali has a sister, doesn't she? Gracie?' She wrinkled her nose. 'An odd name for a baby.'

'Grace,' I corrected.

'Still an odd name for a baby.'

'She isn't a baby.'

'Well, no, but you know what I mean.'

At the car Roz says to Lucy, 'Drop me at the crossroads, will you? I could do with a walk.'

Roz assumes that she will be dropped off first, although the route is circular. Lucy unlocks the doors and I fold myself past the front seat into the back of the car: first in, last out. Lucy and Roz dip onto the front seats and snap shut the doors at their sides. Their necks bend, their heads disappear, their hands trawl beneath the seats and then loop across into the space between them.

'These sodding seat-belts,' strains Lucy. She glances puffing at Roz. 'Are you all right?'

Roz winces, and there is a loud click. 'Yes.' She straightens and settles.

Lucy returns to her own predicament. 'Got it!' she hisses finally, the exclamation punctured by another click. Then she cranes forward and peers at the road. 'Geronimo,' she says flatly, sarcastically, starting the car.

'Handbrake,' I offer.

'Yes,' she agrees, reminded, performing on cue and reaching down to release us.

We roll out of the parking space towards the gate. The gear-stick moves tersely in the space between the seats. For Lucy, changing gear is an uncharacteristically definite act. How did she ever learn to drive?

Desperation and driving lessons, she always tells me.

The driving lessons were a birthday present from her mother.

I watch the waltz of the gear-stick, mapping our progress: first, second, third. We are out on the road.

Roz turns and stares in our wake. 'Thank God it's the weekend,' she says, disgusted.

'But in two days' time it's Monday again,' I add wistfully.

She groans. 'Lalie!'

'But it's true.'

'I don't care if it's true. I don't want to know. Why can't you be thankful for small mercies?'

Because they are not big enough.

The car slides to a stop.

'Shit,' mutters Lucy, thumping the gear-stick around in the gear-box. We are in a traffic jam. 'This always happens here.' *Here* is the High Street. 'Why can't they build a flyover or something?'

Outside, the sunlight is very yellow, baked for too long on the street. Cars are herding around us towards the traffic lights, open windows containing a fold of elbow. Car radios rasp traffic bulletins: *Delays on the East India Dock Road*. Where is the East India Dock Road? London, presumably. Ahead of us, the queue of cars is sifting onto the crossroads. The fumes taste like warm flat cola.

The High Street: there is nothing *high* about the High Street. On both sides of the street there is a row of single-storey shops: butcher, baker, lighting fitter. The shops squat beneath shiny plastic hoardings: *Dee Lite Unisex* and *Pennywise Ladies Fashions*. At the end of the row, around the corner, there is a faint stain of lettering on the brickwork: *Artificial Limbs*. The hoardings form a faulty jigsaw. Above them, behind them, are mysterious windows dark with net curtains: flats, homes, perhaps. Many of the windows are blocked by boards advertising that they are *To Let*.

'We're not going to make the lights this time,' warns Lucy, shunting the car forwards.

Women teem beside us on the pavement, their legs inside thick pale crusts of denim. One woman turns around to harangue a small child rolling along on a Tonka toy: 'Will you hurry up?' Another is bending into a pram, coaxing a baby. The baby is reluctant in frills, its features buttoned firmly against the sunlight. A child totters beside the pram, strapped into dungarees. The dungarees are bright with paint-box colours. A mini-person, useless in utility clothing, the child is waddling next to the pram, frowning at knees and wheels.

The car stops again. I turn away from the window, the pavement, the trestle table of raw meat under a khaki canopy. Joints: the stumps do not look like joints unless they are studded with a bluish blind knot of bone. The dead flesh is pale, leeched, although in some cases a film of blood clings to the plastic wrapping. They are grotesque parcels, demands for ransom. I turn my attention to the shops on the other side of the road. At the newsagent – *Sweets and Cigarettes* – there are wire screens locked over the windows: Mum would say, *It's like Harlem*. Next to the newsagent is the Pet Shop and Parlour: there is a large sign in the window, *Matted Dogs Welcome*. I remember guinea pigs snuffling in cages, and the flashes of tropical fish behind glass. I remember the myna bird, *Not For Sale*, which drew crowds from the street with its renditions of *Hickory Dickory Dock*. One night, it was stolen. 'Imagine,' said Mum, rolling her eyes.

The car edges forward. 'Hurrah,' says Lucy, angrily.

We have reached the greengrocer. Outside, strawberries are glistening in punnets, fat and red like blown kisses. We leave the strawberries and approach the jeweller. Behind glass, watches and bracelets lie on mossy red velvet. I came here to the jeweller to buy my first pair of earrings. They were a birthday present.

'What do you want for your birthday?' Mum had asked me.

Earrings, I decided; some earrings – my first pair to follow the small gold sleepers with which I had recently been pierced, with which I had been learning to cope. At the beginning and end of each day, as told, I was dabbing each frail hoop with antiseptic solution and then winding it into my numb nib of clean skin. The gold winked into the mirror in the bathroom; I had grown bright eyes on my earlobes. I came on the bus to the jeweller one afternoon after school in the black rain of winter. It was the day before my twelfth birthday. There was a new ten pound note in my bag, placed by Mum in an old brown envelope for safety. I stood in the rain and chose from the window. I knew what I wanted. I chose a pair of small thick rings, I still think of them as *gypsy* rings. Inside the shop, the jeweller laid them in a little red box. To me, the box was precious too: the sheaves of golden cotton wool inside, and the gold lettering on the lid.

We have stopped close to the crossroads. Roz steps out onto the grass verge, and presses the open door back into the car, saying, 'See you later.' Lucy twists the car away from the kerb. Roz's face is shadowed by her cupped hands, and flashed with the flame from her cigarette lighter.

'Come home with me,' Lucy says to me. 'For a while, for a cup of tea. Please. I'll take you home later.' And she is indicating to turn at the crossroads towards her own house, not mine.

When the car turns the final corner, I recognize Lucy's house among the others at the far end of the Close. It is not a house but a bungalow. *Bung-a-low-roof-on*. Before I met Lucy, I had only ever been into a bungalow to visit Mum's Aunty Glad. Mum repeated before each visit that *Aunty Glad can't manage stairs any more*. As far as I know, there is nothing wrong with anyone in Lucy's family. They chose to be without stairs. It seems to me that their home should belong to someone else, someone less able. Nevertheless, Mum approves: 'I'd like a flat, to tell the truth,' she once told Lucy's mum, on the doorstep, years ago, when she came to collect me, 'but not with kids.'

Presumably kids need a garden; or, at least, a short fall from windows.

'But I'd like everything at home to be more accessible,' she said.

She would like *us* to be more accessible – me, my sisters, my brother – but she pretends that the concern is with practicalities: less hoovering, less heating. It worries me that the bedrooms in a bungalow are so vulnerable to public scrutiny, it seems odd that they are so close to everything, and not somewhere else. Sleeping downstairs is like wearing slippers to the shops, like Aunty Glad, who cannot manage laces.

The bedroom windows of Lucy's bungalow are blank with net curtain: one, two, three; one for Mr and Mrs Harvey, and one each for Lucy and Elliott. Elliott was a late addition, like the large wooden front door with a brass knocker. What was Elliott's room before Elliott? An empty guest room, perhaps. In the middle of each sill is a vase, crystal and flowerless. There are flowers in the garden, fluffy at the edges of the lawn. Lucy sweeps the car slowly into the wide base of the Close. *No Through Road.* She parks at the kerb. Her home is one of four bungalows in a row. There is a small ornamental willow tree in the middle of her lawn; and a birdhouse, (a birdbungalow?). We leave the car and walk across the lawn towards the side door. None of the bungalows in the Close have fences and gates but most have burglar alarms nestling under the eaves.

Joining the path outside the door, Lucy does a few hopscotch skips: a habit, a reflex. She has lived here since she was a baby. Ten years ago, her father left. He left the bungalow to Lucy's mum. Lucy says that possessions are unimportant to him.

'Good job too,' said Mum when I repeated the story. She often says that *It can't have been easy for Lucy's mum, left alone to bring up a baby*. She means that it cannot have been easy for Lucy's mum, left alone. Lucy's mum remained in the bungalow with Lucy. In the Close, everyone was watching, waiting. Eventually, after several years, the waiting ended when a man came to live in the bungalow: not Mr Evans, but Mr Harvey. Mrs Evans was suddenly Mrs Harvey. A few years later, baby Harvey was born: Elliott.

Lucy has remained Lucy-Ann Evans. I am not sure whether she sees her real dad. She tells me that he is a jazz musician. A jazzian?

Solo sax, she says sometimes; at other times, composer. Usually she says that he is away on tour.

I'll bet, says Mum to me.

Lucy's real dad's tours are perpetual, a purgatory of touring. Periodically, Lucy tells me more: her real dad believes that you've-got-to-do-what's-right-for-you; you've-got-to-make-your-own-life; you've-got-to-remember-that-what's-good-for-one-person-is-not-necessarily-good-for-the-next-so-if-you-find-yourself-in-a-situation-that's-not-right-for-you-then-you've-got-to-get-out-whilst-you-can. You've-only-got-one-life-and-there's-no-dress-rehearsal.

Oh, so did you see him? I interrupt Lucy eventually.

He writes, sometimes, she replies. *He's busy, but he writes*.

I follow Lucy through the side door into the kitchen: my favourite kitchen, quiet and peaceful unlike the kitchen at home. Today Lucy's kitchen is empty but even when it is busy it is peaceful: Lucy's mum in a pinny, pressing icing from a soft white bag onto glistening biscuits; Elliott kneading Play-Doh; the drone of a radio play. Lucy's kitchen is old-fashioned, white, sparkling: white tiles on the walls and floor, a white sink, and white wooden cupboards. There is the smell of Vim. The table is decorated with faint lines, wound like spirogyrae in a biology textbook. There is no hob or hood over the cooker, no stainless steel draining board, no panelling of dark brown formica, no textured oatmeal floor surface, no toaster bearing a stencil of a wheatsheaf. On the draining board there is a mug tree hung with four china mugs, each bearing a name: Mummy, Daddy, Elliott, Lucy-Ann. *Lucy-Ann* is entwined with a skipping rope and surrounded by butterflies. Above the draining board, fixed to the wall, there is dimpled kitchen roll. At home we use dishcloths, damp, cheap. On the wall by the door there is a calendar, the black and red days beneath inky whispers of words, evidence of life.

Lucy takes a note from the table and glances at it before dropping it into the bin. 'Shopping,' she quotes. 'Good. Peace for a while. Do you want a drink?' She opens the fridge door.

'Just tea for me, please. Your mum's shopping?' I am vaguely disappointed. I like Lucy's mum. She smells of handcream.

'Only for an hour or so, I suppose.' Lucy lifts a carton from one of the shimmering shelves. 'I'm having orange juice. Are you sure you don't want orange juice? It's cold.'

'Tea'll be fine.' I take the kettle to the sink, stepping around Lucy. 'What about your dad?'

Lucy has a *dad*, and a *real dad*.

'What about him?' Lucy's voice is muffled. She reappears from a cupboard with a long glass in her hand.

'What time does he come home?'

Lucy waves the glass at another cupboard. 'Teabags on the bottom shelf, mugs on the top. He's not home from work until seven-thirtyish.'

I found out about Mr Harvey's job in a French lesson; I know about Mr Harvey's job in French: our French teacher, Mme Williams, asked each of us to say the occupation of our father in French. She had to be told that Karen Fisher did not have a father, and it had to be suggested that Karen could use an uncle: Mon oncle Max. Mme Williams was expecting us to say *Il est ingénieur* or *Il est professeur*, following the examples of Marie-Claire and Catherine in our text-books, but Lucy requested the translation of Divisional Manager. Mme Williams said that Lucy was being facetious. Roz had no problems: *Il est agent*. We teased Roz after the class that *Ton père est agent secret*. Mine is a car dealer, which was not difficult to translate, *Seller of cars*. Ali struggled with civil servant. 'He inspects building sites,' she said, shrugging. 'You

38

know.' I did not know: I had always imagined civil servants to wear wing collars, not hard hats, because they are known as white-collar workers. There is no one in a hard hat in Miss Killick's careers leaflet, *The Civil Service*. Whenever she forces the leaflet upon me I amuse myself by secretly translating it as The Impolite Service.

Mme Williams decided that Lucy's dad worked in a factory but eventually allowed that he worked in an office in a factory. The factory is on an industrial estate in the countryside. I pass the estate whenever I travel by train with Mum to visit Mad Great Aunt Theda, Great Mad Aunt Theda. The estate is dominated by a huge factory resembling my brother's toy garage: white, with a flat roof. Mum says that *White is not a sensible colour for a factory, considering the dirt*. She says that *They should call a spade a spade and paint all our factories black*. The huge white factory makes breakfast cereal. The lorries parked in rows below the railway line are loaded with breakfast cereal. Lucy's dad's factory is hidden from view. Whenever I ask Lucy for more information she replies, without a hint of humour or irony, that he is *something in cat food*.

'I think I'll go and change out of all this,' says Lucy. It is not a statement but a request for permission. *All this* is a short white dress without sleeves, suitable for tennis.

'Yes, fine. I'll make my tea.' The kettle is wheezing. The tea-bag falls like a dappled feather from my fingers into a dry mug.

Lucy slips from the room. I make my mug of tea and then take it with me into the dining room. I pass the honey-coloured dining table and slide open the french windows: two stainless steel frames and two sheets of glass, double-glazed. The afternoon air in the garden has been baked by the sun and spiced with mown grass. I sit down on the doorstep. At home, an open door does not offer solitude: our lawn is covered with children and their transistor radios and bikes.

Lucy returns. 'More comfortable now,' she murmurs, standing over me on the step. She is wearing a nightdress.

'But you're wearing your nightie.'

'Comfy,' she confirms.

It looks comfy: outgrown and faded. The pale pink print comprises flowers, tiny and indistinct, a smattering of blossom. The bib is bordered by tatters of *broderie anglaise*, with a pair of pink satin ribbons hanging untied from the collar in corkscrew curls. Decorative buttons bob precariously on loops of thread. She squats beside me, the bony part of each ankle a porcelain scroll. She rests her chin on her knees, and cradles her shins. Suddenly I realize that there is music in the dining room: presumably it is one of Lucy's tapes.

'What's that?' I ask. The singer sounds maniacal.

'He's dead now,' she says.

'Yes, but who is it?'

'Cab Calloway.'

'Oh.' We stare together across the lawn. 'Who's he?'

'A singer.'

I look down onto Lucy's big toe: nude. It is disconcertingly free of paint; bare, bald, a detail on a statue. Suddenly it seems to me that her stillness is unusual; and her silence, too. Cab Calloway is gabbling in the dining room but Lucy is staring across the lawn at the swathes of ivy on the fence. She pleaded with me to come here: why? It would be too crass for me to ask, *What's up?* I need clues.

'Did you see him today?' *He* is the new boyfriend.

'Him? Yes.' No trace of interest.

Mum says *Boys, boys, boys, that's all you ever talk about* but it is not true. And nor is it a complaint. She encourages me to talk with my friends about boys because she can eavesdrop. She likes me to have boyfriends: no mother wants her daughter to be a spinster or worse. Predictably she prefers conversation about boys to conversation about famine or nuclear war. Boys are easier on the ear.

Lucy's new boyfriend is in the upper sixth. He is notorious at school for the double bass which he hauls through the corridors to and from rehearsals: is it a huge violin case, or is he a dwarf Mafioso? Sometimes he nods across the corridor at me: the masculine equivalent of a smile. Often he takes Lucy into the cloakroom, where they talk quietly together, keeping their words to themselves but casting their glances elsewhere, guarded. My boyfriend, Ben, is never guarded. Mum says that he is *flamboyant*. I do not consider flamboyant to be a suitable description of any boyfriend of mine. How about *high profile*, instead?

The only musical instrument that Ben carries around school is a silver whistle on a scarlet ribbon around his neck. He plays rugby, football, basketball, squash, tennis, real tennis, badminton; and Lear, Fool, Jimmy Porter: he is a devotee of both the sports field and the stage, simultaneously a team member and a prima donna. He has the muddy legs of a sportsman and the quiff of an actor.

Oh don't you just love him, squeal my friends.

In reply, I delight them with a sceptical wrinkle of my nose. I do not want to seem too keen. Not as far as Ben is concerned. Not too often. Whenever I tell him that I do not know why I like him, he tap dances in his muddy, studded boots and sings *A-I'm-Adorable*.

Why *do* I like him? He makes me laugh. He has always made me laugh, even when we were in the first year and he was no one special. Even then, I had an inkling. I kept my eye on him.

This year, for our anniversary, he planned a trip on a Green Line bus to Wembley to see the Harlem Globetrotters. *A spectacle*, he enthused. Initially, I was not amused. Mum wanted to know who else I could rely upon to take me to see the Harlem Globetrotters. She likes him: he is *An Original*, whereas I am *A Weirdo*. When she found out that he has a passion for downhill skiing she said, giggling, girlish, 'Never mind, because the prospects are better in downhill skiing than uphill.'

Ali's boyfriend is a mystery. He is a student, a friend of Ali's sister. I have not met him but I imagine that he wears a duffel coat and a Rupert scarf. Ali says that he is a student of Humanities, and I imagine a pair of kindly round glasses. Unfortunately, his name is Julian. I remember Julian of the *Famous Five*, clever Ju, too clever Ju, too tall Ju with boorish Dick, graceless George, witless crinoline Anne, and the dog. Enid Blyton has left me with a bias against

41

Julians. Roz's boyfriend is an estate agent. He left school last year with an ambition to be a surveyor. He works instead for George Tilson, the most famous person in the neighbourhood because his name lines the streets. Sometimes I accompany Roz to the pub and endure the company of boys who left school last year to work in their same grey sixth form suits for British Gas or British Telecom. These boys are enthusiastic in the evenings about *pints*.

Lucy is dabbling her fingertips onto her toes. The tapping on the nails is sharper than the tapping on flesh-wrapped bone.

'Have you been to bed with him yet?' I do not like to ask this question. The answer last week was no.

Lucy sighs, folds her arms around her knees, and shifts on the stone step to face me. 'No, actually.'

I know that Lucy agrees with me that if someone is nice enough to kiss, then they are nice enough for bed. No false distinctions. We are choosy, very choosy, and very careful, but realistic.

'No,' she repeats, and shrugs, devoid of explanation.

We focus again on the ivy, on the evening falling from the leaves.

'So, what's up, then?'

There is a pause. 'Nothing.' The word thuds into the silence between us. Nothing at all, or nothing in particular?

'Oh, I don't know.' She throws a shrug from her shoulders. 'Oh, you know.'

We remain together on the step, the stain of sunshine in our eyes and on our skins.

You know: yes, perhaps; but then again, no.

~

I walk towards the front door. The driveway is bright with the crazy paving of bald pink stones. It was left by the people who lived here before us. They also planted a rockery of sparkling silvery rocks. Dad prefers tarmac. Tarmac, like dark muscovado sugar, is burning in the sunshine on the driveway next door. I walk across our pink stones and open the front door. Then I hurry through the hallway towards the kitchen, dropping my schoolbag at the foot of the stairs.

The kitchen is shaded. The blind hangs listlessly at the open window. In the glass bowl on the sill the goldfish sinks in a steamy swamp of water and weeds. I hurry to the bread bin. My sister, Jane, is sitting at the table, doing nothing.

She's at that age, says Mum: the age of doing nothing; nothing except sitting, chin in hand, and glaring. Jane glares at me as I reach into the bread bin.

'What?' I challenge.

She continues to glare.

'*What?*'

Mum appears at the back door, leaving the garden to a fanfare of shrieks and splashes from my little brother and sister in the paddling pool. On the doorstep she is taller than usual. She stares down at us.

'Stop it, you two,' she warns before she descends.

'It was Jane,' I protest.

Jane widens her glaring eyes. 'I wasn't doing anything.'

Mum sighs and rakes her fingers through her hair as she crosses to the fridge. 'I don't care *who*. Just *stop*.'

Jane pouts. 'I wasn't saying anything.'

I protest to Mum: 'She was looking at me.'

Mum's bright head glows at the open door of the fridge. 'Oh stop it,' she mumbles, probing the freezer box, 'both of you. Now.'

Jane transfers her chin from one hand to the other. 'Pardon me for breathing,' she hisses.

'No,' I reply.

Mum straightens and turns towards me. 'Now, that's enough,' she commands, blonde curls bouncing around her face.

I return my attention to the bread bin. 'Is there any brown?' I push around the packets and bags of white bread.

Mum snarls again into the fridge: 'Have I had time today to worry about bloody brown bread?'

I grimace as rudely as possible at her back. 'Just asking.'

She sighs heavily and closes the fridge, turning towards me with a packet of frozen sausages in her hands. 'No,' she admits, 'there's

43

no brown.' She crosses to the cooker. 'Anyway, it's nearly teatime. We're having an early tea because Erin has Brownies at six o'clock.'

'Tea? Now?'

She opens the cupboard and selects a tin of baked beans.

'Tea? Now?' I sigh emphatically. 'It's too hot for tea.'

Mum slams the tin onto the table. 'Oh stop complaining. I'm sick of it. Do you imagine that I want to stand here in this heat and cook your tea?'

I draw two slices from a packet of bread and drop them onto the breadboard. I want to suggest salad, but do not dare.

'And don't mention salad,' she says suddenly. 'You can't live on salad, not all the time.'

I butter the slices of bread and lift them onto a plate.

'Don't spoil your appetite,' Mum says as I leave the table. She begins to prick the sausages, thudding the prongs of the fork into the slushy grey flesh.

I shut the door behind me and walk through the dining area to the living room. Sitting down on the settee, I tear a piece from one of the slices of bread and squash it into a buttery ball. A cloud of net curtain hangs at the open windows: visibility, nil; and just the sound of a pushchair somewhere, of small hard wheels skipping over the uneven surface of the pavement, moving away. I press the buttery ball against the roof of my mouth. The room is scented with dust baking slowly in sunshine.

That's the one thing that I hate about summer, says Mum: *the spring cleaning waiting to be done.*

The room divider no longer divides the room but stands as shelves against a wall: caramel brown in the sun; sticky with fingerprints and dredged with a pale dust. Spider plants flop from shelf to shelf and tangle with the ornaments. On the middle shelf there is a row of books: Reader's Digest, cities and monuments photographed against enamel blue skies. I am supposed to want to visit the cities and monuments when I am older: the Parthenon, the Eiffel Tower, the Sistine Chapel. There is also a book of health, the cover black with the silhouette of a woman with childbearing hips.

I notice Erin's scrapbooks on the floor as Mum opens the door, strides across the dining area, and stares at the debris. She jabs the tip of her tongue against the roof of her mouth in irritation.

'Look at that,' she says to me, pointing at the pile. She hurries across the living room, through the door, and halts in the hallway at the foot of the stairs.

'Erin,' she yaps, 'Erin. Erin. Erin.'

I despair, dumping the plate of bread beside me on the settee.

'Perhaps she can't hear you.'

Mum turns briefly towards me. 'I'll be the judge of that.' She turns again to the stairs. 'Erin. Erin.'

'*All right*:' the voice at the top of the stairs is faint but indignant.

Mum sighs. 'It is *not* all right. Don't talk to me like that. Get down here and tidy your things.'

'In a minute.'

'Not in a minute. Now.'

Erin comes down the stairs so slowly that it must be difficult to balance.

'Take your stuff to your room,' demands Mum: Jane-and-Erin's room.

Mum insists that they share a room: *Your sister is a teenager now, she needs privacy, she has bosoms.*

Erin kneels on the floor and gathers pens and books into her arms. She drops more with each movement than she gathers.

Mum winces. 'Will you look at this?' she says to me, indicating Erin.

Erin rises, stumbles, and drops a pencil case.

Mum turns to me. 'Are you around on Saturday night?' she asks, changing the subject.

I shrug, affecting nonchalance: 'Yes, probably.' I hope that she will ask me to baby-sit. I like baby-sitting because Ben visits me.

'Oh, good. Can you baby-sit?'

I shrug again: I will not baby-sit for Jane; Mum knows that I will not baby-sit for Jane. I will for the others, and Jane can stay with them, but I will not baby-sit for Jane. Sometimes on Saturday mornings Mum persuades me to take Jane-and-Erin to the shops or the pool, and I walk with Erin on one side of the street whilst Jane walks on the other.

'Oh, good,' says Mum. 'I was wondering whether I could possibly borrow that little white top of yours?'

Erin shuffles from the room. I fold a piece of bread between my fingertips. 'Mmmm.'

'Because it'll go so nicely with that skirt of mine.' She leans towards the window and lifts the corner of the net curtain. She peers through the window, squinting into the sunlight, and seems surprised to see nothing at all of interest. 'That green skirt,' she finishes, dropping the net curtain from her fingers. She turns from the window. 'We're off out for a meal with Jenny and Graham.' She walks across the room into the dining area.

I tear a corner from the last slice of bread.

'Poor Jenny,' she says, 'she hasn't been at all well lately.'

'No?' I slur through a mouthful of bread.

'No. Back trouble.' She opens the kitchen door. Sausage smoke billows into the room. 'Mind you,' she calls cheerfully to me as she leaves the room, 'who would feel well, living with Graham?'

I finish the bread and take the plate to the kitchen. Jane does not glare at me because she is reading a magazine: *Nineteen*, although she is thirteen. She reaches blindly across the table into an open packet of biscuits.

'Biscuits are fattening,' mutters Mum at the cooker. She glances over her shoulder at Jane. 'And stop reading that bloody rubbish.'

Jane turns the page and crams another biscuit into her mouth.

Mum is standing on tiptoe and poking a fork into the eye-level grill: *An eye-level grill for giants*, she joked after the kitchen was refitted.

The sausages spit and roll, their blistering skins burnt with thin deep scars.

'Bloody Brownies,' says Mum as I step past her to put my plate into the sink. 'Tea at five-thirty because of Brownies. For how many years have my evenings revolved around Brownies?'

'Perhaps it'll be cancelled,' I suggest.

'No chance,' says Mum, fending sausages from the edge of the grill pan. 'There's Brown Owl, Snowy Owl, and all those other Owls: if one of the Owls is indisposed, there's always another species around to take control.' She turns to the saucepan of baked beans. 'Brownies are invincible: Baden Powell, BP, Be Prepared.'

I am amused by the mention of Baden Powell: I remember pale photographs of a man in flappy shorts.

'Never mind,' I remind her: 'Erin's ten, she will have to leave at the end of term.'

Mum inclines her head towards the back door: my little brother is trundling across the crazy pink patio in his red plastic Rolls-Royce, the pedals churning under the bonnet. 'And then it's Cubs,' she says. We crane our necks: on the lawn, my baby sister is emerging from the paddling pool; fat fists seizing the sides, terry towelling knickers sagging to her knees. Mum sighs. 'And then Brownies again.' She reaches into the cupboard for plates. 'And then retirement, and peace, and oblivion.'

'Jane,' she says, 'would you go and tell Erin that it's time for tea?' She places a bottle of ketchup on the table. 'If you tell her now, she might come down in time for Brownies next week. And if you remind her that it's Brownies, she might not try to come down in a tutu for ballet class or a toga for a fancy dress party or whatever.'

Jane continues reading. 'I'm reading.'

Mum snatches the magazine and throws it on top of the fridge. 'Not any more.'

Jane sighs noisily and leaves the table with maximum indignation.

I fetch the magazine from the fridge and sit at the table to flick through the pages. Mum lays the plates on the table, peering over my shoulder. 'My best friend's boyfriend,' she announces, quoting a headline. She shrugs. 'My best friend's boyfriend had a glass eye.' She reaches for the grill pan and lowers the mass of sausages to the table. 'So I wouldn't have wanted to kiss him, even if he had been the most gorgeous boy in the school.' She flicks two sausages onto a plate. 'Which he wasn't.' She flicks another pair of sausages onto another plate.

'That's an awful thing to say,' I protest, laughing quietly; 'about the eye. It wasn't his fault.'

'No, I know it wasn't his fault,' she replies, dicing a sausage for the baby, 'and I know that it was an awful thing to say, but it's true. A glass eye is somehow worse than a wooden leg.'

'Your boyfriend had a wooden leg?'

She glances at me in surprise and lowers the knife and fork onto the messy plate. 'Did I say that my boyfriend had a wooden leg? No, no wooden leg, or not that I noticed.'

She fetches the saucepan of beans. 'No, my boyfriend was fully ambulant.' She relishes the word *ambulant*. 'Mind you, his father was in the RAF during the war, he was a navigator. And Douglas Bader lost his legs.'

I smirk. 'Douglas Bader lost your boyfriend's father's legs?'

The wooden spoon drips beans onto one of the plates. Mum raises her eyebrows. 'Douglas Bader lost his own legs; or what used to be his own legs, before he lost them, if you see what I mean.'

Beans pool on the remaining plates.

In the distance, in the hallway, Jane is shouting: 'Erin. Erin.'

Mum lifts the plates in pairs to the oven and loads them onto the shelves. 'Did you get a lift home from school today?'

'Yes.'

'Who?'

'Lucy.'

'Oh, Lucy.' She closes the oven door. 'Weird and wonderful Lucy.' Her voice is brittle with sarcasm.

I refuse to rise to the bait. I turn a page and glance at *Holiday Reading, Books for the Beach*.

'And is she still driving around in her mother's car?' Mum leans over the sink to scrub the grill pan with a scourer. The scourer skids on the layer of fat. Does she disapprove of the driving around? or is this an in-my-day story, a story of trams? Does she disapprove

48

of Lucy, or Lucy's mother, or both? I know that she regards Lucy as feckless, and she believes that character traits belong to families: there are good families and bad families.

So, what does that mean for us, for our family? Apparently, I am *uncommunicative, uncooperative, defiant;* whilst Jane is on probation at school for stealing a packet of cigarettes from Matron's handbag in Sick Bay, and Erin cannot find her own way home from the bus stop. Mum despairs of us, but she despairs even more of Dad's family: *The Blaneys.* The Blaneys live in a row of tied cottages on a local farm: Dad's Gran; Dad's Dad; and his brother and sister-in-law, Uncle Tom and Aunty Mo. Dad's Mum left more than thirty years ago.

She was a GI bride, says Mum, *the second time around*.

Whenever she tells the story, she whispers *Scandal*: an unnecessary emphasis.

And who can blame her? she says rhetorically: *Manhattan skyline, or Cold Comfort Farm?*

But there was plenty of blame, of course: Mum tells us that Gran never liked the daughter-in-law, and advised the Blaneys to *never trust a blonde*.

Well, concludes Mum, *as far as I'm concerned, all hope for the Blaneys went to the New World with Blondie Brenda*.

The hopelessness is a reference to Aunty Mo, who is fat with metabolism.

Childless, says Mum of Uncle Tom and Aunty Mo; breathing the word as if it is a curse.

The Blaney cottages are fenced with rusty machinery.

Motorbikes, explains Dad, uncomfortably: *The Blaneys have an interest in machines*.

They're tinkers, says Mum.

They're mechanics, corrects Dad, half-heartedly: a reluctant defender.

They're Irish, says Mum; and there is no answer, because it is true.

Gran Blaney has an interest in clothes.

Finery, sneers Mum.

When worn, Gran's silk blouses and linen suits echo the rustle of the tissue paper in which they are stored.

But where does she find the money? mutters Mum, voicing everyone's thoughts. *I'll tell you where she finds the money, she finds the money by hook or by crook.* When she says *by hook or by crook*, she fixes us with a knowing stare; but we do not know what she means, and nor does she know what she means. No one knows. Gran has a vast selection of wide-brimmed hats. She skewers them to her dark hair with ornate pins. One of the pinheads is a small silver skull.

The Blaneys give me the creeps, says Mum.

She sends me to the cottages with birthday and Christmas gifts. She believes that gifts within families are an obligation.

Why me? I ask before each trip.

Because I can't send your Dad because men are no good with gifts; and, besides, they'll want to see one of you kids, and you're the eldest, and you're one of them.

I am one of them because, unlike my sisters and my brother, I am tall and thin and I have straight dark hair. My sisters and my brother resemble Mum: short, with fair curls; Blondie Brendas.

Whenever I visit Gran I drink dark tea and stare at the stuffed monkey on the mantelpiece.

A stuffed monkey, shrieks Mum: *how unhygienic.*

No one mentions the shrunken heads pinned by their pigtails to the wall above the fireplace. Gran describes them as heirlooms.

Gran serves Jaffa Cakes and asks me about my school reports. Sometimes she suggests that I come along when she is working at one of the local fairs. She trades in a small ivory tent as *NostraMadamus*.

Mum is leaning across the table, staring at me: 'Eh?'

I blink thoroughly: is Lucy still driving around in her mother's car? 'No,' I answer, 'she swapped a book of Green Shield stamps for an E-type Jag.'

Mum turns away in a flamboyant gesture of disgust. 'If you can't answer sensibly, then don't answer at all.' She switches off the oven. 'Fetch the little ones from the garden, will you. It's time for tea.'

I lean from my chair and look into the garden. My little brother is disembarking gravely from the Rolls-Royce, which is not well parked. He is searching for a foothold on the grass.

'Lynd,' I call to him, reorientating him, 'it's time for tea.'

My brother's name is Lyndsay, which horrifies Dad. It was Mum's choice after Dad pleaded for *anything, anything but Ashley*.

Mum relinquished Ashley, and enjoyed the search for a name. The sole stipulation was *no royalty*. She did not want a George, a Charles, an Edward, a William, a Henry: *Stuffed shirts*, she says. She was almost prepared to make an exception for Richard, but was troubled by the notion of Richard the Third: 'No one thinks of Richard the Lionheart,' she said, 'but everyone remembers Richard the Third.'

'Richard the Third, turd,' said Jane.

I pointed out that there had been a Queen Jane.

Mum explained that Jane Grey was Queen for nine days, before she was beheaded by the next one: 'It seems unlikely that she was regarded by them as one of their own.'

Mum likes dissenters, outsiders; and she is not bothered by Queens: Queens are not stuffed shirts, and they have nice names like Victoria and Elizabeth.

For a while, Mum favoured *Corin*.

'Corin?' Jane and I crowed.

'After Corin Redgrave,' Mum informed us. 'Well, not after Corin Redgrave, but that's how I know the name.'

Jane wondered whether babies continue to be named Adolf.

I pointed out that *Corin* might be mistaken for *Colin*, and the option was dropped.

Then Mum wanted *Linus*.

'Snoopy,' we said: Linus was a character in the Snoopy cartoon, the small one with a blanket as a comforter. In retrospect, Linus would have suited my brother.

In the end, she chose *Lyndsay*.

'It's a girl's name,' we said.

'No,' said Mum, 'you're wrong: it's like Lesley, it's unisex.'

'Lesley's vile,' I breathed, 'it's the worst name in the world.'

'Says who?' challenged Mum.

I knew that Lyndsay was a better option than Lesley.

Mum told us that it is a unisex name like Hilary and Shirley: 'Yes,' she insisted, 'there are men called Shirley.'

'You're joking,' we said.

'No,' she said, 'I'm not, I promise.'

I was persuaded when Mum explained that Lyndsay is bohemian.

'What's bohemian?' puzzled Jane.

Mum shrugged. 'Different,' she said eventually, 'unusual, wild.'

She tried to soothe Dad by explaining that Lyn is a man's name in Wales. 'Lyn for short,' she said cheerfully, 'if you like: in Welsh, it means lake, so it's a lovely lyrical name.'

Dad said that we were not Welsh and that he did not want a son named Lake.

'Lyn is a girl's name,' he insisted morosely.

We were worried that Lyndsay would be teased at school, but this was not one of Mum's considerations. She believes that there are more worrying things in life than teasing.

Lyndsay picks his way across the garden towards me. He is followed by the baby, Lauren. She slinks past him. At three years old, she is half his age and half his size but twice as bright. The last of the line, Mum decrees of Lauren. The five of us were born at regular intervals of three years so that no one would mistake us for Catholics.

I don't want anyone to think that some old goat of a Pope dealt with my family planning for me, says Mum. Then she begins to muse: *Come to think of it, there are more than a few similarities between the Pope and my GP; two sanctimonious old gits in white coats.*

There was no difficulty in naming Lauren: Mum continued the theme that began with Erin, the American theme. American names, for Mum, evoke a pioneering spirit. There is nothing pioneering about Erin: she looks like something out of *Sesame Street*. It is too soon to know about Lauren.

I'm surprised that she isn't Laurence, says Dad, sarcastically.

He calls Erin *Eric*; and Erin has only recently learned not to look puzzled and hurt, not to whine *But my name's Erin.*

Mum assured us that Dad was secretly pleased by the decision to name the baby Lauren because he fancies Lauren Bacall. She was changing Lauren's nappy when she told us.

'Isn't Lauren Bacall dead?' asked Jane, peering into the dirty nappy.

'I don't know,' replied Mum, folding a clean square of terry towelling into a triangle; 'and, anyway, it doesn't matter.'

'Doesn't matter?' echoed Jane; 'doesn't matter if Dad fancies a dead person?'

Mum's teeth were bared, clenched on a safety pin: 'It's different for film stars.'

'I'm sure she's dead,' muttered Jane, searching through the basket of baby lotions. She span the lid from the jar of Vic and inhaled the fumes. 'Who is dead, then?'

Mum forced the safety pin into a wedge of terry towelling. 'What?'

'Who is dead?'

'What do you mean, who is dead? Lots of people are dead. Don't be silly, Jane.'

I lifted a bottle of gripe water from the basket. 'Carole Lombard,' I said; 'in a plane crash.'

Jane seemed satisfied with my answer. She replaced the lid on the jar of Vic and dropped it into the basket before leaving us alone.

The meal has been hurried and noisy, the cutlery spinning through the soft food and ringing against the plates. Now there is pudding: at school, it is *afters*; at my friends' houses, it is *sweet*; in restaurants, it is *dessert*. For Mum, it is *pudding: Hurry up, eat your pudding.*

She believes in pudding. This evening we are having ice cream, American flavoured: pecan or praline or butter or something. Mum levers shards from the tub into our bowls with a large flat spoon. I think fondly of the scoops at school that extract smooth balls of mashed potato as the shards of ice cream slither around my bowl, escaping my spoon and leaving thick buttery trails.

Mum takes the plates from the table and dumps them into the sink.

'Come on, Erin,' she complains, 'finish your ice cream.'

Erin has to be accompanied to Brownies. Mum says that Erin has as much road sense as a hedgehog. Jane and I learned to cross roads with the help of Tufty. We were introduced to Tufty at school by the policeman who came each year to the infant class and left his big black bicycle chained to the railings in the playground.

'A policeman came to school today,' Jane told Mum.

'At least it wasn't the nit nurse,' said Mum.

'Nit?' repeated Jane, amused; 'Nit nurse? Nit policeman. The policeman was a nit.'

The policeman bribed us with books and badges to cross roads with care: *Look both ways*. My badge proclaimed that I was a member of the Tufty Club. I had done nothing to qualify for membership, and there was no hint of exclusivity: although I was only five years old, I had a strong suspicion that this was a contradiction in terms. Besides, I did not want to be a member of the same club as Jane. When she obtained a badge, I relinquished mine. For Erin, three years after Jane, there was no club or badge; there were no furry animals. Instead, there was someone resembling Superman, who favoured the Green Cross Code: *Left, right, and left again*. Erin did not benefit from this: she was uninterested in supermen, and confused by the mention of left and right.

Erin struggles from the table, squeezing behind Lyndsay. Her bowl, wet with uncaptured ice cream, tilts precariously above his head. Mum mutters and snatches it away.

'Come on, Erin,' she insists loudly, hurrying to the sink, 'we're late.' She turns to Jane and me: 'I want this table cleared and wiped before I return.' Then she ushers Erin through the door.

Jane glares into an empty bowl.

I reach for Lyndsay's and Lauren's sticky bowls and stack them with mine. 'Off you go,' I command.

They slide from their chairs and scurry from the kitchen to the garden.

I take the bowls to the sink and return with a damp cloth to wipe across the table. 'Don't forget to clear your place,' I say to Jane.

She sighs wearily and raises her eyes to mine: 'Fuck off.'

I slap the cloth onto the table and turn towards the door. 'Mum?' I turn back to Jane. 'I'll tell Mum.' I will not tell Mum because Mum has gone. Also, I do not want to repeat the *fuck off*, and Mum will demand a full account. She will not accept *Jane swore*. She is unperturbed by swearing in general, by *bloody* and *bugger*, but tormented by *four letter words*: it is a rule, *no four letter words*.

Four letter words, I taunt, *like shed or song, perhaps? or town or long?*

Her eyes are narrow when she replies: *four letter nasty words*.

Nasty words? I goad. *How can a word be nasty?*

It is not clear whether *crap* is included in this category.

Mum's zeal is awesome: punishment of offenders is indiscriminate. Whenever I repeat Jane's *fuck off*, I am in trouble; and whenever I protest, Mum becomes indignant and frantic with insinuations: *Who taught Jane to say something like that? You're the eldest*.

Mum's own swear word is *git*, because she is a Londoner.

Nothing nasty, she says: *I might come from Wandsworth, but I'm not common. No pun intended*.

Dad says an occasional *sod*. At Primary School I was delighted to discover *sod* in the Bible.

I suspect that Jane knows that I will not tell Mum, but I call her bluff: 'Mum!'

Jane shrugs. 'You can tell Mum whatever you like.'

I leave Jane and go into the living room. I kneel at the cabinet, and coax open one of the small doors. Mum refers to the cabinet as *the unit: be careful with the unit*, she says. I pull gently on the flat white knob, and the door drops forward. I take the large black bag of photos from the cupboard and then close the door by lifting and jamming it into the frame. The units came from a warehouse in a box marked *self-assembly*. They require constant re-assembly.

I drag the black bag onto my lap. The photos remain in packets in a dustbin liner despite Dad's insistence that they should be in albums.

I delve into the bag. There are too many photos for albums; there are too many children: our dustbin liner is constantly refilled with recent photographs of first smiles, first birthday parties, first days at school. I lift the shiny yellow wallets, and strips of negatives scatter into my lap: the large dark smooth seeds of photographs. Most of the wallets bear a bright motif: on the new wallets it is discreet, an identifying mark, but on the older wallets it blazes as an advertisement for colour, a celebration of technological achievement. It seems that colour photography was once a cause for celebration.

Black and white? gasps Mum in horror whenever she sees me with my camera. For Mum, my black and white photographs are reminiscent of the dark ages: they cannot be included in the category of old-fashioned things such as natural childbirth, herbal shampoo and pine dressers, but belong instead with outside toilets.

On the older wallets there is a picture of a woman in a bikini on a beach. She is holding a beach ball and looking delighted. The pieces of the bikini are too large, and the colour is too light. Nowadays, bikinis are black, or magenta, never sky blue. Nurses uniforms are sky blue. Also, the woman is too pale. Nowadays, beach belles roast in coconut oil. They do not smile, but squint and leer. Nor do they leap after beach balls, but recline instead on burning sand. Today's beach belles are indolent. The woman in the picture is healthy. I can see her tummy button: a firm thumbprint in the pale flesh. She looms: the smile wide, the arms open. Prancing on the sand, bleached by sunlight, she is a Slimcea or Nimble woman: extra light, no mystery, no promise.

On some of the newer wallets there is a picture of a happy family: they are happy because they are smiling. In real life, people smile because they are happy; but the wallets do not contain real life, they contain photography: a gilt of smiles in darkness. Inside our dustbin liner we are a happy family, we are smiling, smiling throughout our coloured lives; our lives of parties and holidays. Would the parties and holidays have taken place without a camera? The photographs in the dustbin liner are presumably more important to Mum and Dad than our birth certificates, which are stored in the loft in a Sealink sickbag.

I sift the photographs. In some of them we have food in our mouths: Mum regards these photographs as failures because the food interferes with our smiles. *Cake-hole*, she says, distressed. Also, eating is personal: Mum complains that *we might as well have a photo of you picking your nose*. Food in our photographs is usually decorative: birthday or Christmas cake. In most of the pictures we are foodless and standing to attention, instructed to smile. These group photographs exhibit the striking resemblance of my sisters and brother to Mum. Indistinct blonde babies in individual portraits carry clues: Jane in the old armchair which was replaced by a brown corduroy bean bag; Erin and the eyeless teddy bear; Lyndsay in the red Rolls-Royce; Lauren in the shiny new buggy which disappeared without her one day in Mothercare. In all the photographs Mum is not unlike the woman with the beach ball. She smiles strenuously. Dad is invisible: he owns the camera, he takes the pictures. Alongside my sisters and my brother I am the eldest, tallest, darkest; the shadow at the end of the line.

I continue to sift. I am not interested in these life stories. I do not need to be reminded that Jane wanted to be a showjumper, that she went with friends every weekend to Gymkhanas; that she stood solid in black boots with a riding hat frown on her face. I have not forgotten that I once wanted to be a ballet dancer: I do not need to see the marshmallow coloured tights flopping into creamy folds around my ankles, stemmed by whorls of pink satin ribbon. I am searching for photographs of the Blaneys. At the bottom of the dustbin liner I run my fingertips over several small pieces of board and some large silky squares. I pull them to the surface and spread them around me on the floor. The faces glow: The Blaneys. There is no pretence of spontaneity in these photographs; they are portraits. In one photograph Grandad is a young man with a motorbike, framed by protruding pedals and pipes; in another, he stands beside a car. Dad once told me that the Blaneys were the first family in the village to own a car. They still have the car; it is kept in a barn on the farm. Among the photographs of motorbikes and cars there is a photograph of Gran. She is close to the camera, her smile encircled by the brim of a hat.

The photographs are old: dark colours, papery smells, odd shapes and sizes that do not slot into yellow wallets. In the dustbin liner they sink below the technicolour celebrations. In each photograph the props are familiar: in a photograph of Gran I recognize the tumbling shadows of a silk-wrapped, fruit-topped sundae hat; the medallion glint of a brooch; the chaos of a charm bracelet. Other photographs show two loose black suits: Grandad and Uncle Tom, the magpies at our family weddings and funerals. The waddings of waistcoat are hidden from view, along with the scarlet braces, hard white cuffs and shiny gold cuff links. In most of the photographs there are engines snarling oil: cars, tractors, motorbikes. I search in vain for the monkey.

The inky gazes of the Blaney faces are as familiar to me as the baby blonde smiles festooning the newer photographs. There have been very few changes in their appearances: Grandad's greased dark head is now a wild white cloud; Gran's smooth skin is now shattered by wrinkles, and the smile is less spry. Mum used to say that *we should all bow out at sixty*, but recently she has revised this to sixty-five. Gran was seventy when I was born: an old woman. She is not old in these photographs. Is she younger than Mum? I take the photograph of the hat and turn it towards the light. Is she thirty, perhaps? By the time she was thirty, she was married. Her husband died before I was born. She was already a widow. I find it hard to imagine Gran as a wife. Did she ever cook his tea? It is difficult for me to picture Gran cooking anyone's tea.

I lay the photograph with the others and delve again into the dustbin liner. I pull a handful of wallets to the surface and lift the flaps. I am looking for a photograph of myself. Presumably I have at least a one-in-five chance of success: I was the first born, posing alone; and subsequently I am present in the snapshots of the others. But unlike the others, the blonde babies, I am not photogenic. In one of the solo photographs I glower under-exposed from the saddle of a seaside donkey. I discard the dim seasides and continue to search until I find my most recent school photo. At school we are photographed individually: most recently, I am thirteen and under duress; but I am visible, I am not a shadow at the end of a line of blondes. I take the portrait, which has never been removed from its brown plastic presentation wallet, to the window; and I examine the reluctant smile. *You're a Blaney,* says Mum; and she is right, I can see what she means: the Blaney eyes are burning like stigmata on the glossy surface of the paper. In the searchlight of sunshine at the window they are wounded stars. I stare into their startling darkness and I realize that there is no escape for me: I am a Blaney, a black-eyed Blaney.

I move away from the light and return the photo to the bag. I recall Mum's theory: the Blaneys have black eyes because they are the descendants of Spanish pirates shipwrecked on the coast of County Cork. Thus, for Mum, the Blaneys are more foreign than Irish, and spectacularly untrustworthy. Piracy suggests rampant opportunism amd excessive cruelty: gang planks; press gangs. Pirates preyed on the vulnerable; they were not Robin Hoods; they did not turn aristocrats topsy-turvy in leafy glades as comeuppance; nor did they tumble in true love with Maid Marion. There were no Maid Marions at sea. Pirates were not part of an English tradition of loveable rogues and likeable eccentrics, of monks and kings and twenty-four blackbirds baked in a pie.

'You never hear of a woman pirate,' said Mum, when she had told me the theory.

'You never hear of a woman anything,' I replied; meaning that they might have existed nevertheless.

Mum remained unconvinced, muttering about the problems of babies and sanitary towels at sea.

Pirates lived on the high seas: *high*; dangerous, unpredictable, not-quite-right, not-all-there, you-never-knew-where-you-were-

59

with-a-pirate. Mum is similarly wary of the Blaneys. I like the theory but remain sceptical: what were Spanish pirates doing in the Irish sea? I am entranced by the idea of County Cork: *Cork*, a strange name for a County.

'What I remember about Cork,' said Mum, who once went on holiday to Ireland, 'is the stink of fish.' Then, seeing my disappointment, she conceded reluctantly: 'But that was years ago, and things change, I suppose.'

I hear footsteps and turn to the window to see Mum and Erin outside on the tarmac. Why Erin? Erin should be in the village hall with the Brownies: socks flaccid around ankles, plimsolls punching softly into wooden floorboards. Mum stops at the door and grinds the key into the keyhole. Her face is hidden from me in a haze of bright curls. Erin stands at her side; dimmer, duller; frowning, puzzled. The Brownie beret is askew. In the uniform in the sunshine she is yellow and brown like a soft bruised fruit.

Erin follows Mum over the doorstep into the house. Mum rustles in the hallway and then comes into the living room: she does not pause as usual in the doorway to survey the scene and identify the perpetrators; she does not stare at me and demand *What are you doing?* Instead, she hurries towards me, taut with excitement. 'Guess what?'

I cannot guess, of course. I lower the dustbin liner, and it sags noisily at my feet.

'There was a car accident, just now,' she waves towards the window, 'outside the village hall, just before we arrived.'

Erin follows, eddying in the doorway.

'All the Owls,' continues Mum, anguished, 'in one car.'

Erin's beret flops across her eyes.

'All in one car, turning into the car park, when some stupid old sod from the Over 65s Bring And Buy comes out in his Range Rover without looking: slam!' Mum shrugs in despair. 'There was an ambulance and everything; a policeman. One whiplash injury, they reckon: Snowy Owl. With any luck, it's just cuts and bruises for the others.' She pauses and shrugs again. 'There was talk of cracked ribs.' She steps closer to me. 'But what worries me,' she confides, 'is Brown Owl's palpitations: she told me that she went to see the doctor last week. She's no spring chicken.'

Dismayed, I murmur my sympathies.

Mum sighs. 'Cars all over the road.' Suddenly she remembers Erin, and turns to smile. 'What a mess, eh?' she cajoles. There is no response from Erin. 'So,' she says, returning to me, 'Brownies is cancelled, and we need a cup of tea.' She moves towards the door. 'Perhaps they should avoid travelling in the same car, like royalty.' When she reaches the door she turns to face me, sparkling with suspicion. 'You *said* it would be cancelled.'

'No . . .' I reply hurriedly.

'Yes,' she muses.

'No,' I refute, 'I said it *might* be cancelled.'

She is unconvinced. 'Same thing.'

'It is not the same thing:' I was aware of the possibility of cancellation; I did not expect it, I did not forsee it.

She opens the door. 'Blaney blood,' she mutters as she disappears; 'you give me the creeps.'

1982

··········

Roz is sitting at her dressing table, staring into the mirror with an expression of amazement. She is not amazed but raising her eyebrows so that she can pluck them. Her face is damp from cotton wool licks of toner. Toner opens pores. Should pores be open? Surely they should be closed. I would not want anyone staring into my gaping pores. Her face, cleansed, is larger than usual, stripped of shading, washed of mystery. I look at the smooth pale cheeks in the mirror and I think of a baby's bottom. A strange compliment: as smooth as a baby's bottom. Why bottom? Why baby's bottom? It seems the worst possible combination: baby's bottoms are uncontrollable and in constant need of zinc ointment.

Roz's face is looming at me from the mirror, but she does not see me, she is not looking at me; she is looking at her eyebrows. Momentarily silent, concentrating, she is hunting stray hairs across her brow with the sharp silver points of a pair of tweezers. She seems to poke, not to pluck. Whenever she jabs, I shift uncomfortably against the cushions. I am sitting on the edge of her bed, propped against a pile of cushions, my feet on the floor. The cushions are lacy and not much bigger than pin-cushions. They roll around and slip from the small of my back like pebbles under the arch of a foot.

Roz lowers the tweezers. The track of an eyebrow is visible above each eye. I have no memory of Roz's unplucked eyebrows but I cannot imagine that they were hideous. Nothing on Roz's face is hideous. I am thankful that my own eyebrows are not too thick or shapeless because I cannot pluck them: at the first tug, my eyes become swollen and red and wet like tomatoes. Are my eyebrows unusually sensitive, or exceptionally deep-rooted?

Mum said that there was no need for me to pluck my eyebrows.

'Look at Elizabeth Taylor,' she said. 'Lovely thick eyebrows. And is she ashamed?'

I do not know whether Elizabeth Taylor is ashamed.

Roz rises from the dressing table. She is wearing a towelling bathrobe, and a towel wound around her head: towelling everywhere, a surreptitious return to nappies. The bathrobe is baby pink, I have never seen an article of clothing so baby pink. Cute, cuddly, helpless, happy: why not? Who wants to look like an adult?

'No,' she says suddenly, in delayed reply to my earlier question, a question I had forgotten, 'but if she arrives first, she'll wait across the road in McDonald's.'

I remember that Roz is going out tonight to a Wine Bar with Kim. Kim is a friend from work, on Reception. The Wine Bar is in Barnet: *The Greedy Grape*. I have never met Kim or been to the Wine Bar. I have never been to any Wine Bar. I go to pubs, here, at home: *The Sun, The Vic, The Brewers, The Wheelwrights*. But I have been to Barnet. I have been to Barnet High Street, with Mum, shopping late on cold Saturdays when there was nothing left in the shops near home and, in the end, not much more on the shelves in Barnet. Barnet, the last resort. It is on the end of the tube line: Barnet, the terminus. The map in the station names High Barnet, implying hills and countryside. But there are no hills or countryside. Instead, there is the first – or last – of the London hospitals, The General. There is also a McDonald's, and a record shop where we spend record tokens. So we go to Barnet at the end of Saturdays and after Christmas and birthdays; we go for take-aways and stitches, and for one-way transportation into London. I cannot imagine going to Barnet for a night out.

Roz hurries from the room, through the open door, across the landing at the top of the stairs and into the bathroom. There is a squeal of water unleashed from the shower head and then a drumming on the shower tray. 'What time are your parents going out tonight?' Her voice arrives odd from the bathroom: raised, rinsed. She is washing the conditioner from her hair. *Leave*, it says on the bottle, *Work to ends of hair and leave for 2 or 3 minutes*.

'Eight,' I reply.

I glance at the digital green numerals slotting into position on the black face of the bedside clock: six-twenty.

Roz said to come around on Saturday, at teatime. Her open window presents me with a view of the sky. It is smoky after the heat of the day, the heat rising, disappearing. Somewhere, the sun is fizzling against the hard cool surface of the horizon. I have not seen Roz for a long time, for several weeks, because we do not meet often now that she has left school.

'Why don't you come around on Saturday at teatime,' she said, 'and help me to get ready.'

But Roz needs no help. Once again, I realize, I am Roz's Lady in Waiting.

The sound of spraying water ceases and Roz comes back into the bedroom with the towel re-wound around her head.

'At least you're seeing Sweetiepie this evening,' she says, returning to the stool at the dressing table. 'You're so lucky, he's such a darling.'

Ben: so much of a darling that she cannot remember his name.

She spreads the contents of a make-up bag onto the dressing table. The plastic tubes clatter together on the white wooden surface.

'Gavin's out tonight with his wife.'

Gavin is the man from work, the man – what? – is Roz going out with him? Surely it is impossible to *go out with* someone who is twenty-seven. Twenty-seven and married means *affair*. Anyway, Roz and Gavin do not go out; they go out nowhere, or at least not very often, because they must not be seen together. But does it have to be affair? Is Gavin the man with whom Roz is having-an-affair? Roz cannot have an affair, she is too young for an affair. Affairs are for men with suits and partings, and for ladies with car keys and the inconvenience of children. Roz will not say *affair*. She says that it-wouldn't-be-an-affair-if-he-wasn't-married-and-he-just-happens-to-be-married-and-it-was-a-mistake-and-it-isn't-really-a-marriage-or-not-much-of-a-marriage.

Roz told me about Gavin several months ago, sitting on this bed with me. It was an evening, late, nine o'clock or later, late for during the week. There were – and still are – few opportunities for us to see each other: late evening, after everything else, or early, before. On that evening, Roz was partially depleted of work clothes: the dark shiny shoes were splayed under the dressing table and the navy blue box jacket was hanging pertly on the back of the door. Thick white cuffs had been peeled away from her wrists and stuffed into the folds of cotton above her elbows. Mascara had dislodged throughout the day from her eyelashes to her lower eyelids, and her hair was not as straight as she likes. Between us on the bed there was a ripped packet running with Maltesers. Outside Roz's room, on the landing, her brother was moving to and fro between the bathroom and his bedroom, followed by his mum's voice: *Matthew, did you wash your hair? Properly?*

Roz was leaning, crunching, whispering. 'He's going to leave his wife.' Then she shook her head hurriedly, in denial, although I had said nothing. 'He was always going to leave his wife.' She was breathing chocolate over me. 'He doesn't love her, he never loved her, not really.' Someone else's words? 'In fact,' she elaborated, 'I don't think that he even likes her any more.' She tried to coax a response from me with a leap of her thin eyebrows. 'Isn't that awful?' Then she shrugged, and the eyebrows dropped with the shoulders. 'Isn't that an awful way to live your life?'

Awful for Gavin, she meant. I said nothing.

Now, this evening, Roz is spreading the tubes of make-up across the dressing table by rolling them beneath the palm of her hand. 'It's a Dinner And Dance for Gavin tonight,' she continues. She sighs sadly. 'Poor Gavin, he hates that sort of thing.' She selects a stalk of eyeliner.

I can think of nothing to say. I did not come here this evening to talk about Gavin.

'It's Rotary,' she says.

Rotary? I think of *carousel*, of the frozen prance of the white wooden horses stuck with beads of paint.

'Kim says that Wifey will be in her element, that she comes to all the office parties in a purple ballgown.' Kim is the only other person to know about Gavin. Kim is on Reception, so it is inevitable that she knows about Gavin. Roz's naked green eyes are looking at me from the mirror. 'Purple ballgown, I ask you.'

True. So I cannot stop myself: 'What does she expect?'

Roz laughs. She draws the rod from the container of eyeliner, returns her attention to the mirror, glances back into her own eyes.

She wants to marry Gavin. She talks of a flatshare near him, with other girls from work, nice-and-convenient; followed by a rented home together whilst he is divorcing his wife; and then a mortgage of their own. When she left school last year she was talking in the same manner about becoming a lawyer: in stages, working as an assistant whilst studying at evening classes and law school. She presented the stages as the real route, the authentic route, the superior route. And she sounded credible. But as soon as there was the offer of a job in Small Claims, she abandoned the plans. She mentioned good prospects for promotion from Small Claims, but was unconvincing.

I know by now that the stages were an invention, a yarn to be spun whilst she was plotting an escape from school and college. It was the end of last summer, at the beginning of the new school year, when she told me of her decision to leave. We were three weeks into the Upper Sixth.

'Not now,' I pleaded, 'not yet, wait a while, wait and see.' I had been gathering brochures from universities as if I was planning a holiday; and I was relishing the jargon: Oxbridge, Oxbridge Reject, collegiate, campus, redbrick, LSE, UEA, UCL, defer, combine, sandwich. I wanted to say, *Don't leave me, this will be no fun without you*.

She said, 'I've made my decision.'

Which was unusual. What could I have said in reply? Could I tell her to leave this pink and white bedroom? I could not have talked, like Mum and Dad, about A Good Job: four years of poverty and then you too can be a teacher, Return To Go. It is different for me because all I want is to leave home. Roz wanted a good job. As far as she is concerned, she has a good job now. She travels to London each day on the train, dressed in a dark narrow skirt and a loose blazer, chained with a security pass – Miss Roz Smith – and she earns money.

The green pupils are resting now on fine black lines. 'Lalie,' she says, relinquishing the mirror and bowing again over the dressing table, 'could you check in my bag for headache pills?'

I reach to the end of the bed for the bag.

'We working girls are prone to headaches.' She is smiling, flicking open a compact of eyeshadows.

Working girls: I am sick of these working girls. What does she think that we have been doing, Ali and Lucy and me? During the last year I have taken three sets of exams: weeks of exams, three hour papers in the morning and afternoon, three and a half hours of Practical Criticism; months of revision, of folders full of slithering papers, the declining heavy industry of South Wales in Merthyr Tydfil, Llantrisant, Ebbw Vale. Ebboo Vale. All year I have worked days, nights, and weekends; not because I am interested in South Wales, or in Hoover, and not because I care about King Lear, but because the slip of paper which will arrive next month from the examination board is my passport to somewhere else.

In the bag there is a red leather purse, a black address book, a hairy hairbrush, half a tube of Tunes, a shiny white make-up bag, a bottle of *eau de toilette* rattling in its box, a ring of keys, an emery board, and two tampons. The tampons are pellets, without applicators. I do not like tampons without applicators. It was always the sole way in which we failed each other: *Oh no, not those,* I'd shriek at Roz in my times of emergency in school washrooms; and similarly she would reject mine, my unwieldy batons.

'Try the purse,' she calls. Her eyelids are dappled now like leaves: green, brown, white.

I open the purse: banknotes, lots of them, soft, doubled, cupped; a travel pass of yellow velvet card; and a metallic strip containing painkillers. 'Yes,' I confirm. 'Six.' I take the emery board and begin to scrape at the edge of a troublesome nail.

Downstairs, the door slams: Roz's mum. 'I'm home, darling,' she sings from the porch. 'Give me a shout when you're ready, and I'll run you to the station.'

Roz continues prising the upper lid from her eye with each slow sticky stroke of mascara. She and her mum have similar sturdy black eyelashes. Their eyebrows are identical, too: untethered by longer hairs, drifting weightless to the top of the brow. But Roz's eyes are green, and I have never noticed the colour of her mum's eyes. Dad refers to Roz as *That friend of yours with the striking eyes.*

Striking is a word used by Mum and Dad when they are reluctant to use *pretty*; similarly, *unusual*. Perhaps *unusual* is less so: *Striking?* – Mum will frown doubtfully, eager to withhold a compliment, forcing negotiation – *Well, unusual, certainly.*

I have noticed that people will praise something, anything, rather than nothing: I have lovely eyes and lovely hands and a lovely neck, even a lovely voice, so I know that I do not have a lovely face.

Roz and her mum share other features: pink-painted fingernails; and clothes without shiny patches, clothes smelling of washing powder. And they smoke the same brand of cigarettes, made for women. Roz has always modelled herself on her mum. Soft blonde hair, a baggy black leather handbag and a yellow car: Roz's mum is desirable but substantial. She seems central to the lives of so many people: Roz and Matthew, the ex-husband, the current boyfriend, two extended families (perhaps three, now?), and everyone on Victoria Ward at the cottage hospital. For Roz, a divorce is not a disadvantage: there has been a husband; and there is the chance of another. In the meantime, as a divorcée, Roz's mum has everything that Roz wants: house, car, kids, man, wedding ring, wedding photos in which she looks beautiful, and an ex-husband to resent.

Roz's mum is the sort of mum who would say to her children *I just want you to be happy, darling.* I imagine that my mum might say the opposite. My mum's favourite saying is *I've never shirked.* She would never say *darling.*

68

I'm home, darling. Give me a shout when you're ready, and I'll run you to the station.

Mum would say, *What are you doing up there?* Or, *When are you going to eat your tea, do you think I cook this stuff for my own amusement?* Or, *Tidy your room, I've told you a thousand times, it's a pigsty.* And she would not run me to the station because she cannot drive.

Roz turns the mascara brush to the other eye. Notwithstanding the eyes, Mum regards Roz as a *pudding:* small, regular features. Mum favours women like Sophia Loren. She praises interesting noses. I would rather have Roz's regular face than risk a big nose.

I can't see what they see in that Roz, insists Mum.

That-Roz: What's *That-Roz* doing these days? And *That-Roz* is trouble. Roz *is* trouble, not the *cause* of trouble: according to Mum, Roz is trouble itself, a little devil on my shoulder.

Roz sighs. 'Do you think those black shoes will be all right with that blue dress?' She is staring at me from the mirror with the jewel eyes, and biting an unpainted lower lip.

I reply into the mirror: 'Yes, fine.'

She comes to sit beside me on the pink duvet so that our feet are resting lightly side by side on the tufts of the carpet. Her feet are bare: this little piggy went to market. I am wearing plimsolls. Her shins are bare, colourless, hairless; I am wearing jeans: *Jeans,* says Mum, *in this weather, and what on earth is wrong with a nice summer dress?* I relish my reply: *Show me a nice summer dress and I'll tell you.*

Roz lifts the towel from her head and lowers it onto the floor where it is borne around her ankles by the tufts. She shakes loose her hair: it is highlighted, selectively depleted of colour so that she appears to be hurtling headlong towards an early second childhood. 'What are you doing about a holiday this year?'

'What are *you* doing? What about Tenerife?'

Roz sighs. 'Oh, Tene-bloody-rife. I don't want to go to Tenerife. I want to go to Majorca with Kim and her cousin. But what do I tell Dad? Me, Matthew, Dad: Hotel Isabella, every year.' She sighs again. 'It's not that I don't like going to Tenerife.' She is staring at the whorl of towel on the floor.

'Can't you do both? Doesn't your Dad pay for Tenerife?'

She turns mournfully towards me. 'It's not money, Lalie, it's time. I have ten days holiday.'

Ten days? Shamefully, I contemplate my three and a half months.

'But, anyway,' she continues resignedly, 'what about you?'

'I'd like to go away for a while at the end of the summer but I suppose I'll have to find a job.' I have to find work during the holidays but she has to find a holiday during work; I have time but no money, and she has money but no time.

'Temping?' she asks.

'Yes,' I lie: I am quite sure that no one will want my services, even temporarily; especially temporarily. It will take time for me to learn about offices and machines. *You couldn't organize a night out in a brewery*, Mum says to me.

Night out?

I have already been on holiday for a week, but not my holiday: it was a holiday for three children from a local Special School. Their Headmistress had written to Miss Killick – a magic circle of mistresses – because she needed a volunteer: there were staff shortages at the school and there could be no holiday without a volunteer. Miss Killick came from her office with the letter to find me during Free Study: 'It's your sort of thing,' she said, 'people and their rights.'

I almost replied that it was not my sort of thing. I wanted to work with disadvantaged children, not disabled children. I had been reading about disadvantaged children in paperback books bought from the secondhand book room at the back of the bookshop in town. The paperbacks are written by women who are Dames. The women were not Dames when the books were written: due to the books, the reports, the policies, they *became* Dames. The paperbacks have black and white photographs on the covers: terraces and basements; or high-rises. They are washed with tints, green and brown like slime. Freeze-framed children in the streets or on the balconies are distant, small, stunted. The books told me that these children are limited, denied, rejected. They are powerless and impoverished. They can do no right. They are intended to fail: factory fodder; and, I suppose, family fodder. Small-minded, big-bellied.

The books were written for teachers. The Dames are clear that none of this is the fault of the teachers: children are failed by the system; in a system that passes or fails, not everyone can succeed. *Pass or fail* smothers *Learn and develop*. The failures become listless and bitter. Reading the books, I began to wonder why Mr MacKenzie continues to teach A level. Why isn't he working in a school like Summerhill? When I asked him, he laughed and said, 'I know what you mean.' What kind of an answer is that?

At our school there is a faded notice in the entrance hall: VISITORS MUST REPORT TO RECEPTION. When I visited the Special School, the entrance hall was bright with words: fresh words, bold words, words not issued as threats on notices or shut into books.

TODAY IS TUESDAY.

THE WEATHER IS – .

A small girl was affixing SUNNY. She was standing on tip-toe, reaching up the wall. Hearing my footsteps, she turned towards me. For an instant, I thought that I recognized the face. It was a smooth round face with smooth round features. It was the Down's Syndrome that I was recognizing. Mum cannot even manage *Mongols*, mistakenly saying *Mongrels*: a hash of chromosomes.

'Hello,' said the girl, 'I'm Emily.'

She took me to the Headmistress, and the Headmistress took me around the school. I looked into classrooms and saw that these children were not limited, like those in my books, by high-rises, or not solely by high-rises, but by the smallest things, by steps, stairs, and stares, by numbers and words, written and spoken, spoken too quietly, unspoken. They were equipped with wheelchairs, hearing aids, spelling boards. I saw classrooms,

71

kitchens, tropical fish, a pottery studio, a hydrotherapy pool. My tour finished at the Special Unit. The Special Unit in a Special School: 'Mobility and behavioural problems,' the Headmistress had told me in the introduction before the tour. I stopped outside the door.

'Go on,' said the Headmistress. 'It's Amelia's class. You'll be going on the holiday with Amelia's class.'

Now-she-tells-me?

I opened the door. The classroom was busy. Children – five of them? six? – were sitting around the room in wheelchairs and on cushions. One child was banging his head against the wall: deliberate, sonorous head-butts. Another was crying silently, staring at the floor. Two women in pink nylon overalls were rushing quietly across each other's paths like drip-dry nuns: *There, there; now, now*. In the far corner, opposite me, a woman wearing jeans and a T-shirt was sitting on a floor cushion with a boy. The boy was gnarled, stiffened, downcast. 'Hello,' the woman called to me, laughing. 'You must excuse us, but it's like Paddy's Market in here today.' She turned, muttering, to the boy in her arms: 'Isn't it? eh?'

The Headmistress chuckled, stepping past me, drawing me towards them: 'Meet Paddy. And Amelia.'

That afternoon, Amelia began to teach me everything from the beginning.

Eye contact, she explained to me, is the first step. She had been trying to establish eye contact on the cushion with Paddy. I watched Paddy twisting away from Amelia and I thought of the blonde babies at home who used to attach themselves to me with their blue gazes, searching my face for familiarity: if I poked out my tongue, they copied me; and if I smiled, too. My own schooldays had begun with Peter and Jane (always Peter-and-Jane, never Jane-and-Peter). After eye contact, Amelia mentioned manipulation skills and showed me Clara's pegboard. Clara held the pegs in her fists and aimed at the holes. Later in the afternoon, trying to assist Clara to drink from her beaker, I felt the lack of strength in her grasp, the stiff fingers, the poor judgement and co-ordination.

The two classroom assistants were kind to me: Doreen and Shirley; perms, pinnies, sandals. They brought their homes to work with them, the news of their children: Jody-and-Jason; Graham-Glenn-and-Samantha. It was Doreen who came with us on the holiday: Amelia, Doreen, and me; with Paddy, Clara, Mohammed. We went to a caravan near Brighton.

'Brighton! And me, a vicar's daughter,' said Amelia. It was Amelia's catch phrase: *And me, a vicar's daughter*.

All day, every day, for our four days near Brighton, we went out: beach, town, castle, Downs. We travelled in the minibus – Variety Club Sunshine – with the wheelchairs, three of them, black leather and chrome. Clara's wheelchair was different from the others, longer, extended for her legs: the unbending, unbendable legs lay on a platform, tickled by sunburn. On the seafront, in the shops, on the bone-coloured hills, people fluttered around Clara: bowing over her, murmuring praise, flattered by her smiles and entranced by her sandy pigtails. Clara laughed and clapped to say Yes and to indicate pleasure: desire and delight exploded like twenty-one-gun-salutes throughout the holiday. Mohammed, immobile, nudged us with his gaze. The gaze clung to Amelia. Amelia conducted conversations with him: *You want to saunter along the pier this afternoon, do you? Candy floss? Yuk*. They allowed us to glimpse their private jokes: *Look at Mohammed, here, listen to this giggle, we're not even out of the car park and he's found the tea shop*. Paddy looked nowhere, bowing his head and rocking to his own rhythm.

Amelia told me Paddy's story, one afternoon, in a café, when we were carrying trays from the counter to our table: 'Paddy's thirteen. When he was nine, he was knocked down by a truck. He spent nine months in hospital: nothing. And then they sent him home: *There's nothing more we can do*. They sent him home, carried him into the house, and left him on the sofa. And that was that. His poor mother.'

In the distance, Paddy was slumped in his wheelchair next to Doreen. Doreen was chatting over the table to Clara.

'And the others?' I asked tentatively.

'Mo has cerebral palsy, of course. You know about cerebral palsy?'
I nodded. 'But Clara?'

'Oh, a list as long as your arm, from birth.' She shrugged. 'I'm
not a doctor.' Across the room, Clara was clapping for some more
strangers. 'And it's a shame, because when she's older, without
the pigtails, when she's no longer cute, people won't want to
know.'

In the evenings, when the children were quiet in their beds, when
music was humming from our tape recorder, we would rip open
a packet of biscuits and Doreen would leave the caravan with a
handful of coins to phone Jody and Jason. Amelia was writing a
letter to her husband. I had written a few postcards. I sent a
postcard of Brighton seafront to Roz.

'You went to Brighton, of course,' says Roz, now, beside me on
the bed.

'Yes.'

'Not much of a holiday, though, I suppose.' She is dragging a
hairbrush through the wet tangles of her hair.

'No.'

'Depressing, I suppose.'

'No,' I correct hurriedly, 'but hard work.'

'Yes.' She glances down at my hands, and frowns. 'Lalie, look
at that emery board; you can't use that old thing; let me get you
another.'

Before I can protest she is across the room at the dressing table,
sifting the contents of the drawer. 'Here.' She turns to me with
another.

'Anyway, where do you think you'll go for a holiday?' She sits
down again on the bed.

'France, probably.'

She grins. 'A romantic trip to Paris for two?'

'No, he's off to the States, to stay with relatives for a month or
so.'

74

She grips my forearm. 'And you're not going with him?' She is horrified.

I laugh into her face. 'With his sister?' My rhetorical question provokes a predictable response: Roz recoils. We do not remember the details, or perhaps there are no details, merely instincts, but we know that we do not like his sister.

'And to Cousin Kay?'

She protests again: 'I never knew about any American cousin.'

I want to say *She's hardly Edie Sedgewick*, but Roz will be foxed. 'In New Jersey,' I say instead. Roz stares blankly at me. I explain, 'It would be like going on holiday to Dagenham. And I'm told that she's big in the local church.'

Roz wrinkles her nose; I pinch it gently between my thumb and forefinger. 'And *small* in the local church would be bad enough.'

She laughs, rolls away from me, and crosses the room to the hairdryer. I settle back on the bed, composed, cross-legged, straight-backed: I am Thinking Tall; I once watched a yoga programme on television and the woman told us to Think Tall, to imagine that we each had a spirit rising up our spines and escaping from the tops of our heads. It had seemed like a good idea at the time. But now, when I close my eyes, I see a genie stuck in the neck of a bottle.

'So,' says Roz, brandishing the hairdryer, 'Cousin Kay, non; La France, oui.' She turns to the mirror and switches on the hairdryer. The blast of air screams from the barrel, splattering her hair against her head. 'But who with?' She was required to shout this question over the roar of heat.

I pause to consider my answer. 'Ali.' Then I shrug, to imply — what? — doubt? nonchalance?

Roz has turned towards me. Perhaps she is reading my lips, because she is peering very closely at me through a fog of blown hair. 'Ali?' she screams, the hairdryer rearing in her hand. 'Just you and Ali?'

I stare up at her from the bed. 'And Deborah.' I realize that my answer has risen like a question, waiting for confirmation or permission.

'Deborah?' She echoes, frowning, staring, grasping my words. 'Deborah who?'

How many Deborahs do we know? 'Steiner.'

Roz's expression explodes into incredulity. 'Debbie Steiner?'

I stare impassively from the bed. Ali and Deborah are going to France, to practise their French, and they have invited me to join them.

Receiving no reply, Roz returns to the mirror. 'What's she doing now?' she asks.

What is she doing now? She means *What did she ever do, what does she do, who is she?* I remind myself that Roz knows Deborah as someone who sits across a classroom, frowning over books.

'She's waiting, like the rest of us, to go away in the autumn.'

Roz is concentrating again on the mirror. 'Doesn't she have a brother or sister or something already away at college?'

'Yes.' All of them, two sisters and a brother.

All of them, says Mum, breathless with excitement. *Aren't they clever? And both parents are teachers. Aren't they clever?*

'Isn't she Jewish?' asks Roz, switching off the hairdryer.

'Yes.' I do not understand what this means. We did Jews in the first year at school, in Religious Education. We drew candlesticks with six branches, and we wrote out a menu for Passover. I have seen men in Golders Green wearing hats and beards, and I have seen a documentary about Anne Frank, but none of this seems pertinent to Deborah.

Isn't she Jewish? Mum says the same, with a similar lack of malice.

At first, I challenged her: 'How do you know?'

'Jewish names.'

Code name: Steiner, Deborah.

Mum says that Deborah is A Nice Girl, that the Steiners are A Nice Family. She seizes opportunities to learn more: *Oh Deborah, hello, have a cup of tea, just sit yourself down here whilst the kettle boils.* Neither Roz nor Lucy are given tea during their visits: I suspect that Mum considers them to be Not Quite Right because there has been a divorce in the family. She is not happy with divorce: *People should talk more*, she says.

I cover my ears and raise my eyes.

People drift if there's not enough talk, she shouts.

I remove my hands from my ears to shout my reply: *Well, there's no chance of me going anywhere, then, is there*.

I am convinced that there is another explanation for Mum's fascination with the Steiners: they are exotic. There is nothing exotic about Roz's and Lucy's families: there is no chance for them to be termed Sephardic or Ashkenazy. Roz's parents came from Rainham in Essex; Lucy's mum was born in Slough. It does not seem to matter to Mum that Deborah's parents came from Manchester. Neither does it matter to Mum that there are four Steiner children: Mum usually implies that a large family is tasteless or indiscreet, presumably indicative of too much sex, or careless sex, or perhaps just sex – other people's sex. Her own family is an exception, of course, an ambition. The Steiner family is another exception, a noble institution, a valiant effort to preserve a heritage: almost royalty.

One day Mum told me, 'Deborah's brother is studying politics.' Presumably she had learned this from Deborah.

'I know.' A reply, yet no reply at all. I stayed studiously calm, over the newspaper. Which was difficult because, for some reason, I find the mention of Deborah's brother anything but calming.

'So,' she prattled, 'I asked Deborah, Will he be an MP?'

I glanced up from the newspaper. People study Politics to overthrow-the-system, don't they? If they want to become politicians, they study law.

'And she said: "No, he wants to go into housing." '

I looked down, turned a page.

'So what's that?' Mum asked me. 'Building? Design?'

'Policy,' I replied reluctantly.

'Oh, town planning.'

It was not the first time that Mum had raised the subject of Deborah's brother with me. I do not want to discuss him with her. Because if I start, she will not stop. Because I detect a fixation; hers, not mine. No, hers as well as mine. And I refuse to share a fixation with my mother. Hers is ridiculous because she has never even seen him. I suspect that she imagines him studying books by candlelight, bowed over pages of indecipherable script: a young Lenin, or a priestly Montgomery Clift, serious, passionate, emaciated. Which is not so far from the truth but lacks a crucial element: Deborah's brother is very laid back. Literally so, when I met him. When I met him, last month, he was lying on the settee, watching a Lassie film and eating bacon flavoured crisps. He had returned home from university for the summer. Deborah introduced me in passing – *Oh, this is Lalie* – and he raised a hand slowly, smiled slowly. As we left the room, the hand remained above the settee in good-natured surrender.

The other day, when Deborah came to see me, Mum followed us into the kitchen towards the kettle. 'I've just been shopping,' she told Deborah, 'and, believe me, we could do with your brother and his policy.' She stood at the sink with the kettle, staring out of the window. 'This is a God-forsaken hole.'

I do not know whether it is permissible to say God-forsaken to a Jew.

She turned off the tap. 'Why on earth did anyone decide to put it here?'

My knowledge of Geography provided the answer: 'It's a dormitory town.'

She continued to stare out of the window. 'Dormitory,' she echoed incredulously, despondently.

Roz sits at the dressing table and eases her hair into the tight grip of a black hairband. She frowns into the mirror, reluctant, fearful that it will dry with kinks. The frowning forehead is a canvas which she marks with a dab of foundation from a tube.

'How's Ali?' she asks the mirror. 'I haven't seen her for ages.'

There is a dab of foundation on each cheek, on the chin, the nose, the neck.

'Oh, she's fine.'

I saw Ali last night, en route to Deborah: 'Coming?'

She had declined, laughing apologetically. She was wearing pyjamas, large, cotton, loose and cool; she smelled of a bubbly bath time. 'I'm knackered,' she said. 'Friday night. A busy week.' I was sitting on one of the leather armchairs and she was sitting opposite me on the settee. On the coffee table between us was the photo album: Ali and Grace as children; Brownies and bridesmaids.

'I don't know how you can bear to go to work,' I sympathized. She laughed again. 'It's not forever, that's how I bear it. I work until lunch and then I work until home time. Simple.' She smiled kindly at me. 'Four more weeks, then France and freedom.'

Roz is smoothing the foundation over her face. 'She's working, isn't she?'

'Yes. Typing.'

The foundation is melting into Roz's skin. 'Typing,' she repeats, wrinkling her nose. The face in the mirror is enriched, sealed, matt. 'She said that her exams went okay?' The voice is doubtful, or perhaps merely preoccupied: the eyes are scanning the skin.

'Yes.'

'So she'll be going away in October?' Roz waves a small soft brush at one side of her face, and a cheekbone appears.

'Yes.'

Like Deborah, Ali wants to study French: French and Spanish for Deborah; French for Ali. Initially it was English for Ali, for all of us; all of us except Deborah. But then Ali perfected her French with Deborah during the Upper Sixth. They were the best students in the small French class, which was a closed order to the rest of us. For me, French has become their language, the language spoken by them, invented by them: no longer a lesson in a classroom hung with maps of wine-producing regions, no longer a tape in a booth in a language lab fecund with creepers of graffiti. And if French is taking Ali away, then Deborah, with two languages, is going even further. And Spain, of course, is even further away than France.

French was the language in the magazines read by Ali and Deborah in the Common Room at lunch time. The magazines came from Claudie, the French Assistant. Claudie was their friend. For me, she would have been simply another language Assistant, nameless, foreign. An Assistant came and went every year, walking jauntily through the corridors in scuffed ankle boots, in corduroy trousers and blouson, swinging shapeless shoulder-length dark hair; too young to be a teacher, too old to be one of us, and forming peculiar liaisons with both. But the last one became Claudie. Claudie would touch Ali and Deborah's shoulder blades in passing, muttering *Ça va?* as if it was natural; which it was, I suppose, for her.

We were new to the Upper Sixth when Ali and Deborah began waiting together every lunch time outside the Conversation Room for Claudie to arrive with the key. At that time, Roz was making the decision to leave. Later, when Roz had gone, Deborah began to sit next to Ali in the Common Room, opposite me. One day, I leaned forward in my chair and asked her, 'What about Games?' Deborah was Head Girl; everyone knew that if *I* had been Head Girl I would have fought for the abolition of compulsory Games lessons, especially for Sixth Formers. Deborah did not seem to be the fighting type. When she turned towards me, I saw the grey ripple of her eyes. 'What about games?' she asked me calmly, emptily. It was the first time that we had spoken directly to each other.

'They're compulsory,' I snapped, 'and they shouldn't be compulsory. I don't want to play hockey. It's demeaning.' I was pleased with *demeaning*.

She frowned. The frown was dense with thought.

'So can't you do something?' I asked her.

She shifted nearer to me in her chair. 'What about alternatives to hockey?' She placed equal stress on each word; unlike me, presumably, because Mum tells me to *Stop bloody shouting* when I have not raised my voice.

'That's not the point; the point is *freedom*.'

'I know, I realize; but suggestions are likely to be more successful than refusals, and, anyway, it might be nice to be able to make some suggestions, some choices.'

80

I sat back in my chair. 'Like what?'

She shrugged. 'Riding, yoga, swimming, dancing. We could present a petition,' she said.

Ali and Lucy had abandoned their conversation to listen to us. They were waiting for my reply.

I shrugged. 'Okay. But what shall we say?'

She sat back in her chair. 'Perhaps we should do some research.'

'Why?'

'To find out what people think.'

'But we *know* what they think.'

She laughed as if I had made a joke, her eyes running briefly elsewhere, everywhere, with their strange dull sparkle. 'We *think* we know what they think.' The frown settled again. 'It might be best to use their own words, on paper. It'll mean more. They'll be less likely to go back on their own words. It might be best if everyone agrees on some statements.' She paused and then smiled. 'To be honest, my only statement is that I hate the PE skirt.'

Later, at Christmas, after our victory over Games, we started another campaign, for a school magazine. Deborah negotiated the use of a room as an office, an ex-storeroom, to remain unlocked for us at all times. Mr Allan praised our *enterprising initiative* and often lingered outside in the corridor. With my teeth clamped onto my blue printer's pencil, I would flounce past him into our office. I was using the blue pencil to edit. I liked to edit. Lucy was providing illustrations. I liked to tease that she was giving new meaning to the term *artist's impression*. 'It's certainly an impression,' I'd say, handing a sketch of Mr Allan or Miss Killick across the office to Deborah, 'but is it libellous?'. One day, poised with my blue pencil over something written by Deborah, an account of a visit to a relative in an old people's home, I remarked that she was going to be a journalist. Deborah glanced at me from the sticky, blotchy paste-up version of a cover. 'I'd rather be a dancer,' she said lightly.

I had seen Deborah dancing in the school hall. By then, Sixth Formers had permission from Mr Allan to propose individual activities to the horrified and resentful Games staff. Deborah had chosen ballet practice. Apparently she had been going to ballet classes for years. The Games staff granted permission for her to dance in the Hall if she could find some space beyond the punches of the volley-ball players. I was granted permission for Rambling because I had enlisted the support of one of the Geography teachers: *Meet In The Car Park For A Walk Through The Cemetery*. I was walking through the Hall on my way to the car park when I paused to watch Deborah. The volley-ball players were characteristically vigorous, but a small space settled around Deborah whilst she plugged in a tape recorder and bent over her shoes. She began dusting the shoes with resin, to prevent slipping on the parquet floor. Behind me, in the Games corridor, a Rugby team was crashing studded soles onto the tiles. When Deborah's pink leather slippers were assured an invisible grip, she returned soundlessly to the tape recorder. She was wearing a leotard, a cardigan, tights and leg warmers: layers, wrappings, bindings; her joints cushioned and strengthened. She depressed the button on the tape recorder and then stretched; and suddenly there were muscles in her slim legs, firm and full like little pillows.

Deborah's ballet classes are on Saturdays. For most of Saturday she is missing. She misses our notorious elevenses-and-lunch-all-rolled-into-one in the Patisserie, joins us late in the afternoon for shopping. She has been going to classes since she was nine or ten. I started classes when I was four but stopped when I was eleven, when everyone else's Saturdays became more interesting: clothes sales, and take-away milkshakes by the penny-filled fountain in the shopping centre. My sister Jane went to three ballet classes before deciding to stay at home as usual on Saturday mornings, watching *Banana Splits* and eating heaps of sugary cereal soaked in the cream from the top of each milk bottle. Erin has no sense of balance, Lyndsay is a boy, and it is too soon to know about Lauren. Until I was eleven I wanted to be a dancer. Whenever I told Mum, she said that all little girls want to be dancers. This meant that she had wanted to be a dancer. And, of course, it meant No. She told me, time and time again, ballerinas work so hard that their feet bleed. I was fascinated, and sceptical: how could flesh bleed without cuts?

Now Roz is using a pom-pom to splash powder from a small tub onto her face and neck, monitoring the progress in the mirror. 'So when did you last see Ali?'

'Last night.'

'Go anywhere nice?'

'No, she was too tired.'

After Ali, I had gone to visit Deborah; and Deborah's house *is* somewhere nice. I wish I could tell Roz about Deborah's house, it is unlike anyone else's house: it is without the pale fluffy carpets and silky walls of Roz's rooms, the bright white kitchen of Lucy's bungalow or the squeaky leather armchairs of Ali's glass-plated, stone-effected lounge. On my first visit to Deborah's house, I marvelled at the bookshelves lining the walls. There are no books in my house except the Reader's Digest picture books of the wonders of the world; and, upstairs, children's annuals, many of them donated to us by family friends – who needs enemies? – or bought from Brownie jumble sales, the covers featuring children ecstatic on sleighs. Now I look briefly around Roz's room: clutter, controlled and colour co-ordinated clutter; a box of tissues in a lacy holder, a pristine white fluffy toy on the window sill, the lacy cushions on the bed.

I realise that nothing in Roz's room seems to have been made by hand. I notice that there are no pots or vases ribboned by traces of fingertips; and no flowers, picked. The room is untouched by human hand: there is no trace of Roz here, no sign that she lives here, or dreams here. There is an appointment diary on the dressing table, with illustrations from Kew Gardens, too nice to use, and a birthday book on the bedside table, with a cover drawing of girls in lily-pale Victorian dresses, bowling hoops through a field of daisies. Downstairs there are no books – not even an Ali-and-Grace album of childhood photos – but a fresh pile of magazines and catalogues next to the biscuit tin in the kitchen.

In Deborah's house the rooms are insulated by books. The house

83

is not quiet, not at all quiet: outside noise is kept out but inside noise is kept in. The inside noise is musical. I have been to her house three or four times now, and on each occasion I have noticed a new musical instrument. On the visit before last, I saw a banjo on the wall in the downstairs toilet. On my last visit I noticed a second piano, in the distance, in the study, hidden beneath pot plants, stacks of scores and a few metronomes. '*Two* pianos?'

Deborah merely said, 'Well, we all play.'

Other instruments, smaller, portable, are in the hallway or on the stairs, in cupboards and beneath tables, their distinctive shapes obscured by the hard black shells of the cases. There are music stands, feeble chrome scarecrows, in the corners of every room. Deborah's mother is a music teacher: 'Music and Remedial,' Deborah informed me casually, recalling for me Music-and-Movement, a class of prancing five-year-olds in knickers and vests. Unlike Remedial, Deborah's mother teaches music from home. Whenever I have been to the house I have seen her receiving individual instrument-burdened pupils into the hallway and leading them to the study. It seems to me that Deborah's mother's favourite word is *Nonsense,* of which she is emphatic that she will have none. Whenever I go to the house I hear her, as she swipes another sheet of music from another pile and leads another pupil into the study: *Can't play the piece? Nonsense. No cake with your cup of tea? Nonsense.*

On my last visit, someone was playing a flute upstairs. 'Who's that?' I asked Deborah.

'My sister,' she replied, appreciatively. 'She's home for dinner tonight.'

I have never seen the two sisters. 'What instruments does your brother play?'

She laughed knowingly, indulgently. 'Oh, *him*. He plays *nothing.*'

I questioned closer: 'But you told me that you all play the piano.'

'Oh, the piano, yes,' she allowed dubiously, as if the piano did not count. 'Yes, he can play the piano.' Then she brightened, lightened: 'Actually, he's a natural, he'd be brilliant if he tried, but he's a lazy sod.' She laughed again. 'You'd have to tie him down before he'd practise.'

Deborah's father plays records. When I first went to the house, when I was standing with Deborah in the hallway, hanging up my coat, he called to us from the front room: drawing a record from a boldly labelled, densely packed box, he enthused, 'Listen to this, girls; this is what counts.' It was an old record, cut from a thick shiny black material like a mineral. Her father's records are pressed with scratchy black voices; black voices singing-the-blues. He seems to like rueful complaint. Whenever I have been to the house he has been busy with his own complaints, proclaiming and bellowing from the bathroom, the kitchen, the hallway, the cellar, about lack of toilet roll, lack of biscuits, lack of money, lack of spirituality, lack of cynicism, lack of peace and quiet. Also he reads aloud from his newspaper, which complains. 'He likes an audience,' Deborah told me; 'So, ignore him,' she murmured kindly, indulgently, meaning the opposite.

Ali has begun to go to Jazz Clubs in London on Saturday nights with Julian. And my Dad has a boxed set of jazz records entitled *Swing*. It is kept in the cupboard beneath the stairs with the other things that belong to him: his tool box, some old log books, a wallet containing three pale photographs of friends during National Service, a trophy won in a driving contest, a pair of best shoes, and a bottle of Scotch received several Christmases ago from a customer. He never listens to the records, but sometimes the car radio plays Radio Two: *Jazz*, he says, *easy listening*. I recognize this music from airport lounges and planes before take-off: travel sickness, motion sickness, Swing. I know that Roz and I agree: who would want to go to an Easy Listening Club?

Roz is drawing a thin red line around her lips. 'So is she still going out with Julian?' she mutters between long strokes of the pencil.

'Who?' I ask, focusing again on Roz.

She directs a dark green flash at me from the mirror. 'Well Ali, of course. Who do you think I mean? Debbie Steiner, Good God? I might be out of touch, but I'm not *that* out of touch.'

85

'Yes,' I reply resignedly, rebuked. 'Yes, she's still going out with Julian.'

Roz replaces the pencil on the dressing table and selects a small tubular enamel case. From the case, she raises a core of lipstick. She has said nothing about Julian. Her silence is a subtle comment: she wishes to imply that she is uninterested in Julian; moreover, that Julian is uninteresting. She is wrong. Julian is very interesting; pale and interesting, as Mum would say. His faded olive complexion matches the faded olive raincoat that he wears thrown onto his shoulders like a failed disguise. Roz's lips are momentarily sealed on the subject by the sliding stub of red wax. For Roz, Julian's crime is that he is not Gavin.

Roz has learned all about Julian from me because she has never met him. I see him often with Ali. In the days before Gavin, Roz was interested: sceptical, and derisive sometimes, but interested. In the early days, I would describe Julian as nice and Roz would wring a mocking red smile from her face: *Nice?* And then, laughing, I would insist – *No, really* – before making the mistake of describing him as *Quiet*. Roz would tickle me with another hidden smile: *Nice and quiet? How scintillating! An evening in the company of Ali and Julian, how scintillating! I envy you.*

But Julian is nice *and* quiet. Like Ali, I suppose.

Roz is looking at me from the mirror: relenting, pausing, poised with the lipstick. 'What's up?' she whispers, not a question but a statement: *Something's Wrong.* She is looking knowingly at me.

I am surprised. 'Nothing.'

The faded eyebrows arch over the eyes like toppled question marks.

'No, really, nothing.'

She shrugs to signify offence, and twists the lipstick down into its case.

'Anyway, why?' I probe, curious.

She shrugs more emphatically, abdicating responsibility for explanation, hinting at intuition. 'You look miserable.'

'Thanks, Roz.'

She laughs, on cue, turning towards me. 'I'm sympathetic, Lalie; take advantage.' Then she leaves the stool and comes to sit beside me, peering into my face with a smiling expression of benevolence and vague fascination. She reaches briefly for my wrist, and squeezes: a chivvying motion.

'What?' I interrupt, faintly alarmed. 'What?'

'You've seemed a bit miserable lately.'

Lately? When, lately, have I seen Roz? 'Lately?'

She withdraws the hand.

'I'm always miserable, Roz.'

Unhearing, she proceeds with an increasingly indulgent smile and another manual chivvy. 'So there's nothing?'

'Nothing.'

Nothing. Mum says that I worry about nothing. On my way here, there was nothing as usual in the streets: the lampposts at regular intervals on the hill, with the long grey necks and tiny heads of dinosaurs; the bus travelling its route, crawling alongside the kerb, growling and rattling, quarter-past-the-hour but ten minutes late, half-full with shoppers sitting alone, driven by the staring bus driver with the thatched wig. On the hill, I narrowed my eyes against the thin slices of sunlight spilling from the bunting of parked cars. The small gardens, behind the small gates, inside the low fences, were empty of people. They are boxed displays of lawn and shrubbery inherited from previous residents; Harvey perennials. I turned from the hill into Roz's road, passing the Sub Post Office, glancing at the ribbons of handwritten postcards in the window: *Gardening Done, Sideboard For Sale, Garage To Let*, each marked faintly in pencil with a future expiry date.

In front of me, Roz's painted face looms on the blank canvas of the window-framed sky. What can I say to her? She would not understand me. For Roz, there is no problem: Miserable? So spend an evening in The Greedy Grape. I cannot tell her because this life, the life that I hate, is her life: weekends at The Greedy Grape in the company of the car-keyed regulars, Dave, Andy, Mandy, Tim, Kim; a flat in Southgate, a nice enough area. In ten years' time where will they be, Roz and the regulars? In The Greedy Grape, perhaps, but less often? More often at home in Southgate, with the kids? There will be kids by then, there are kids eventually: two kids, two cars, four bedrooms. Unlike me, Roz does not seem to worry that everything is pointless. Perhaps she knows something that I don't know. And perhaps not.

Roz likes work. At my feet, the yellow travel pass is protruding from the handbag. A pass restricts access, confers status: the yellow pass implies that everyone wants to travel on the seven-fifty-seven. Work, Roz tells me, means that she is someone. Who? Roz Smith, Assistant, Small Claims? Then, sometimes, she says that work is a laugh. Bathing Roz's dog is a laugh, but barely. There are good laughs and less good laughs, and there must be better laughs than work. Sometimes she praises work as something to do. I have plenty to do. At work, Roz is doing something for someone else. All day, every day, from seven-fifty-seven in the morning, Roz's life belongs to someone else. What does she do in the evenings? What would I do? Exhausted, I'd watch the repeats of *The Good Life*. Tea, telly, bath, bed, and my nights would be haunted by mornings. I could bear three days each week, perhaps, or four, but five? A five-day week leaves a day for collapse and a day for preparation, and nothing in-between. And who wants a free day on a Sunday, when there is nothing to do?

How can I tell Roz that I am afraid that university will not be enough to take me away from all of this? Mum and Dad want me to graduate to a good job. Apparently there are good jobs in accountancy. But what do accountants review with satisfaction at the end of their lives? Their accounts? There is no shortage of occupations that I have chosen: archaeologist, art historian, ballerina, florist, pharmacist, pilot. Florist, I had forgotten florist, I would still like to be a florist. But somehow it seems now that these occupations are for other lives. How? Why?

Mum and Dad suggest that a good job will bestow me a nice house, and travel. But when will I spend time in the nice house, and when will I travel? On Sundays? Watching Roz as she spills away from me across the bed, roly-poly, reaching towards the chest of drawers, rummaging for knickers, I realize that I am very tired, that I would not want to go out tonight. I shut my eyes. How can I tell Roz that I am tired? She works, all day, every day, and I do nothing. How can I be tired? I do nothing except wait. I wait to be somewhere else. Mum likes to say that waiting is tiring, but not to me: to me, she says *You should be outside in all this lovely sunshine whilst you have the chance.* The sunshine is here all the time, in my room and on my bed before I wake, downstairs at breakfast, in the garden, staying until bedtime and leaving a smoky smell in all the rooms. Everywhere the sky is raw and open. What would I do, outside? Perhaps Mum wants to tether me in the garden like a pony.

Roz is muttering: 'Why do I never have any decent underwear?'

Decent underwear? I open my eyes. She is picking through the drawerful of frilly knickers. I smirk: 'Decent or decent?'

'Decent:' recent.

But all Roz's knickers are new, always. Mine are Marks and Spencer, Mum-bought, less new. If I complain to Mum about my clothes in comparison to my friends' clothes, she replies, *And since when have you wanted to be like everyone else?* Again, I shut my eyes on Roz. Although I have been away from school for weeks and weeks, exams remain with me, inside me, and whenever I shut my eyes there is a map of South Wales on the inside of my eyelids. Sometimes I wake during the night and try to remember . . . what? . . . the declining heavy industries of South Wales? I am allowed to forget about South Wales, now. I am supposed to forget, now.

I forget during the trips with Lucy into the countryside. Most days, Lucy's car arrives on the crazy paving beneath my window: *A drive,* she calls to me from the driveway; *Town, or something.* Sometimes we go into the countryside: a left turn at the church. The countryside has villages with village greens, some of them sprawling spectacularly like sick lakes inside the rings of old houses. The villages are deserted, the inhabitants at work in London. Our destination is a bench outside a pub; our reward, a cold drink. We buy the drinks with Mum-money, borrowed. They are soft drinks, but they do not seem soft, hissing in our glasses and sharp with ice. There is a pub on the road into each village, and one on the road out, and one in the centre with the church and the shop. The village shops stock desperately priced boxes of breakfast cereal and packets of processed cheese. I do not like the villages but I like the windy drives through tunnels of hedgerow, furry with flowers. The intoxicating drift of pollen burns our eyes and stiffens us with sneezes.

'I forgot to tell you about Lucy,' I say to Roz. How did I forget? The news has been lost for a week or more in the silence between us. Roz turns to face me with a handful of knickers. Her eyes are smaller than usual beneath the gilded lids, concentrated, intent on extracting information. 'What news?'

'She painted a mural on the bungalow.'

'She what?' The eyes are wide now, and she is braced, a hand jammed on each side of her into the mattress.

'It's true,' I relish.

'No.' She is thrilled.

'Yes.'

'She's mad.' The whisper tingles with awe.

'I know.'

'I'm serious,' she insists.

'I know, I know.'

'She's *mad*.'

She sags, creeping across the puffy bedclothes towards me, seeking my confidence. 'Where? Where on the bungalow?'

'On the garage wall.' I bite into my lip. 'On the lovely big white garage wall.'

Suddenly we spill our suppressed laughter all over each other. 'What kind of a mural?'

I shrug. 'Snakes and things.' I do not know much about murals. I presume snakes. Lucy likes jungles. At school, there were jungles in the margins of her notes and essays: jungles around King Lear,

90

jungles in the Wars of the Roses. Roz used to doodle flowers. Girls usually doodle flowers. What do boys doodle? Cars, planes, trains, machine guns?

'So you haven't seen it?' Roz is momentarily disappointed, deflated, denied.

I shake my head.

'But how big?' Her eyes are wide again, the question rattling with renewed vigour.

'The whole wall.'

Gratified, we wail our laughter.

'But what about her parents?' continues Roz, noisy with anticipation.

'Mr Harvey provided whitewash. Promptly.'

We press our fingertips against our lips, conserving the ticklish giggles.

'No,' breathes Roz, goading me.

'Yes. And then Lucy complained bitterly to me about the splashes of whitewash on her boiler suit.' Lucy has adopted a boiler suit which she wears every day, a Michelin mass of dim dusky blue topped by swathes of black lace which she winds around her head. Above the dark bandage of lace is Lucy's hair, the spikes crowding pale and sticky, suggestive somehow of the scene of an accident.

'But the mural's gone?' Roz is woeful.

'Gone.'

She is frowning, baffled: 'Why did she do it?'

I splay my hands in the air. 'You know Lucy.'

No one knows Lucy. Everyone knows that no one knows Lucy. She seems to live by whim alone. But if Lucy is a bundle of whims, then they are multiple whims, complex whims, not whimsical whims. She is forever busy, preoccupied, propelled. The whims are not mere, yet everyone remains reluctant to credit Lucy with intent, and even more reluctant to suspect malice. At school, Miss Killick would tell Lucy to *remove that clothing* – hats, feathers, kilts, capes – but there would be no punishment, whereas Roz was Litter Monitor for a week because she wore a bracelet around her ankle.

91

And years ago, on the Third Form day trip to Calais, when Lucy was found with a group of smoking schoolboys from Cheshire, she was warned to *behave in future;* while Roz, tuning her transistor on the quayside, was sent back to the coach. This year, Lucy has had four or five boyfriends, accepting them without interest and rejecting them without regret, but she has no reputation. The same cannot be said for Roz. So, Lucy Evans walks on water? She could step clean from an oil slick.

~

As soon as I come through the front door I can hear the drone of the unattended television, the soft rain of applause. The darkness of the hallway fractures with electric blue lightning. I open the kitchen door. Mum is wiping the work surfaces and Jane is sitting on a stool beside the boiler, reading the newspaper. Mum is bound in huge towels, around her head and her body. The curse of the mummy?

'At last!' she trumpets, pausing dramatically with the dishcloth. 'Where have you been? I thought you weren't coming back. It's ten to eight. I have to leave in half an hour, and every child in this house needs bathing.'

Jane and I glance at each other: almost an exchange, and almost sympathetic. We know from years of experience that there is no point in us insisting that we will bath the children, or they will bath themselves, or do not need baths; or, moreover, if we resist the temptation to count Erin, that there are only two children. Mum likes an opportunity to complain.

I sit down at the table. 'Of course I'm back. I said that I'd baby-sit.'

Mum rubs vigorously with the dishcloth. 'Yes, Miss, but what you say and what you do are often two different things.' She flings the dishcloth across the kitchen towards the sink, and wipes her hand on her towelling toga.

'When?' I stare at her with dismay. 'When have I ever said I'd baby-sit and then not come home?'

She scowls to imply that I am pedantic. When it suits her, she is less interested than usual in fine detail.

'I don't ask much of you,' she hisses.

I shrug. There is no point in answering. I intend to remain sitting at the table until she leaves the kitchen. Soon she will hurry upstairs to dress: *Glad rags*. My bedroom guarantees little privacy because she talks loudly into the hallway from the bathroom, and then finds excuses to disturb me with armfuls of clean laundry. She shakes pillow cases at me as she files them into drawers, whining, *How do you think they get here? Do you think they walk?*

There is no lock on my door. Mum's excuse is young children: no locks on doors, no music upstairs after seven o'clock, no swearing, and no peanuts. She denies our requests by reminding us that Lauren is four. Lauren is four so all of us are monitored, muted, and forced to eat peanuts outside on the driveway. But Lauren seems forty: I suspect that she is baffled by the whispering and the antics with the peanuts.

'There's a lovely big potato in the oven for you,' Mum's recital is without enthusiasm. 'And some cottage cheese and salad in the fridge. Swiss Roll for pudding. And if you don't want the sponge, then leave it for Lyndsay. He loves it.'

'I know.'

'God knows why. But put it on a plate so that he can have it with his bedtime drink. He deserves it, he's been a good kid today, following me around the shops.'

Is this a hint that I should have offered to baby-sit for him this afternoon? Jane could have obliged. She is old enough now to be left alone. I crane across the table and see that she is inking moustaches and spectacles onto the photographs in the newspaper.

'He's exhausted. If he tries to tell you that I said that he could stay up tonight with Erin, it's not true: send him to bed with Lauren, please, as soon as I leave.'

Mum and Dad are going to a wedding reception: Buffet-and-disco, Mum had informed me with approval. I know about buffets-and-discos. The DJ will stand behind his High Altar. There will be long tables covered by sheets of crisp clean white paper. Platters will lie along the tables with impressive symmetry: *vol-au-vents* showing a smear of something chicken, and dips which become dollops on people's plates. The puddings are always difficult to reach through the quiche-eating crowds. The puddings are unnaturally long gâteaux wearing frills of fake cream, studded with dead mandarin segments and slimy flecks of fake chocolate.

The bride is the daughter of one of Dad's clients.

'No wonder you're going to the wedding,' I goaded Mum, when she told me, 'since you have such an intimate relationship with the bride.'

Mum's eyes shrank with suspicion. 'Your dad has known Bob since before you were born,' she snapped.

'And it's Bob's wedding?'

'Well, yes,' Mum hooted jollily, 'I suppose so, because he's paying for it.' Then she sank happily into a babble of gossip: 'It's Bob's eldest daughter. Sherry. Cherry. Something.' She paused to puzzle. 'And he's a lovely lad, apparently,' she started again.

'Sherry-Cherry is a lovely lad?'

'No,' she continued, unfazed, 'the groom. He's a manager at John Lewis. Kitchenware.'

Now she retreats to the sink, retrieves the dishcloth and hangs it neatly over the taps to dry. 'What a day! Barnet was Purgatory this afternoon.'

And home is Hell.

'Your father offered me a lift – and I do resent the local prices – but while I was unloading the kids from the car, he broke the news that he couldn't pick us up again until six. Oh well, I said, I'll cook the tea on the pavement outside Sainsbury's: I'll serve at six o'clock prompt, please bring a paper plate.' She is reclining against the sink unit, and showing no signs of leaving. 'We're so late this evening.'

I contemplate the kettle.

'Lyndsay's blister!' she exclaims suddenly, 'I must tell you about Lyndsay's blister, you've never seen such a blister. I wonder whether I should call the doctor, because I don't know what else to do, and I'm worried about gangrene.'

Would Deborah's mother ever have this kind of conversation with anyone?

I am drawn inevitably towards the kettle. Mum does not move, so I loop the kettle around her to the tap.

'But your father refuses,' she continues. 'Your father wouldn't call the doctor if one of you was dying.'

'Nice of him.'

'Because he thinks that we can't afford the doctor.'

'But there's an NHS.'

'Yes, nowadays, but you must remember that he comes from a family which couldn't afford the doctor. And poverty is ingrained. You've seen the way he eats.'

'The way he eats?' I leave the kettle and peer through the door of the oven at the potato. I see my reflection on the splattered brown glass. I do not look my best. I need to wash my hair.

'He eats fast, as if it's the first and last food for a long time. If you've ever been hungry, if your ancestors have ever been hungry, you never forget. It's ingrained.'

I open the fridge and lift a bowl of salad from one of the shelves.

'Cottage cheese,' says Mum.

I take the tub of cottage cheese.

'So, anyway,' she finishes, 'I'm going to take Lyndsay with me into the shoe shop and wave his heel in their faces. You don't expect blisters from Clarks, do you.'

I replace the cottage cheese in the fridge. 'It's with pineapple. I hate pineapple.'

'Erin loves it. Can't you pick out the pieces?'

I wrinkle my nose and shut the fridge door in reply.

'Nothing's ever good enough for you, is it,' she mutters, stirring and glancing around at the clock on the wall.

'I like the one with chives,' I reply, plunging my hand into the oven to reach the potato.

'There's everyone else to consider,' snaps Mum.

'I like plain,' says Jane. 'We never have plain. Why do we never have plain? What's wrong with plain?'

'Anyway, the chives taste of soap,' says Mum.

I make a deep incision into the potato.

Mum sighs. 'Well, I suppose I should go and change.' She ambles across the kitchen to the door. 'Erin has asked very nicely if she can watch a bit of the ice-skating on telly tonight.'

'She hasn't asked me.'

'Perhaps she's scared to ask you.'

I pause with my first forkful of the steaming fluffy starch. Could anyone be scared of me? Me? People like Roz are scary. Not me.

'What time is Lover Boy arriving tonight?' Mum adds from the doorway.

I plug my mouth with potato. There is no point in objecting to the term *Lover Boy*; Mum is encouraged by objections.

'Lover Boy,' titters Jane.

'Jane!' Mum barks. 'Stop that!'

Jane stares at her. 'What?'

'That.' Mum points at the defaced newspaper.

'What?'

'That.'

'What?'

I drop my fork onto my plate. 'Oh just stop it.'

Jane turns to me. 'Stop it yourself.'

'Stop what?'

'It's not yours to scribble on,' shrieks Mum. Then she swings forward from the door to hiss into Jane's face: 'This is typical of your attitude.'

Erin squeezes through the doorway. 'Mum,' she announces, 'Lyndsay's blister has burst on his bedroom floor. Yuk.'

Reluctantly, Mum turns from Jane to Erin. 'On his bedroom floor, Erin?' She pauses, confused. 'Go and tell him that I'm coming.'

She opens the most inaccessible, child-proof cupboard for the first aid box.

'That's all I need,' she snaps. She removes the lid from the box, and peers inside. 'And where's your father?'

'Not in the first aid box.'

She glances at me without expression. Then she pokes into a plastic wallet containing plasters. 'Anyway, where were you this evening?'

I chew for a while on a mouthful of potato skin. 'Roz's.'

'Oh, Roz.' Huge emphasis. 'I saw her mother in town the other day.'

'Did you?' Bored sarcasm, How-Very-Interesting.

'Yes, young lady, I did.' She is examining a tube of antiseptic ointment for an expiry date. 'They're very alike, aren't they, those two, Roz and her mum. The mother's a bit softer looking, though. That's age, I suppose. But it makes all the difference. A nice-looking woman. She smokes, though, doesn't she?'

I heap more salad onto my plate. 'Have there been any messages for me?'

'Nothing from Casanova, if that's what you mean.'

I quell my irritation with a deep, slow breath. 'No, that's not what I mean.'

She presses the lid onto the first aid box. 'Well, Lucy rang.'

'Yes?'

'She's off to visit her grandmother for a few days and she'll call you when she gets back. The grandmother is in Kent. Nice, I like Kent, or most of it. So I said, are you going to drive all the way in that car?'

Why the continuing obsession with Lucy's car?

'She said no, she's going on the train. So I said, I hope you've arranged a mortgage because you'll need one.'

'What's wrong with the car?'

Replacing the first aid box, Mum booms inside the cupboard: 'Nothing.'

'So why isn't she driving?' Lucy drives everywhere.

'Her mum has the car.'

'Her mum never has the car.' Something is wrong.

97

Mum emerges irritably from the cupboard. 'Lyndsay!' she calls to the ceiling, 'I'm coming! Just hang on for a minute!' She begins to search in one of the drawers, pushing aside folded plastic carrier bags. 'The car belongs to Lucy's mum, doesn't it? So why shouldn't she have it?'

I am musing. I take my plate to the bin and reject three pieces of soggy tomato. 'Lucy's dad drives Lucy's mum everywhere. Lucy's mum hates driving. She says that she learned to drive in case something happens and she is the last person left on earth.'

Mum draws a pair of scissors from under the pile of carrier bags. 'And where would she drive, if she was the last person left on earth? The supermarket?' She waves the scissors in the air. 'I'm moving these to the cutlery drawer,' she announces loudly. 'I'm sick of being unable to find them because you kids fail to return them to their proper place on top of the pile of bags. So, cutlery drawer: please pass on the word to the others.' She slams shut the drawer of bags. 'So why does Lucy's mother have a car, if she never uses it? Is she in a permanent state of readiness for Armageddon, with a full tank?'

'It was Mr Harvey's car, before his company car. It's a spare car.'

Mum pauses with scissors and plasters and ointment at the door. 'That Roz, what's she doing nowadays?' The question is laced with suspicion. 'She's working, isn't she? Is she still going to be a lawyer?'

'No. A clerk.' I am unpeeling my portion of Swiss Roll.

Mum sighs. She was once a clerk in an insurance company, at the beginning, before we were born. 'Well, it's understandable, I suppose. A decent wage. It seems an awfully long haul to train as a lawyer. The same for doctors, architects, anything.' She sighs again. 'These professions aren't designed for women. You'll all be married so late, having babies so late.'

'Perhaps marriage and babies aren't designed for women.'

She frowns at me, puzzled.

In the distance, upstairs, Dad shouts to her: 'Where are you? Are you ready? We're leaving *now*.'

1983

....

Mum looks around at me, looks up from the pile of sliced cabbage, when I come back into the kitchen. I know that she wants to know who was on the phone. I want to resist, but it is easier to comply. 'It was Roz.'

It was Roz: 'Can I speak to Lalie, please?'

'Roz,' I said, 'It *is* me.'

Usually people complain that I sound like Mum. But not Roz, not today, or not specifically: 'Oh, Lalie, you didn't sound like you.' Nor did she sound like Roz. She sounded more cheerful than Roz. It struck me that I prefer Roz to whine and worry, to assume intimacy.

'Roz?' says Mum. She sifts pale green strips of cabbage into the colander. 'At last,' she adds, disparagingly.

She knows that I have been trying to contact Roz this week. I have been leaving messages with Roz's mum: *Can you tell her that I called? I'm at home for a few days.* When was the last time that I spoke to Roz? Last summer? We exchanged cards at Christmas, of course. She had signed the card with the familiar flourish: Roz. No message. Short and sweet. Why did I not see Roz at Easter? Where was I at Easter?

'So you're off out to see her?' Mum levers a knife into the surviving hulk of cabbage.

'Yes.' She told me that she will be home early from work this afternoon after an appointment at the Migraine Clinic. 'Let's meet,' she said. I suggested that I go to her house. 'It's easier,' I said. We both know that there is no choice: where would we go, here? We would have to sit in the kitchen with Mum, or go upstairs into Erin's bedroom, or dodge Lyndsay's plastic vehicles in the garden.

Mum sighs ferociously, cleaving the remaining cabbage. 'One call from that Roz, and once again you're running around after her.'

Pointedly, glaring at the cabbage, I take the biscuit tin from the cupboard. Mum scowls. 'Be sensible with those biscuits.' She takes the colander to the sink and flashes it into a stream of tap water. 'I saw that Roz the other day, in town. But she avoided me.'

Mum assumes the worst of Roz, of course. There is no possibility that Roz did not see her.

'I was with the kids.'

Perhaps she *did* avoid them, and no wonder.

'And Jane said to me, *Look, there's that Roz Smith; she loves herself, doesn't she.*'

'Just like Jane. Jane loves *her*self.'

Mum thumps the colander onto the table so that the flints of cabbage shudder. 'We're not discussing Jane.'

'A pity,' I sneer, 'because someone should, before it's too late.'

'I have my eye on Jane,' Mum concedes from the vegetable rack.

I think of Jane's blue eyes, embedded in blue powder: eyeshadow is not the word, there is no *shadow*. Eye*stress*, perhaps. I remember when Jane began wearing make-up to school. Mum protested: 'Good God, what do you look like?'

'What do *you* look like?' challenged Jane, unnecessarily, nonsensically, before protesting eventually and predictably that *Lalie does*.

'Lalie's older,' decreed Mum, similarly predictably.

'Lalie's *always* older,' screamed Jane, thwarted.

Then Mum changed tactics, adopting a confiding tone, warning Jane to be careful: 'Unlike Lalie,' she said, 'who is lucky, you have a tendency to look common; the word is *brassy*.'

This was tactless and has allowed Jane to hate both of us ever since with increased self-righteousness.

But Jane and Roz have boyfriends; lots of them; *all* of them. Jane and Roz are girlfriend material. So how do the rest of us manage? How do I manage? Pulling another crispy raisin from another Garibaldi, I contemplate my own history of boyfriends. How have

I adapted to being non-girlfriend material? Is there survival of the fittest? It occurs to me that Jane and Roz are perhaps unfit and lazy. One day, when they are older, when they have lost their looks, romance will be more difficult for them. They rely on being noticed, whereas I have to make my way into people's lives. People tell me that I am A Good Listener. (They do not seem to consider that they are good talkers). For me, listening is easy. It does not seem to be easy for Roz, who will fidget, flinch, challenge, explain, dismiss. And Jane? I have never tried to talk to Jane.

Mum is noisily discarding withered carrots, weeding them from the vegetable rack and posting them one by one into the bin. 'So Roz has made the effort at the eleventh hour,' she pronounces. 'When are you going over there?'

'In an hour or so.'

'Do you want me to keep your tea for you?'

'Just the vegetables, please.'

Mum pauses emphatically with a lurid carrot. 'Just cabbage? You can't have just cabbage.'

I do not respond.

'Well, I suppose it's fibre,' she admits wearily.

'I'll grate cheese onto it,' I add, to pre-empt the protein problem.

'Yes, you should have some protein.'

I have to see Roz today because tomorrow I am going to stay with my boyfriend and his family in Liverpool for a week before I go camping with him in France. And then it will be the start of the new term.

Come and tell all, said Roz.

Mum has been professing to be unable to understand why I should want to go to Liverpool.

'Why Liverpool?'

'You know why.'

Now she begins again: 'Liverpool tomorrow!' It has become The Liverpool Mystery.

What does she want me to do? Does she want me to bring him here? Does she want him to sleep with me on the floor in Erin's room?

101

'Liverpool!'

I could insert the name of anywhere in the world into her mouth and the emphasis would remain unchanged — although the reason would vary: Canada, cold; California, crime-ridden; Australia, crude; Jamaica, poverty-stricken; Paris, expensive; Switzerland, even more expensive; Sweden, the Swedes. For places in Britain the reason for the expression of horror is rain, litter, or sixties' architecture.

'You'll be going back to your roots,' she remarks with fake cheeriness, raking cabbage from the colander into a saucepan of boiling water. The Blaneys came to Liverpool from Ireland. For Mum, Liverpool represents the leak of Irish people into England. The Blaneys percolated as far as Nottingham before Grandpa was born.

'If Grandpa Blaney was born in Nottingham then he's English,' I propose, 'not Irish.'

This is a radical critique: she frowns into the simmering cabbage. 'I expect that he was brought up on potatoes all the same.'

She takes the biscuit tin from the table. 'You haven't seen the Blaneys for a while.'

The Blaneys: I *am* a Blaney.

'Your Gran is coming around here every week or so now,' continues Mum, 'loitering on the doorstep as if she's here to sell lavender.' She shudders.

I smirk.

'Don't smirk. She is having another phase of weekly visits, another phase of I'm-not-long-for-this-world-and-I-want-to-spend-some-time-with-the-little-'uns. And what kind of talk is that for children to hear? And *this world?* Which other world is she planning to visit? I'll tell you which world.' She fixes me with a knowing stare but does not tell. Finally she adds, 'Every time she leaves here I shout *Get Thee Behind Me* but she doesn't seem to hear.'

I laugh. 'She hears.'

'Don't laugh: one day she'll be on your doorstep, asking to see *your* kids.'

I look into the cupboard for muesli and find a box containing a crunchy version, boasting pieces of dehydrated apple. The box is small, old, and stacked behind huge boxes crackling with various forms of bright sugared maize and bearing excitable cartoon characters. Most of the muesli remains uneaten and the recommended sell-by-date has expired. Perhaps it was bought for me; I cannot remember. I replace the box on the shelf.

'Throw it out if you're not going to eat it,' says Mum. 'I bought it for you and it's old now.' She sighs and sits down at the table. 'Blaneys . . . Liverpool . . . I hope you realize that you'll have to bring up your kids as Catholics.'

I stare at her. 'I'm not going to have any kids.' No? 'Not necessarily. Not yet. And he's *not* Catholic, he's not *Irish*.' She has confused me. 'Mum,' I begin again, recovering myself, 'he lives on the Wirral.'

She shrugs. 'I don't care if he lives in Buckingham Palace: once Irish, always Irish. And it's the same for you: off you go, off to Liverpool, off to an Irishman. Water finds its own level.'

I am always confused by this talk of water, blood, bone, this talk of breeding, mixing, strengths and levels. 'He's not Irish,' I repeat wildly. 'And I'm not Irish.' And our children will not be Irish. And both of *Ben's* grandfathers *were* Irish, but I do not want to mention Ben.

Mum rises again from the table. 'I'm only warning you,' she says mildly, glancing through the door at the garden, 'that the church has a tremendous grip on people.'

'Yes.' It is easiest to agree.

'Remember Brenda, your grandmother: when she married Grandpa Blaney, they insisted on a Catholic wedding, with Latin. There was a lot of mumbo-jumbo, and she didn't know what was happening.'

How does Mum know? Blondie Brenda Blaney was long gone from Cold Comfort Farm when Mum met Dad. I suspect that Mum is addicted to a vision of the young bride bound helplessly in the ivory silks of a wedding dress: a young Mrs Rochester.

'Perhaps it was an exorcism,' she giggles suddenly. 'A free exorcism courtesy of the church whenever you marry a Blaney.'

'I never know what's happening at any wedding,' I say sourly. And then I add, more gently, 'Mum, I'm going to Liverpool, not Amityville.'

Planning to escape soon from the kitchen, I ask, 'How are they, the Blaneys?'

Mum shrugs. 'The same as ever: still rotting away on that farm. As ever, your grandfather looks as if he has tried to put himself out of his misery and failed. And *she's* as strong as an ox, of course.' *She* is Gran Blaney. Mum often likes to imply that Gran will live longer than any of us, and sometimes she hints at immortality. Immortality in books and films means eternal youth but it seems to me that Gran Blaney has always been old. She was seventy years old when I was born. Perhaps no one ages much after seventy. In fact, she looks younger now, with a decent pair of glasses, than in the photos taken when she was fifties-frumpy and bespectacled. Mum abandons the excessive-longevity and immortality theories in more rational moments and implies instead that Gran Blaney will die eventually of natural causes. For Mum, natural causes are rare and covetous. She assumes that natural causes are painless, representing weathering, a smoothing away of moving parts; so that there is no great change in state, and death results in a subtle alteration to the landscape, similar to the loss of a tree. Nothing nasty, and life goes on.

But Mum judges this to be an unsuitable fate for Gran Blaney. When she mentions Gran Blaney's limited immortality she sighs, sags, grimaces, raises her eyebrows and rolls her eyeballs. The implication of these facial contortions is that Gran Blaney is undeserving; or, perhaps, not as deserving as Mum and the rest of us. Another implication is that evolution, preserving the Blaneys, the solid stolid Blaneys, is playing safe. I suspect that Mum is disappointed by evolution. In Mum's day, evolution was the champion of the classroom, not to mention the British Museum. It was an assurance that everything would be all right in the end.

Evolution was a hero for Mum, a ruthless but discerning hero. But now it cannot be relied upon to appreciate her small blonde troupe of neo-Blaneys. And Mum is convinced that we are suitable candidates for evolution. In kinder moments she says that we are *intelligent*, or *sensitive*. She is dismayed that we must remain shooting stars in the dark ages of the dark Blaneys.

So I have been brought up to believe that the Blaneys will live forever or die natural deaths because they are enduring, obstinate; or perhaps because they have made a less than natural pact.

But what about Gran Blaney's husband, long-dead before I was born?

Mum has an answer, or two: *Drink*; or *She probably poisoned him*.

I have been brought up with a sense of doom, with Mum's sense that that the neo-Blaneys cannot share the Blaney good fortune, that little blondes are less substantial and destined for deaths more complicated than natural. For the blonde Blaneys, soft and pale, there is cancer, a melting of tissue but also a growing of tissue, a bloating of tissue, a knotting and wrenching of tissue, but nevertheless a disease of tissue. Blondes are tissuey; you can see their tissue. And children are insubstantial, especially your own children, who were once nothing more than indigestion and then a bump on which the doctor could rest the stethoscope. Children swooping from you into the world but bearing someone else's fingerprints, NHS standard issue fingerprints, a stranger's prints in a soft new scalp. For Mum, the threat to the neo-Blaneys starts at the beginning, the decay starts as soon as the outside world makes its mark; the inky, oily outside world which will push inside and eventually trigger some giddy genetics.

But what about me, a neo-Blaney but not a blonde? Darker, sallow, a lanky writer of diaries, Mum's prediction for me is TB: chronic, but not fatal.

You'll outlive us all, grumbles Mum, *in your own way*.

In my own way, with neither the fearsome constitution of the Blaneys nor the pretty frailty of the blondes. She expects me to linger, wheezing: almost immortal, but not quite; almost tragic, but not quite. Rest Home material. I suspect that she is wrong; I know that she is wrong about Gran Blaney. Gran Blaney, who is eighty-nine, will not be here much longer.

'Are you taking that box of books with you when you go?' Mum interrupts my thoughts. She is spilling handfuls of cutlery onto the table.

Which box, which books? I try to imagine an inventory of the loft: box, *Jackie Annuals*. 'What will I do with a box of books?'

She scowls at me and mistakenly places Lauren's small spoon in Dad's place. 'And that blue jacket? Do you want the blue jacket? You could give it to Jane.'

'No. And she wouldn't want it.'

'Erin, then.'

'Or Lyndsay.' I smirk.

'Don't:' a reference to Dad's fears for Lyndsay's masculinity. *Poor little chappie, surrounded by women.*

Mum retorts that being surrounded by women is preferable to being surrounded by men: *He might turn out human, which is more than I can say for his father.*

'And do you want to take this old sandwich toaster?' Mum opens a cupboard door with her foot.

I peer into the cupboard which is filled by the pressure cooker. I have vague memories of sizzling sandwiches. Eventually I see a small chrome machine. It has lost a leg, a small leg, and is slumped over a pile of folded paper crowns. 'No thanks.'

'But what do you do for toast?'

I grin into her face: 'I don't; I starve.'

She shuts the door with her foot, buzzing with anxiety. 'Eulalia . . .'

'I make toast in the toaster in the kitchen at the end of the corridor. *All* the time. *Constantly.*' I rescue a ladybird from the dazzling chaos of her hair. 'There's no space for a toaster in my room. Honest. So thanks, but no.'

She turns po-faced from me, still unsettled by the threat of my starvation, by the thought that she is failing in her duty to ensure my survival, and reaches into the cupboard for a bottle of ketchup. 'It's a pity that you're not here next week,' she says suddenly.

Why? What now? Which fête, jumble sale, gang show?

'Because you could have gone to the school one afternoon to fetch Lauren.'

Lauren started at school last term. She is in Mrs Harper's class. Fifteen years ago I was in Mrs Harper's class. Fifteen years ago Mrs Harper was a mother of two young children: Hamish, in my class, who was famous for his collection of Knock-Knock jokes, and Ruth, in the Big Class, who broke an ankle on Sports Day. Now, Mum tells me, Mrs Harper is a grandmother.

A grandmother twice over, she says, as if Mrs Harper is a winner of the Grand National.

Who feels more aged by this, Mrs Harper or me?

I was surprised when Lauren started school. She seemed too young.

'Schoolkids are becoming younger and younger,' I complained to Mum.

'She's a *Rising Five*,' said Mum.

I like this expression, *Rising Five*, and I try to provide opportunities for Mum to explain to me again: *Eulalia, I've told you, she's a Rising Five*.

Now Mum is enthusing about my visit to the school: 'They'd love to see you.' They: Mrs Harper, Mrs Gray; and Mrs Jones, the cleaner, the domestic.

'No fear.' *Mrs Harper: Lalie, you know what happens to little girls who giggle at the back of my class*. I did not know, and still do not know. Mrs Gray: *Tuck your skirt into your knickers, Lalie, and stop letting down the rest of the team*.

Mum sighs with disappointment: 'Why not?'

I shrug. 'Everyone will think that I'm Lauren's mum.'

'Mrs Harper will know who you are; and Mrs Gray, and Mrs Jones.' She wipes clots of ketchup from the top of the bottle. 'They'd love to see you. And, besides, there are worse children to mother than Lauren.'

She rinses the clots of food from the dishcloth into the sink. 'I tell them all about what you're doing, of course. They're very proud of you. You're their success story. Brains Blaney, they call you.'

'That's that: I'm never going there.'

'And they want me to ask you if you're in The Footlights.'

'No,' I snap, 'and I've never even seen one.'

'You're a spoilsport,' she mutters, wringing the dishcloth, 'you're a misery guts.' Then she turns, sprightly from the sink. 'I think it'll be a good term for Lauren. She'll be a good angel in the Nativity Play, of course, like the rest of you.'

I protest: 'I wasn't an angel.'

'No?' She is surprised. There have been so many Blaney angels; she has become blasé about Blaney angels. Suddenly she laughs: 'What were you, then? Half of the donkey?'

'I was a shepherdess.'

'A shepherdess?' She considers the notion of shepherdess. Usually she is more than willing to advocate equal opportunities in Nativity Plays: she doubts that angels are men. *Gabriel, Gabrielle,* she says, suspiciously.

'I had Elaine Miller's mum's hockey stick as my crook. Remember?'

'Poor little Elaine Miller,' breathes Mum, remembering Elaine Miller rather than the hockey stick, 'she was covered in eczema. I wonder what happened to her?'

'She went to a convent,' I reply absently. Inexplicably, fifteen years on, I am subjected again to the overwhelming urge to impress upon Mum the importance of my role in the Nativity Play. It seems to me that the role of shepherdess exhibits all the leadership qualities that she holds so dear. 'You can't have sheep running amok.'

Mum frowns at me, puzzled. 'Surely there were no sheep on stage.'

'Well, no, but you were supposed to use your imagination.'

Lauren's role as an angel does not seem plausible. Despite the blonde curls, she is not at all angelic. Somehow she is street-wise although, as a Rising Five, she has probably not yet been out alone into a street. During Herod's census she would have been touting rooms at Jerusalem Central.

Mum begins tapping a fingernail onto the lid of the steaming saucepan of cabbage. 'Perhaps I should have sent Erin to a convent, or something. I hope she'll settle at school this year.'

'Erin?' Erin will soon be going into the second year of secondary school.

'She's flower monitor for the class now.'

I am puzzled. 'They don't have flower monitors.'

'It's an invention of the Form Teacher, for Erin.'

'They don't have flowers.' Where were the flowers, at school? There was a clump of bullrushes in the Biology Pond.

Mum looks at me with irritation before returning her attention to the shiny lid. 'The Form Teacher can only do so much, though. Erin would be happier at home.'

Everyone would be happier at home: pupils and teachers. Perhaps, one day, someone will say so, and everyone will agree, and everything will change. In the meantime, school survives as a giant con trick. But why the selective sympathy from Mum? My pleas to stay at home were brutally dismissed: *What would happen if none of us went to school? And don't give me one of your fancy answers*. Now she sighs sadly. 'Erin is such a dreamer,' she says dreamily. 'She's not tough enough to cope.'

I resent the implication that I am tough, that I coped. What do *you* know? *Did* I cope? I came out the other side of school, but did I *cope?*

Erin in the Second Form, little Erin in the big Second Form. When we reached the Second Form, Roz, Ali, Lucy, and me, we were confident that we were grown-up. It was in the Second Form that Roz began wearing make-up: the ripe damson blush around the bitter green flesh of her eyes. When we were First Formers, the Second Formers had seemed to us to be the most frightening people in the school: newly risen from the bottom of the pile, they were eager to exact revenge. And they exacted revenge on the defenceless. I remember the names of those Second Formers, I will

109

always remember the names: Mandy Cochrane, Julie Harris, Kathy Slater, Sally Jones, Jane Simms, Jane Jenkins, Jane Porter. They were never without their navy blue canvas bags, wielding them on their shoulders. The bags contained the vital ingredients: combs and brushes bound with tangles of bleached hair; tiny palettes of bruise-coloured dusts; and hand-held mirrors folded away with noisy blinding blinks. But the Second Formers preferred the big mirrors in the washrooms: they lined in front of the mirrors, blocking our view, blocking our way. By contrast, as First Formers, we ducked, skirted, scurried our way through school. Unlike the Second Formers, we had no united front, not then. As First Formers, we were still dressed by our mothers in the mornings, and did not yet possess our own canvas-bag-carried-language.

When we were First Formers, we were disliked by the Second Formers. Or, rather, Roz was disliked. The rest of us – Ali, Lucy, and me – were disliked through our association with Roz. The same old story: somehow, I am placed with Roz. And somehow I remain with Roz. She is my friend, after all. Somehow she is my friend. But why was she so disliked? Certainly she was competition for the Second Formers.

Too big for her boots, Mum used to say.

But competition for what? She was girlfriend material, so she was in competition for the boys. Again I remember the names: Darren Ingham, Peter Marks, Richard Dean, Paul Grant, the Petrie twins. But it was more than boys. The boys were not important, the boys were an excuse, another aspect of territory. Perhaps it was Roz's eyes: the challenge, the gritty green glint from the mirrors in the washroom.

Perhaps it was the sight of the code, their code, the code shown clearly, expertly, inventively in the mirrors by Roz: the length of the skirt, the roll of the sleeves, the number of buttons undone at the neck; the colour of the tights, the thickness of the soles, the type of clasp on bracelets, the size of the links in chains, the arrangement of rings on the fingers, the articulation of felt-tip graffiti on hands; and the hair, of course, the style and colour of the hair.

110

For Roz, it seemed so effortless. But now, in the kitchen, effortless in dungarees, it occurs to me that this cannot have been true. Somehow Roz *disguised* the effort, *thrived* on the effort. She was gifted.

Faddy, Mum used to say.

But she was not faddy. The image was carefully crafted. In another world, Roz would have been a cheerleader but in England there is no cheering.

You all follow that Roz, Mum used to complain.

But this was Roz's gift: Roz spoke louder and more cleverly than me in the language that was mine; the language that was ours, the language of Ali, Lucy, and me. So what could I have done? Should I have retreated into the blank silence of Peggy Crane and Carol Denby, Ginny Smith, Sarah Gresham, Mary Pitt; into laced shoes, pleated skirts, middle partings and Kirby Grips at Christian Union meetings at lunch times on Thursdays?

You all follow that Roz, Mum would whine. *Why can't you be different?*

But Roz *was* different. Was.

I glance beyond Mum to the clock. In three quarters of an hour I will see Roz. Roz was free of the bullies when we became Second Formers, when the Second Formers became Third Formers. Third Formers are almost Seniors, and want to minimize their association with Juniors. So they were suddenly unconcerned by Roz. Third Formers appeared alongside us in the washroom mirrors but seemed to inhabit a different dimension. So, from the Second Form onwards, life at school was kinder to Roz and the rest of us. And eventually I made friends with girls in the Form above us; perhaps not with Mandy, Julie, Kathy, Sally and the Janes, but with the others, particularly on field trips in the Sixth Form. Roz did not stay long enough in the Sixth Form to make friends.

'Now, *Jane* . . .' muses Mum, struggling at the sink with the saucepan of steaming cabbage.

Not Jane, please not Jane. I look again at the clock: forty minutes. I look at the door.

111

'. . . Jane's O levels . . .' Mum slops the mass of cabbage from the saucepan into the colander. The movement is equivalent to a huge hopeless shrug. 'Maths is out of the question, of course, but I am adamant that she tries to get English. She needs English.'

I have a brief vision of Jane opening her mouth and speaking Portuguese. Jane speaks nothing but English, and very forcefully. What does it mean to be unqualified in your own language?

'Poor Mr MacKenzie, Jane must break his heart.'

Mr MacKenzie? Mr MacKenzie, fossilized at school.

'She must break his heart, following you, I mean. Because you were his star pupil, don't forget.' She eyes me suspiciously through the steam. English, to Mum, means debauched poets and essays entitled 'Spoons'.

'Poor man, he is probably at the end of his tether with Jane, and he hasn't taught Erin yet.'

Mum opens the oven door and begins to rake cabbage from the colander onto the seven warming plates. 'But he tries to be brave. He says that Jane is a character.'

Mr MacKenzie believes that everyone is A Character. This belief is the sole comfort in his job: as a teacher he hopes to meet characters, preserve characters, develop characters. As an English teacher, he has a chance of success: discussions of debauched poets and dramatic interpretations of 'Spoons' are more inspiring than chalk diagrams of alluvial deposits. There was nothing for us to learn from Mr MacKenzie, no charts or tables, but somehow we learned more with him than in any other classroom.

'A secretary, perhaps; I thought that Jane could be a secretary, perhaps, but nowadays she'd need five O levels and two years at college.'. Mum slams shut the oven door: another effective substitute for a shrug. 'College seems a bit unnecessary. And then I suggested that she should become a travel agent, but again there's the problem of college: day release, apparently.' Mum is tipping frozen Brussels sprouts into a saucepan: septic hailstones. 'Day release,' she repeats sceptically. 'It sounds like prison.' She chuckles. 'Mind you . . .'

And we chorus, 'Prison's-the-best-place-for-Jane.'

Mum adjusts the flame beneath the saucepan of sprouts. 'I've decided that we're having Brussels. Do you want some?'

'No:' spoken with vehemence. Mum frowns at me, and I modify my tone: 'No, thank you.'

'Anyway,' Mum continues, signalling a grudging acceptance, 'if you ask Jane about careers . . .'

Unlikely because I do not speak to Jane at all.

'. . . then she'll tell you that she wants to work with children.' She stuffs the depleted bag of Brussels into the freezer box. 'But they all say that. I said to her, "You have lots of children at home, all around you, all day, every day, and you hate them." ' She turns towards me from the fridge. 'Just like you.'

An old argument: *All these handicapped children*, Mum says to me, *And that's all very well, but what about your own siblings?*

What does she expect me to do with Jane, Erin, Lyndsay and Lauren?

She opens the oven and lunges with a fork at the steak and kidney pie. 'But we've had everything from Jane, of course: fashion designer . . . air hostess . . . war correspondent . . .' She pauses, puzzled, at war correspondent. 'And all the time she is intending to marry Brendan.'

Brendan is the boyfriend.

'I said to her, I wish him luck.' She retreats from the pie. 'He's only fifteen,' she tells me.

'*Jane's* only fifteen.'

'Yes, but that's not the point. Girls mature faster. And she bullies him. I said to her, *What makes you think that the poor lad wants to marry you? Look at you.*'

The Look-at-you is a reference to Jane's Heavy Metal appearance, a recent affectation. Brendan is a Boot Boy, if anything. 'What's all this Boot Boy business?' Mum once asked me; and, on another occasion, 'Dare I ask about skanking?'

Now Mum sighs loudly to communicate despair. 'What will become of Jane?' she laments.

113

'Nothing much.'

She looks at me for a moment before returning to the sink; and if she says anything to me, the words are lost in the water streaming from the taps.

I am intercepted on my way out of the kitchen by Lyndsay who rushes in from the garden. 'My shoelace is undone,' he announces to me with an air of interest. I look down at him to find the shoe offered for inspection. Prompted, I bend down to rectify the situation. He has been followed by Lauren. 'I'm thirsty,' she sings out across the kitchen.

Mum hauls a saucepan from the sinkful of water. 'Are you, poppet?' she calls back. 'Fetch your beaker, then.'

I slip through the door into the hallway and climb the stairs. I do not have a bedroom: when I left home, Mum donated it to Jane. Now Erin shares Jane-and-Erin's room with Lauren.

'Why not Lyndsay-and-Lauren?' I asked Mum.

'Lyndsay's a boy.'

'Hardly.'

Mum disapproves of banter about Lyndsay.

'He's not old enough to be a boy,' I explained quickly.

I am sleeping in Erin-and-Lauren's room because I hate Jane and Lyndsay is adenoidal. On my first night at home I lay on the floor alongside Lyndsay's bed. Somewhere above me, with a golden halo of hair on the pillow, Lyndsay was a snotty snoring angel. Sleepless, I moved onto the floor in Erin-and-Lauren's room. Mum claims that Erin and Lauren enjoy sharing a room. This is speculation: she has not consulted them. And, in the meantime, Erin complains to me that Lauren is messy, and Lauren complains to me that Erin is boring.

In Erin-and-Lauren's room, Erin is lolling on one of the beds and turning the pages of the *TV Times*. I walk between the beds to the window. I have been robbed of my own view, the view from my own bedroom window, by Jane. It was a view of little lawns, laid clean, soft and green between houses like napkins. The view from Erin-and-Lauren's window is the same as the view from the living room window, but more remote. The Scout Hut, across the road, is lower, smaller. When I was small, playing around The Scout Hut with my friends in the long grass, it was *The Witches' House*; simply because of the long grass. For children in a neighbourhood of laundered lawns, long grass means witches. For the adults, it is worse.

An eyesore, spits Mum.

One day, The Scout Hut will disappear beneath redevelopment and Mum will say the same about the replacement.

But where are those friends of mine? When I pass them on the High Street, and we swop greetings, are we no longer friends? When did we cease to be friends? Certainly we are not enemies. Shopping in the same High Street, it seems to me that we occupy different worlds, smiling at each other through plate glass windows. I know more about them than their smiles because Mum, like a medium, relays their stories to me: I know that these old friends, these ex-friends, are occupying various stages in their job-engagement-marriage-children plans. Sometimes I come face to face with one of the girls in the Bank or the Building Society: Rowena or Lisa or Clare, across a desk or behind a clear plastic screen. They wear thin, stiff, paper-pale blouses and regulation acrylic two-piece suits.

How-are-you-fine-and-you-fine.

Sometimes they ask me what I am doing nowadays. Once, questioned closely, I admitted to studying English.

'Oh, so you plan to write books?'

If I had been studying biology, would I have been expected to create species?

The boys have gone into the army: a cliché but true. Even Sebastian Tilman has gone into the army. Once upon a time, I had hopes for Sebastian Tilman.

'Private Tilman, now,' Mum told me despondently.

Surely he is less than private, now, in his uniform, in his barracks.

Mum hates the army. *Male*, she complains vigorously. *And if Lyndsay tries to enlist, I'll shoot him*.

Since I came home last week Mum has talked endlessly at me.

Did she always do this? Perhaps I did not notice, beforehand; perhaps my distance, now, enables me to hear. The words are amplified, deafening. I can predict the justification: *I'm keeping you up-to-date*. But the people populating Mum's stories were long gone from my life before I left home; even sweet Seb Tilman, with whom my last contact was a game of Postman's Knock at someone else's party eleven years ago.

Michaela Pond is having another baby and she's not yet married; and there's talk of an October wedding but she'll be seven months' gone and you can't get married at seven months, because what's the point?

Michaela Pond? The elder sister of one of my primary school classmates, Gina Pond. Whatever happened to Gina Pond? But Michaela Pond, Michaela Pond, I dredge my memory: pale hair and a fistful of rings; a baby in a buggy on the road towards the council estate; a boyfriend with a removal van.

And the Walmsley girl, third baby on the way, said to be a mistake, said to be twins, so third and FOURTH baby on the way and an even BIGGER mistake; but, then, she never does anything by halves. Veronica.

Veronica Walmsley?

Veronica Simpson.

Veronica Simpson, helper at Guides; Veronica Simpson, Ranger.

I've seen him a lot lately, lounging around outside the pub.

He is not Veronica Simpson but Veronica Simpson's husband.

He's a lanky sod, I'd like to see him cope with their baby day-in-day-out. And the Richards' boy is getting married!

According to Mum, Derek Richards steals cars.

And to a convent girl!

And Mrs Lacey has had a breast removed, Mrs Wadham has had a stroke, and Mr Deal died of a heart attack in the supermarket. For a moment it is peaceful here, without Mum, in Erin-and-Lauren's room. I gaze at the ponies in a distant field. When I was young, I wanted a pony more than anything else in the world. I named one of those distant ponies, as if she was mine: Little Nell. I can see Little Nell, now, in the field. When I was young, I entered the WH Smith Win A Pony Competition every year. Year after

116

year, I knew that my answers were right. Perhaps I lost the tie-breakers.

No one else listens to Mum. Jane claims that Mum listens to no one. 'Tell her,' Jane seethed yesterday, directing her fury at Mum via me, 'tell her what Chemistry is like. Tell her that Mrs Clement is an old cow who can't teach and picks on people for no reason.' The occasion was Jane's E grade for Chemistry and Mrs Clement's comment that *Jane could not try harder to displease.*

Mum was pondering. 'She lost a child, didn't she? Mrs Clement?'

'In an sailing accident,' I confirmed.

Mum turned on Jane. 'So how can you be so cruel?'

Jane was bloated with incredulity. 'It was twenty years ago or something.'

Mum stiffened, repulsed. 'So? Pain doesn't lessen with time.'

Yesterday Jane shrieked at me, 'Tell her that everyone goes to all-night parties. *You* did.'

'No, I didn't,' I said hurriedly, lying.

'You'll drink,' boomed Mum.

'So? Just because *you* don't.'

'No, I don't, you're quite right. I don't want to become a fat slob.' She was shimmering with anger. 'You don't want to turn out like the Blaneys, do you?'

'Yes.'

'Well, that's a lovely way to thank your mother for bothering to bring you into the world.'

Now I can hear noises from Jane's room. There are always noises from Jane's room. The dragging of heavy objects, the banging: it always sounds as if she is burying someone. Erin's silence is wonderful. I can hear the hoarse growl of a bus on the main road in the distance. Soon I will be back at college, in my room, and there will be no sounds of buses, no nearby roads. Instead there is the chiming of the clock in the courtyard and the creaking of ducks on the river. There are no little girls, either, reading the *Radio Times* or playing AC/DC tapes in the next room. At college everyone is twenty. I have never been on a bus at college. Where would I go?

Lauren joins us, swinging onto the other bed and lying with her hands behind her head.

I turn from the window, irritated. 'What are you doing?'

'Thinking.'

Did I think when I was five years old?

Lyndsay has followed Lauren. He stands in the doorway. 'I can't spell Eulalia.'

He can't spell, or he can't spell Eulalia?

'I can't spell it.'

Lauren shifts her head on her hands. 'I.T.'

'And Mum says to ask you.' He is staring at me from the doorway.

'Logical, I suppose,' I concede. 'But now?'

His eyes widen further, impossibly. 'I'm making you a Goodbye Card.'

'Oh Lyndsay,' I cross the room towards him, between the beds. 'You don't have to make me a Goodbye Card.'

He frowns, disappointed. 'Aren't you going?'

I pause before I reach him. 'Well, yes, I'm going.'

I help Lyndsay with my name and then leave him in the bedroom. I pause at the top of the stairs. 'I'm going,' I shout to Mum. 'I'm going now.'

She appears instantly below me in the hallway. 'Early.' She is frowning too.

'I'm going to leave some books for Ali with her mum.'

'Ali,' says Mum. 'Now, *she's* a funny one.'

~

I am walking to Roz's house. I have decided to walk rather than to catch the bus. The journey by bus takes three or four minutes; the walk, twenty. The road is bordered by fields for a mile or so; for a mile or so there are no houses. The last house is behind me. It is a strange house, somehow, perhaps because it is designed to be a last house: a wide verandah, and hooded windows bulging from the scaly skin of the roof. It has a name like Good View or something; I can't remember. The view is a mile or so of fields but the garden is small, fenced, planted with flowerbeds. In the spring, white tulips swarm at the fence, swaggering and curious like geese.

The road is a main road: I am safe. Safe, paradoxically, because I am visible. Safe, now that I am no longer a child, now that I can take care of myself, almost. A succession of cars swings along the road towards the town. The occupants observe me, observe each other, so there is safety for me in numbers. The cars are travelling too fast to be an intrusion. The eyes of the occupants return from me to the search for the destination beyond the fields. When I lived at home, I came here for walks in the evenings and at the weekends, alone. Amid all the people in the cars, I was alone. But I was not lonely. My walks were noisy with imagined conversations. During these walks I fell in and out of love, married (sometimes several times, because everyone makes mistakes), had children, became famous, won fortunes, and bought big houses with stables. 'Good walk?' Mum would ask me when I returned, glowing. *Walk?*

But today I am walking, quietly, intently, to see Roz. Roz Smith, 24 Apple Tree Walk: an address that I last wrote on a Christmas card, one amongst many. *Acacia Avenue*, the rest of us used to tease, Ali and Lucy and me, but our sarcasm was lost on Roz. Apple Tree Walk is surrounded by other Walks, Crescents, Avenues and Parades beyond the fields. I remember that Number 24 has a china blue garage door. And in the porch there is a tall bin full of umbrellas. Shielding my eyes from the sun, I look over the low hedge into the distance: nothing but fields, trimmed, undulating. High summer. Why *high?* High temperatures? Somehow the temperature does not feel high, but sunken, or perhaps flat, floating. It feels even, indistinguishable from my skin. High implies turbulence. High seas. It implies swell. Perhaps it is true that high summer promises storms. Mum talks a lot about summer storms. I do not recall any. Surely storms are rain and wind, and rain and wind are winter.

119

I glance up into the sky. It is lit by huge platinum clouds. Suddenly I pass under a tree which rises from the hedgerow. I remember that, in springtime, these horse chestnuts glow in the fields in isolation, the waxy ivory blossom like candles on exuberant Christmas trees. Then I remember the blossom filling the small trees in local gardens: pink, puffy, chaotic. And, less common, the tight vermilion blossom teeming on an occasional cherry tree. I look again over the hedge at the panorama of fields. Several of them, in the distance, are yellow: a startling, mad shade of yellow; a thick, glowing yellow. The colour is unnatural, artificial, and there is no evidence at this distance of individual plants. The fields are silky blobs on a palette.

Previously, I had never noticed this mad yellow. So is it new, or was it always here? Was it waiting for me to come back and walk here without my dreams? It is a shock for me to realize that there is nothing gentle about the summer. These lanes are bloated and extravagant. This year, I have been surprised by summer; and last year, too, perhaps, after the exams, in these lanes in Lucy's car. Now it is difficult for me to imagine winter, to imagine the pain of cold air, the cowering in the icy wind. But it is almost always winter, almost everything takes place in winter: terms, Christmas, Easter, bank holidays and birthdays. It is difficult, now, in the warm air, to imagine layers of clothing, and the exhausting considerations: the right number of layers, the right combination of layers, the laundry of layers. Mum has exacting standards for layers, incorporating vests.

The depths of winter: an accurate description for the endless absence of the sun in a thick cold pile of sky. In the depths of winter it would be dark now. Dark at half past three? How can a day end in the middle of the afternoon? But it does not end because it has not started. It slides into the darkness which has lingered all day on the horizon. Daylight in the depths of winter is a mere interlude. Morning arrives late, for a brief hard sweep through the sky. And when darkness comes it is spiked with rain, it is cold, colourless, without the glow of day. And it is a noisy darkness; not a throbbing, droning, soft-sounding darkness but banging, bleating. I have started to notice summers but also to dread the return of winter.

The doorbell conjures synchronized slices of Roz in the frosted glass of the front door. The Smith doorbell chimes, announcing guests with ceremony, but at home we have a buzzer. Now the peace of the Smith doorstep is punctured by the opening of the door. In the past, Roz's opening of the door was a sweeping movement, sweeping her away into the hallway and up the stairs, leaving me to follow. Today, she pauses on the doorstep. We are smiling at each other, and, I suppose, examining each other.

'Roz,' I say appreciatively.

Her smile widens. I think vaguely of a hug, but she turns away. I have forgotten that she does not like displays of affection. And nor do I.

'Come in, come in.'

Is it possible that she is less pretty? I shut the door behind me with a twinge of panic. The smile in the doorway was filled with a light silt of make-up. The hair was brittle. Where is the soft snowy skin and silky, difficult hair? Surely she is too young to be less pretty already?

'Come up, come up,' she is saying above me, climbing the stairs.

The clothes are strange, fussy, dress-by-numbers, peaches-'n'-cream.

'How are you?' she sings as she reaches the landing.

'Fine. And you?'

'Fine.'

Fine.

The bedroom is a dressing room, a room for dressing, a room elaborately dressed. I am reminded of Mum's strange covetous mutterings in British Home Stores: *valance, border, broderie anglaise, louvre.* Roz's room is so different from the rooms occupied by the rest of us, by Lucy, Ali, Deborah, and me. Lucy has been at home this year, with nowhere else to go, but her bedroom is unlike Roz's room. It has white furniture and a tidy bed but I do not think of it as Lucy's room. It is yet another bedroom in the Harvey house.

And Lucy does not take me into her room. We do not need to go away together into rooms. We meet elsewhere. We have made places our own. Where would I go with Roz? If I imagine Roz away from home, I imagine the forecourt of the local railway station. I realize that we have no common ground.

Roz waves at the bed. 'Sit down, sit down.' I comply. She takes the stool from the dressing table and sits opposite me, facing me, crossing one leg over the other, folding forwards. I notice that she is wearing tights, or stockings: a tight, fine mesh of pale nylon. I cannot remember when I last wore tights. I push back into the cushions.

'Do excuse me,' says Roz suddenly, quickly, with an indecipherable wave or shrug, 'but I've been at work, I'm such a mess.'

Mess? A peaches-'n'-cream mess? I smile but glance at my shoes, risen above the Crufty white tufts of the carpet: Chinese silk slippers, orange, embroidered with a few small black flowers. What must Roz think? There would be no point in telling her that they were bought in the King's Road.

Roz's room is so unlike our rooms at college. At college they are study bedrooms: I was sent a letter informing me that I would be *allocated a study bedroom*. But the difference between Roz's room and the college rooms is greater than the absence of a desk or the presence of a dressing table. In Roz's room there is no cork noticeboard stuck with invitations, letters, tickets, supposedly utilitarian but confirming popularity; no cork-pinned bunting of doodles, badges, beer mats, supposedly significant, supposedly personal but on display as annotations to an engaging life, *A-I'm-Adorable*. And in Roz's room there are no posters, no moody blue Picassos. Roz's walls bear small wallpaper roses. There is no kettle here, no mugs or cups, no crusted teaspoon, no coffee jar of pale brown powder; no traces of food, no torn packets of Ritz or Tuc biscuits, no flecks of cheese rind. And there are no piles of laundry, clean or dirty, no stray nightdresses.

'So how *are* you?' Roz is leaning towards me, smiling hugely.

We had this question on the stairs, so this is the second round, but there is a crucial difference in emphasis: *How ARE you?* The emphasis implies that this is the real version of the question. But I know, we both know, that it is no more real, that it is a sitting How-are-you to follow the How-are-you on the stairs.

'Fine, fine.'

'Did you *walk*?'

'I *like* walking.'

She exaggerates exasperation. 'You're *mad*. There's a *bus*.'

'It's lovely out there.'

She glances briefly at the open window. 'So you're off to Liverpool tomorrow? To The Long Haired Lover in Liverpool?' She laughs. 'Tell all.'

So I begin to tell Roz about Tim. I say everything that he would say about himself, that he is twenty years old, an economics student. I am loyal to him: he is my friend, after all. So perhaps I am po-faced, but I feel vindicated. And Roz is behaving appropriately, nodding soberly. Suddenly I am compelled to say, 'But he's very nice.' Why do women habitually say this, claim this for their men? Whenever a woman confides a new love, she will stress that he is *very nice*. What do we expect? Presumably we expect the worst. Do men say the same about women? *No, really, she's very nice*. No, they say, *She's all right*. We mean *He listens to me, he talks to me*. And men mean *She doesn't make a fuss, she's fun*.

Roz is still nodding. My attention wanders to the photograph on the dressing table: eight or ten people crowded into the frame, pressed beneath the glass, their roars of laughter plugged by the glossy finish. Several of them are waving baguettes. Baguettes? Roz follows my gaze. 'Gavin,' she announces. She lifts the frame and holds it briefly in her hands before passing it to me. 'A picture of Gavin smuggled into my room, disguised as a picture of the office staff on a day trip to France.' Hence the baguettes.

'Don't tell my mum.' She smiles.

So it remains a secret from her mum. I am surprised. I am surprised that Roz can live here, like this, and keep secrets from her mum. I follow Roz's fingertip across the glass onto Gavin.

'Mum would go mad,' Roz says. 'Because of Dad.'

I stare hard at glossy Gavin, to avoid Roz, to avoid the mention of Dad. I realise that this is a reference to an affair, and to the divorce. She has confirmed my suspicions; or, rather, Mum's suspicions. I had no suspicions.

'Oh yes,' said Mum. 'Mark my words. An affair. He's a policeman, so he's the type.' Then she laughed and said, 'He's a *man*, he's the type.'

Does Roz's mum care about this, about Roz's dad's affair, after so long, and when her boyfriend's giant grey car is parked every evening in front of the china blue garage door?

I remember that Mum says *Betrayal is betrayal and it never goes away.* The eternal optimist.

Examining Gavin, I remember that Mum also says *If they've done it once, they'll do it again.* Will he do it again, to Roz?

'Nice smile,' I say about Gavin: not true. Gavin lunges across the photo, a self-styled mascot for the crowd. The smile, accompanied by a baguette, confronts the camera as an obscene gesture.

I do not comment on *Dad*: I accept without question. Without question, without comment, the intimacy can remain painless for Roz. I know that she prefers to confide obliquely. I remember, years ago, when it was important to confide in each other about sex, so that we could gauge acceptability, she told me about a conversation with one of her boyfriends: 'He asked me for a blow job, at the Fourth Form Christmas party, so I said . . .' and she puffed with sarcasm, '. . . *Oh, yes, of course, why don't you just slip underneath the buffet table here?*' I know Roz, I knew Roz, I knew that she was implying to me that the problem was the location rather than the act. So, Roz did blow jobs: this was a revelation to me. But I smiled genially and said nothing.

'He hasn't left his wife yet,' she says without expression. 'She's been ill, she's been made redundant.'

Ill, redundant: which? both? is one the result of the other?

124

'He says it wouldn't be fair yet.'

Yet? Fair? *For richer, for poorer, In sickness and in health.* 'No,' I murmur in confused agreement.

But she has not asked for my opinion, and she does not respond. Silence sinks between us like the photo which I lower into her hands. I am missing the usual routine of her questions: *What do you think? Why . . .? Should I . . .?* Questions are as vital as confidences, as involving. But she turns away, returns the photo to the dressing table. Perhaps she is wary of criticism. But my criticisms were never a problem: they were expected; they were challenging, confirming: *I know, I know, I know he's a bastard, Lalie, but I love him.* Perhaps she is afraid of prediction. But not mine, surely. Not me. Anyone, everyone, can see the future of Roz and Gavin.

Not For You: Mum's voice would rise to stop me in the doorway when she was in conversation with a friend. There was no answer to Not For You. Roz's silence, now, is saying *Not For You*, saying *Out Of Bounds.* She is insisting that she is somewhere else and does not want me there. Why not? Is it because I will see that trust is as absent in this relationship with Gavin as a decree nisi? I suspect that she wants to tell me that *I know nothing*, knowing that I know too much. She is running for her life, the life with Gavin, the life in the house in Southgate, and I know too much. I know about the life with Gavin, and I know about the running. She is vulnerable, now, and I know.

There is no music in Roz's room. In rooms at college there is always music; coffee and music, as soon as possible. Records slip with a rasp from their sleeves whilst the kettle is boiling. Roz does not have a record player. There is a portable cassette player on the bedside table, and a small stack of tapes selected from the collection downstairs. The cassettes have colourful sleeves. They have been bought from shops. Mine have been recorded by friends and returned to me in inky wrappers proclaiming *The Doors* but containing Bowie, or Bauhaus rather than Vivaldi. My collection is regularly tilled, Neil Young transformed into Brian Eno. I suspect that Roz plays tapes when she is alone. I imagine that she likes to have a rhythm to accompany preparations for a night out. For Roz, music absorbs silence. And we have never needed music between us until now.

She says no more about Gavin.

'Is Ali still going out with Julian?'

'Yes,' I tell her, 'as far as I know.' As far as I know, they are in France together, picking grapes, and due back in mid-September. 'When did you last see Ali?'

'Christmas Eve,' Roz replies. 'She was in *The Sun*.' With her sister, no doubt. 'We arranged to meet for a drink sometime between Christmas and New Year, before she went away again, but she went down with 'flu.'

'Have you seen Lucy?' she asks.

Have-you-seen-Lucy? It sounds like the title of a television serial.

'Last Saturday.'

'She's working, isn't she?'

She worked part-time until the re-takes in the winter; and then – now – full-time.

'In a café?'

'A bakery, yes.' *Tea, Coffee served here.*

'It would be nice to see her,' Roz says.

Would it? Roz gives no indication of any intention; not even a cursory I-must-ring or We-should-all-go-out-for-a-drink-sometime.

'She was a good laugh,' she adds briefly, quietly. Then she puzzles: 'Did she take any more exams this summer? What will happen to her?'

'Maths,' I reply, 'as ever.' O level Maths is essential for progression to college: a career in Art without O level Maths? Unthinkable! And Lucy cannot do Maths. I scraped a pass. I remember the terror of equations but I cannot remember the name: simultaneous? differential? There is a redundant vocabulary soggy in the back of my brain. I remember vectors, co-ordinates, moving pencil marks across graph paper: why? why bother? 'And she's going to a college in Staffordshire, I think, to do Combined Studies or something.' Sentenced to Staffordshire; where is Staffordshire?

'In the middle of the country,' Mum told me, 'somewhere.'

'The Midlands?'

'No, The Midlands is Birmingham.'

And what is Combined Studies? Combined with what? Lucy says that it is Art, English, History, Psychology, Education, that sort of thing. The entry requirements are minimal. Lucy passed her English re-take in January. Last summer, she had been expected to pass English and History with average grades. And she was expected to excel in Art – she was going to go to Art College, somewhere famous. But she passed Art with an average grade and failed everything else. There was no explanation. She was mortified by the grade for Art. She returned to school in the autumn, without us, for occasional classes in English. And Miss Killick suggested a career in teaching: Juniors.

'I hate kids,' Lucy told me in despair at Christmas.

'But your little brother is nice,' I tried.

'My brother is a *child*, Lalie,' she said. 'I'm sure that he'll be lovely *one day* but for now he's a *child*. Children are children and nothing else, not funny, not interesting, nothing. You can't have a conversation with a child, Lalie. You can't go for a drink with a child.'

Art, English, History, Psychology, Education? Lucy reassures me that Combined Studies is not a qualification in teaching but it seems to me that it is a BEd without the Ed.

Last Saturday I went to the bakery to meet Lucy at half past five.

'Get me out of here,' she sighed, pushing through the door ahead of me. She was wearing the required uniform: a pale brown nylon housecoat. It is difficult to believe that anyone could design a pale brown uniform, and even more difficult to believe that anyone else would accept the design. Perhaps it was a mistake. Or a joke, The World's Worst Uniform. Or a conspiracy; a conspiracy of uniform designers against the baking industry, a vendetta.

'The next person who asks me for a toasted teacake will need to suck it through a straw.'

127

Her thin legs were bare and pale. She paused in the middle of the shopping centre to wait for me beside the yellow display of the AA. The shopping centre is new; it is not called a shopping centre, it is called a *pavilion*. Lucy was illuminated by the slow burning low light of static. She was wearing black plimsolls, a negation of shoes, plainer and flatter than bare feet. She resembled a nurse, or worse; worse, because there were no pretentions to smartness, starchiness. So, a domestic, perhaps, or an orderly. Lucy is an unlikely orderly.

'And, Lalie, the endless talk of toilets! Where's-the-toilet-Where's-the-toilet?'

I reached her. 'Do you want to go home and change?'

'No. Let's go and have a drink.' Then, as we walked away, she turned to smile at the AA man to tell him, 'I'm having a breakdown.'

'Poor Lucy,' says Roz.

She does not ask about Deborah. I wish I was in Deborah's room rather than here in Roz's room; Deborah's college room, which I have visited several times this year. Whenever she is in the room, her door is open, ajar: a seam of light in the stone stairwell, a drizzle of music. Inside, there is the lamp, my favourite lamp, on the desk: an old glass lamp, a shimmering bauble on a wooden stalk, draped in a sheer red scarf, a Deborah-scarf; a hot pink cloud low on the sturdy little curtains. And there are flowers, velvet posies in party dress colours, purple and scarlet and white. And there are neat rows of books, a wall built from soft smooth shiny spines. On the wall above the desk is a large print of tall tapering trees, an avenue somewhere.

Whenever I visit Deborah, I see Peter. He was introduced simply as Peter; I know no more. Or, if I know more, it is not because I have been told. Perhaps Deborah assumes that I assume; or perhaps she has forgotten that she has not told me. And what would she say? *Boyfriend* is prissy. Should she say *We're sleeping together?* But why should that be an adequate description, a more accurate description of their relationship than all the other statements? *We went to see that play* or *We are going to London on Saturday* or *We had a good trip to Nottingham at the weekend*. I have seen them walking together slowly, arm in arm, heads inclined towards each other to bracket their conversation from the rest of the world.

Peter is nice. What would I say about Peter to Roz? He is nice-looking, although his hair is slightly too long. He is going to be a vet. I would not mention the jumpers with holes, or the satchel. And Deborah: what would I say about Deborah to Roz, if she ever asked? Deborah is busy, frighteningly busy. She does everything that I would like to do, as well as so much that I would not want to do. She acts and directs, which I would like to do; or, which, once upon a time, I felt that I would like to do. Whenever I visit Deborah for the day, she is spending the evening in a rehearsal or performance. In her spare time, now, she runs: 'Which is for stamina without muscles,' she told me jollily, 'which is good for the dancing.' *Spare time?* Her words. She runs daily, three miles.

On Saturday mornings she goes shopping with patients from the local psychiatric hospital, and on Sunday afternoons she records herself reading books onto tapes for blind people. One night each week is spent on duty beside the phone in the student advice centre. And, in between, she goes to meetings: the notices on the mantelpiece announce lunch time meetings of Third World First and the Women's Group, each of them bearing a handwritten plea, *Deborah Steiner*. Also on the mantelpiece is a column of coins. On one of my visits I rippled this cool spine between my fingertips and checked incredulously, 'For 'phoning home?' Because who else? But if I rang home during term, Mum would be suspicious. And what would we say to each other?

Deborah laughed knowingly, as always, as if there is something that I do not understand. 'It keeps them happy,' she said breezily. And then, with a smile which was a compressed but deeper version of the laugh, she added quietly, 'I ring my darling brother, too.' The *darling* was dry but slow, and her eyes sent mine away in a hurry, in search of a change of subject.

Now, momentarily, Roz presses a row of beady red fingertips to

129

her lips. 'Oh Lalie,' she murmurs, 'I didn't ask you whether you wanted a cup of tea or something.'

I shrug dismissively.

'No, really, do you want a drink? Shall we have a drink?'

'I don't mind.'

'Let's,' she says, and shifts in the chair, reaching backwards to the dressing table for a large black handbag. She places the bag in her lap, frowns into it, delves fretfully, and calls towards the footsteps outside on the landing: 'Matt?'

So, sometime in the last few years, *Matthew* has become *Matt*. 'Matt?'

The door opens gradually into the deep pile of the carpet. Matthew, Matt, is braced in the doorway in a pair of tight jeans, the tough dry denim yielding with familiarity around the neat hips and long legs, creasing into smile lines. But he is not smiling. And he is no longer thirteen. He peers through a dark tumble of hair, and then nods at me. 'All right?'

I shudder because I am wondering whether he thinks of me as Jane Blaney's sister.

'All right,' I confirm nervously.

'Matt,' sings Roz, busy with the bag, 'do you have a light?' She inserts the filtertip of a cigarette into her mouth and flashes the packet at us. She does not wait for an answer from me, and Matt waves the packet away with a furious frown before tapping his chest and demonstrating a cough. Does he not smoke? Or not today? He slides his fingertips into a tiny pocket in his jeans and extracts a box of matches to throw at Roz.

'Thanks,' she calls to him as he leaves. 'You're a life-saver.'

1984

....

Deborah and I are sitting on the edge of a dry, drained pool in Trafalgar Square. Nelson's Column towers above us in a thick sheath of blue plastic, a straight siphon filled with bright blue sky. Deborah is hunched on the warm stone rim, her arms folded around her skirt-covered knees. The tapering toes of her shoes are poking beneath the hem. I am swinging my legs, thudding my heels against the stone wall, and shifting warily from the pigeons.

'I hate pigeons,' I complain to her. 'They're like moths, but worse: bigger, with beaks.' Worse. 'And feet. And necks.' Worse still. 'Fleshy. Slimy.' Why do we never see baby pigeons?

Deborah laughs cheerily. 'You're in the wrong place, then. Do you want to move on?'

I shake my head, tipsy on sunshine.

She administers a reassuring tap to my knees. 'Don't worry, they won't peck you. I'll act as scarecrow.'

Briefly I glance from the pigeons to Deborah, to see the pewter shine on her hair. Is there anyone less like a scarecrow than Deborah?

The low loose rattle of taxis surrounds us. They are moving in gleaming black swarms. And the Square is sparkling with another sound, faint but unbroken like the ghost of the sea in a beached seashell. I listen carefully for a moment, and realize that it is the call of distant traffic across the city, swelling above the streets in a cloud, showering a song of distant horns. Nearby, gusts of conversation come to me from the spinning crowds like thin sharp voices pricking into a doze. 'Alex!' calls a woman, 'Alex, come along!' There is the inevitable siren of protest from the child, and a contemptuous morse of footsteps in the opposite direction.

131

'Well, all right,' the woman brays in reply, 'two more minutes.' Their limbs, passing me, are washing lines flapping thin pale loose clothes.

Ali is not here.

'She forgot that it's her sister's wedding,' Deborah told me a few moments ago, when I arrived.

'She *forgot* her sister's *wedding?*' Not Ali. I could believe this of Lucy – if Lucy had a sister – but not Ali.

'No, not exactly: the wedding's tomorrow; she forgot that she would have to stay home and help.' Deborah frowned in an effort to comprehend. 'I don't think she forgot July the third, the wedding, but I think she forgot that July the third is preceded by July the second, if you see what I mean.'

And today is July the second. It had been Ali's suggestion, weeks ago, that we meet this evening – a meal, Italian, somewhere cheap in St Martin's Lane – because she and Deborah are going abroad soon for a year: Ali to Paris, Deborah to Seville.

'No worries about marmalade!' Mum had trilled when I mentioned that Deborah would be shopping in London today for supplies.

I have been at work today, as usual, as a Playleader Assistant in a local Community Centre, Waltham-way. My job will last for a month. So, for a month, I am staying at home. Work was relatively easy today. There were no trips with the children to Casualty, and no visits from the police. And I am no longer exhausted at four o'clock, no longer saturated with the massed voices of children. Today there was a Treasure Hunt in the morning and Rounders in the afternoon. The sole disaster during the Treasure Hunt was one of the smaller children stumbling into a pile of something less than treasure. The others celebrated noisily as one of my co-workers carried him from the field to the washroom, confiding to me in a stage whisper that, 'It's *utterly* between his toes.' Our daily activities are devised by Brenda, the boss, the Playleader. Brenda The Boss is twenty-one, slightly older than me but belonging to my generation, and yet she is called Brenda. And she is a Brenda.

Who would call a baby Brenda? She has *become* a Brenda. She seems thirty. She says prayers before sandwiches. She is training to be a Primary School teacher.

Brenda organized Rounders in the afternoon, but she knew better than to include me. I have made a niche for myself with the Rounders Refusers. By tacit agreement I offer alternative activities. Today, to my shame, I relied on a competition. The non-competitive activities – the potato prints and drama workshops – degenerate on each occasion into chaos: the younger children babbling amongst themselves in rings-o'-roses about bikes and Rubik's cubes; the older girls slouching in a tight knot of contempt against a distant wall, and the older boys snaking away across the playground behind their self-proclaimed leader, Joey Jordan. A competition, however, produces concentration, regardless of any prize. And today there was no prize, no pack of fun-size Mars Bars. But – inadvertently? – there was the word *best*: Let's see who can produce the best picture of night-time. This provoked reverent silence and intense activity above each roughly torn giant piece of grey fibrous paper.

And this afternoon there was less trouble than usual involving Dean. Mum says *There Is Always One*, and at the Garnett Street Playscheme, The One is Dean. As Dean is a Rounders Refuser (or, perhaps, Rounders is a Dean Refuser) he spent the afternoon with me. I am more sympathetic to Dean than the others. The children bounce him around the room with their shouts and shoves. *Dean Brenton, Fuck off*. The staff sigh and stiffen. *Dean. DEAN*. I try to be more sympathetic. Why does Dean do what he does? *What* does he do? He does nothing. He is not naughty. And he is a nice-looking child, not fat or dowdy. What makes a Dean? Was there one mistake, once? Did he wet himself or cry in class or something, some faux pas or failure? Surely there was more than one mistake. If I have a child, how can I ensure that it is not a Dean? Why was I not a Dean? How did I escape his fate?

Dean does not seem to recognize my sympathy; or, rather, he is not satisfied, he wants more. I want to say, *Be thankful for small mercies*. Or perhaps I want to say, *Give me my due*. But why should he? And why should he not want more? He craves. Everywhere I turn, he is there, surrounded but alone, yelping. *Miss! Miss?* His protests and sulks are dramatic, directed at us, at the staff. He appeals to us all the time for attention. And he extracts it from us, but it is the very worst kind of attention: *Dean, DEAN.* And, similarly, from his peers. They could have been his allies but they have become his enemies. It is a vicious circle, very vicious, increasingly vicious.

I am haunted by visions of Dean at twenty, at thirty: what will happen to him? Is it possible that this is simply a phase? Or will he continue to amass unhappiness until it spills from his life into the lives of those closest to him? A lover, a child, who knows? I have seen his mother. She came to fetch him one afternoon, early, for a dental appointment. She is not much taller than him. It was a wet afternoon and she was wearing a grey plastic mac and a transparent plastic rainhood which bore traces of having been recently unfolded from its tiny plastic packet. Her short wellies were rainbow-coloured. She stood bent towards Dean as if she was trying to catch his words although he remained in petulant silence. Dean has a brother, too: Wayne. Dean-and-Wayne, too much of a cliché to be true. But it *is* true. Wayne is six years old, three years younger than Dean. And he is universally adored. Somehow Dean *sulks* but Wayne is *cool*. Dean shrieks but Wayne raises an eyebrow. Until I met Wayne, I assumed that everyone was condemned for the sins of their siblings.

At my primary school, traits came in family-sized batches. I remember Clodagh and Melanie Bright: Clodagh was bossy and acquisitive, Melanie was resentful and spiteful. The Matthews brothers: Sean Matthews was always late, slow, smiling, reading, declining to wear any shoes other than a pair of red plastic sandals and missing swimming lessons due to ear trouble; little Jason Matthews wore clip-on bow ties and was inseparable from his portable chess set. Katy and Emma Hanley were famous for their party dresses, seersucker in summer with bright silk sashes, velvet or tartan in winter with ruffs and cuffs of lace. It is difficult to imagine any of them now, ten years later, although Mum tells me that Emma Hanley is an ambulance driver in Birmingham.

'You're tired,' says Deborah suddenly.

'Yes. No. I'm thinking.'

She turns respectfully away. I follow her gaze into the crowds. Almost every face is eating ice cream, nudging into a glossy white hand-held pile of sugary fat.

'What about Lucy,' she says eventually, slowly, full of awe.

Not Lucy, but Lucy's parents. Lucy's parents? Lucy's mum. Mr Harvey is no relation. He is married to Lucy's mum. Or, was. Or, rather, they are still Mr and Mrs Harvey, but not for long now, not forever, not now. The white bedroom which once contained Lucy now contains Mr Harvey. And he is refusing to move. So he has left, but not left. Lucy is away at college, she will stay away, but what will happen to Lucy's mum? If Mrs Harvey is no longer Mrs Harvey, who is she? She ceased to be Mrs Evans so that she could become Mrs Harvey. And if Mr Harvey has left but not left, left her but not left her house, what can she do?

'Did you know?' Deborah's gaze swims towards me from the crowds.

Did I know what? Did I know before Deborah? Did I know before *Lucy?* I *should* have known. I should have known from Lucy's spectacular failure in her exams; her obvious confusion, exhaustion, misery, hopelessness.

I shrug. I knew nothing until, in the course of a phone conversation several months ago, Lucy complained that Mr Harvey had recently thrown the contents of her bedroom outside onto the lawn. Then she called him a few names, indicating that the rift was serious and total. 'Mum rang me in tears,' she told me, her tone rich with vindication.

'Did you hear it from Lucy?' I ask Deborah.

'I've written a few letters since Christmas.' Diligent Deborah. 'But there was no reply. And then Ali told me that Lucy had been hinting at problems at home.' *Problems at home*: Deborah talks like

135

a teacher, like her parents. 'But Ali hadn't asked her about them, of course.'

We exchange smirks: typical Ali.

'So,' Deborah returns brightly, tentatively, 'is it all true?'

All true is weak on details but captures the mood.

'Apparently. Apparently there was an affair with Darren Fish's mum. Did you know?'

Deborah frowns dutifully.

What do I know? I have nothing but Lucy's word; Lucy's big blue-eyed accusations. Mum's designation for people like Lucy is *fertile imagination*. There is nothing wrong with imagination – the more fertile, the better – but I wish that Lucy could be a more reliable informant. I have learned to rely on the tone of Lucy's statements: she elaborates the details, but the tone is accurate.

'Darren Fish,' mutters Deborah.

'Darren Fish's mum. But Lucy thinks that it's over.'

'Darren Fish,' repeats Deborah, incredulous.

'Darren Fish's *mum*.'

She smiles distractedly. 'Yes; but I was thinking about Darren Fish.'

The name has always sounded to me like a description, a cross between *dry fish* and *barren fish*. Darren Fish was – is – two years older than us. He left school – when? – six years ago? At school he was famous for his smile, the black ghost of a missing tooth, and also for Mr Allan announcing in assembly that *I want to see Fish in my office*. After Darren Fish left school, I saw him sometimes in town, sitting with friends and beer glasses on the wall outside The Jolly Bricklayers. This was appropriate because Darren Fish was a bricklayer, and jolly. But then he seemed to go into a decline, a few years later, after breaking his leg; or perhaps he broke his leg because he was already in a decline. The leg seemed to stay broken for a long time. He thumped around town on a pair of tall wooden crutches, and his hair was wildly unwashed. Perhaps it is difficult to wash your hair with a broken leg: perhaps it is difficult to balance, perhaps the plaster dissolves on contact with water, I don't know.

And then there was an article in the local paper about his conviction for shop-lifting.

'Don't tell me,' laughed Roz at the time, 'but he stole a bottle of shampoo.'

'Whatever happened to Darren Fish?' Deborah's gaze ripples into the crowds.

'Shall I ask Lucy?'

She returns to me with a faint smile. 'Perhaps not. And perhaps we should avoid all mention of fish to Lucy.'

'No meals out, then, with Lucy.'

'No seaside jaunts.'

'But there's more,' I continue, conspiratorially.

'Isn't there always?'

I am surprised by Deborah's cynicism. But she is frowning gently, without focus, at the tuppence-a-bag man.

'Poor Luce,' she mutters.

'Yes, poor Luce,' I agree.

I try to remember the other details. 'Mr Harvey either kicked or killed the cat: I couldn't quite hear, on the phone, and I didn't like to ask.'

Deborah presses a small pink pyramid of fingertips to her twitching lips. 'Don't.' *Don't laugh.* 'That's awful.'

'And he is saying nasty things to Elliott.'

We raise our eyebrows simultaneously: I am conjecturing, she is questioning.

'I don't know. Don't ask.' I shrug. 'Things about Lucy's mum, I suppose, or even about Lucy.'

There is a pause before Deborah ventures, 'And there's a sports car?'

'It was the first sign,' I confirm confidently. 'He sold Lucy's car – Lucy's *mum's* car – and bought himself an X19. And now he has a perm.'

'A perm?' she interrogates, alarmed.

'A *horrid* perm,' I elaborate, using Lucy's words.

Deborah laughs lightly, with relief. 'Perhaps it was a mistake.

Perhaps it was an inverse Sweeney Todd, so that he left the barber with more rather than less.'

'Nice try, Deborah, but men don't make mistakes about perms. For men, perms are premeditated. They don't perm by default, not like women. No, the perm was the second sign.'

It seems to me that certain kinds of perms and cars are specially designed for men's mid-life crises. If there was an affair with Darren Fish's mum, then I suspect that it was a symptom rather than a cause. I try to visualize the original Mr Harvey. I can see a pale grey suit moving slowly around Lucy's bungalow in the evenings, partially dismantled, jacketless. The thick column of grey twitches in the living room like the tail of a mermaid. Then I see Lucy's mum in the kitchen, bent over a dark green bottle, tipping silky gold sherry into a small glittering glass, *For Daddy*. I had thought that sherry was for grandmothers; and, similarly, slippers. But Mr Harvey had slippers, and they moped around the bungalow in front of him. He had a moustache, too, cloaking his mouth. In my mind's eye I see him staring down over the moustache at Lucy as if she were mad.

'Is it true that he dumped Lucy's stuff on the front lawn?' Deborah's enquiring gaze struggles against the sunlight.

'Yes.'

Deborah doesn't ask, *Why?* Roz would ask, Roz would require me to offer explanations. Roz would continue a conversation with the explanations: *But why? . . . perhaps . . . but you'd think . . .* Because Roz thinks aloud. Or did.

Deborah simply says, 'Imagine the neighbours!'

Presumably the neighbours were horrified enough by the mural. Now they know that the mural was a warning to the neighbourhood: Abandon all hope, ye who enter here.

'Imagine Mr Harvey . . .' Deborah is frowning.

The unbroken hoop of sunshine on Deborah's crown flexes as she turns again towards me. 'But how is Lucy?'

'You should see Lucy.' She has not seen Lucy, of course, but I saw Lucy last month. 'Lucy's in love.'

Avid, she hugs her knees. 'Who?'

'You should see him.' He came along when Lucy drove over to see me; or, rather, he drove Lucy. Lucy is car-less.

'You've seen him; tell me.'

'Clean jeans!'

The hoop of sunshine slips sideways.

'Polite haircut. Aran sweater and everything.'

'Everything?' She is sweetly sceptical.

'Well, Aran sweater.'

I want to say that he is like a big brother, but he is not like Deborah's big brother. Deborah's big brother is not *big*, he is skin and bones: small bones nestle under the skin at the base of his neck. His narrow chest is nothing but a cage for a heart. But bones are tough. Tough white bones slither beneath Deborah's brother's skin. Shadows collect at the corners of his eyes and mouth. Sea-water eyes and uneven teeth. I imagine that his uneven bite is as peculiar and particular as the print of a scarred fingertip.

'He's not like your brother,' I try.

'So?' She laughs, tipping her own rows of bright teeth towards the sun. 'Since when has my brother been the be-all-and-end-all?'

I do not answer.

Lucy's Love is a few years older than us, but he is like a baby; full and soft like a baby.

'He's Ents Officer at their college,' I inform Deborah.

She shrugs happily. 'Nice little number: free tickets.'

'Seriously.'

The grey gaze concentrates on me. 'But, Lalie, why is he so awful?'

'He's not so awful. He's nice, really.' *Nice, really?* So conspicuously different to *really nice*. I shudder: does anyone ever refer to me as *nice, really?* How can I guard against this?

'But?' Deborah is peeking, with avid interest, from behind the shiny length of her hair.

But. 'He's studying accountancy.'

The same kindly laugh. 'So?'

'Deborah, listen to me, for God's sake: he's going to be an accountant.'

She frowns hopefully. 'Perhaps he has a sick mother to support.'

'He's not Lucy's type,' I counter in desperation.

'What is Lucy's type?'

Good question. 'Lucy couldn't even count out a bus fare. Remember?'

Deborah soothes a faint scuff on the toe of one of her shoes. 'Opposites attract,' she offers faintly.

'Initially, yes . . .'

'Perhaps she needs someone to count out the bus fares.' She is concerned.

'But we can do that for her; and, into the bargain, we don't play rugby.'

'But we're not *there*.' She applies spittle to the scuff. Without looking up, she says clearly, confidently, conclusively, 'Give her time. She'll come round.'

Before I can answer, or perhaps query, she adds, 'Perhaps he has hidden attributes.'

Is this innuendo? I need to shock Deborah from this cheerful complacency. 'He calls her Loopy Lu.'

She looks sharply but amusedly upwards into my face. 'No!'

'I told you,' I trumpet, vindicated.

'But you didn't tell me *that*.'

'How do you know that she's in love?' Deborah is frowning doubtfully into my face. 'Did she say?'

'No, but it was obvious.' When Lucy came to see me, she was no longer moving with the striking elongation of a flying swan. She stood very still next to him, silent, smiling, shining. Was she on display? Or was she in awe? 'She brought him to see me, didn't she.'

The news of Lucy settles silently between us. We are both reluctant to move from the fizzling sunshine. We are supposed to be going for a drink. We have changed our plans and decided not to go for a meal. Of course, Deborah is right: half past five was

140

a convenient time to meet but it is not necessarily a convenient time for a meal. And spontaneity is not one of Deborah's gifts. Especially not when she has just been taken to lunch by her mother. But I have had no lunch and I can detect the smell of garlic sweltering in fiercely hot butter, a civilizing smell filtering through the traffic, suggesting a human pace of life, the end of the working day and the start of the evening. And the scent is tugging at the lining of my stomach. Why do smells travel so much further on hot days? And sounds, too. I like to think that they melt in the warm air, and run. But it is probably because there are more windows open.

'Debbie Doo,' I ask, 'how are you and Pete?'

'Fine, fine.' She nods satisfaction. 'He has gone to be a vet, now, of course.' She continues nodding.

'Where?' Not Seville.

'Potters Bar.' She smiles sympathetically. 'Hardly Herriot country.'

'Fewer cows,' I say approvingly. My childhood was ruined by the Herriot exposés: vets, for me, before Herriot, wore clean white coats and administered to grumpy cats in baskets. Before Herriot, I wanted to be a vet; I even took an interest in the neighbour's rabbit.

It strikes me that Deborah's Pete chose to be a vet instead of a doctor because he is so shy. What other explanation is there for the rejection of a chance to wear the heroic bloodied coat of the doctor? But I suspect that he is mistaken, that there is no passion like the passion of the owner of a sick scottie. I know that Gran Blaney's will has been written to benefit abandoned donkeys. I know this because Mum tells me whenever I go home: *Well, blow me if she isn't leaving everything to a load of donkeys!* I doubt that the donkeys will be inheriting stupendous riches. I wonder whether they will be inheriting the stuffed monkey. If not, where will it go? Mum will refuse it. And surely stuffed animals are not allowed in dustbins. Someone will have to ring the Council.

141

'I'll see him at Christmas, of course,' Deborah is continuing, 'and he'll come out to Spain for a couple of holidays.'

And suddenly The Troublesome Notion crosses my mind again despite a conscientious attempt at suppression: The Troublesome Notion is that I cannot imagine Deborah and Pete having sex. Talking politics, yes; cooking pasta, yes; anything, everything, but not having sex. I glance with intrigue at Deborah. Her face is held towards the sun, eyes closed. Pete would never close his eyes in a public place. I realize that my mental block concerns Pete, not Deborah. Pete is too self-conscious for sex.

For Ben, my first lover, star of stage and stadium, sex was one of life's pleasures. He proceeded with enthusiasm, buoyancy, gusto; the same attitude, I noticed, with which he tackled meals and jogs. *Tea for two. Anyone for tennis?* He liked participation, team spirit. I was, literally, his partner. Love is the stuff of dodgy declaration, but I know that he *liked* me. Because he *chose* me. Often I must have been a disappointment to him, reluctant with my colds and headaches, cynically distant: not the sporting type. Not that he ever complained. On the contrary, he seemed to think that I was a scream: I remember all the names that he liked to call me, Little Miss Muffet, The Duchess, and HM which stood for High-and-Mighty. I loathed this at the time, of course, but now miss it. Now that I am nothing but Lalie. No one else has ever had names for me, then or since.

Now I realize how *much* I liked Ben, *liked* him, so much more than any boy whom I have met since; *any* boy, from those who come to drink coffee with me in my college room, to the boyfriends of my friends. I know that I would still like Ben if I met him, but the point is that I do not meet him. He is training to be a Games teacher, not because he wants to teach Games but because he wants to spend his life on a field in a tracksuit. For me to miss Ben would mean missing that whole world, the world of school and home. And I do not. But sometimes I wonder about him; I wonder about him without wondering about school and home, focusing firmly on him, constructing a keyhole. Deborah liked Ben and, whenever we meet, she asks after him. Reminds me of him. But today, so far, there has been no mention. So now I ask her, 'Have you heard anything of Ben?'

She peeps through the sunshine, her eyes sprung with surprise. 'No. But you're the one who knows everything about everyone.'

Not everyone. Not everything. I tell her, 'I had a postcard from him . . .' Before or after Christmas? Not *at* Christmas: I remember that he did not send me a Christmas card. But boys tend not to. 'He said nothing, but my sister Jane told me that he has been seen with Madeleine Wren.' Told me with relish. Told me that he was engaged to Madeleine Wren. Which I refuse to believe. Not that there is anything wrong with Madeleine Wren. In principle. She was in the year below us, and Queen of Long Jump. Deborah, eyes sticky with sunshine, shut, sends a smooth laugh into the sky. 'Noooo.'

'No?' Does she know something that I do not know?

'No,' she confirms 'Because if he went for someone like you, then why would he be interested in someone like Madeleine Wren?'

Precisely: so perhaps he did not go for someone like me, perhaps he never liked me, or not much, or found that he was relieved to see me go, recognizing his error and turning gladly to the Queen of Long Jump. Common-sensical Deborah, can she not see this?

Suddenly she swings around to me. 'What's up?' Her enquiry is polite, almost cheerful.

I prickle hotly. 'Nothing.'

She does not shift. 'Are you missing Ben?' There is surprise in her tone but nothing else to suggest that it is disgraceful for me to miss Ben. Which I do not.

'No.' But I am missing something. What?

Sex, for Tim, is the discharge of an urge. *Healthy sex life.* In thirty years' time, when his charisma has gone, along with his hair and his waistline, he will lecture his kids liked a pitied nudist: *Don't be silly, it's perfectly natural, there's no need to feel ashamed.* Tim tells me that he does not believe in marriage, and I agree with him, but what else can I say? *Marry me anyway, because I say so, because I don't*

care what you think, because I am everything in which you do not believe?
At the beginning, I did not feel that we needed to marry: why marry your best friend? Now I think that we would need marriage to keep us together. Which means, surely, that we should not be together at all. Perhaps everything would have been different if I had been certain that he would never leave. But even marriage is no such guarantee, not nowadays; nor ever, because what of my own grandmother, Brenda Blaney? Marriage does not mean that someone will never leave, it means that they have said that they will never leave. Which can be said without marriage, is said whenever we fall in love. So where does that leave us?

I ask Deborah, 'Will you and Pete get married?'

She flinches in surprise. 'Not *yet*.'

'Which is not what I asked.'

She frowns, her face sprinkled with sunny lines, sun rays. 'We don't feel the need,' she replies doubtfully, 'it's not on our list of priorities.'

I am interested: 'So what *is?*'

She loosens, her frown fizzling away into the blank white light. 'Oh, I don't know. Getting this degree, I suppose. Some travel, perhaps. Jobs. Somewhere to live.' She shrugs inconclusively.

I muse, 'Odd that it used always to be the other way around. Married first, then doing everything together, settling down together.'

She smiles and slips back to the sun.

'But you will?' I urge. 'Marry, I mean.'

She returns sleepily, sunnily, to me. 'How do *I* know?'

Try again: 'Do you *want* to marry?'

'Lalie,' she says emphatically, amused but exasperated, 'I don't know.' The words ring faintly with the tone which Mum uses on me whilst adding *If-that's-quite-all-right-with-you.*

But as usual I cannot stop myself. 'Don't know about what? About Pete?'

'No . . .' Her head inclines in front of the sun, considering.

'So what do you need to know, in order to know? Surely it is something that you *want* or do *not* want.'

She laughs and smooths the palm of one hand down her length of warm hair. 'You're a touch too absolute, as ever, Lalie.'

It has been said before. Although perhaps never so nicely. (Is it possible to be a touch too absolute?)

'Because how do I know what will happen?' She sounds happy about this.

I challenge her, 'What *can* happen? The future is easy to guess. Nothing ever happens. Not *really*.'

She asks me, kindly, 'Do you want to marry Tim?'

Quickly I tell her, 'Tim doesn't believe in marriage.'

'With whom?'

I look at her sun-shrivelled eyes.

'Lalie,' she starts gently, 'why don't you talk to me about you and Tim.'

But suddenly I have come far enough to be certain that I do not want talk to Deborah about Tim. Not this evening; I do not want to spoil our evening, our last evening alone together for a long time. Tim is spoiling enough of my life. 'There's nothing to say,' I tell her, lightly. Except one thing: 'You are in love with Pete?'

She is distracted, and sinks into a smile. 'Yes. And you?'

We are suspended in a tiny pause before falling into a laugh.

'In love with Tim, I mean.'

Tim never talks to me about love. 'Yes,' I say, carefully copying her confident tone. But the answer rings false for me, which is exactly what I needed to know.

'What news of Roz?' Deborah changes the subject.

'Nothing.' I have heard nothing from Roz since the annual Christmas card, the annual signature. 'I presume everything is the same:' Gavin; the office.

Deborah nods knowingly without opening her eyes.

It strikes me that there is very little news from any of us. We are in limbo. But Deborah and Ali are breaking free for a year.

'My big sister is having a baby,' she murmurs to the sun.

145

Surprised, I turn sharply to her. 'No!'

'Yes.' The eyelids lift briefly, barely, so that she can scrutinize me.

'Deborah, you drop it into the conversation as if it's perfectly *normal*.'

A frown sparks on her face.

'*When?*' I ask quickly.

'February.'

'Are they pleased?' *They* are sister-and-sister's-boyfriend.

'Of course.'

Of course? 'Will you come home?'

'I hope so.'

I want to know so much but Deborah sits silently, warm with Steiner secrets.

'My brother is converting to Law,' she adds.

I experience the familiar tingle at the mention of him. And I grin to myself. 'You make him sound like a reformed criminal.'

Once again she peers at me. 'Well . . .' Then the mock concern relaxes into a little laugh and she returns blindly to the sun. 'And my Dad,' she continues, 'my newly-retired Dad tells me that he is going to write some songs about unemployment.' The indulgent smile remains.

'Tell him that I know a good one: *Maggie, Maggie, Maggie, Out, Out, Out*.'

She concedes with a lift of her eyebrows. 'I've tried to suggest to him that it has been done before, that he should listen more closely to his old records, *Railroad Blues* or whatever. I said to him, *They're not lamenting the price of Supersavers*.'

'Daddy-got-the-blues,' I sympathize.

'Oh yes,' she says mildly. 'As ever. Loudly. And giving them to everybody else in the house.'

I open my mouth to ask whether her dad ever wrote for *Grange Hill* – a rumour originating recently from Lucy – but she is swinging onto her feet and asking, 'Shall we move on?'

I nod, non-committal. Pigeons rise in a thick grey dust around our feet. Deborah shooes ineffectively, directing an ostentatious frown of disapproval at them. Then she relents, turning to me with a wide smile. 'So, how are the Blaneys?'

Is the question designed to distract me from the pigeons? They are flying in front of my face: fat, swollen, muscular. 'The Blaneys? What can I say? What is there to say about the Blaneys?'

She is uttering notes of polite protest.

'No, really. They're not like your Steiners. They're not grown-up. Nothing happens to them.'

Her skirt, hair, limbs are swinging, swishing, rustling beside me. 'One day they'll surprise you,' she says.

I wonder if she would be surprised if she knew that I am considering leaving university, that I am deciding whether or not to return. But of course she would be surprised. Because no one ever leaves. Not before time. Not even the people who spend the first term in silence and the second term in hospital. Even they follow the route: growing up, going from school to college to graduate to a job. Tim is the very least of my worries. I do not want to discuss Tim but I do want to talk to Deborah about leaving. I have been wanting to say something ever since I saw her across the square, as still as a stone beside the empty pool, waiting for me. Or perhaps before, on all the occasions in the past few months when I sat with pen and paper and wrote *Dear* before giving up and continuing to scribble more notes for the same old essay. If I do not tell Deborah, then who do I tell? But I know that if I tell, she will feel not solely surprise, she will also feel hurt. Because, somehow, leaving the route means leaving everyone else; and it hurts to be left, like when Roz left me in the Sixth Form.

I do not want to spoil our evening, because what would be the point? What can Deborah say or do? Usually she can make everything seem all right, but not this time. Which feels odd. She can either say *Do* or *Don't* – what else can people say? – and both are misery for me. No, she will say *Do what you want to do* and this is worse. Because what do I want? I was always the one – in their opinion, in Roz's, Ali's, Lucy's, Deborah's opinions – who knew what I wanted. I-know-what-I-like. And, conversely, what I do not like. But now nothing is unfolding as I expected. So, what did I expect? More options, more and more. Instead, there are fewer and fewer: school, university, degree, job. I do not want to be at university but I do want my degree, no, I *need* my degree to secure myself a job. I do not want to be at university, but nor do I want to be here, home. Nor do I want a job; or not a *job* job, a proper job, nine-to-five, or, more likely, nine-to-six, six-thirty – seven-thirty after the train journey home. A job-job. I do not want, I do not want: whatever is happening to me? I am losing my nerve.

But I do not want to spoil this evening, I do not want to spoil *my* evening, I do not want to hear the words which are stale from storage inside my head. I was always the one who could talk my way out of anything. Not this time. This time I must make a decision. Deborah is only momentarily here, with me, then gone, for a whole year. I cannot send her away with my problems. Besides, by the time she returns, everything will be resolved for me. Either way, if I stay or if I go, university will be over, for me. No more topics. *That's your lot*. When I was at school, university seemed to stretch forever into the future, a whole new life. Now, whatever my decision, life looms: tinker, tailor; or, rather, accountant, management consultant. If I close my eyes I can see the names: Prewitt, Hewson, Nelson, Neal, Partners, plc. Recruitment, graduate recruitment. Deborah has an extra year before making these decisions. Whenever I ask about her plans, for jobs, she replies happily that she has no idea. But if I am unsure about my exact interests, and increasingly reluctant to go back into classrooms despite the preference in special education for sand-pits in place of blackboards, then I am certain that Graduate Recruitment plc is not for me. What is the graduate equivalent of flat feet? The wrong attitude? Flat attitude?

In any case, everyone says that there are no jobs any more, no real jobs. Instead, there is management, the management of the demise of other people's jobs. Rationalization rather than creation. When I was at school, university meant journalist, researcher, copywriter. Nowadays university means nothing and experience is essential. But Mum and Dad do not realize this. Whenever I go home, they question me: *What kind of job . . .?* Dad favours the BBC: *East End Boys,* he says approvingly, *Reith and the others.* He knows that I am not a boy, but I suspect he thinks that our suburb is a modern equivalent of the East End. I try to explain to him that there are training schemes nowadays for the BBC: eight places per year? ten? Eight, ten, what does it matter? I knew one of last year's successful candidates by sight: who didn't? He wore a long black cloak. He was not an East End Boy. And he directed plays, wrote plays, wrote reviews, locally, nationally. What do they call them, these success stories? high calibre graduates? I am not a high calibre graduate, working away in my room on my weekly essay.

Law, growls Dad, on his way through the house. I suppose that law means people, to some extent. But law means two years of further study, without a grant. Dad does not realize that, nowadays, a degree is nothing; or, rather, that it is known ominously as a first degree. Teaching is an easy option, one year more of training. But teaching means school. *Special* school means fewer job opportunities. Primary teaching is for people who like papier mâché, and secondary teaching is slavery. And there is no money in teaching. Social work? *Busybodies,* says Mum, *toffee-nosed busybodies.* What is the origin of *toffee-nosed?* Stuck up, literally stuck? But there is no money in social work, either: for staff or clients. There is the Civil Service; I suppose I could take the Civil Service exams. *Idiots,* says Dad, *useless, clueless, parasites.* What have civil servants ever done to him? (What *are* civil servants?) *Good pension, though,* he says. Pension? I have decided that I did not choose to go to university to graduate to office work; I could have gone to the local college with Jane and taken the Office Management course, which included *Grooming.* 'Secretary or stablehand?' I demanded from Mum, pointing to the curriculum in Jane's copy of the prospectus.

'Courses for horses,' she replied absently.

I remember now that I was going to write to the Principal to complain, but I never did.

If I do not go back in October, where will I go? I cannot come back here, back home. It is not home, not any more, or not mine. The goal of going away was staying away. What would I do, Waltham-way, with my A levels? So I have left, but not left. And if I do not keep moving, I will be stuck, nowhere. Purgatory.

When I go back in October, if I go back, I must cover enough topics in a term for two papers. *Papers*, why *papers*? Exams. But when I close my eyes I can see papers, smaller than friendly, ordinary A4: A5, meaner, precious, precise. I can see that the instructions on the papers are in italics, fierce, angry, unrelenting: *Answer three questions*. Each paper will threaten me with three questions, so I will learn five topics to be safe. Ten topics in total next term. Ten topics in ten weeks. A weekly essay. The essays are about books, the tutor gives me a weekly reading list for each essay. It takes a while to find the books, and then I spend several days reading them. There is no time to think. There is hardly any time to write. My handwriting has become strange, hurried, cramped. It is not my handwriting. What would Mr MacKenzie say about all this, if I told him? Why did he not warn me?

I will go back to a little room in college. The rooms are bigger than my old bedroom at home, so why do they seem so small? They are study bedrooms, fitted for the purpose. The prominent feature of each room is the desk. I have never been able to work at a desk. Mum and Dad bought me one when I was ten, when I was selected for the Grammar School. They took me to John Lewis, late night shopping, to the Furniture Basement. Their furniture used to come from John Lewis, but now it comes from MFI. Whatever happened to my desk? I do not remember having seen it at home. Presumably one of the others has it. Erin will have built a den underneath; or it will be Lyndsay's workbench. Or Lauren will be Chairperson of General Motors, spreading her papers and borrowing the most formal chair from the kitchen. I have never seen Jane near a desk but it is conceivable that she might spread photographs of herself across it.

At home I worked on the kitchen table or on the living room floor; in the warmth, and near the kettle or television. My bedroom was for my bed, for lying in it or on it, dreaming or day-dreaming. It was for privacy, or, at least, in a household of Blaneys, the tantalizing possibility of privacy. It was a room of mirrors: hanging oval on the wall; swinging long, sleek and silver inside the wardrobe; folding into a compact in a drawer; and shining darkly inside window frames, polished by night.

Living in a study bedroom is living-at-the-office. At college there is nowhere to hide. And the main gate is locked at midnight (*Later By Prior Arrangement With The Porter*). Dinner is at six each evening, at long tables in the refectory. The refectory is open until seven but it is empty of all food except cabbage by twenty past six. And latecomers face the possibility of having to sit at the end of a long table next to an isolated and miserable PhD student or avuncular trainee clergyman. I would say that it is like a boarding school, but what do I know about boarding schools? Unlike many of the students, I have never been to a boarding school. Nor have I ever been to a holiday camp – contrary to their expectations? – but I suspect that college is like a holiday camp without the holiday.

At my side, Deborah is striding, smiling. At college I do have friends, not a group of friends but satellites: I met Clive outside a party, and he makes me laugh; Gaynor is politically active and puts me to shame; Sam fries bread solitarily and vaguely in the kitchen, next to my room at the end of the corridor, late at night, activating the fire alarms; Kate gossips, shops, and swims with me on Ladies' Night each week at the local pool. There is also my next door neighbour, Caroline, and her recognizable, routine, reassuring tread on the weak floorboards outside my door. She appears in my doorway at regular intervals throughout the day, in outfits ranging from tracksuits to ballgowns, pleading and wailing: *Just ASK me if I have any coffee/ink/toothpaste*.

I have friends there, so why do I feel so lonely? I shut my sun-scorched eyes momentarily, guided by the steady sway of Deborah beside me, and I think of university, of October. I see a thick frill of posters lining a corridor, each one handwritten with enthusiastic squeaky sweeps of marker pen: *Film Soc., Third World First, Jewish*

151

Soc., Rowing Club; Old Hall, Common Room, Archaeology Dept., H3;
7.30, 8.00. I open my eyes wearily. I am not a member of anything.
I do not know how or why I became a member of nothing. When
college is all around me, I feel that I am somewhere else. College
is for someone else. Everyone else. Like home, like school. At the
beginning, before the beginning, when I was at home and school,
I felt that college would be mine.

Tim left before the very end of term, in the blaze of celebratory
end-of-term fireworks. He was still slightly drunk, probably, when
he boarded the first train on the Saturday morning for the North.
He is in Liverpool now, working all day every day for three and
a half months: a summer job, all summer. But he wanted the job,
this job. His overdraft is no motivation. He wants to work. Last
term he spent a long time in the Careers Library consulting the
shelves of royal blue plastic folders. Now his queries are specific:
exactly which organization, and exactly when?

I went to the Careers Library, to the seven long shelves of labelled
folders: arts administrator, archivist, acupuncturist, operating
department assistant, psychiatric social worker, publisher, indexer,
public relations officer, probation officer, prison governor. I could
be a prison governor; no one else wants to be a prison governor
so there would be a job for me. I could be what the newspapers
call a Liberal Prison Governor. I decided I wanted to be a Careers
Advisor, but when I asked the Careers Advisor for details she
thought I was joking.

I have the time to go to Liverpool but I do not have the money.
And he has the overdraft, still. So there are phone calls and letters
instead. So he does not know that I think I am pregnant. He will not
know, he never knows, when my period is due; or was due. It is six
days late. Too early to test. I will test soon and if it is positive I will
go to the doctor. But for now, I will say nothing, not even to Deborah.

～

It seems that everyone has gone to bed. I ease the front door gently
into its frame behind me. There is a faint glow in the gloom of

the hallway: a trick of the light, perhaps, or, rather, of the dark; or perhaps the fizzing dial of the stereo, mute and forgotten in the living room behind the ribbed glass door, or perhaps the plastic coals of the electric fire, recently extinguished. When I was small, coming downstairs in darkness for drinks of water, I would aim confidently for the living room and find no one there. Now, nevertheless, I open the door tentatively, and I find Mum. She is sitting on the settee, staring at the plastic coals which are smarting and winking inside the wooden fire surround. I have spent a lifetime staring at those coals, too. I know that the electric flicker beneath the undulating plastic terrain is cast by the shadow of a tiny fan turning like a weather vane over a red bulb.

Mum must have been dozing, because she is doing nothing: there is no newspaper in her lap, no emery board in her hand.

'Oh, it's you,' she says, shifting inside a soft purple sack of tracksuit.

'Yes, it's me.'

Her slippers are toy lambs, the two puckered faces popping from the bitter blue veins of her feet. I remember that they were a present from someone: who? Erin?

I remember that I used to find Mum breast-feeding a baby in this room, sometimes, in the night. In this dark red light; one of the indistinguishable Blaney babies laid across her lap in sleepy ecstasy, small bald head and slack limbs, and the smell of freshly washed towelling in the room. Mum would be sitting tall on the settee. Her hair was long in those days, much longer, a shiny yellow shawl around her head and shoulders and the baby. She did not feed me in this room. When I was a baby, we lived somewhere else. *A nasty poky little flat*, Mum tells me, *I couldn't wait to leave*. We left before Jane was born. We moved here for Jane.

I aim hungrily for the kitchen. Why isn't the television on? Why silence? At college I have only the small distant voice of the radio. At home I like the throb of the television.

'Was it nice?' Her drawl follows me across the room.

'Yes, thanks.' But the trip was marred by the wait at the station for a bus: forty minutes. I can walk home from the station in half an hour in the daytime, but at night the road is dark amid fields.

'And how was Deborah?' Her drowsy gaze follows me through the doorway into the kitchen.

'Fine.'

There is a loaf on the table, truncated, the flecks of crust splattered across the breadboard. There is a tub of margarine, open, shiny yellow, and a pot of red jam with lumps. My evening meal.

'How's that brother of hers?'

I shrug. 'Fine.' I take the breadknife. 'Her sister is having a baby.'

I hear Mum shift again on the settee. 'Really?' The tone is lighter. 'When is it due?'

I shrug again. 'Winter, sometime.'

'Tell me when it's born,' she says, more excitedly, 'and I'll send a card.'

I start to shave a slice from the loaf.

'Cut that loaf properly, Eulalia.'

I turn to search the fridge for pickle or mustard or something, anything but suppurating margarine. 'Well, I think she's mad,' I goad Mum.

'Deborah's sister?' I can hear the gathering frown. 'Why?'

I examine a jar of piccalilli. '*Childbirth*.'

'Oh, childbirth.' There is a pause. 'Childbirth's the least of it,' she says vaguely. 'It's over quickly and you forget the pain.'

I rotate towards her in my struggle with the lid. 'Seems unwise, don't you think? To forget?'

She shrugs. 'Evolution,' she pronounces eventually. 'It's what we're here for.'

'Speak for yourself. It's not what *I'm* here for.' The lid pops from the jar.

She turns away from me and smirks into the flickering coals. 'Ah, *you*.'

Yes, me.

'I hope you don't want any hot water,' she says as I approach with my tray, 'because Jane has used it all. As usual.' The words slough with disgust. 'I've switched on the tank for your dad. He'll be delighted if he comes home to a cold bath.' Her gaze arcs as I pass. 'He's still at work,' she adds wearily as an explanation.

I know. I avoided phoning from the station for a lift because I knew that he would be at work, or only recently home and tackling a re-heated meal.

'And I hope that you didn't try to ring from the station,' she continues, raising her voice, 'because Jane moved from the bathroom to take up residence on the phone. What can she need to talk about, for so long, every evening?' This is not a question but a cry of despair.

'And then we had World War Three because I forgot to buy low-fat cottage cheese for her lunch.'

I have noticed that Jane takes a packed lunch to the office every day. She leaves the packages overnight in the bottom of the fridge, obstructing the crisper compartment. They are wodges of greaseproof paper, thick and dull like hide, or silver foil, imprisoned in polythene: surgically sterilized.

'Don't I have enough to think about, without trying to remember a prissy little tub of cottage cheese?' Her blue eyes are wide with terror and outrage. 'I forgot,' she challenges. 'It's as simple as that: I forgot. No great crime.'

'Chuck her out,' I offer reasonably.

'She says, *What else do you do all day?* She says, *It's one tiny thing to remember.* But that's just it: it's one more tiny thing to remember, in a houseful of tiny things. I'm supposed to have to remember *less*, as time goes on, surely; not *more*. Where will it all end?'

I have forgotten a glass of water for my bedside. I set down the tray in the nearest armchair – 'Don't balance that tray there, Eulalia' – and dash into the kitchen. Mum's voice continues despite the loud hiss in the long sleek silver neck of the tap and the tinkle of falling water in the glass. 'Shopping has been terrible, horrible,' she pipes, 'since you turned Lyndsay into a vegetarian.'

Terrible? Horrible? Yes, of course, all those bloodied carrots! I snap shut the tap on the stream of water and glance back into the hot gloom. 'I did not turn Lyndsay into a vegetarian . . .'

'You said something about lambs . . .'

'*He* said something about lambs. He said something like, *Look at all those lovely lambs*, or *lambeys* or somethings; and I merely remarked that he seemed to like to eat them for his tea.'

Mum frowns heavily at me as I approach with the gleaming glass. 'He's sensitive,' she admonishes with a murmur.

'So sensitive,' I reply jauntily, 'that he doesn't want to chew on someone else's carcass at least once a day.'

She folds her arms: a big huff of a movement. 'A lamb isn't a *someone*.' She glowers at the fan spinning beneath the coals. 'And we hardly ever have lamb. You *know* that. It's too fatty. It's too dear.'

'Cow, pig, whatever.' I cannot find today's newspaper: with my free hand I have been spinning the papers which are in a pile on an armchair, and glancing at the dates next to the headlines. But today already feels like yesterday, so I stop the search, and swipe the *TV Times*. I used to enjoy the *TV Times* problem page. It is preferable, tonight, to the Durkheim which I am supposed to be reading.

Mum bends forward with a wince and extracts a wad of newspaper from behind or beneath her. She throws it sharply across the room to me. I catch it, checking the date, noting that the prime minister's upper lip is wet with ink, and place it on my tray. 'Thanks.'

'I mean,' she has started again, 'what do you buy for a ten-year-old vegetarian?' The question is addressed to no one, to anyone, to the ceiling. I know that she is pondering the impossibility of beefburgers without beef, fishfingers without fish. (Fingers?) 'And it has caused trouble at school: *Mrs Blaney, is there a medical reason for this?* There must be a *medical* reason, you see, or *religious* reason, for a special diet. No fads. *Is there a religious reason, Mrs Blaney?*' The irritable gaze flicks towards me. 'I said, *Well, you could say God had spoken* . . .'

I notice a small dish of peanuts, a jam jar lid filled with ten or so peanuts, on the floor beside the armchair: so, there has been a show, this evening, for Mum; the Lyndsay-and-Lauren show. Laurel-and-Hardy: hardly. When I was small, I did shows in here: closing the curtains, fetching bowls of peanuts or crisps, or a plate of bourbons, hurrying Mum and Dad to the settee, pushing Jane into cartwheels.

'And now Erin has started to ask questions – *Why this cheese croquette for Lynd? Why no sausage?* – and I don't want Erin to get any ideas.' Startled, we glance at each other. Mum's taut face relaxes into a faint smile, and she lowers her eyes. 'Well, no,' she corrects, quickly, quietly, definitely, 'it would be nice for Erin to have ideas . . .'

'But not vegetarian ones.'

She nods, the same smile seeping from the lowered gaze.

'With Erin . . .' she looks around the room for the words, 'well, there's a problem with the flowers, now, at school.'

I sprinkle the peanuts from the jam jar lid onto the sticky slice of bread on my tray: an open sandwich, peanut and piccalilli.

'She is flower monitor but she won't pick flowers. She says that it doesn't seem right.'

I shrug.

Mum shrugs. 'Oh, I don't mind about the flowers, I can understand about the flowers.' She rubs the palm of her hand into her blonde curls. 'But they were the last hope, for Erin, at school. I don't think Erin will ever pass exams, or play hockey . . .' she glares at me, '. . . or even *cause trouble.*' She sighs. 'Nothing.'

I pick up the tray.

'How do I face those teachers at that school?' Mum stares accusingly at me. 'First, you; then, Jane; now, Erin.'

'And next, Lynd.'

'Lyndsay!' She searches the ceiling again. 'Lyndsay's not a bad lad, but he's so . . .'

'Sensitive.'

'*Sensitive.*'

'And Lauren . . .'

157

She waves a hand, dismissive. 'Lauren's a bright little spark.'

'Which spells trouble.'

'But *you*,' she returns her attention sharply to me, 'you got the exam results, but why the incidents? Would it have been so difficult to conform, nine-to-four, for a few years?'

'Mum, the word which springs to mind is, *impossible*.'

'You should have had my old biddies.' She nods with grim satisfaction at the coals. 'Navy blue knickers,' she adds without explanation.

I open my mouth to say good night.

'Old women, all of them.' She glances perfunctorily at me before returning to the electric glow. 'All except Mr Allinson, I suppose.'

She supposes?

'Mr Drake. Mr Something, for a term. And Mr – what? – Cauliffe? Cunliffe? MacCauliffe?' She looks enquiringly at me. 'MacCorkindale?'

I step backwards into the doorway.

'*Why*,' she says suddenly, 'didn't she *try*?'

Jane. Exams.

'What will she do *now*? Is this it, is this all, living here and working in a bank? What is she going to *do*?'

The ferocity of the questioning keeps me in the doorway.

'She's still on about modelling.' *Modelling* is a wail of despair. 'She says that Christine Binky earns a million pounds an hour or something, I don't know.' Mum gestures vaguely. 'And it sounds good to them, these girls; of course it sounds good to them: earning huge sums for who you are . . .' she shrugs, '. . . like the Queen, I suppose. But she's *not* the Queen.' Mum's blue eyes loom towards me.

'No,' I admit.

She exhales and flops back onto the cushions, 'The Queen coins-it-in even when she's an OAP. But models are finished at thirty, twenty-five.'

I turn away towards the stairs.

'And Jane's not Christina Brinky. But, well, good luck to her, I suppose,' she murmurs grudgingly.

'Mum,' I begin, pausing on the bottom stair, 'I was going to go when the job finishes on Friday, but what about Aunty Mo?'

'What about Aunty Mo?' The voice comes from deep inside the dark red room.

'Well, you know.' There is a pause. 'The funeral.'

'Oh.' The tone suggests confusion.

'I mean, shall I stay around for the funeral?'

Surely there will be a funeral? Aunty Mo is dying. She is in hospital now, this time for the last time. *She's riddled*, Mum told me. Why does Mum persist with this, the word *riddled*? How would she like to be described as *riddled*, like a lump of rotten wormy fruit? Aunty Mo is in Cressington Park Hospital. Throughout my life I have heard Mum saying, *Once you go to Cressington Park, you're lost*. When I was small, I understood this in a literal sense: it seemed possible to me to be lost – physically lost – in the long corridors. But Cressington Park has no long corridors. And Aunty Mo is in a room now rather than a ward: this was related to me by Mum with pleasure, or perhaps with relief. Later, when I visited, it seemed to me that Aunty Mo had been lodged there hastily, prudently, temporarily.

I visited Aunty Mo last week. I do not remember whether I had been expecting her to look different. All I remember, now, is the shock. Years ago, when I was very young, I saw a film in which a woman grows old in seconds, contracting and shrivelling, shrieking with rage and terror as she is punished for her magic and robbed of her spell for immortality. She became a pile of dust, and then a speck, and then nothing. It was a living death. Aunty Mo was laid in front of me under a strong white sheet, propped for me on thick white pillows. I looked around at Mum. Had she ever seen the film? Did she know it? Why had she not warned me? But Mum was smiling, cooing at the tiny face. The hair on the pillow was vivid with grey. It looked as though it had been splattered with white paint, but the change of colour was unimportant. The texture

159

was changing. It was dying, dead, dried. And Aunty Mo was so thin, too thin. Once she was too fat, now she was too thin. Suddenly she was an old woman, an old dying woman. She was not dying young, as Mum had told me, but dying old. Is it possible to die young of disease, or does the disease inevitably bring age?

Mum's latest refrain is, *They say she won't last the weekend*.

They: who are these people with the power to decide? And, anyway, it is Mum who says; or, rather, it is Mum who says so to me. Mum says that Aunty Mo won't last the weekend. Once again she implies inadvertently that Aunty Mo is something in the fridge with a date on the lid.

Aunty Mo, cradled by the thick white sheet, is a reverse sleeping beauty. The weekend is looming. Yesterday Mum went with Dad to the hospital on a visit.

'Mo's on stacks of morphine now,' she informed me in the evening, her face pinched with pity. 'She's hallucinating, she thinks it's her wedding day: *Something old, something new*, you know. She wanted to borrow something from me: *Something borrowed*.'

'What did you lend her?' I asked.

Mum focused a frown on me, puzzled. 'Well, nothing.' A spasm of a smile came with a flutter of exasperation. 'Nothing. Of course.' Each utterance was lifted between us like a question. But I did not reply. Instead, I bit my lip. The frown scissored again into Mum's forehead. 'I mean, what use . . .?' Then she stopped, and turned away.

Now Mum replies lightly from the shadows. 'Oh no, don't wait around for the funeral.'

Don't *wait around*? She is confident that there are better places for me to go.

'No?'

'Noooo. Funerals are morbid. Avoid them like the plague.' Once again there is the patient, definite tone: she is not joking.

'What about a wake?' I am curious. I leave the bottom stair, and drift back into the doorway with my tray.

'Awake?' Across the room, the purple tracksuit stirs.

160

'A *wake*, a *wake*: the Blaneys are Irish.'

'They're not really Irish.' The voice is gentle. 'Or, they haven't brought the best of the Irish with them. No gift of the gab, no wakes. Not the Blaneys. Spam sandwiches at Gran Blaney's. And, anyway,' she adds, 'Mo's not a Blaney, she's not Irish, she's Isle of Sheppey.'

'But shouldn't I go? Anyway?'

I glimpse a shadowy purple shrug on the settee. 'Well, so says the whole world, I suppose, but I don't think so. I think you should stay away from funerals for as long as you can, while you still have the chance.'

This means nothing to me because I have never been to one. What would I wear to Aunty Mo's funeral? I begin to panic. I do not want to buy anything: it is disrespectful, surely, to go shopping for new clothes − my favourite indulgence − after a death. And surely it is disrespectful to wear the clothes elsewhere, afterwards, for any occasions other than funerals. So I will have an outfit in my wardrobe, ready for funerals: isn't this disrespectfully cynical? And isn't it disrespectful to be thinking now of clothes? But I own nothing which is black and respectable. Except my old school skirt.

'People say it's an excuse for a family get-together,' Mum is saying, 'but what a get-together! And what an excuse! What *kind* of family needs *death* as an excuse for that *kind* of get-together?'

I stare blankly at the purple presence on the settee.

'Good God,' she finishes animatedly, 'the kind of family that shouldn't be *allowed* to get together.'

I am very tired. 'Night, then,' I say hopefully.

'A lot of spam sandwiches for nothing,' she replies distantly. 'Don't come to my funeral. Go out for the day, go anywhere, go shopping, go to McDonald's . . .' she sighs wearily '. . . oh, no, I forgot, you wouldn't want to go to McDonald's . . . But go anywhere, anywhere but Gran Blaney's.'

'Gran Blaney won't be around,' I correct with a smile. I do not say, *When you die*. I turn away with my tray.

'No?' The tone is suspicious. 'Remember Brenda, and think of Mo: women who marry Blaneys only ever run or die.'

161

1985

....

I am selecting from the first aid box: plasters, a selection, including tiny ones for toes; and painkillers. How many painkillers? Should I think in terms of one illness, of three, five or seven days? Or should I consider daily debilitation from headaches, sore throats, cystitis, period pains? It is so long since I have been abroad that I have forgotten how to pack. I decide on the daily option. And now the worst possible scenario: two doses per day, four tablets per day, and an extra one for luck, so five tablets per day.

'Remember tampax,' says Mum. She is standing at the draining board, working through a rackful of clean dry plates, wiping each one with a damp dirty tea towel and then inserting it noisily into the crockery cupboard. Beneath the draining board, the washing machine is masticating some laundry very thoroughly and contemplating the spin cycle. The washing machine is new, or fairly new: two years? three? I remember the twin-tub with its rubber tubing and puddles.

I have lost my train of thought: painkillers? tampax?

'Oh, yes, of course,' I rejoin in exasperation, 'I'll remember to take tampax, because Spanish women don't have periods; a well-known natural phenomenon . . .'

'Don't be sarcastic,' Mum reprimands across the noise of the plates. 'Because tampax are expensive in Spain. And you're the one who has been complaining about a tight budget.'

I take several foil leaves from the box of painkillers, add them to the pile of plasters, and close the lid. Presumably there is pain in Spain, and so, presumably, there are painkillers.

'And put that box back where you found it, Eulalia.' Mum is deep inside the crockery cupboard, reorganizing a casserole dish.

So, tampax: how many days, and how many per day? And a selection of Regular and Super, or solely Super to cope with all eventualities? There is a Mini size, now, too. Mini must be for girls like Erin. Erin cannot even cope with a Lemsip. She is sitting now at the table, chin propped in hands. I presume that she is watching us, because she does not seem to be doing anything else. Above, on the ceiling, the fluorescent strip sizzles, dilute in daylight; below, on the table, Erin's yellow hair glows like a lampshade.

'What time are you leaving?' Mum is retreating on her knees from the cupboard.

'About five.'

Crouching, she twists to face me. 'I thought it was a night train.'

'It is a night train. It leaves Victoria at about eight. But, first, I have to get into London and across.'

'Oh, well, then,' she rises awkwardly, 'you won't see your father.'

So? When do I ever see him? I have never seen him at home before five. I presume he knew that I was here, and I presume he knows that I am going away. Perhaps Mum thinks that I was expecting a lift to the station.

'He left this morning without a word,' she informs me. 'Without a word.' These last three words bear equal heavy stress. She stares at me.

Is she waiting for an explanation? If so, why stare at me? I know nothing.

'What have I done?' Her eyes are popping beneath the soft muddle of curls.

'I mean, what have I done?' Once again there are the slow stresses, like a threat. 'I'd just like to know.' *I'd just like to kill him.*

Erin has not moved, she is still bearing her face on her hands into the light. Mum draws a chair from under the table and creeps into it as if she has been wounded. 'All the time,' she says. 'All the time.' She slumps onto the table. 'His moods, I mean,' she adds, glancing at me.

'Yes,' I reply. I lived with Dad for eighteen years, I know his moods.

The door opens and Jane hurries in from the hallway. She is wearing her bathrobe. It strikes me that it has been a long time since I have seen her wearing clothes. What sort of clothes does she wear, nowadays? She prances around me, opens the cupboard, takes the first aid box, extracts one of the few remaining foil pieces from the packet of painkillers, scowls at the packet, shakes the packet, scowls at me, throws the box into the cupboard and leaves the room. A trace of fresh deodorant remains.

'*Bye, Lalie,*' I mutter as the door closes, '*Have a good trip. Why! thank-you Jane.*'

Mum is staring at the closed door but she does not seem to see it. Unusually, she does not complain in a loud voice that Jane *uses this place like a hotel*. Jane lives in hotels now. She travels a lot with her work as a model. The house is scattered with sachets from hotels and planes. Jane's room – my old room – is semi-deserted in semi-darkness at the end of the hallway. It seems that when she has been at work, she comes home sick with jet lag and air conditioning and goes to bed. Then she leaves the house in the morning before anyone wakes. So, despite the swelling tide of sachets in the bathroom, no one is aware of Jane's presence, or absence.

When she has no work, though, she trips endlessly around the house, shedding towels and half-eaten pieces of toast, accompanied by the ringing of the phone.

Mum nods finally in the direction of the door. 'She earns more for a week's modelling than your father earns all year.' This is the economic equivalent of *She uses this place like a hotel*. It concerns *attitude*.

I make the obvious reply: 'Dad tries hard but he hasn't the figure.'

Mum smiles grudgingly.

But Jane's figure is non-existent. When she began modelling I started to notice that models are plain. They have regular, standard faces. They are not paid to attract attention to themselves; they are paid to sell clothes; they are clotheshorses. Mum told me that Jane was modelling for several well-known chain stores but I had to search the billboards to find her. *The disappearance of Jane Blaney*.

On a billboard she becomes a milky insubstantial presence behind a splash of clothing. Under the lights she bears a faint sheen of sauciness, or fitness, or serenity, or whatever else is required. And by the end of the working day, when she comes home, it has evaporated.

Mum sighs. 'No wonder he wonders why he bothers.'

Dad? I was not aware that he has been wondering why he bothers. Bothering was always the most important thing in the world, for Dad. It was self-evident, the meaning of life. I have always wondered why he bothers: day in, day out, from eight in the morning until eight at night, just so that he can pay the bills. But what else would he do?

Mum returns her attention sharply to me. 'I wish *I* could go off for the summer.'

It is not my fault that she stays here. I do not live here any more. I am not responsible. All the other Blaneys, the blonde baby Blaneys, keep her here. But perhaps it *is* my fault, perhaps I began a chain reaction, the Blaney chain.

Lyndsay swings slowly from the patio into the kitchen, dropping down from the doorstep. 'Where's my penknife?' he asks Mum.

'Where you left it, I imagine,' she replies, without looking at him.

He waits for a moment before swooping back into the garden.

'Kids,' damns Mum. 'They have no respect for their mothers, nowadays.'

To me, this is progress. Who wants mass civil obedience? *Respect* smacks of *Il Duce*. Mum surprises me. Surely she knows that if she wants my respect, she has to earn it. And has she considered the logical implications? Has she considered that if children must respect mothers, then Grandpa must respect Gran Blaney? But, according to Mum, Gran Blaney is *Beyond the pale*.

'Penknife,' she says derisively, 'is that all Lyndsay can think about? Good God, I went shopping the other day and spent hundreds of pounds on him – hundreds of pounds that we don't have – on his new school uniform.'

Lyndsay is changing schools, from primary to secondary, at the end of the summer. 'None of your hand-me-downs for him,' she adds with grim satisfaction.

'He's a *boy*.'

'Precisely.' She straightens, and pivots on the points of her elbows. 'All new, all of it, every last football sock.' She pauses to consider.

'Hundreds of pounds worth, and it's all horrid: poor Lynd; poor me; poor Dad.'

Poor, now, in more senses than one.

'At least there won't be any scenes about the pinafore.' The pinafore haunted us, me and Jane, throughout our years at school: the threat of the pinafore. The school regulations decreed the pinafore *Or similar*. We wanted approximations, from Chelsea Girl or Miss Selfridge. Mum had faith in the pinafore, which she said was *better quality and less faddy*. We refused. Erin seemed destined for the pinafore, until, unexpectedly, Mum took pity.

'And does he thank me?' Mum crows about Lyndsay. 'No. Of course not. He complains. He complains that he doesn't want to go to your old school, he wants to go to Bankbridge.'

'And why not?' I add cheerfully. I know that this will goad Mum, because she has always been inexplicably compelled to defend my old school, and because she believes in families. Families, according to Mum, pose for photographs together, go on holidays together, and go to the same school. Also, Bankbridge was never a Grammar School.

'But Bankbridge wouldn't have him!' she explodes.

I raise my eyebrows. In my day, Bankbridge took anyone from my primary school; even the Lauder twins, who threatened our teacher with a rounders bat on Sports Day, telephoned a bomb hoax to the Swimming Gala, and reached into the Nativity Scene to furnish Joseph with a piece of erect Plasticine.

'Boundaries,' Mum warbles. 'Catchment areas. Gone are the days of Grammar. Instead of the eleven plus, the 272 is the important factor.' The 272 is the local bus. 'Lyndsay is in the wrong area for Bankbridge.'

'Why did he want to go?'

'Friends,' disparages Mum, distaste tightening her lips and placing inverted commas around the word. 'Harry Porter, the Daniell's boy, the youngest Lauder.' Then she adds, 'Also, Spanish, Silversmithing, you name it: anything and everything that your old school doesn't offer, Lyndsay has decided that he wants to study. Archaeology.'

'Archaeology? O level?'

She shudders with irritation. 'I don't know.' Then she thinks again. 'Digs.' She picks at a cuticle, unsure.

'Well,' I sigh expansively, 'my school had English, History, Geography. The spice of life, eh?' I smile coldly at her.

She looks sharply up at me from the cuticle. 'Your school got results, Eulalia. Where would you be now with a term of Silversmithing on your CV?'

I ponder this. The possibilities seem endless. Where am I with my English, History, Geography? I am in this kitchen again, passing through, going away, coming back. And where will I be when I am back? I will be living somewhere with friends, renting, claiming dole. *Friends*: I recall Mum's belittling pout. But Mum is friendless, alone, here.

'What will you do now?' she wailed when I arrived with my bags.

I suggested voluntary work, for a while. I did not tell her that I need to discover what I want to do, what I can do. Nor did I tell her that I intend to forget all this for a while, on holiday.

'But you were going to be a teacher!' Her despair was laced with the remnants of Wait-until-your-father-gets-home.

'Mum,' I said, 'I was seven when I was going to be a teacher.'

'No,' she countered, 'you want to teach handicapped children.'

'Mum . . .'

'Voluntary work?' She was horrified. For Mum, voluntary work is a contradiction in terms. Work earns money: nothing more, nothing less.

Mum worked in an office until I was born. Her tone, when telling Blancy babies about the office job, implies that this was success:

she was the-one-who-got-away; a white-collar worker. *White collar*, plain and clean, stiff, starched. She continued to swap cards at Christmas with Renée, a colleague, until Renée died a few years ago of breast cancer. My-friend-Renée, My-friend-Reen, who had gone to Australia, who she had not seen for years and years, who she will never see again. Mum hated the office. 'Some people go to work for company,' she explained to me once, 'but I was never keen on people, except Reen.'

The office was Mum's escape from her neighbourhood, and I was Mum's escape from the office. I was the ultimate freedom. I was the meaning of life, for Mum.

She says that she loves babies. She says this to anyone and everyone, a declaration. And whenever she says it, she screws her features into an itsy-bitsy shrug of a smile, *Li'l-ol'-me*, implying that we Blaney babies are a mere indulgence, like chocolate. If she loves babies so much, why did she not become a midwife or a nursery nurse? There are no babies left here now, not even Lauren, not now.

Moreover, the tale of the office is not the whole truth. I remember other tales. She was a white-collar clerk by day, but in the evenings and at weekends she had jobs as a tearoom waitress and a telephone operator.

'I spent my days and nights running,' she told me once, 'from one job to the next, while I was saving for a home of my own.'

It seems to me that she spent those days and nights not running but standing or sitting, silent and still, whilst other people's conversations rolled back and forth across the dressed tabletops or crackled and connected somewhere in the air near her ears.

On another occasion, years ago, she remarked to me that, when she was a child, women were required to resign from their jobs when they married.

I did not believe this, of course.

'It's true,' she protested crossly: 'no married women teachers.' Then she inclined her head and looked mournfully at me. 'Which wouldn't have suited you, eh?' The mournful expression was cloaking a count-your-blessings rebuke.

'But why did they have to resign?' I asked. I was trying hard to imagine why married women were so dangerous.

She threw off my concern with a shrug. 'Why did they have to work? They had husbands. And they were taking men's jobs, there was a shortage of jobs. Who wants to go out to work? Not me.'

I did not know, in those days, when I was young, that the world is made by those who work for those who work; that it is a man's world. Instead I objected to the fallacy which seemed obvious to me: 'Why couldn't men stay at home?' It was a sincere enquiry.

Mum peered at me for a moment as if she could not see me. Then she shrieked briefly with laughter before slapping her fingertips onto her lips. 'Men wouldn't know what to *do*,' she stressed kindly. 'Men operate machines. They don't rear children. They'd rear a race of monsters.' She gestured vaguely in the air, incredulous, feeling for words. 'There would be no clean knickers in the mornings . . . no milk in the fridge . . . they'd rear a race of stinking, starving monsters.'

Mum's best friend, Aunty Jenny, was a hairdresser until she contracted dermatitis.

'Caused by all those perms,' Mum explained with an air of tragedy throughout my childhood, mourning wasted youth. She was keen to dissuade any of us from becoming hairdressers. The idea never crossed my mind. And the others, the other Blaney babies? With their hair, their moppy Blaney hair? Physician, heal thyself.

Now, suddenly, I decide to escape Mum and find Lyndsay: my brother, the silversmith. I cross the kitchen to the door, into the doorway, and balance on the balls of my feet on the smooth dull wooden doorstep. I can smell the tang of rain in the air. The garden is drenched in sunshine spilling through the luminous clouds which have been flapping all afternoon in front of the sun. The puddles on the patio are furred with wind. Lyndsay is crouching in the corner, at the foot of the fence, his back to me. He is hunched over a line of ants, a loop of ants entering and leaving our garden beneath the fence, a diversion of ants linking the pink stones. His hair needs cutting. It lies, uniform length – uni-length? – over his collar. It strikes me that he has lost his baby curls – puppy curls? – in the increased weight, length, strength of this bright hair. The overall effect is perilously close to a pageboy style. Poor Lynd, he suffers in this household of girl-children. Mum knows nothing about barbers, and enlists instead the voluntary efforts of Aunty Jenny, ex-hairdresser, to *trim the ends*. Presumably Dad knows about barbers; but, to Dad, Lyndsay is one of the children, and the children are Mum's responsibility.

As I approach, Lyndsay transfers his gaze reluctantly to me from the trail of ants. He has the longest, darkest, thickest eyelashes of any of us: is this fair? But, then, boys lack the option of mascara. Or do they?

'Hi.' I join him, respectfully, in perusal of the ants.

He is holding a twig, the tip resting on the ground.

'I hear that you don't want to go to my old school,' I begin: jocular, hopeful.

'No.' The voice is distant; the gaze follows the pulsating thread of ants.

'Oh? And why not? Don't you want to follow in the footsteps of your dear old sisters?'

The twig twitches on the ground. The ants maintain their purposeful trot. 'No.'

'Oh.'

'It's a boring school.' The tone is without emotion.

'But all schools are boring.'

The line of ants is carrying away a few small unrecognizable pieces of the garden. Small for me, enormous for them. Are they triumphant, or is this a tiresome necessity? Is it pleasure or pain?

Lyndsay drops the twig, and stands. His face darts beneath the thick bright crown. He slips his hands into the pockets of his jeans: small slats wedged into tiny tight pouches. If I meant what I said about schools to be a comfort to him, then I have failed. He slinks away from me, across the patio, behind the bins and into the alley at the side of the house.

I return to the kitchen, determined to pass through, to go to the bathroom and pack the tampax. Erin looks at me on the doorstep and I notice that she does not have Lyndsay's huge eyes, flaming blue, edged with darkness. Her eyes are pale – grey? – and luminous like eggshells. Her hair is darker, though, than Lyndsay's: a ripe glossy woven yellow. Perhaps the Blaney babies are differentiating. But like Lyndsay, Erin no longer has curls. Her hair is tucked demurely behind an Alice band. So, unlike Lyndsay, she has nowhere to hide. I look into her face, at the slightly long nose bridged by a pollen of freckles, and I see that she is very different from pallid Jane, angelic Lyndsay, or fiery Mum.

Mum is saying something. My attention shifts in a lazy blur to the heaped figure in the chair next to Erin. Mum's hot red lips seem wet and swollen, full of angry tears.

'. . . and so there was silence all morning. Disapproval. Resentment. And I had only asked him if he could run Lauren to Latin American, to the Dance Centre on the High Street for five o'clock – not far, not too early, not unreasonable, *surely* – because I needed to be with Lyndsay at the Dentist at the other end of town at four-thirty . . .' She pauses and frowns at me in confusion. 'I mean, I have spent my *life* on buses with children. I doubt whether he has ever been on a bus, let alone with kids.' She pauses again and frowns at her hands contracting into fists on the table. 'I *know* he's busy.' Suddenly the hands spring through the chaotic curls, damming them, and she blinks at me from her flushed face. 'You see,' she says slowly, almost calmly, 'he's not interested. He's not interested in kids. He didn't want kids. He wasn't bothered. He *let me* have kids. I wanted kids, and that's all I wanted. So he *let me* have them.' She shrugs expansively. 'Everyone has kids, I suppose he didn't see any problem.' The lip droops again. 'But now there are so *many* of you . . .' She gestures helplessly, liberating the curls. 'And he blames *me*, you're *mine*, you're *my* responsibility.'

Poor Mum, gathering babies. But surely Dad wanted me, the first baby. If everyone has kids, then everyone has a first one. There is nothing exceptional about me, but there was nothing wrong with

171

me. So why did Mum continue? Perhaps it was a quest for the perfect baby. And perhaps the quest was not so unsuccessful: first, there was me, small and dark, full of Blaney blood; then there was plain Jane, insipid; then rich, golden Erin; then lovely Lyndsay, and perfect Lauren. Lauren: I realize that I have been hearing Lauren's voice for the last few minutes, a wordless murmur, an undertow sweeping below Mum's complaints and dragging my attention towards the garden.

I glance back through the doorway. Lauren is in the garden with a friend. I know that she is not alone although, from here, I can see no one else. She is supine on the lawn, regardless of the damp grass; the head raised on cupped linked palms, the thin brown legs slung together to cross at the ankle like a long loose knot of twine. She is talking into the sky, eyes shut. On her face, the confident spread of features is weighted by long smooth cheekbones. As she talks on, lips shifting, it occurs to me that she does not need to look at people to hold their attention.

'I'm sick of it,' says Mum flatly. She is looking at me. 'Sick of it.'

I look at Erin. 'How's school?' I ask compulsively. What do I mean? How are lessons? How is the building?

'All right.' Erin is surprised too. The reply comes back to me as a question, raised: What do I mean?

I do not want to know about school, I want to know about Erin. *How's-school?* was appropriate for me and Jane because we *were* school, our *lives* were school, despite our efforts to the contrary. But not Erin. Erin's life is here, home. *How's-school?* is as meaningless to Erin as *How's-the-Republic-of-China?*

'School's school,' barks Mum protectively, suspiciously.

'What do you think you'll do when you leave?' I continue desperately.

Erin frowns with concentration. 'I don't know.' But she sounds curious. Then she shrugs away the frown. 'Something,' she says.

This strikes me as the most optimistic statement I have heard today. I suppose that *I* will do *something*, after my jaunt abroad.

'I wish *I* could leave,' Mum whines. 'I'm sick of it. Complaints from him all the time, complaints from you kids: whatever I do, I do wrong. I'm spending my life skivvying for people who don't give me the time of day.'

'So leave, then.' This is cruel, but what else can I say?

I lose my nerve, and cringe, anticipating her fury.

But she looks sadly and steadily at me. 'Where would I go? What would I do? I've nowhere, I've nothing. I've no friends of my own, no money of my own, no skills, no experience.' She pauses, but then says no more. Instead, she lowers her head into her hands. The blonde curls creep through the dry brown hands, camouflaging the fat gold wedding ring. Her children – Erin at the table, Lynd returned to the patio, Lauren on the lawn, and even the frost of Jane in the air – are hovering around her; little mirrors to send her back to herself.

~

I am offering myself on a plastic sunlounger to the hot sheen of the late afternoon sky. Ali is sitting on the neighbouring sunlounger, supported at the small of her back by a bulging beach bag, writing a letter. The writing paper is pressed onto a paperback in her lap. Deborah is swimming in the pool at our feet; I can hear the shivers of the water. She is alone in the pool. A few moments ago two men vaulted from the shallow water onto the hot stone rim and I heard the water spilling down their bodies into the pool with a fizz and crackle like distant applause.

I left home – when? – two days ago? Two nights ago. I left at night, and there were two sleepless nights, two lost nights spent on trains, with Ali, who met me in Paris. A train to Madrid, a train from Madrid: two nights in compartments ironically termed sleepers. Now we are in Cadiz. Deborah has finished her year in Seville and has come to Cadiz for the summer. Seville is too hot, too busy. She has come for the sea breeze. Cadiz is the oldest city in Spain: so says my guide book. Certainly it is the furthest city in Spain. It is a Southern tip, poking towards Africa. We have seen a roadsign for Africa: a normal roadsign, a Hatfield-and-the-North sign with no suggestion of ferries. Bear left for Africa, bear right for the centre of the city. My book says that the city was founded by Phoenicians. My ancient history is poor: who were Phoenicians? people from Phoenicia? Now it is full of Spanish sailors, barely older than Lyndsay, on leave very briefly with their mothers. No one else comes to Cadiz. Tourists stop in Seville.

We walked past the Cathedral this morning, squat in a large empty plaza, across the road from the rocks and sea. It was closed, and seemed derelict. My guide book mentions renovations. All the streets in the old town seemed too narrow for cars, or too narrow for foreign cars, or confused cars: narrow one-way dead-ends. The names of the streets are spelled out across the walls, each letter on a ceramic tile: large tiles, and elaborate names of saints. We have come to the tip of the town, to the sandy gardens planted with palms, to an hotel for drinks and a swim. The patio overlooks the Atlantic. I had not expected the Atlantic to be so very different from the pastel blue Mediterranean of my childhood holidays. But it is a bottomless blue, a boundless blue. We have been swimming this afternoon in the bleached domestic water of the swimming pool; swimming beside the sea, but not in it: heaven.

Ali puffs with irritation. I prise my eyes open a little against the heavy sunshine. The direction and expression of Ali's gaze is hidden behind a glossy black visor of sunglasses. But her lips are mean. This is familiar to me from our journey. The mean lips were focused variously on the zip of her bag, our disintegrating train tickets, the banana in my bag, the trilling games machines in the cafés and the soft thuds of the long chrome levers on the coffee machines. I would laugh at her and she would transfer the furious focus to me. *Give it here*, I'd say; or *Put it here*, or *Have mine*, or *Have one of these biscuits*, and she would do so, numb and obedient. Travelling is an irritation to Ali. I hate it, but I hate it so much that I am better equipped.

Now Ali flicks her pen into the air, three times, before scribbling hard on the writing paper. Apparently these efforts were futile because she slams the pen onto the lounger, and sighs ferociously.

174

'In my bag,' I offer.

The sunglasses turn sharply to me. She seems stunned by the sun.

'My bag,' I tell her, 'my bag, my bag.' I flap my hand in the direction of the bag.

She re-directs the black gaze, hauls the bag from the ground onto her lap and glares inside. The lips remain sullen.

'Look at you,' I exclaim fondly.

'I'm tired,' she says immediately, without ceasing the thorough investigation of my bag.

I tease with a lift of my eyebrows.

'And my hormones are raging,' she adds resentfully.

'Plenty of fluids,' I murmur, sliding back beneath the blanket of sunshine. 'And no chocolate.'

'No chocolate?' She pushes the sunglasses away from her face onto her head, forming a hairband of flashing black. This is a mark of exasperation, and wisps of hair – usually such wispless hair – drift and loop on cue around the frames. It is also a mark of vulnerability, because her face is bare. Her naked eyes drag their eyelids over them to escape the sun.

'I hope you've brought some tampax,' I lecture with relish, playing Mum.

She squints intensely at me. 'Why? Don't they have them here?'

At the edge of the pool the water ruffles, and Deborah appears. Her soaked hair is darkened and drawn, but she is wearing a huge white T-shirt which sparkles against the dull stone of the poolside. 'Have what here?' she asks cheerfully, helpfully.

'Snack-sized Benzedrines for Dozey,' I tell her.

Ali snaps the glinting black visor back down over her face. 'I feel like I've been speeding for days, thank you,' she complains.

I stretch between our sunloungers and snatch her wrist between my fingertips. Then I pause thoughtfully for a second, pretending to assess her pulse. 'God!' I exclaim finally, and urgently.

The black visor swivels sharply towards me.

'You're clinically dead,' I pronounce.

She turns away in disgust and resumes writing. Deborah smiles

175

and lowers her covered, protected shoulders into the sunlit silver pool. I close my warm eyelids and listen to the steady sloppy turning of her feet in the water, increasingly distant; and, nearer, the scratch of my pen on Ali's brittle airmail paper.

Afraid of dozing and burning, I reach up to my head and slot my sunglasses over my eyes. Then I survey the darkened poolside. I can always see so much more in sunglasses, not because the glare of the sun is gone but because no one can see me seeing. In sunglasses, I can look at everything and everyone. I am learning to see. Whenever someone stares into my face – and it is usually a man – I do not have to look away, look down; I do not have to relinquish my claim to, and miss a whole moment of, the world.

I am watching a woman, now, though, on the other side of the pool. I am looking at a man and a woman, but the man is behind the woman. Something catches my dark, hidden eyes; but what? They are talking, I can see that they are talking, although I cannot hear the words. Her skin is leather, and a golden pony-tail dangles bright and blunt from the back of her head. The hair has been lifted upwards and backwards from her face, smooth and simple; deceptively simple, somehow exclusive, like a good scarf. She is wearing a towel, held in place by a tuck beneath an armpit. It is a beach towel, tough and dark. The pattern, distorted, is probably palm trees. The woman is not young: the skin and muscles on her shoulders, arms, calves are hard. The man is much older. Tanned, hairy skin hangs heavy and uneven on his chest and legs.

And suddenly I know: the man and woman are standing fractionally too far apart. They are talking and smiling but they do not know each other, or not at all well. Her arms are folded, she makes no superfluous movement, presumably commanding attention with her voice. She is guarded, standing her ground. Unlike Mum, who would flap, snatching attention in terror and then throwing it in different directions with gestures and shrieks of laughter. Now the woman is joined by a man who has walked out onto the patio from the bar. He halts very close to her, slightly behind her. She cranes briefly upwards and backwards to smile at him, to greet him. Her face, momentarily lifted to him, is puffed with approval. Then they smile in unison at the older man.

I close my eyes and slide the sunglasses away from my face.

'Are you writing to Julian?' I ask Ali. This is not nosiness; it is conversation.

'No,' she replies. The whisper of the pen on the paper does not falter.

I know that she is still fond of Julian, friendly with him, close to him. I know because she told me. I have known about the split for some time, although no one seems able to tell me the details, probably because there are none: there were no rows, and she has been in Paris without him for most of the year. Deborah's comments were elusive in gauzy airmail letters. Ali shrugged yesterday in the tiny couchette and told me only that, 'We had been growing apart for a long time.' They have been *living* apart for a long time, certainly: was this the reason? is there hope? 'He's lovely,' she said in reply to my questions, leaving the *but* unsaid and unexplained. 'We still see each other,' she said. Then she shrugged again. 'We still write,' she revised.

Growing apart seems inappropriate: *growing together* is understandable because something *grows* but *growing apart* results in nothing at all. But perhaps I am wrong, perhaps two separate lives grew for Ali and Julian from one. A scene from a microscope drifts through the yellow darkness of my closed eyelids: a cell bloating to two cells, two shivering, sticky buds of pale pink jelly. Replication. Perhaps Ali and Julian have replicated rather than torn apart.

I tore from Tim, or he tore from me: we tore apart. There were lots of rows but none of them were important. I am left – even now, even here, in this steaming gleaming sunshine – with a cool flutter of dismay. It is dismaying to fall out of love. Surely it is more serious than falling *in* love. Falling in love is always hopeful; falling out of love admits misjudgement. So, I was wrong. Or perhaps I was right, once upon a time, before something changed; or perhaps some*one* changed, me or him, or both of us. But surely, if we were in love, we should have been able to anticipate changes, to adapt, to survive: *the course of true love . . .* and *true love conquers all*. It certainly conquered me.

Perhaps the secret of success in love is to know when to stop. *Mutual* is a lie. It was only mutual in the end because I had stopped caring. Because he had not cared for a long time. Perhaps it is impossible to love someone who cannot return love. Perhaps there can be feelings, so strong, but they are not love. By definition, they are not love. They are everything else. Everything but. Perhaps, with Tim, this was always so. I hear the crack of another sheet of airmail paper in the air, flicked to the underside of the pad. And I am glad of the distraction. 'So,' I ask Ali, 'who are you writing to, then?'

'Elinor.'

Elinor: I remember Elinor from a brief visit to Ali's house several years ago. The house was shared by four girls, Ali and Elinor and two others. It was wonderfully real in comparison to student halls of residence: there was a living room with a saggy velvet settee and a coffee table sopping with magazines; an old portable telly, space-age rounded, with chrome switches; and a real phone purring in my hands. I had been surviving for a long time on an armoured payphone at the end of a busy corridor. The girls had bedrooms: plump beds with austere headboards, jumbles of wardrobes and chests, relics of ornate fireplaces, and fluttering curtains. Desks were wedged into corners. The bathroom was small, the floor furred with old carpet, the cabinet full of contraceptive devices and boxes of tampons, the glistening ghostly rims of the sink and bath littered with bottles, a wooden chair bearing a wadding of towels, and the door stuck with a poster of a teddy bear sitting mournfully above a caption about diets. After my tour of the house, we went into the kitchen and saw Elinor.

She was pouring boiling water from a kettle into a cup, standing with her back to us at the small enamel sink in front of the window. Her feet were bare, she was wearing nightclothes. She turned towards us, clutching at her billowing dressing gown. It was a long

178

dressing gown, although not long enough to reach her ankles. It was silky, with no fastenings. It was more like a shawl, somehow: a shawl with sleeves. It seems to me now that the silky material was Chinese: an intricate coral of small bright flowers. But the most striking aspect of Elinor was her hair: long, straight, thick, shiny, blonde. It was hanging so heavily from the flawless parting that it caused a gentle incline of her head. Why is Blaney blonde hair so different from Elinor's hair? It lacks the glossy sweep. Any swing is broken by the remnant of Blaney curls. Jane's hair is colourless and brittle. Erin's hair is prone to frizz and tangles. Lyndsay's hair, although too long for a boy, is not long enough to move. And Lauren has curls: like Mum's hair, it bounces rather than swings.

Elinor passed us with a strange sweet smell. I glanced down into the cup and saw lurid yellow knots floating in the hot water: camomile.

'I remember Elinor,' I tell Ali. 'She drinks camomile tea.'

'Only when she has a hangover.' There is no pause in the rapid, purposeful rub of Ali's hand on the paper.

'What's she doing now?'

'She's in Paris.'

'Oh?' Paris, a coincidence, because we were in Paris – when? – thirty-six hours ago? forty-eight hours ago? We were *recently* in Paris. 'What's she doing there?'

'She has been in Paris this year.'

'With you?' I am surprised; I had imagined Ali alone in Paris.

The pen pauses. Light washes into my eyes and I glimpse Ali staring reflectively into the distance. Perhaps the distance is a function of the non-focusing sunglasses.

'Alongside me,' she says eventually, pedantically.

I close my eyes again. There is a fierce dense network of sparks inside them, and a sizzle in my skin. I listen to the gulping gurgling of the pool. I could go to the edge and jump, breaking the surface of the water and shearing the heat from my skin. But I am heavy on the sunlounger. I am baked in honey. 'Have you heard from Roz?' I ask Ali.

179

'Nothing.' The voice is small because she is folded intently over the writing pad again. 'You?'

'She rang me on my birthday.'

'Did she?' The sunglasses flash momentarily in my direction.

'Which is unusual. And I was on my way out, so it was brief.'

'*When was* Roz's birthday?' She lifts her head from the letter, and lifts the pen to tap on her teeth.

'It's on the twenty-fourth. Of April. Never difficult to remember because it's Deborah's birthday a couple of weeks before, on the twelfth.'

How was Roz? What did she tell me? She told me that she had been on holiday and was very brown. I glance at Ali. None of us were ever as brown as Ali. None of us could match the soft dark burr of Ali's skin during summertime. And she never went abroad. Her parents favoured Cornwall, hotels on cliffs. *Cornish* hotels. I have never been to Cornwall, but at home we used to have Cornish ice cream in a snappy plastic tub in the freezer. Dad bought the freezer so that Mum could freeze whole animals. It was his idea, inspired less by love of meat than by notions of economy and self-sufficiency: no more expensive weekly trips to the supermarket. He was delighted with the idea, boring us by reading aloud from the white shiny floppy manual at mealtimes. He seemed to want to freeze the entire contents of the world, a modern Noah. *Ask your butcher*: Mum did not have a butcher, she had the supermarket. Eventually Dad bought a carcass with Aunty Jenny and Uncle Graham, to share. I do not remember eating it. The freezer was soon filled with thin yellow packs of fishfingers and beefburgers. The Cornish ice cream – *white-flavoured*, according to Erin – came not from Cornwall but from a weekly shop at Budgen.

Several years ago the transparent rectangular tubs of Cornish ice cream in Mum's freezer were replaced by colourful round tubs of New England ice cream. This new ice cream was white but not white-flavoured; it was filled with thick woody pecans and sticky clots of maple. Why was the old white vanilla ice cream *Cornish*? Perhaps this was due not to the vanilla, the black pods of vanilla

180

– because I suspect that there are no vanilla farms in Cornwall –
but to the cream. *Made with clotted cream*. But surely clotted cream
comes from Devon? A small pot of it came to us every year from
Great Mad Aunty Theda, on holiday in Devon. It came
miraculously through the post: wrapped, padded cream. How did
it not go off? Inside the soft swaddling the cream was still, stiff,
folded, intact. There was a ripe yellow bloom of sheer excess on
the surface. It was the cream of creams, the essence of cream.

Roz went abroad every year on holiday. Her tan was always *tan*.
After the holiday her shoulders, nose and knees were tough
gleaming chestnuts. And then, soon, the white skin from
underneath was back again, on the surface; she seemed to have
turned inside-out.

'She had been on holiday to Malta with Kim,' I tell Ali.

'Who's Kim?' The question whines sideways from the small space
above the letter.

Where's Malta? And, yes, who is Kim? 'Roz's friend.' It feels
strange to say this because we are Roz's friends. Is she one of us?
No. But perhaps we are not Roz's friends. And perhaps this feels
strange.

'What happened to Gavin?' The voice is fuller, more interested.

I shrug my shoulders against the sunlounger. 'Everything was
the same.'

'Not married, then?' Ali slaps the pad of paper onto the ground,
followed by the bag from the small of her back, and then lies down
on the sunlounger with a flourish, sweeping her hair away from
her face and neck with her hands. The thin tip of the nearest ear
is ruby red.

'No. But her mum is getting married. To that man.' *That man*
will suffice because Ali is nodding. I am pleased that I resisted the
temptation to call him *Mr Suave*. It does not seem fair to think
of him as *Mr Suave*, because he was always very nice to me. But,
then, suave men are nice; that is what suave means. 'Roz is going
to be a bridesmaid.' Why does this seem so incongruous? Is it the
dress, the tucks and flounces of the dress? Or the obligatory false

181

hairstyle, the tucks and flounces created by a hairdresser at nine o'clock on a Saturday morning? Roz is not Roz without the silky floppy hair with the tease of bleach. Or is it the shoes, wedding-day shoes, tight, shiny, hard, florid, like enormous blisters at the end of hot tired wedding-day legs? Or is it the smile, Roz's smile at someone else's wedding: *Cheese!*

'Her Dad got married a year or so ago,' I continue. 'Not to the woman . . .' How can I put this? 'Not to the woman . . .' I pause hopefully.

'Oh,' says Ali eventually, comprehending.

Roz had explained very well to me, in a very Roz-like manner: *In the end, after all, he has married an innocent party*. I wonder what happened to the guilty party. I wonder everything about the guilty party.

'But what about Gavin?' Ali insists.

'He says,' I report, 'or he was saying, when I heard from Roz, that it was the wrong time to leave his wife.'

'There's a right time to leave his wife?' A sceptical smirk settles on Ali's lips. Suddenly she turns with urgency, her hair rasping against the sticky sunlounger. 'Do you think she was pregnant?' The black glass stare is unflinching.

It is my turn to be sceptical. 'Who? Roz?' Roz has always been the Queen of Contraception. When she was fifteen, her mum told her to say if she wanted to go on the pill when she was sixteen. I suspect that *When you're sixteen* meant *Sometime after your sixteenth birthday*, but nevertheless Roz went on the pill when she was sixteen years and four hours old. It was a birthday trip to the clinic. She spent the rest of the afternoon in her room with her boyfriend, sweet Tim Castell, exploring the contents of the packet and reading the leaflets. Now, years later, I worry about Roz's cervix, about the years of exposure of Roz's young cervix. I prefer a barrier method. I like to see a barrier, feel a barrier.

'Not Roz,' Ali counters impatiently. 'Gavin's wife.'

'If she was, then it was the longest pregnancy in the history of the world because he has been saying that it is the wrong time to leave his wife since the very beginning.'

'Oh.' She relinquishes this theory, turns back to the sun.

'And if she was, then it would be a big surprise for Roz because she thinks that Gavin and his wife don't sleep together.'

'When will women ever learn?' Ali mutters, barely moving her lips.

I smile and reach for my book. But it casts an inconvenient shadow. I am worried by the prospect of a pale patch on my chest. This is always a problem on holiday. And I have so much holiday reading to do, a backlog of books that I want to read. If I turn onto my front to read, I will strain my neck and shoulders. It seems that I must choose to go home mottled or crippled or poorly-read. I drop the book to the ground. 'Do you think your sister will have a baby?' Ali's sister, Grace.

Ali chuckles. 'Kids? Grace? Noooo.' This is a definitive, dismissive No; a broad sweep of a No.

So why did she marry? I dismiss this qualm immediately: merely because she is married, she does not have to have children. Yet it nags. 'So why did she marry?'

'She doesn't have to have children.' Ali sounds tetchy. 'It's a personal decision, whether or not to have children.'

'But isn't marriage a public statement about all that? Don't they say something in church, or the vicar says something, about having children?'

Ali shoves her sunglasses through her hair and squints irritably at me.

'The church words are just a load of incantation,' she says.

'It's not *Latin*, Ali,' I reply, remembering Brenda Blaney and the Latin wedding. 'Everyone understands what they're saying.'

'No one understands what they're saying when it comes to love and marriage,' she answers frostily.

I smile to myself again.

'They have a dog,' Ali offers grudgingly, deadpan: their consolation, my consolation.

'There you are, then,' I goad, 'a reason as good as any: dogs *love* children!'

Ali's sigh is bitter with despair.

'And did she say *obey*? Did your sister say that she'd obey Mike?'

'I doubt it, knowing my sister.' The reply is crisp. She is confident, even smug.

What do I know about Grace? I know that she is In Publishing. (Why are people *in publishing* rather than *publishers*?) I know how she looks, I have been looking at her – up at her – ever since I was eleven, new at school, and she was thirteen.

A lovely-looking girl, that Gracie Mortimer, Mum used to say; *but boy! does she know it. Sophistication itself.*

Ali, unlike Grace, according to Mum, was a *touch tubby*. But Grace is, has always been, the shape and colour of Dracula, languid with white skin, black hair and long nails. No doubt she goes to an embalmer rather than a beautician.

Ali's body is slumped on the sunlounger but her neck is taut so that her blinded, blackened face is tipped towards the sun.

'The sister who you know so well agreed in church to have children, and you never even noticed,' I object cheerfully.

'Will you stop this?' she squeaks. 'I'm trying to sunbathe.' As if sunbathing requires contemplation, concentration. 'I am *not* responsible for my sister's actions.'

'Of course not.' I pause. 'But you helped with the wedding, which makes you a collaborator.'

Ali's lips part with a sticky click of exasperation, but she says nothing.

'At least you weren't a bridesmaid.' I remember being told that the bride had a cutesy trail of child cousins. I fear that there was even a pageboy among them: sailor suit? mini kilt?

A woman slip-slaps in flip-flops across the patio towards the hotel. She is wearing a white towelling robe, the hood sagging between her shoulders: Ku-Klux-Klan, or an escapee from a nearby bathroom? Her weight sinks onto each step: touch-slouch, touch-slouch. Above the mass of white towelling, woolly brown hair hangs loose to her shoulders. Below the towelling, white shins show a wash of sunburn. I suspect that she is British, but why? As she comes closer, I see the benign smile, a smile at nothing, a distant horizon of a smile. Her weak double chin belongs to a sitcom. She raises a hand to someone hidden from me inside the hotel, and I see the mark of married womanhood wedged down onto the appropriate finger: gold band, standard issue.

Why does Roz want to marry? She wants to be the centre of attention for a day (*for a day? Roz?*). But after a year or more of planning, the day – or half-day – is over very quickly. She wants to be beautiful in photographs, a beautiful bride. But all brides are beautiful. Roz is beautiful without bridery. Years ago I took a photo of Roz, my favourite photo of Roz, on the school field; a close-up, by accident (and it seems strange, now, to have been close to Roz, even by accident). The sun-scrunched face winks from the surface of the photo with the sharp sparkle of a cut diamond.

Roz wants a significant day, one significant day in her life, so she will make one, with the help of her mother, from taffeta, flowers, and awnings. She has not yet had any truly significant days, of births and deaths. The fake significant day, though, becomes a day for everyone else: the hall with signposted toilets; the tables and chairs, tablecloths, napkins, and little vases with carnation plus fern; the drink, food, music. The bride is merely the icing on the cake. No one talks to the bride because they assume that she is busy. Eventually she leaves early.

Roz wants *to marry*, to have a wedding, but also she wants *to be married*. Everyone is either married or single – there is no room on official forms for anything else – and who wants to be single? The only single woman known to Roz is Miss Killick. Single means unwanted. Roz wants a husband. *Husband* slides into *hubby*, cuddly, a comfy domestic arrangement. Husbandry, the management of a household. For a woman, husband means home, and home remains the prime ambition: Mum and Dad used to lecture to me to *Wait until you have a home of your own*, rather than bother themselves with any notion of adulthood; *Wait until you have your own place, Madam*.

Years ago, Roz used to tell me that she could hardly wait until

185

she was able to say *My husband*. To me, a husband was a man who wanders around his own living room in the evening in shirt-sleeves, frowning at the babbling television. There are people whom I say are mine: *My* mother, but no one can avoid having a mother, there is no choice. But lovers are chosen. Why stuff that glorious act of choice away forever under *my*? Why turn him into a mere *my*? If I was so much in love, I would want to speak his name, to conjure him whole into conversations. But I suppose that *my* is convenient: *my husband* fits neatly into conversations. Similarly *my boyfriend*, although boyfriends are for teenagers. But *My* says nothing about anyone other than the speaker. *My mother, my baby, my milkman, my doctor*: featureless figures of speech, all suggesting *me*.

Roz wants to disappear and reappear twice as important: no more Roz Smith, but Mrs Gavin Somebody. Women are slippery in history, slipping under different names, untraceable, to re-emerge under cover. Who was Brenda Blaney before she became a Blaney? and who is she now? But, legally, I can call myself whatever I like; I can disappear and reappear without having to marry. Are joint surnames a possibility? Not those fake American surnames for women, the maiden name stuck between the Christian name and the conquering surname of the man, the final word on the matter. No, not Roz Smith Somebody, but the Smith-Somebodies, a genuine compromise, or, of course, the Somebody-Smiths. But somehow the Smith-Somebodies or Somebody-Smiths would be even more irritating: this-thing-is-bigger-than-the-both-of-us. But, then, this problem is common to all family names. Mum thinks that Blaney is bigger than me. All my life I have been trying to be something other than Blaney.

I glance across at Ali, whose chin is jutting towards the sun. 'I haven't seen you for so long,' I observe.

She lifts and turns her head to stare at me, silent, soggy with recent memories of days and nights on trains.

'Before this holiday,' I explain, 'I hadn't seen you for so long.'

The head thumps back onto the sunlounger. 'That's because we're never at home.'

186

'We're not at home now.' Home: the place which is not home, the place where we do not live.

No one has mentioned Lucy. I did not think that we would talk about Roz — what is there to say about Roz? — but I am worried about Lucy. Lucy came from her college in Staffordshire to see me several months ago. She was waiting for me to return to my room, sitting outside my door on the soft, scented floorboards.

'Lucy!' I said when I stepped from the stairwell into the corridor. She did not rise, but watched me unlock the door — a reflex action. I stared down at her as the key turned familiarly in the lock, and she stared up at me. Her wide eyes were widened further by the tilt of her head: the china blue eyeballs of a doll clunking backwards into ceramic sockets.

'Oh Lalie,' she said with a tone of weary disappointment, 'do you think I could stay? I need to get away.'

From what? Lucy is always away, away from home, from a home which is not a home.

'Of *course*,' I said: not an answer, but a reassurance, a bossy reassurance, *but you MUST!* For how long? Rapidly I considered my timetable: essay due on Wednesday, trip to London on Friday for the weekend. I withdrew the key from the lock and pushed through the doorway: another reflex action. Behind me, she stood, reached across the floor for her bag, and followed.

Suddenly my room seemed smaller than usual. And messier. I picked my nightdress from the floor and flung it at the bed. 'What would you have done if I hadn't turned up?'

Lucy dropped her bag and shrugged: less I-don't-know than I-don't-care. Her blue eyes were invisible beneath bare bulbous eyelids. Little muscles were collecting and sagging at the corners of her mouth.

'What's wrong, Lucy?'

She passed me soundlessly and settled on the bed.

'It's Andy,' she said with the same weariness of the *Oh Lalie* at the door, but with an added tremble of tears.

Andy The Ents. Andy The Aran Sweater. Andy The Accountant.

187

I recalled his slab of shining golden hair: Andy The Golden Boy.
I began to fill the kettle.

'I've had enough of him,' Lucy sang flatly with the splashes of
the water in the sink.

I rinsed two cups quickly and turned off the tap.

'I've just had enough.'

I turned towards Lucy, and waited.

'He has to decide; you know?' The eyes flicked towards me and
froze. The *you know?* was a strong appeal for solidarity.

But I did not know. 'Decide what?'

Her face shut again. 'There's this woman . . .' All the bitterness
fell onto *woman*. She halted, and I tried to think of a suitable
question, but then she added, 'She really is an old cow.' This was
spoken without emotion, as fact. 'You should see her.' The eyes
rose briefly. I nodded fervently, I-trust-your-judgement, although,
of course, Lucy was not the person to make an unbiased judgement.

'I just . . .'

Why *just*? Why use *just* for emphasis? Just means only, merely,
barely.

'She's . . . I just don't know how . . . ' She jabbed both hands
into her hair to seize the spikes.

She was angry at the wrong person. Of course.

'I'm sick and tired of it. He has to make up his mind. Or I'm
going. I won't hang around to be messed about.'

She stayed the night, and the next night. Two sleepless nights.
They were sleepless for me because they were sleepless for her. I
was listening for low, slow whistles of sleep but there was silence.
Once I woke to the silence and she was sitting looking out of the
window: a magic transformation from asleep to awake, from
blankets to chair. The dawn air was empty of light and darkness.

What would I have done if I had heard sobs in the silence? I would
have waited for them to stop. And if they did not stop, I would
have reached above my head into the cobweb sway and tickle of
the light switch. The sudden flush of light would have made us
both self-conscious in our pyjamas and blankets. We would have

188

sat up, and then I would have made tea. But what would I have *said*?

During the daytime she followed me around – around the room, the building, the street, the refectory, the shops – speaking quietly in questions: *Do you think I did the right thing? Do you think I should call him now? Or later? Do you think I should have called him yesterday? Do you think he wonders where I am? Do you think he knows where I am? Do you think it's possible to love two people at the same time? Did I tell you that we've been together for eighteen months? Does that count for nothing? Did you know that we're booked to go to Crete in September? What do you think he sees in her? Am I so awful? Did I tell you that she has a PONY? Could you fall in love with someone with a PONY? Do you think she realizes what she is doing? Do you think he has lied to her? Do you think I should speak to her? Is there anything else I can do? Do you think he'll come back?*

I said to my friends, in passing, in the corridors and courts, 'This is Lucy.' And suddenly, briefly, Lucy's questions were silenced, and there was a polite twitch of the skin around her eyes and mouth. What did my friends see? An uninterested girl – woman? – with thick dull features and hair like ash. When we were walking to the coach station she said to me, forcefully and fearfully, 'He can't do this, he just can't.' When she rose above me into the coach I patted the rising rucksack and reminded her to write to me. She turned stiffly on the stairs and looked down at me kindly. 'OK, sister,' she smirked wearily. But, of course, there has been no word.

I had another visitor, a week later: Deborah's brother. I have told no one, not even Deborah, especially not Deborah. I wanted to wait and see if he had told her. And she does not seem to know, but is this good or bad? He knocked on my door at the end of an afternoon. He had been in town for a conference. 'And I thought I'd drop by,' he said with a lazy smile, sitting down on my bed. There was nowhere else for him to sit because I was sitting at the desk, turning in the chair, suddenly free from the dry smell of the open book. Drop by? On me, the friend of his little sister? I was blinking, adjusting. Then I stood and began to make tea,

189

thankful for the soothing rhythm of kettle-sink-cups. I was asking questions – *for the day? on the train?* – and thinking of more questions whilst pretending to listen to the replies. Talking, he left the bed and wandered around the room, touching with his pale precise fingers: the book on the desk, a leaf on my plant, a magazine, a candle, a cassette case, a postcard from Ali.

Later he sat on the windowsill to smoke, lifting his face towards the cigarette and searching with his lips. He winced when dragging the smoke down the frayed length of tobacco, but he held each mouthful for a long time. Holding, he nodded when I spoke, slow and definite nods. When he spoke, his drawl made me his co-conspirator: *Why don't they . . .? Do you think they . . .? The bastards . . .*

After an hour or so, he said that he should start the journey back home. I said nothing, watching the swing of his jacket from the bed to his shoulder. When I was thirteen or fourteen, I worried about being seen in bed without make-up: how could I look across the pillow without mascara and kohl – with bald and ill-defined eyelids – into the eyes of a man? Now, suddenly I felt worried again: could I ever lie next to Deborah's brother at night, bare-faced and scented with Nivea?

'Thanks for the tea,' he said cheerfully. I followed him to the door. I could smell him, I was following him to catch the smell of him. He turned before he reached the door and I stepped backwards and felt the rim of the strayed wastepaper bin against my shins. He smiled down at me. (Had he heard the jumpy twitch of the bin?)

'See you around,' he said. Yes, but where? And when?

I glance across at Ali. Is she asleep? 'I saw Deborah's brother a while ago,' I try, carelessly, loudly.

On Ali's sunlounger nothing moves. 'Deborah's brother?' she mutters eventually, without interest.

I bite my lip.

'I wouldn't trust him with my chihuahua,' she sighs.

I prickle, and skip the obvious reply, You-don't-have-a-chihuahua. 'Why not?' Immediately I regret my defensive response.

'No reason.' Her tone is fey, nonchalant. She wants to be cantankerous, but without much effort.

I do not reply. I wait and listen but she says no more. Then I sit up, ripping myself from the sticky plastic lounger, a scar tissue of sweat freezing the warm skin on my back. I pause, sun-dizzy, swimmy. The pool water is wobbling inside the basin of pale blue tiles, throwing lassos of sunlight across the surface. My looming legs look tanned but I remind myself that I am wearing sunglasses. Should I remove my sunglasses for a more realistic appraisal? No: why seek disappointment, especially so early in the holiday? Instead, I dab at one of the gleaming brown shins with a fingertip: do my legs need shaving? The skin is rough. I peer closer and see the hairs, so many, and so uniform in colour, shape, length. These do not look like hairs: hairs are soft, surely; silky and wayward. Hairs are long. There should be another word for these un-hairlike hairs. But, then, I suppose there is another word: stubble. How does this stubble appear to other people, people who are not peering at my shins but looking at the whole of me? Do I need to shave? I shaved before the train journey. So, the old question: do hairs grow faster in the sun, or are they merely more noticeable?

I lower my feet gently onto the hot stone floor, tapping to test the temperature. Then I struggle from the low lounger and walk the few steps to the poolside. Deborah is swimming along the bottom. Her body is a hot cloud below the surface, like blood released into water.

1986

....

When she sees us, Mum pauses in the doorway. 'Lucy.'

Lucy startles me with the sudden smile across the table, the flash of blue flame in her swivelling gaze. 'Hello Mrs Blaney,' she says cheerfully. I remember that she has the enviable knack of talking to grown-ups; even now that we are grown up.

Mum swells in the doorway with a bountiful smile. She saunters into the kitchen with a small sack of cat litter. 'Hello Lucy.' She nods towards me: 'You tracked her down, then?'

'Amazing powers of observation, Mother,' I interject.

Mum pointedly ignores me, glancing meaningfully at Lucy, her new ally. Lucy, who is returning to oblivion, can only grin inanely in response.

Apparently Lucy has been trying to contact me over the last few days. A week ago, she met Erin at the bus stop and learned that I was due home. I am home on holiday. I have not been here, in England, for a long time. I cannot afford the time or money to travel so far. This week I have been in London, moving around London, meeting and staying with friends.

'How's your mother?' Mum enquires brightly of Lucy, shoving the sack of cat litter into the cupboard beneath the sink. She did not ask How-are-you? Was this intentional? Lucy looks terrible.

'Well . . .'

Mum fails to listen to Lucy's tone. 'Good. And little Elliott?'

'Fine, fine,' Lucy agrees gladly, genially, nodding and smiling.

'And is he doing well at school?'

This is a ridiculous question; what does she expect in reply? Well-no-he-has-trouble-with-joined-up-Zs-and-he-has-an-allergy-to-the-class-gerbil. But it is an easy question, unlike Does-Mr-Harvey-pay-

192

maintenance? and Does-Mr-Harvey-still-ring-to-accuse-your-
mother-of-infidelity-with-that-nice-Dr-Clements-and-his-wife?

Lucy remains nodding, smiling, murmuring: 'Oh yes, fine.'

I can see that Mum has nothing more to say. Her smile is fixed.
'Well,' she sighs finally; and the smile brightens briefly, anxiously,
in compensation, as she backs through the doorway to disappear
into the hall. Lucy droops again. Her forearms are flat on the table.
Putty-pale skin binds her solid limbs. She is fingering her fingers.
Her downcast face reminds me that I saw a programme on special
effects for television in which an actor stuffed his cheeks with cotton
wool to become Henry VIII. (What is *special* about cotton wool?)
Lucy seems to be sucking on two cheekfuls.

'For once in my life,' she announces flatly, 'I don't have to pick
up Boy Wonder from school this afternoon. Mum is off work for
a week, on holiday.'

'You fetch Elliott every afternoon?'

'Three o'clock, with plimsolls.' She blows a big hot sigh across
the table. 'You don't know how awful it is, here, Lalie. I am so
bored.'

'Are you sure you don't want a cup of tea?'

'I don't drink tea.' Her face is resting now on one hand; the
handful of cheek swells beneath one eye. 'No caffeine.'

'Do you mind if I do?' I rise from the table.

'I'll have a glass of water.'

I take a long glass from the cupboard and run the water from
the tap onto my fingertips until it comes cool from somewhere
other than the sheath of hot steel. I fill the glass and place it on
the table.

'Thanks.'

I fill the kettle.

'It's so boring here,' says Lucy after taking a sip of water. 'There's
nothing to do, nowhere to go, no one around. And I've no
money.'

I turn towards her, leaning back against the sink, but she
continues to talk to the glass of water.

'The only day that's different to the others is Tuesday because the bin men come: Commotion in The Close.'

I turn back and look through the window at the garden. I live in a flat, now, without a garden. So, now, I notice gardens. I notice this one: the small square lawn of short rough grass and the dark crumbly soil of the borders, all inside a pen of thin orange fencing. Who does this gardening, and when?

'I've been here for a year now,' mutters Lucy. 'And all day, every day I have mum telling me to get-a-job. And I'm trying. But what job?'

I hear her shifting in her chair. So I turn from the window, and reach for a cup from the draining board. She is staring at me with one eye, rubbing the other very slowly and thoroughly. 'I don't want to end up in some office,' she whines.

I sigh my agreement. I remember that she worked in the department store, Hinton's, over Christmas; she sent me a Christmas card, claiming that *Darren Fish is Santa*. Was she serious?

'Mum wanted me to go for a job in the supermarket. Trainee Assistant Manager.' Her voice prickles with outrage.

I can think of lots of reasons for not wanting to work in the supermarket, but it strikes me that I do not know Lucy's reasons. I never know, with Lucy. So I wait.

'I'm worth more than that.' She sucks another sip of water with urgency from the wet rim of the glass.

Is she? Is she worth more than the supermarket? Who is worth the supermarket? What am *I* worth?

'Donna Lawrence works in the supermarket,' she protests. 'And all those YTS kids. Can you imagine?'

'Donna Lawrence? I thought Donna Lawrence was a jockey.'

'I am not going to spend the rest of my life in a supermarket.'

'Your mum wants you to spend *the rest of your life* in the supermarket?'

Lucy's pale blue gaze crawls across the room to mine, and she frowns. I wiggle the teabag inside the cup of scalding water.

'She's on at me all the time,' she says eventually. '*Don't eat that, it's for dinner*, or lunch on Saturday or whatever; *Don't stay in bed all morning*. But why should I get up? What's the point?'

I take the cup to the table and sit down again. 'Are you doing any sketching?'

'No.' She rotates the glass of water in one hand under a close gaze. I cannot judge this No: dismissive? despairing?

'Did you see Ali before she went away?'

'No.' The same flat *No*. But now there is a flash of the damp blue sheen of her eyes. 'Where has she gone?'

'Ali?' Now? She finished her exams and left for France a week or so later. 'To teach English in Bordeaux.'

Lucy's flat face writhes suddenly in irritation. 'Ali is *always* abroad. And especially when you need her.'

You? Me? Or *one*, when *one* needs her?

I close my eyes to savour a mouthful of tea.

'I don't regret leaving college, though,' Lucy says wearily. 'The thought of finals!'

'Finals,' I agree, baffled, in an effort to be supportive. In a sense, finals come and go in a week.

'And what would have been the point, for me?' crows Lucy, with new enthusiasm. 'What difference would it have made?' She drinks thirstily from the glass, looking at me over the rim. The frail surfaces and corners of her eyes redden at the shock of the cold. She lowers the glass, takes a deep warm breath, and blinks her eyes blue again. 'I hated them, at college,' she says brightly. 'All of them, supercilious bastards.' She reaches to the floor for her bag and brings to the table a bottle of pills, a small maraca of sepia glass. The child-proof lid snaps off into her hand. 'One, three times a day,' she comments, shaking a tablet from the bottle, 'to keep me jolly.' She smacks the open palm of her hand onto her mouth and winces, reaching frantically for the glass of water.

'I don't know of any pills for jolliness,' I say bleakly.

'Oh, I do.' She raises her eyebrows. 'But not these.' She replaces the lid and drops the bottle back into her bag. 'But these are free and I don't have to sleep with Dr Clements to get them.'

195

'Talking of which . . .' I prompt happily, in a whisper.

She stares blankly at me. 'What? Dr Clements?'

'*Nooooo. You* know: *is* there anyone?' If all else fails, then gossip. I stretch from my chair and push shut the door from the hallway.

'Oh.' She smiles. 'I was going to tell you.'

'Well?'

'Do you ever go into the bookshop in town?'

I shrug. 'Well, sometimes, rarely, when I'm home.' The bookshop: for me, a few shelves of paperbacks to browse, and a section labelled Secondhand; for others, picturebooks of Princess Di and *I-Spy Ancient Monuments*.

'Well,' she says, 'it's him.'

'Who?'

She sighs with impatience. 'The boy in the bookshop.'

'Oh.' I try in vain to remember a boy in the bookshop. 'Lucy,' I admit, 'I haven't been into the bookshop for years.'

'Brian Swann,' she urges. 'Works in the bookshop. Went to St Dominic's. Was friends with Kyle Fenton, Graham Dawson . . .'

'I know Graham Dawson . . .'

Her face brightens.

'I know *of* Graham Dawson,' I clarify.

'Oh.' She frowns. 'Brian Swann,' she tries again, 'Brian Swann. Dark.' She gestures faintly, helplessly. 'Tall.'

I laugh. 'Handsome?'

She pauses, and smiles. 'Well, *I* think so. Fairly. Not bad, for here. I went into the bookshop a month or so ago for a bookplate, on Mum's orders, and . . .' she shrugs, momentarily fey, '. . . came out with Brian.

'He's nice,' she says lightly, conclusively. She dabbles her fingernails onto the glass. 'And the sex is good,' she adds. She looks coolly at me. 'I mean, *really* good.'

I chuckle. 'What *is* really good sex, Luce?'

She grins in reply. 'If you don't know by now, I'm not sure that I can enlighten you.'

I shrug, deliberately obtuse. 'I'm either in the mood, or I'm not.'

I ease a spare chair from beneath the table and rest my bare feet on the seat. 'They're either doing things right or they're doing something wrong, and if they're doing something wrong, you correct them.'

Unruffled, she insists, 'I mean passion, Lalie.'

Passion. Yes, me too. But I cannot imagine passion with any of these local boys, any nice normal local boy, what could he possibly know about passion?

'Anyway,' she continues, 'I'm on the pill, and I've never been on the pill before.'

'Me neither, although my GP told me that it was more dangerous to cross the road.'

Lucy glances uncomprehendingly at me before returning her attention to the tall glass kaleidoscope of sunlight in her hand. 'Anyway, I like the pill, I love it, but . . .' she wrinkles her nose, 'I don't like the way it runs out of me for ages afterwards.'

It takes me a second to realize what she means. 'Lucy.' I slap my cup down on the table in mock protest.

'Well,' she says blithely, 'it's the truth.'

We both take a salutary sip of our drinks. To me, the pill is for those who are unable to cope with contraception; prescribed by doctors for sixteen-year-olds.

'What about you?' Slowly she stirs the skin around one eye again with those blank fingertips, devoid of ink and paint.

'What *about* me?'

'Is there anyone, up there in Edinburgh?'

'Oh. No.' What is the expression? *Leave me cold?*

She drifts backwards from the table into the chair, sinking, dangling her arms to the floor. 'You should make an effort.'

Effort is exactly what would be required. Huge effort. I stare listlessly at Lucy, at the web of tributary veins spanning each falling eyelid. Do we have our own unique pattern of these veins, like a fingerprint? Or do I have the same faint criss-crosses, two perfect copies, standard-issue? Surely a web so insubstantial, and in such thin skin, is vulnerable to change?

She says, 'It certainly livens up the weekends for me around here.'
She hauls her bag from the floor and extracts a packet of cigarettes.
'Not in here,' I warn.

Lucy pauses, packet aloft, and looks at me with wide blank eyes.
I nod towards the closed door to imply that the problem is Mum,
which is not strictly true, because I hate smoke.

'The garden?' she suggests.

I shake my head: too close to Mum. 'Let's go for a walk.'

Presumably we are walking towards the playing field; a spare field
among fields of purposeless cows and ponies. The playing field is
festooned with tatty fencing, and forever partially mown (by whom?
The Council?). There is a slide-swing-roundabout set in a bed of
hot sticky tarmac; and a wooden bench, bumpy on tufts of grass.
Towering storm-clouds of dark green leaves mark the boundaries.
When I was younger there was a rumour that, in the shadows of
the huge trees, on Sundays, our local boys had sex with girls
wandering free for the afternoon from the grounds of the nearby
boarding school. Gordon Low, Simon Allinson, Peter Coe: did
they? was it true? And who are the local boys now? And does the
rumour still exist, independent of them?

Lucy's knees, small shells turning over and over, are bouncing
the sagging hems of her baggy shorts. Dust puffs around her feet
from the blunt black toes of her plimsolls. She sniffs frequently,
sighing faintly afterwards, and occasionally exhaling a single dry
cough. We are walking past The Architect's House. I have always
thought of it as The Architect's House. It has belonged for the
past ten years or so to the Devonshires, none of whom are
architects, but it was obviously built by an architect: huge angular
planes of brick and tiles and glass, and sweeping views of open-
plan rooms. Surrounding the house and garden is a high brick wall,
with gates of barbed black iron. I have seen the gates operating
by remote control for cars, yawning open and smashing shut. But
where do the *people* go?

Lucy dips down, sits suddenly on the grass verge beneath some
trees. What can I do but sit with her? I crouch, fussing momentarily

over the grass, the threat of damp and prickles. Lucy is busy with the cigarette. We have a perfect view of the road; and there is a perfect view of us from the road. I long for the playing field, the forgotten field, the hush of the forgotten field. Lucy is concentrating on the bitter burn, scowling. I look upwards at the gleaming green canopy. There is a slow uneven swell of branches in the breeze. I hear the dry rattle of the leaves, the flutter of thin silvery tongues. 'Roz is married now,' I muse. 'Did you know?'

Lucy nods.

I am surprised. '*How* did you know?'

The scowl flicks towards me. 'You told me.'

'I did?' When?

'Christmas card.'

Roz told *me* on a Christmas card: *I got married August 15th, he's really nice and I'm v. happy!* Underneath, she signed the card *Roz and Martin Beecham*. The address, written along the bottom of the card, was numbers and meaningless abbreviations, a code. But, of course, I understood *W. Germany*. And I know that he is in the Air Force: I know this because Mum told me.

'Forces,' Mum said with a derisive wrinkle of her nose. It sounded like a verb, vaguely unpleasant. 'RAF,' she added. *Raff*.

The RAF, that great rugby club in the sky. Mum knew because someone told her (Mrs Harper? Mrs Illingsworth?). And she was told much more, too; much more than the mere fate of Roz. She was told that the Smiths of Appletree Walk no longer exist.

'Her mum has moved away,' she recounted for me. 'A new life, and all that,' meaning with the new husband. 'Cheshire, apparently.'

'Cheshire,' I repeated, full of wonder. Where is Cheshire, exactly? Why move there?

'I do remember that Chester has lovely shops,' Mum finished unsurely.

Roz was married in Cheshire, or so said the Harper-Illingsworth News Conglomerate. Presumably brides marry at home, home is mum, and mum is in Cheshire. Perhaps this explains the lack of invitation for me: too far away. But I am hurt that she told me, months later, on a Christmas card. But, then, I knew nothing of Martin; there had been no letters or phone calls between Roz and me for a long time. I wonder how she met him. I wonder what happened to Gavin. Does Martin know about Gavin, the years of Gavin?

Lucy sighs smoke into the air. 'So, she . . .' the free hand flaps, 'tied the . . .'

'Knot.'

Lucy nods rhythmically, heavily, gazing unfocused into the road.

'And do you know to whom?' I try, or tease.

She is still nodding. 'Action Man,' she utters suddenly.

I bite into my smile.

'Ken,' she concludes.

'Ken?'

'Ken-and-Barbie.'

'Lucy!' I have never thought of Roz as Barbie. But it strikes me as wonderfully appropriate. 'That's a bit rude.'

She shrugs, and glances blankly at me. 'What did Roz ever do for me?'

True.

There is a regular pulse of passing cars on this section of road; lorries, too, loose and rattling. I hear them, see them, but realize suddenly that I am thinking of Edinburgh, of my new home; of the wide streets, wide European streets, filled with the shrieks of braking buses and the ticking of black taxis. I am missing the ripple of tyres on cobblestones. It seems to me that all the streets in Edinburgh are wide, sweeping; even the backstreets, even my street. And tall, the streets are tall with tenements, so cool, the stone façades quiet with rows of huge communal doors and the thick wooden shutters of shops. Everyone lives in tall buildings of thick stone, except those who live – who were placed – in vast prefab wastegrounds on the edges of the city, and those who own bungalows along the routes of Sunday afternoon trips to the shores of the Forth. The centre of the city is built on stairs: almost everyone lives on a close – a tall, dark, steep stone staircase – and their addresses bear rickety codes, my own being TFL or 3FL (Top-Floor-Left, or Top-Flat-Left, or Third- Floor-Left). I miss the smell, in the stairwell, of so many kitchens. Here, Mum's kitchen smells very briefly of the food defrosting beneath the grill; and sometimes the rich smoke from a neighbouring barbecue passes over the garden. But there, in Edinburgh, in the close, there is a comforting smell of pantries and of old crumbs in the seams of wooden kitchen floors.

I am missing, too, the clear boundaries of Edinburgh: the sea to the North, the Pentlands to the South, the crags on the East, the trees of Corstorphine on the West. And, of course, I miss the middle, the peak of the castle, the broad plain of Princes Street and the New Town, the stony vales of Stockbridge and the Grassmarket. Here, there are no landmarks; no centre, no boundaries. I can see nothing; I do not know where I am. In the quietness of the night I can hear the distant running of the M25, some section of the M25, somewhere. In the daytime, the horizon is the Blaney farm. Travelling here, last week, on the train from the North to the South, I watched the world shrinking to a low widespread rubble, a terminal moraine of Wimpey homes.

In Edinburgh my purse contains a baffling mess of small banknotes; and I tend to forget that the banks close for an hour at lunch time. Then there is the strangeness of the language, not simply the strange expressions – through which I can merely feel my way, and against which I bounce my own words – but also the distinctive thread of names: *Isobel, Helen, Ailsa, Christina, Duncan, Drew, Kenny, Ian, Ewan*. The Scottish accent, sing-song, sang-song accent chimes so suddenly at the border, at the non-existent border: I remember that the voices behind the counter in the coffee shop in Jedburgh were so very different from those a few miles back at the petrol station in Northumberland. On my first trip, at the end of last summer, an aimless end-of-summer visit to a friend from college, I marvelled from the coach window at the countryside between England and Edinburgh, so much countryside and no main road. Snow gates were resting open in the warm sunshine. The scoured uneven surface of the land was low beneath the sky, the fields soft with a frosting of sweet hay. Clouds budded from small hills on the horizon into the sky, linking and drifting away. I know what I like about living in Edinburgh: I am a stranger in a strange land, but only slightly; and I am far away, but not too far.

'My mum is saving up for one of those,' says Lucy, blandly.

I look at her; and, with a nod, she redirects my attention to the passing car.

'No,' I object immediately. 'They're rust-buckets.'

A tweek of incredulity lifts her expression. 'How do you know?'

How do I know? I consider, but no answer comes to mind. 'I just know.' I pause and try again. 'I suppose it's difficult to live with a car-dealer for eighteen years and *not* know.'

She checks, dubious: 'And they really are rust-buckets?'

'Oh, definitely,' I agree rigorously. 'The worst.'

Strangely subdued, we watch the next car pass and disappear.

'When are you going to learn to drive?' Lucy complains suddenly. 'Your dad could find you a nice little number.'

I feel smaller. 'No,' I say, faintly.

'Why not?' she persists.

Why does she persist? Her words tug at me, and my muscles clamp still and hard, all except the muscles of my heart.

'Too dangerous.' And this paltry utterance is a signal, a sign from a shared language; a signal that surely she cannot fail to recognize.

'Oh go on,' she nudges me, 'live a little.'

But I have not wanted to go inside a car since Deborah died.

I do not know when Deborah died. It was sometime between this summer and last summer, during those short faint days of stagnant skies, of roaring tyres ripping into rainwater on the roads, of the hiss and puff of hot dry breath from lungs into the streets to make small white grazes on the darkness of the afternoons. But I do not know exactly when Deborah died: I have no day, no date; no *month*, even. The month has sunk without trace into the sludge of winter. Deborah died, and I forgot about months: February, March, what is the difference? The day, the date, was gone by the time Deborah's mother called me with the news: I could not ask, *Excuse me, Mrs Steiner, but when was this, exactly?* It did not seem important. But it is important; it is important now. If I had a date, I would have something of Deborah. I would have something for Deborah, too. What would she say if she knew that I do not know the date of her death? We should share the date, Deborah and me: Deborah's date, but mine too, looming huge every year on my calendar. A date is precise, certain, everlasting. And a date would gently and gradually mark the ever-increasing gap between us: three months ago, six months, and then, sometime, inconceivably, a year ago, two years ago, ten years ago.

The telephone voice had said, 'Hello Lalie, it's Deborah's mother here.' It was a very weary voice. So I knew immediately that this call did not concern a visit to Edinburgh, or any other possible reason for a call from the mother of a friend; I knew that this was serious. But did I know how serious, then? No doubt I said Hello in reply, if only to indicate that I was listening.

'I'm afraid that I have some very bad news for you,' she continued. 'Deborah has been killed in a car accident.'

She continued, slowly but evenly and without pauses, (how many times had she done this?), 'We've had a family funeral at home in Manchester, but we're having a memorial service down here next week for Deborah's friends, and I'd like it very much if you could come.' There was a tiny break. 'I realize that it's a long way for you to come, and at such short notice,' she said, sounding suddenly very sad.

'Yes,' I said, 'I mean, no; I mean, yes, of course I'll come.'

She gave me the details of the service: date, time, place. *Yes-yes-I'll-be-there-of-course-I'll-be-there*. Where? Some void, some building, somewhere without Deborah. *I'll-be-there* but I was not there when Deborah died. It was all over. After giving me the details, Mrs Steiner said, 'Thank-you, Lalie.'

I rang Ali, without pausing to catch my breath. She answered too soon, unnaturally soon, snatching away the beeps: 'Hello?'

'Ali, it's me.'

'You've heard.'

'Just now. *You've* heard.' My voice was carrying little feeble breaths into the air.

'Just now.'

'Are you going?' To the memorial service.

'Yes. Are you?'

'Yes.'

'Thank God.'

And then, frantically, we made arrangements to meet before the service; hurried, elaborate arrangements, with layers of safeguards. It did not occur to me, at the time, when I replaced the receiver, that nothing else had been said.

Next, I started to dial Lucy's number, but stopped. I turned away from the phone, and looked around at the walls of the hallway. They are pretty walls, pale green. There is a huge, new, white, reassuring radiator. There was no sound in the flat; no one else was home. Doors had been left in varying states: closed, half-open, wide open. Amanda's door was wide open, but distant, half-visible; the empty space lined with daylight, like silver foil. Nearer, Coralie's collapsible umbrella was a green chrysalis against the skirting board. I turned back to the phone and started to dial Deborah's number and that was when I realized. Or that was the first time that I realized. A few days before the memorial service I rang Lucy. She had decided not to go. 'I can't face it,' she told me flatly, without elaboration. Then I rang Mum, to ask if I could come to stay. As soon as I announced myself, she said, in a stage whisper, 'What terrible news.'

I talk to Deborah, every day, silently, in my head. I keep in touch. I am talking to Deborah while I am buying stamps or sitting on the bus or surveying the spines of books in the library. Life-goes-on, in the Post Office and the bus and the library, although I am not sure that I do. The world has not noticed that Deborah has gone, will never notice. The world closed instantly over the wound.

The same Post Office exists with the same staff, the same queue, the same troubled video croaking about orthopaedic beds. There has been no increase in bus fares, and few new books in the library. Yet I dread change, I am holding my breath in dread of change. Not long after Deborah died, her dad's favourite newspaper was re-designed; so, suddenly, one morning, in one more little way, Deborah was consigned to a different time, to the olden days.

I want to know what happened to Deborah, but she cannot tell me. What did she see or feel in the moment before impact? Was she frightened? I hope not, I hope not. Did it hurt? And how much, and where? When did she die? Did she hear them arrive with their sirens and their crackling, slithering waterproof, bloodproof jackets? Did they hurt her when they moved her? Did they frighten her with their sparse, urgent words and blaring sirens, or did they soothe, and inspire hope and confidence? Did it seem to Deborah that they had come to save her, or did it feel like the end?

Often I imagine the disappointment of the ambulance crew. It was probably the first call of their day. And I have the details now from Ali. (I do not know how she knows; I did not think to ask). She told me that Deborah was taking care of her sister's car for a month. She was driving into college, early in the morning, seven-thirty – why so early? – on the outskirts of town, when she was hit by a car travelling in her lane in the opposite direction. It was overtaking another car on the brow of a hill. Why do that? Why drive into the other side of the road with no view of the oncoming traffic? No one needs driving lessons to be able to spot the snag. Was it a dare? There were two men in the other car, early twenties; one lived, one died. I doubt that it was a dare, Tails-you-live-Heads-you-die. There is nothing daring about dying, too quick and too final for boasts.

No doubt it was momentary mindlessness. This was not a car accident but a car manslaughter. *Man*slaughter? The *slaughter* is appropriate. Sometimes I see the car rearing suddenly in the road in front of Deborah. (Is it best to swerve? But swerve *where?*) What was playing on Deborah's radio at the time? (And do I really want to know?) And, of course, of course, why was she there, just there, on the brow of the hill at that particular moment? She was taken to hospital but she was dead on arrival. She died among strangers, twisted among strangers.

Ali tells me that Deborah died of head injuries. Head injuries? Brain damage. Perhaps necessarily vague. Ali says that it is a relief that Deborah did not live with head injuries. *Not Deborah*, she says to me; *you've seen those people, people with brain damage, in the newspapers*.

But since when have you believed what you read in the newspapers, Ali? Deborah's leg was broken, too, and the leg bothers me. Legs are easy to fix, compared to brains, and I do not like to think that she was buried with a broken leg. It seems to me that she was left incomplete, neglected; however much I tell myself that no one would or could mend the broken leg of a dead person.

I do think of her, in the grave, although I try to stop. It horrifies me that I think about decomposition, but I want to know if she is still there, if she still exists, if I could see her if I wanted, if I dug. How long will she be there? I do not think solely of the inside of the grave; I think about the flowers growing on top, and the colour of the sky. I try to imagine the Manchester sky, day by day. And I do not think solely of the grave. I think of her room, her desk and drawers: where are her belongings? Letters, diaries, photos. After the memorial service I went through my own personal papers, destroying and tidying, fearful for my privacy. But what about the inconsequential items, the odd pair of earrings, not valuable but indestructible? Where are her clothes? Have they been thrown away? Or given away, to charity? And if they have been given away, is it wrong to pass them back into the world without a word, as if nothing has happened? Fearfully, I have been through my own clothes and thrown away the secondhand bargains, the favourite cashmere cardigan, linen shirt, limp kid gloves. What about underwear? No one gives away underwear, so where did it go? Surely a dustbin is too drastic.

What happened to the clothes at the hospital? Were they burned in the incinerator with dressings, or given to the Steiners to take home? I want to know what Deborah was wearing, how she was wearing her hair, on the final morning. It is more and more difficult for me to remember her face, her hair, her walk, her laugh. I have photos, a few. But photos are colourful shadows, nothing more. And photos were *then*: Deborah with a face which is too young, clothes which are too old, and becoming more so, day by day. In the last year or so before her death two faint folds had formed a pair of tiny brackets around her mouth, and I cannot find these lines anywhere in my photos.

I was uneasy, in the beginning, that it was not Deborah: not Deborah in the car, not Deborah dead. I had not seen her; I had to take their word. But if it was not Deborah, who was it? (Someone to whom she had lent the car). And where was Deborah – the live Deborah – now? (She was abroad, oblivious; or shocked, gone mad with guilt, in hiding). I worry less now, or hope less. I remind myself that she would have been identified, formally, by one of the Steiners, although I am still sceptical about the ability to recognize anyone who has died of head injuries. But then I worry that she was not dead. And perhaps no one is ever dead, so that everyone wakes in the coffin or the fire, because how would we know? And I worry about Deborah naked and cold under the sheet in the mortuary. Morticians work with plugs and bungs: the bodies bound and gagged, no doubt by junior technicians who are singing along to Radio One. I want someone to stay with me in the mortuary when my time comes; every minute, to protect me, to care for me until the last possible moment, the final moment of earth or fire.

These thoughts, all these thoughts, are with me all the time, a background hum. Once a day or so, or at night, the volume increases and fills my world for five minutes, ten minutes, an hour, longer. And I am ashamed of these thoughts, morbid thoughts: what would Deborah say? She would hate this. But, then, she does not know. So, this-hurts-me-more-than-it-hurts-you, Deborah. And it *hurts*; there is an actual pain, a freezing-thawing burn down my throat and in my chest.

I do not know where Deborah is buried. If I knew, if I went, then perhaps my frozen core would return slowly to life. I suppose that I could ask someone but the name of a cemetery in Manchester would mean nothing to me. And how would I find a cemetery in Manchester? But it is my ambition to do so, one day. I went to the memorial service, and, afterwards, outside, I followed Ali across the gravel to Deborah's parents. I was unsure and unrehearsed. In turn they grabbed my hands, exclaiming wordlessly about the cold although I do not know whether they wanted to warm my fingers or warm their own. They implored me to keep in touch, and I promised but I have not done so. I want to write, but *what*? A Christmas card will be convenient, Jewish or not. *Seasons Greetings! I hope you are well.* But I have heard, from Mum, that Mr Steiner is not well. He stays at home, early-retired, with angina and back pain and other pain.

Pete, Deborah's lover, ex-lover, also asked us to keep in touch but by the end of the afternoon we had lost him. He was cast adrift. Deborah had been our link. We have no address for him. It is possible that the Steiners will have an address for him, still, for a while, for a few years yet. At the service he bobbed around them, constantly the object of their self-conscious efforts to include him in the family circle. He bore the sad status, non-status, of the lover, ex-lover. He was closer to Deborah than any of them, in a sense, in an important sense, but the world insists that blood is thicker than water.

After we had spoken to Deborah's parents and to Pete, Ali went home before me, on a different bus, in the opposite direction. Then I crossed the road to wait in the shelter for my bus. And I stood where I could watch Deborah's brother, Simon. Stood? Hardly. I had forgotten the breath-holding of infatuation, I had forgotten how the sole sound of me becomes the hot buzz of blood in my ears. I could not believe that, in spite of myself, during the service and afterwards, my body had grown different around me under his eyes. I had become taller and faster, somehow; perhaps, more economical; I hope, more graceful. In spite of myself, I had felt every movement, mine and his, etcha-sketched onto the concentrated atmosphere of the afternoon.

I had said Hello to him in passing, after the service, in the doorway. He was tall over me in his black suit, taller than I had expected. 'Hello Lalie,' he said, and his use of my name seemed oddly formal. A simple Hello would have been more kind. As *Lalie* I was one of the crowd, requiring an effort of discrimination. I avoided his sea-green, see-all eyes; I passed by, with a mere reply. But when I was standing alone in the bus shelter, waiting to go home, when he was standing in the distance on the gravel driveway with his parents, I felt that he was watching me. Nervously, I turned away, looked for the bus.

The sloshy dusk of the road was staked with drowsy streetlamps. Cars passed at regular intervals, creaming the slush of the kerbside. When Simon came into the shelter behind me I was squeezed momentarily by panic. But he came and stood beside me so that we both looked out together for a while onto the wisps of drizzle. Neither of us spoke, and the cue for the kiss was his hand on my shoulder: the touch too feeble to turn me towards him, but a request, perhaps a reminder. Suddenly there was the warmth of him in the cold space, the sudden warmth and size of him in my small cold space, and his taste, his pace: I was stunned and I did nothing to resist, did nothing but kiss.

Nothing was said then nor since. Then, there was no time to speak. I had no mouth to speak and when, after a while, the bus came, swooping wet-wheeled alongside the shelter, doors slapping open, we sprang apart. Frantically I smoothed myself, pulled my clothes into place and soothed the graze left in my hair by the gritty concrete wall of the shelter, before snatching into my pocketful of loose change. High above me, behind the windscreen waterfall, the driver was hot and damp, woozy on diesel fumes, and I could see that he was in no mood for goodbyes. I have wondered ever since why I did not stay, but at the time there seemed to be no option. *No*, there *was* no option, because *stay where?* The bus shelter? From the bus I saw that Simon had turned away, had begun to return to his parents who were waiting in the distance on the gravel driveway and saying the last of the goodbyes.

I have said nothing to anyone. What would I say? *Guess what I did in the bus shelter after my best friend's memorial service, with her brother?* Next time, when I go to visit her grave, I will do everything right. But, for now, what do I do about Simon? If the bus shelter was not the time nor place, when, where? I live in Edinburgh, he lives in London. So, was this Brief Encounter, even briefer without the boat scene? But if I give up on the possibility of Simon, then surely I give up on life, go back on the most important lessons of life, the lessons I have learned from Deborah, because of Deborah: Life-is-short; and Opportunities-exist-to-be-taken; and Ultimately-nothing-matters-but-love. I will not give up on Simon because I cannot give up on him. I must accept that I am in love with him because anything else would be denial, *anything else would be denial*. I have no choice.

So I exist in limbo. Will I feel like this forever? Why am I always so out of place? First, there was Deborah's death, and I was in the wrong place at the wrong time, unable to reach out and stop something so random; and since then, my endless queasiness, the whole world out-of-kilter still, helter-skelter. And now Simon, the finger-clicking luck of finding him, the heart-flipping shoot at each and every mention of him. Yet I am unable to reach out and start something which I know is meant to happen.

Lucy has finished the cigarette. She is sitting very still, eyes closed, face slack. 'Lucy,' I begin the impulsive lie, 'I have to go now, I have to pack.'

She turns towards me, momentarily wide-eyed. 'You're going? I mean, going going?'

I echo her surprise. 'Didn't I tell you?'

'You're going *now*?'

'Overnight.' I stand. 'I'll walk back via the bus stop, if you like.'

She rises slowly, frowning at her watch. 'Yes,' she says, 'I can catch the half past.'

~

As I come through the door into the hallway, Lyndsay bumps into me. His head is bound by a pair of headphones. He stumbles deafly onwards to the stairs. I remember the days when teenagers deafened everyone else. I open the kitchen door.

Mum turns in surprise from the sink. 'That was quick.'

Thanks for the running commentary, Mum. But, of course, it was not a comment, but a question. I do not answer. I check the kettle for water and flick the switch.

Mum pulls the plug and lifts her hands above the basin to shake them free from the crackling froth of bubbles. 'Lucy,' she says: a faint exclamation, the old mixture of incredulity, disdain and fascination. She dries her hands on the tea towel. 'Is she all right?' she asks finally.

How much of this is genuine concern? I make a sound – 'Mmmm' – to indicate that I heard the question, to prevent a repeat.

She shrugs and places the tea towel on the hook. 'Now . . .' the tone is brisk, bright, '. . . would you take over a card and tin of sweets for Aunty Barbara? It's her birthday. I haven't had time and now I'm late with the tea.'

I open my mouth to protest but she frowns frantically and asks, 'Are you eating with us tonight?' she is pushing the peeler against the dry skin of a potato. The blade is a thin reed emitting faint chirps of friction.

'No.'

The frown remains, a spasm containing the effort of computation: 'And your Dad will be late because he's at an auction. And Jane is going out. So that's four for now, and one to keep for later.' The eyebrows lift and part. 'Are you sure that you don't want me to save you something?'

'No, thanks.' But I succumb to curiosity: 'What is it?'

'Liver casserole.'

I display my disgust, in full sound and vision.

She huffs. 'Not for you. You could have the peas. Anyway, liver is full of goodness. And it's your Dad's favourite.'

'But he's not even here.'

'But he will be here. There are no soup kitchens at car auctions.'
She sighs into an open cupboard full of pans. 'More's the pity.'

I try to leave the room but she twists towards me and repeats
cheerfully, 'Will you take the card and present to Aunty Barbara?'

Aunty Barbara is married to Uncle Tom. She is Aunty Mo's
successor. We have never met. She and Uncle Tom met in the
waiting room at the health centre. She has agoraphobia. (He had
a boil; caused by stress, said the doctor). Mum is confident that
agoraphobia is an ideal condition for members of the Blaney farm
household: *Thank God she hasn't claustrophobia, can you imagine?
Cooped up, over there.* Her first husband died years ago. *Heart*, said
Mum to me, as if hearts are lethal. And there is a daughter, but
in New Zealand. *And now she has Gran*, says Mum; *now she is at
the old lady's beck and call all the time. If you ask me, Mo is best out of it.*

I know that everyone wants Gran to move house to somewhere
more suitable. But Gran refuses.

'She has an outside toilet,' Mum said to me yesterday, her voice
hot with horror and shame.

But I remember that Gran likes outside toilets; I remember that
she said to me, during a visit to the farm, when I was small and
fascinated, 'Who wants a dirty great chamber pot in the middle
of the house?' Yesterday I tried to explain this to Mum. 'And
gypsies are the same,' I finished enthusiastically. I know this because
I read it in a book.

'Gypsies?!' she wailed.

But Mum is afraid that Gran will move into the block of flats
which has been built opposite our house: *Sheltered Homes For The
Elderly*. (The elderly *what*?) Yesterday she moaned, 'I hate old
people.'

'Mum,' I said patiently, 'you are an old person, or nearly.'

'Not until I retire,' she countered after a moment of indignant
speechlessness.

This seemed fair until I realized that she has no job, and so will
never retire.

Now she says, 'The card is in the stationery drawer and the present is in my bag in the hallway.'

'No,' I say firmly.

'Eulalia . . .' she pleads.

'No. Why should I go? I've never even met the woman.'

'Well, now's your chance.'

'No. What is she to me?' Secretly, I regret this disregard: it is, after all, the poor woman's birthday.

Mum glowers. 'You invite yourself here, you mooch around my house, and you won't even – where are you going?'

'To pack, since that's how you feel.' I saunter further away into the hallway.

'Don't be silly. If you go to the farm, you can see Gran; when did you last see Gran?' This is a whine.

'Mum, you *hate* Gran,' I reply reasonably.

'*But when did you last see her?*' Fury pricks the red face.

When did I last see Gran? At Aunty Mo's funeral. I went with Mum and Dad. 'Ah, Jane,' she greeted me, but presumably she saw my expression of horror, and said quickly, 'Lyndsay.'

'Lyndsay's a boy,' I found myself saying in dismay. For some reason she chuckled jollily at this. What did she think I had said? She laid her left hand on her huge chest; a soothing, containing gesture. At the base of her throat it became momentarily a massive brooch, a dead, dried claw worn for good luck. 'Erroll,' she said, 'you are full of surprises, didn't I always say?' I had never heard her say this; and I could not imagine Erin full of anything, especially surprises. For the rest of the afternoon she called me Laurie; or perhaps it was Lollie. Once, during the sandwich session, she waddled over to Mum and me, black silk rustling, to ask me pleasantly, 'How are you getting along with that mother of yours?'

Now I reply flatly to Mum: 'I saw her at the funeral.'

Mum frowns in response to the word funeral, and the jutting features retreat. She sinks back to the cupboard of pans. 'Perhaps Erin can do it for me, when she comes home,' she says quietly.

No doubt, because Erin will do anything – even attend school, or eat meat – when persuaded that life will be difficult for someone if she refuses. I come back into the room to tackle an unopened box of tea.

'Erin is shopping,' says Mum suddenly, apparently making conversation. 'With a few of her little friends.' She peeks over my shoulder. 'Eulalia,' she says too loudly, 'don't spill that tea.'

'Why not?' I ask sarcastically.

'Eulalia, if you pull the wrapper like that . . .' The tone of her voice is rising. 'Here, give it here.' Now she is gruff.

I relinquish, as usual. And she rips the cellophane expertly.

She settles the frying pan on the hob. 'And Erin's haircut,' she continues mildly, 'do you like Erin's new haircut?'

Erin's hair has been bobbed.

'Yes, I do, very much.'

'Yes,' agrees Mum enthusiastically, 'isn't it nice? She went off by herself one Saturday, a few weeks ago, and came back with it done.' She takes a small bloody package from the fridge. 'No doubt shorter hair is easier during exams,' she muses. Erin has been taking O levels.

I retreat from the sight of internal organs falling into the frying pan. 'What about the boyfriend?' I ask, from the table.

'Oh, Louis,' she crows, implying that she has known him for years. Her voice rises over the spitting of the livers in the pan. 'What a nice boy. Very well-spoken.' She is hunched, heaving a tin-opener around the top of a tin of tomatoes. 'He's leaving school to work with his mother, in her shop: she's a florist!' The tin cracks. She exhales and pauses briefly. 'I said to Erin, *Hang on in there, perhaps there'll be a job for you, you never know.*' The tomatoes slide from the tin into the pan, lowering the sizzles to sozzles. 'You know that Erin wants to work in a shop?'

I nod in reply, even though Mum is engrossed in the spice rack. But I do not know what Erin means by *a shop* – a clothes shop? a food shop? a bookshop? – and I have never known anyone make such a strange claim. To *own* a shop, yes; but to *work in* a shop?

'I'd prefer a travel agency,' says Mum, choosing dried basil.

'Oh no,' I counter: 'Those screens . . . those phones . . .'

'Ah, yes, but think of the discounts, the opportunities for travel.'

Now Erin comes into the kitchen and sits immediately, heavily, at the table. Mum glances over, puzzled. 'Is it hot out there?' she asks Erin. 'And did you remember to buy those envelopes for me?'

Erin nods.

'Do you want some tea?' Mum indicates the teapot. 'It's still warm.'

'Yuk,' Erin replies emphatically, sorrowfully. The wide sweeps of her head, from side to side, fluff the sleek bob.

I rise from the table. 'I'll fetch you a glass of water.'

'Are you sure?' Mum bellows at Erin over the noise of the liver. 'I'll make a fresh pot.' She fits the lid onto the pan.

Erin gazes appreciatively at the glass as she takes it from me. 'Lovely,' she whispers. 'Thanks very much.'

She drinks dutifully for a moment, and then lowers the glass half-empty to the table. The liver drones under the cover of stainless steel.

'So,' I say finally, cheerfully, to Erin, 'how does it feel to have left school?'

The enormous blue irises float to the surface through the thick pale curds of eyelid. 'It's nice to be free,' she tries.

Mum swings around, a potato half-stripped in her hand. 'Free?' she yelps. 'That *was* free. Just you wait.'

And now Lauren. She sweeps through the door, the hallway echoing with the tom-tom of her bare feet on the stairs. 'If anyone phones for me, I'm out,' she announces happily. She is nine years old; I was much, much older before I needed Mum to lie for me. Passing, Lauren snatches the sunglasses from my head and disappears with them into the garden. Mum's forlorn gaze follows to the doorway. 'She was my last baby,' she sighs, 'the baby to last me for the rest of my life, but she was a teenager from the moment she could walk.' Lauren reappears swiftly, returning the sunglasses to my head. She is wearing the cat on her shoulder. It is perched daintily, crouching, nosing the air. Mum drops the potato onto the chopping board in noisy protest. 'Lauren! Put the cat down!'

The cat, a tabby, six months old, is *The Cat* to Mum. To Jane and Erin, it is *Poppy*; to Lauren, *Poppet*; to Lyndsay, *Jimmy Dean*. Lauren continues on her way, cat wobbling. 'Relax, Mum,' she calls from behind its head, 'you worry too much.' She rubs her long fingers over its frail furry butterfly-wing ears. It thrills, butting softly. Mum's flaming blue gaze flickers and switches to me. I glance helpfully at Erin. Erin's face is hidden in her hands. A cupboard door bangs and Lauren lowers a jar of peanut butter in both hands, a trophy.

Jane steps soundlessly from the hallway, but recoils from Lauren and the cat. 'Lauren!' Her pale face, under a dark wet mess of uncombed hair, is sharp with rage.

Lauren glances perfunctorily in Jane's direction. 'Jane!' she pipes ridiculously in reply. She is constructing a huge peanut butter sandwich.

Anger pokes from Jane's widened eyes, tipped nose and bared teeth. 'Lauren, leave Poppy alone!'

Lauren ignores her.

Jane ventures forward, apparently assessing the possibility of snatching the cat from Lauren's shoulder. The cat is hunched, bony, and too high. So she transfers her scrutiny to Lauren's awesome sandwich. 'You big pig,' she says.

'You big *prig*,' Lauren replies immediately.

Jane exaggerates the effort required to reach around Lauren to open the cupboard. 'Where are my sodding Scandabrots?' she wails.

Mum thuds another potato onto the muddy chopping board. 'Jane! Why don't you try the bottom cupboard?' This means Try-the-bottom-cupboard.

Opening the bottom cupboard onto Lauren's shins, Jane whines, 'Mum, tell Lauren, it's cruel to Poppy.'

'Lauren,' says Mum, scraping again.

The packet of crispbreads floats from the cupboard, drawing Jane upwards.

Lauren moves away slowly with cat and sandwich. 'Come on, Poppet,' she says, loudly and confidently.

Jane slams the packet of crispbreads onto the table, making no sound at all, and glowers at Lauren's back and the cat's tail. Then the translucent eyeballs swivel towards Erin. 'What's up with you?' she demands.

Erin's face rises sleepily, surprised, from her hands. 'Nothing.'

'Mum,' continues Jane, snatching at the tab on the packet, 'will you tell Lyndsay to give me back my headphones?'

Mum sighs.

'And if Duncan comes before seven, I'm in the bathroom.'

Mum's face shimmers with sarcasm: 'Oh dear me, Jane, you in the bathroom? Never! He'll think that I'm making excuses for you, that you're still out with the milkman.'

Jane tears into the internal cellophane and extracts four brittle brown slices. 'The bathroom is a tool of my trade,' she pronounces stiffly. 'And I'm the only one around here who does any work.'

'Work?' Mum chuckles humourlessly at the diminishing potato in her hand. 'You call that work? Preening in front of a camera? You've been doing that since the day you were born.'

I am slow to realize that Jane's comment about work, or lack of work, was probably intended for me. I have been thinking about Jane's Duncan. Yesterday I quizzed Lauren about Duncan. 'He must be thirty,' she replied, horrified, disgusted. For Lauren, it seems, thirty is ultimately old; she can imagine no worse. In fact, he is thirty-six, or so said Mum; and, Mum added, 'divorced.' This *divorced* was whispered in a manner more suitable for an accusation such as *war criminal*. Then Mum turned to Lauren and protested, 'I was in my prime at thirty.' Lauren stared back, unblinking blue, and replied eventually, incredulously, disdainfully, 'You mean that you spent your prime having babies?'

Having confirmed Duncan's age and marital status, I wanted to know about his work.

'Apparently he's in entertainment,' said Mum. (Apparently, I discovered later, he owns an amusement arcade).

Lyndsay, passing us with a half-pint glass of milk, began a Welleresque chorus: *'That's* en-ter-tain-ment, *That's* en-ter-tain-ment . . .'

'Lyndsay!' barked Mum, flinching and covering her ears.

And I wondered, for the first time in a long time, about my old tapes and records, the ones which I did not take away with me: where are they? And has Lyndsay found them? (And if so, which ones does he play? And did he notice the Hawkwind tape? He will not know that the Hawkwind tape is in the box by mistake; and Simon and Garfunkel, too). And where are my old clothes, the silk chinese dress and the straw boater? And my old photos, of school day trips to Calais, and Guide camp?

But Jane's comment about work, or my lack of work, is inaccurate. I clean houses in the mornings, and baby-sit for two little girls in the afternoons; and for one evening each week I work voluntarily, and wait for a vacancy. I teach an evening class, or small group: Slow Learners. I saw an advert in the local paper: *Wanted, Volunteer Tutors, Slow Learners*. I went on the training course, a week of evenings filled with the squeals of marker pens and the stagey thunder of flip-charts, with the constant threat of role play. Now my small group meets with a few others in an old school on the outskirts of the city. I had never been out of the city to the west. It is a long bus ride from the centre. Leaving the centre, the bus travels almost immediately into a poor area: I remember my Geography lessons, the zones of cities, the inner *twilight zone*. Presumably the twilight zone is the red light district, but *red light* was deemed inappropriate for Sixth Formers. The emphasis on light, or lack of light, hazy and unnatural light, is strange because the overwhelming impression is the *smell*, due to the abattoir and brewery.

The bus follows the lines of thin dim tenements. Along the route, marked by new perspex bus shelters, are several huge old buildings, ex-dance halls and Co-ops with thick stone crusts of pillars and inscriptions. Nowadays they are bingo halls, each with three or four pristine vinyl billboards. Each billboard shows an individual posing as an ecstatic compere or winner. Further along the bus route, the tenements shrink to houses with gardens. I know that the houses are council houses, but how do I know? I do not know from the style, because all the styles here are new for me, different from the rows of orange semis down the road from the Blaney farm. Uniformity is not the clue because all housing estates are uniform, like the new crescents of mock-Tudors which were built behind my old school. Perhaps the clue is the extent of the area. But I feel certain that the fences and gates are important; the short white fences of plank-gap-plank and the gates with flicking latches. These houses have fences, but the fences are so inadequate. Privately-owned houses do not often have front fences; the slabs of lawn are separated casually by rows of bushes or driveways, or even decorative loops of chain strung between tiny posts. For privately-owned houses, fences are hidden at the back: high, thin, brown, scented wafers of wood.

The old school building displays the date of origin in stone above the main door. Why were so many schools built at the turn of the century in the same style, a style unique to schools? A modern school, stripped of the wooden sign – name of the school, name of the headteacher with DipEd or MEd, name of the caretaker – could be a branch library or a health centre. But Victorian schools, Edwardian schools, are all small fortresses of thick stone with smatterings of gables. What did this style mean, at the time? Why did it mean school? Inside our old building, the huge high windows are stone-rimmed viewless slots of sky: plenty of light, but no distractions.

Our old building, so typically a school, is no longer a school in the sense that it no longer contains schoolchildren. Presumably the schoolchildren were moved to a colony of flat-roofed slot-together buildings of cement and reinforced glass. Our old building is now an Adult Training Centre, run by the Social Work Department for those with Special Needs, because education finishes for them when they are sixteen years old. And for one evening each week those who come every day with their Special Needs can be Slow Learners, and come voluntarily to the building for extra teaching. Teaching takes place in the old classrooms for an hour, followed by half an hour in the Hall for drinking tea and playing records.

There are four people in my group: Frazer, who wears the tight white suits and studded belts of end-stage Elvis, and needs no encouragement to give demonstrations of outstanding pelvic gyration during tea-break; Sadie, sulky, bossy, self-conscious, stooping, wrapping herself in cardigans and anoraks, a rich grain of dark hairs on each shin underneath a pop sock; Tom, with faint frail stuttering speech and a card in his wallet to record that MY NAME IS TOM MCMANUS I LIVE AT 48 PERTH VILLAS; and Louise, who brings a briefcase and unpacks very carefully with stubby fingers, laying on the desk the exercise book, pencil-case, slide-rule, calculator, diary, address book, and small framed photograph of her dead father.

On my first evening, Louise wanted to continue with the exercises in the big thin book which came from inside the briefcase. 'These,' she muttered, indignant, her small riven hand smoothing the open page: HOW MANY? When she writes the answers, her bulbous eyes are unblinking inside her glasses but her large tongue flips frequently onto her lips. Frazer took a book, too, *Workbook 6D*, from his carrier bag which also contained a pencil, a pencil sharpener, an umbrella, and Elvis records. Tom sat smiling with his hands folded in his lap. Sadie's objections rattled among us: *Louise, put that pen down when She's talking to you; Shut up, Frazer, or I'll put your fucking records in the BIN; Tom, for Christ's sake; AND you, Miss.*

HOW MANY APPLES? Louise dabbed at the drawings, reciting quietly, 'One . . . two . . . three.' Then she began writing the answer. Sadie was insisting to me that Tom's book was in the chest of drawers: 'THERE, I'm telling you.' I was searching the drawers while she shouted after me, 'I can tell the time. It's quarter to seven, no, sixteen minutes to seven, one minute to go. And I was born at half past three in the morning, imagine! My poor old mum!'

The drawer was full of collages of fruit and vegetables. 'I was born at seven in the evening,' I said. 'What is a good time to have a baby?'

'Breakfast time,' Sadie replied immediately.

'Breakfast time?' My fingers slipped over a small pile of books. 'But then you'd *miss breakfast*. I *love* breakfast.'

'But you're *you*,' she said wearily, 'and I'm *me*, and I *hate* breakfast.'

I returned to the table holding a small plain book marked *Thomas McManus*. 'Ay, that's it,' Sadie said, satisfied, 'that's it, Tom, ay?' Tom stuttered politely, agreeably, indistinctly.

Frazer was adding a third fifty pence piece to two on his desk. 'Money bags,' commented Sadie, disgusted.

'Yeah,' agreed Frazer, laughing, rubbing his dry hands together, 'I'm a millionaire.' He deposited the third piece with a small flourish, and folded his arms. 'There's three,' he said to me.

'Which makes . . .?' I was smiling encouragingly, teasingly.

'Three.' Very definite.

'Yes . . .' I slid onto my stool, and leant avidly towards him.

'Dickhead,' said Sadie.

'But what are they?' I waggled my forefinger at the coins.

'Fifties.' Very confident.

'Yes, exactly.' Wonderful. 'And three fifties . . .?'

'Ay, three,' he pronounced conclusively. He was smiling broadly, smiling at everyone, even Sadie. And that was when I glanced down at the book in my hands and saw the pages and pages, years and years, of copying and improvising: MY NAME IS TOM MCMANUS TO M T MC.

Ever since then, since the first evening, I have tried to avoid copying and workbooks. And I try to reserve the first half hour for discussion, despite Sadie. I bring a newspaper, sometimes several newspapers; sometimes magazines, but *current* magazines – passed on by my flatmates – and not the dental surgery flotsam that fills the drawers behind my desk. Louise persists in taking her book from her briefcase at the beginning of the evening, and sighs with enormous sadness when asked to join the discussion, but she listens actively, nodding and muttering. Once she told us about Heaven during our discussion of an IRA bombing, earnestly illustrating the lecture by wielding the photograph of her father. 'Christ,' Sadie repeated throughout Louise's lecture, quietly, unfathomably: 'Christ.'

One of the other tutors, the only man, Raymond, seems to be reponsible for the urn. At half past seven the steam is roaring and rattling beneath the silver cymbal lid. Once Raymond was away and everyone forgot the urn; and the Hall was shockingly silent until someone organized Elvis, Abba, and Showaddywaddy. There seems to be a rota for clearing and washing up, but unfortunately it is enforced by Sadie: *YOU, you fucking eejit, get the cups.* The Regional Organizer, whom I know from the induction course, usually arrives for tea. She comes in a little ladies' car, carrying a cavernous handbag. She is known by her first name, like a queen: Lena.

Lena is greeted with excited shrieks and protestations of affection from everyone; including Frazer, who stops dancing briefly before launching into a special demonstration, and even Sadie. Lena wears outfits, and it seems that there is a new one for every visit: colour co-ordinated, navy, lemon, burgundy, from chain stores and catalogues. She is very large, larger-than-life, but she has a tiny high voice and is jacked onto stilettos. She is the-tart-with-the-heart-of-gold, welfare state version. Her layers of experience drop a soft sand of anecdote: *When I worked with old folks . . . When I was with the blind kids . . .* She smokes on me and tells me about her son: *I said Davey, it's harder for kids these days, don't think I don't know, dear, no one is expecting the moon from you.*

The other tutors are a mystery to me; none of them come from my induction course. They seem to have been born in the building, measuring the years since in Christmases: *Do you remember the panto...? Do you remember the party...? Do you remember the snow...?* Shona is the only other tutor under thirty, and she is eighteen. I know that she is eighteen because we had a birthday tea break in her honour. The record player managed *Happy Birthday* by

Altered Images, and Shona was presented with the card that we had been asked by Raymond to sign in secret during the evening. Shona showed everyone the frail gold outline of a key hanging on a fine chain around her neck; and, thanking us for the card, added, 'Thank God there's no cake.' Raymond explained to me that Shona works all week behind the counter in a bakery. Then Shona returned to us, to the tutors, to the urn, sitting on the table to smoke. She is always stiff in crackly jumpers and clean jeans but her feet flop free in flip-flops. It was Shona who said to me, a few weeks ago, as if she was commenting on the price of bread, 'Did you know that Sadie's sister has AIDS?'

'No,' I said carefully, 'I didn't.' *But I do now*.

'Ay,' she said, 'and the kid, the wee baby.'

Now, suddenly, I realize that I have been worlds away, that Jane has turned on Lyndsay who is suddenly lurking in the doorway, fiddling with his volume control.

'Tell him,' she is shrieking through a mouthful of crispbread. 'They're my headphones.'

It seems to me that the headphones are administering electric shocks to Lyndsay, who is dazed and jerking. He cocks a speaker, baring an ear, and asks innocuously, 'Excuse me?'

Jane opens her mouth but Mum interrupts without turning around: 'I do hate that expression. It's not *Excuse me*, Lyndsay, it's *Pardon*.'

Seemingly deaf, Lyndsay takes a handful of sugar lumps from the bowl on the table.

'Lyndsay!' bawls Jane in protest – at the headphones, the sugar lumps, or both? – and her cry is sticky with gritty Scandabrot saliva.

Lyndsay crunches emphatically on the sugar.

'Mum,' I say, 'they're the same: *Pardon me* and *Excuse me*.'

'*Excuse me* is American,' she replies calmly, the peeler rasping regularly on the latest potato.

'But you like American,' I protest. 'Your favourite programme was *Hawaii Five-O*.'

223

Jane approaches Lyndsay, biting savagely into another crispbread. 'Give me the goddamn headphones. I need them.'

Mum emits a hurricane of a sigh and pauses dramatically over the potato. '*Hawaii Five-O* is Hawaii, not America. Moreover, *Hawaii Five-O* is Steve McGarrett.'

Electronic whispers fill the room because the headphones have been ripped from Lyndsay's ears. Jane's claw retracts. 'I need them for the bathroom,' she insists.

Mum turns briefly, horrified. 'No electronic equipment in the bathroom.'

'Batteries,' mutters Jane.

Mum turns again. 'What did you call me?'

Jane flames with indignation. 'Nothing!'

'*Streets of San Francisco*,' I say quickly, 'you loved *Streets of San Francisco*.'

'Michael Douglas,' she replies.

Lyndsay has adjusted the headphones to fit once again over his ears. Now he shoves Jane. She stumbles into Lauren who is coming back through the door. 'Christ,' says Lauren to Jane, derisively.

'*In The Heat Of The Night*,' I try again.

'Sidney Poitier.'

Now I remember how Mum hates the Kennedys. She was at Ante Natal when she heard about the first assassination, and she upset the nurses by saying, 'He had it coming to him.' Once, I made the mistake of asking the reason for this hatred.

'Irish womanizers.'

She had assumed that the assassin was a woman, A Woman Scorned. She showed little sympathy for Jackie: 'She did all right, marrying Old Man Yacht.'

Jane, rubbing her arms, is shouting again, 'Tell him, Mum.'

Mum plants the heels of her palms onto the chopping board, to brace herself. 'Will you *please*,' she pleads to no one in particular.

'It's *Lyndsay*,' Jane continues wildly.

'I don't think so,' comments Lauren, looping a forefinger inside the neck of the open jar of peanut butter.

Lyndsay is watching Jane, very closely. 'I wouldn't mind if you *asked*,' he says, distrustful, disgusted.

'Why *should* I ask?' The famous furious whine again. 'They're mine.'

'Jane . . .' starts Mum, slowly.

'Lyndsay . . .' warns Jane.

Mum mutters to her own brisk twisting hands, 'And to think that I – an only child – was naive enough to assume that all you kids would play nicely with one another.'

'Mum,' objects Lauren, sucking her finger, 'we're grown up now.' She spins the lid down onto the jar. 'Well, some of us are grown up.'

Mum slips a dark blue glance towards me. 'And, sometimes, lately, I find myself wishing that you'd all been boys. Boys are no trouble, compared.'

Lauren deposits the jar of peanut butter in the cupboard with a flourish. 'Yes, Mommy Dearest, but we look better in dresses.'

'Speak for yourself,' I mutter.

Lauren smiles benignly at me. 'Don't do yourself down.'

Lyndsay has been laboriously extracting the headphones from his head, coiling the lead. Now he hands the bundle to Jane. Jane's muscles are in spasm, she is all fists and frown.

I remind Mum, 'You named your children after Americans: Erin from *The Waltons;* Lauren Bacall.'

To my horror, Mum whirls around to face me, the peeler dripping peel. 'Am I not allowed to change my mind, ever?' Her voice is surging and bubbling with despair.

In the background, Jane's threats are bumping Lyndsay towards the door – 'Don't you . . . and next time . . .' – and as she turns away from him with her precious bounty, the bundle of wires and two tiny speakers in bobbles of orange sponge, she treads on Lauren's foot.

Lauren winces and says, 'Pick on someone your own size, Granny.'

Jane replies sourly, 'Sod off, Know-all.'

Mum howls, 'Why don't you *all* sod off? Leave me alone. This is *my* house, *my* home. Go away, *all* of you. Leave me in peace.'

For a moment, no one moves, no one says a word. Then Lauren says reasonably and very confidently, 'Mum, this is *our* home.'

And it occurs to me that I have never before seen Mum turn pale.

1987

....

'Your post is on the table,' says Mum, following me closely into the kitchen, knocking the buckles on the huge bag on my shoulder.

Whenever I visit there is post for me, propped against the salt cellar in the middle of the table. It is mostly obsolete, always impersonal: stray Reader's Digest suggestions of riches, and mailshots from London theatres and from college. The letters from college, appealing for donations, begin, *As you know* . . . and then detail the continuing renovation of the Master's Lodge.

I drop my bag to the floor.

'Aren't you going to open it?' Mum's question whines with irritation rather than excitement, and her arm arcs over me towards the solitary envelope.

'In a minute,' I complain. I take the envelope from her. It is patched with obviously foreign stamps and postal marks. It is thin, light, probably a card or an invitation. The handwriting – *Miss E Blaney* – is familiar. I ease the tip of my forefinger beneath the flap and along the fold, cracking open the pale thin shell of paper. The card is overwhelmingly pink, a drawing of a fat laughing baby. Inside, my name is written at the top, *Lalie*. It strikes me that this bold black name is a reminder for the sender, a name from a list, rather than a greeting, a real *Dear Lalie*. Beneath my name extends a script of both written and printed words: . . . *Martin and Roz* . . . ARE PLEASED TO ANNOUNCE THE BIRTH OF . . . *Danielle Clare* . . . ON . . . *21 May* . . . WEIGHING . . . *7lbs 6oz.*

Underneath this is a handwritten message: *She's lovely! Well worth the obesity and incontinence* . . . *Hope to see you soon, Love M & R.*

'Roz has had a baby,' I tell Mum.

'Where?' she exclaims from across the kitchen, meaning Let-me-see. 'I must send a card.'

'Mum, you don't *like* Roz.'

She is craning over my shoulder. 'So? New babies are fair game.'

I point to the top line, *Martin and Roz*, and then the bottom line, *M & R*. 'Look,' I say, disgusted.

'Oh, for God's sake, does it matter?' she shrieks, too near my ear, and stalks from the room. Not an inappropriate response, I suppose, for someone who has spent her whole adult life as the invisible part of Mr and Mrs John Blaney.

The pink baby on the front of the card is not a newborn baby. But, then, neither is Roz's baby, not by now. Roz's baby will be chuckling, now, and wriggling, fully receptive to doggies and choo-choos and careful spoonfuls of sloppy solids. Newborn babies are soft blind bundles, striving to suckle. Their tiny useless legs are cold white tassels.

The door bounces open again and Erin comes towards me, her baby jutting from her hip. The baby swivels to face me. The rudimentary bones of her skull still bear a thin coating of luminous white hair. Erin is smiling broadly but the smile is not so much for me as for the baby. 'Heeere,' she sings, 'here's Lalie.' The baby responds perfectly to Erin's tone of excitement, and my expression of delight. Her face expands into a huge smile.

'Weeell,' I sing in reply, 'you're looking remarkably good for a baby born in a hospital lift.' As I take her onto my lap, I glance upwards at Erin: 'How's she doing?'

'Three teeth,' Erin replies proudly.

Smell-of-baby sweetens the air around me: milk, talc, towelling. Dory's sleek white head turns below me as she looks to Erin for reassurance. 'Theeere,' Erin says to her, 'Nansie told us that Lalie was here, didn't she? She said, "Guess who's in the driveway with a huge black bag?" '

'Well, Nansie is in a huge black moodie with me now.'

Erin looks at me with concern. 'Is she? Why?'

'Oh, nothing. The usual sort of thing.'

'That's odd,' she muses with a faint frown, 'because all we've been hearing all week is Lalie-this and Lalie-that, and When-Lalie-comes.'

'Obviously over-excitement,' I mutter, unconvinced. I am slipping my fingertips over the veil of Dory's hair.

Dory was born in a lift between Casualty and Maternity. Mum tells us that the nurse was pleading with Erin to *Hang on*. Then Mum adds, *And I thought, Yes, hang on for a decade or so, please, Erin.* She likes to tell everyone that the birth in the lift was the least of the surprises. I had not been around when the news of the pregnancy broke at the end of last summer. I was in Edinburgh. The phone rang, I picked up the receiver, said Hello, and a voice said, 'Erin's pregnant.' Luckily I recognized the voice.

'Mum,' I said, 'I could have been one of my flatmates.'

'But you're not,' she replied crossly.

'What do you mean, Erin's pregnant?'

'What do you mean, What do I mean? Erin's *pregnant*. Four months gone.'

Four months gone. She told me about Erin's weary, faint confession – 'Mum, I'm Pregnant' – in the queue at the check-out during the weekly shop, and the glass of water fetched by the Shift Manager for Mum, the congratulations and commiserations to them both from staff and shoppers. She told me that Erin had had two positive tests and a trip to the doctor. I lowered my tone to a solemn setting: 'Does she realize that she doesn't have to continue with this pregnancy?' I meant, *Do YOU realize . . .?*

'Oh yes,' chattered Mum, 'I've tried everything but she says this is what she wants.'

Then she said, 'What will your father say?'

'You mean he doesn't know?'

She blew irritation down the line. 'Of course he doesn't know. What will he say?' Her voice weakened in terror.

'Why does it matter? What is it to do with him?' I tried.

Another gust of distant fury. 'Don't start all that nonsense on

229

me, Lalie. He's the breadwinner around here.' There was a pause. 'He'll kill her.'

Because, for Dad, this invisible out-of-wedlock baby would be a deepening womb rather than a future bundle of milk-and-talc-and-towelling, rather than a future shrieker of choo-choo, a future paddler in the shallow end of the pool, a future owner of gerbils, a future star of a series of birthday photos. His own invisible Blaney babies were promises of family and future but somehow Erin's invisible baby would be nothing more than evidence of sex, and – worse – *pre-marital* sex.

Unfortunately this raised a question which I could not resist: 'How did Erin get pregnant?'

Mum squeaked. 'I always thought I'd be explaining all that to *Erin*, not to *you*.'

'Mum,' I chided, tiring, '*Who?*'

'Who do you think? That silly little boyfriend, Louis.'

I imagined a sixteen-year-old Louis: skinny, nervous, embarrassed, horrified, with a sports bag. 'And what does he say about all this?'

'What does he *say*? He says that his mother says that he is to keep away from Erin.'

I was surprised: surely grandmothers are grandmothers, grandly maternal, doting into their dotage. 'And?'

'And what?'

'And so how are they coping, him and Erin?'

'I've told you. He's keeping away from Erin. He hasn't been here for a week or so.'

'Because of his mother? But love-conquers-all, doesn't it?' I was thinking of the telltale whisper of gravel on the blinding blackness of my windowpane during the sleepless nights before exams, the honey-colour of human below me on the lawn, the cold stairs beneath my silent soles, the warm body next to mine in bed: love-conquers-all, including curfews.

'Well, in this case, Mother conquers all, because it seems that Someone Has Got To Him. If-she-wants-to-ruin-her-own-life-then-that's-fine-but-don't-let-her-ruin-yours: that sort of thing, I imagine, don't you?'

No, I did not imagine, I could not imagine. 'Apron strings,' I said weakly, doubtfully: why are apron strings only for *boys*?

'No,' said Mum firmly. 'Purse strings: the florist shop, remember? A budding career in floristry.' She faltered, surprised by her own words, and laughed. But immediately, she was serious again. 'Whoever would have thought that a florist could be so unfeeling?'

Apparently, when Dad was told, he said very little, mostly involving repetition of the word *stupid: You have been so stupid, Erin; This is the most stupid thing you have ever done; How could you be so stupid?* Eventually Erin said, 'This is a baby, Dad, not an exam.' Then he yelled, 'And what are you going to do?' And Lyndsay, lurking, grinning, said, 'She's going to have a baby, Grandpops.'

When the baby was born, I went to stay with friends in London and travelled out to the hospital. Erin, sitting on her bed, was holding the baby in the conventional position, in the crook of her arm, convenient for both mother-and-baby intimacy and public display. At the foot of the bed stood four girls with careful hairstyles and short, simple clothes. Presumably they were Erin's friends. Mum was sitting in the only chair, at the head of the bed. Lauren was reading the cards on the locker; Lyndsay was looking out of the window, humming. The four eager faces at the foot of the bed were wide-eyed, easily triggered into wide smiles, forming a dutiful chorus to Mum's conversation by responding on cue with appreciative nods and murmurs.

Mum explained to me: 'Your Dad said that we're to call him when we're ready, and he'll pop in again and pick us up.' She nodded towards the baby, which was inanimate, unresponsive, asleep. 'And he reckons that she looks like Jane.'

Jane?

I asked Erin, 'Does she have a name?' I detected a seething sigh from Mum but Erin was oblivious, realigning the baby's limbs.

'Dorothy,' she said.

'Jesus Christ,' Mum whispered sadly, but resigned.

231

Lauren spoke from the inside of one of the cards. 'Mum is such a pooper.' Then she slotted the card back among the others, and leaned over the baby, one small perfect nose nudging towards another. 'Isn't she, eh, Dory?'

Another of Erin's surprises was the four O level passes. And, at the end of last summer, she enrolled for evening classes with the ultimate aim of chiropody. When I went to the hospital, I asked Erin about the classes. Mum loomed from the chair to interrupt: 'Erin, how can you? It's *feet*.'

'Yes,' Erin replied patiently, practised, 'I know it's feet.' Between her thumb and forefinger she was rolling one of the baby's feet, a tiny toggle. 'But, well,' she shrugged, 'it's useful and I can work on my own, at my own pace, have my own business.' A chiropody shop. Then she frowned and added inexplicably, 'I would have preferred osteopathy.'

Now I ask Erin, 'Are you still going to the evening classes?'

'Yes,' she replies cheerfully, squatting to undertake some mysterious motherly function involving Dory's bib and mouth.

'But how do you manage? With Dory, I mean.'

There is a cursory blue flash from Erin's intent face. 'But Dory goes to bed at six,' she tells me gently.

'Oh, yes, I suppose so.' I nod towards the card on the table. 'Roz Smith has had a baby.' And then it occurs to me: 'Do you remember Roz?'

Rising, Erin is frowning, doubtful. Then she tries: 'Blonde streak?'

I nod. 'Green eyes.'

'Oh yes!' she sparkles with recognition, 'like those fake contact lenses.'

'Yes, well, she has had a baby, a little girl.'

'Oh,' says Erin, fairly gladly.

'Who has had a baby?' Jane asks flatly, bustling through the doorway, sheer nylon squeaking faintly against the lining of her skirt. She directs a prim cold little smile at me and says, 'Hello,' as if the previous question was directed as someone else, or no one in particular.

232

'Roz,' I answer.

'Oh, Roz.' The glance glints with superiority, but she says nothing more so I cannot answer. She swings into the fridge, extracts a small bottle of mineral water, and leaves the room.

Our gazes drop from the doorway and link again. 'Lovely Aunty Jane,' I say. And then I return to Dory: 'Isn't she, eh?'

Below me, Dory's mini face, captured briefly by anxiety and incomprehension, reflects my own big smile.

'And I think you would be a brilliant bridesmaid,' I tell her, 'despite your buggy.'

It was when I was at the hospital, visiting Erin and newborn Dory, that Jane flounced down the ward with Duncan, with magnanimous smiles for all of us, to announce, 'We're getting married.'

'To whom?' asked Mum, to the quiet delight of the chorus of girls. Erin smiled politely at Jane, dreamily; and Lyndsay's deep blue gaze swung from the window and then back again, expressionless. And now, today, it is the day before the wedding, and I am here, home, under duress.

It'll be a small wedding, Mum insisted to me whenever she was trying to persuade me to come. Lately, it has become a *tiny wedding*. 'Please come,' she begged me, last week, 'for the photos.' The photos of the Blaneys in lines like skittles. Then she said, 'Please come to keep me company.'

'Mum,' I said sarcastically, 'what about all those other daughters of yours? *Jane* will be there.'

She puffed derision and despair into the phone. 'Don't remind me.'

But why such a small wedding for Jane? I had been expecting plans for a video with the soundtrack from *Chariots of Fire*. Is it an attempt by Jane to deny her disappointment at the prospect of the registry office? Mum comes back into the room with a pair of shoes in her hands. 'You've seen the blushing bride, then?' she asks me, flatly.

I shrug. 'She didn't look much like a bride.' And she was blushless as usual.

Mum is on the floor, foraging through the contents of an ice cream container full of shoe-cleaning materials. 'She's home from work early, to transform herself.'

Lauren, following, calls ahead, 'And she'll want the bathroom all evening.'

Erin murmurs and hauls Dory from my lap. 'Bathtime,' she announces, her lips grazing the baby's feathery white scalp; and she retreats with the hot soft bundle, passing Lauren in the doorway.

Lauren also has a pair of shoes in her hands. 'Lalie!' she beams. 'Ça va?'

'Ça-va-bien-merci.'

Mum, on her knees, on the floor, is sifting the contents of the box, a complicated coinage of flat round tins, and muttering unhappily, 'Here, Lauren, this one, or maybe this one, here.'

Lauren, distracted, glances downwards. 'Mum, I want to get into the bathroom before Jane,' she explains patiently. 'I can't wash my hair tomorrow because it'll frizz.'

'B.J.,' says Mum sourly, '*Before Jane*. I'll be glad when she has gone.'

'Why hasn't she gone?' I ask.

Mum pauses, one hand gloved by a shoe, and says, 'They have been gazumped twice recently. And he has sold his flat. He is staying with friends.'

'In an old folks' home,' laughs Lauren.

'And, so, her bedroom . . .' Mum jerks her head towards the ceiling, 'is full of that stuff.'

'What stuff?'

'Underwear.'

'No, Lalie,' corrects Lauren impatiently, urgently, 'it's underwear to sell.'

'It's Jane's business,' grunts Mum, scrubbing the shoe with a harsh sooty brush.

'I was only asking,' I reply petulantly, affronted.

'Nooooo,' Lauren warbles with delight, 'it's Jane's business. She runs a business selling underwear.'

Mum glances very briefly at me over the darkening shoe. 'I thought you knew. She sells it on a motorbike.'

I look to Lauren for aid. She is shimmering above Mum with secret silent laughter. 'Personal delivery by motorbike courier,' she says, swinging a shoe by the heel.

'What?'

'Noooo,' growls Mum, changing shoes, 'Jane doesn't *ride* the bike.'

'But who wants underwear delivered by bike?'

Mum's head is bowed and shaking with effort, and I can see pink skin inside the blonde mesh of hair. 'City-types, apparently.'

'Men,' elaborates Lauren, 'who want to give lingerie as presents but are too embarrassed to go and choose, or can't be bothered. Or, perhaps, ladies who suddenly have a date for the evening . . .'

'Lauren . . .' warns Mum, pained.

'I'm only saying what Jane says.'

'Well, Jane shouldn't say. Not to you.' Mum's exasperation leaps across the kitchen in a wide-eyed shrug to seek support from me. 'I'd like to see Jane bringing up a ten-year-old.'

'Let's get tomorrow over, first . . .' I suggest.

'Don't remind me.'

'So what is it like, this underwear?' Has anyone peeked inside the boxes?

Lauren says mildly, 'It's OK if you want to be trussed up in bits of shiny nylon.'

Mum looks doubtfully at her.

'How erotic,' I agree sarcastically.

'Eulalia.' Mum's troubled gaze has transferred to me. Presumably *erotic* is out of bounds.

'What seems so odd to me,' expounds Lauren, 'is that all this stuff is for *women*, when *men* are so unalluring. And, what's more, men don't care what women look like, not really, not once they're . . .'

235

'Lauren!' Mum reasserts authority.

Lauren turns archly. 'Everyone knows that, Mum.'

Mum looks blankly at me. 'Sometimes I think I'm on the set of *The Omen*.' The gaze returns sharply to Lauren. 'You're ten years old and you're not supposed to talk like that.'

'Mum,' replies Lauren calmly, ominously, 'these are facts of life.'

'The only fact concerning me, at the moment, is the fact of your dirty shoes.'

Lauren flails the shoes. 'I must wash my hair.'

Mum snatches the shoes and shouts, 'Off you go, then.'

Lauren bounds from the room, her perfectly clean hair bouncing on her shoulders. It is more than a year, now, since she came with Mum to stay with me in Edinburgh. Mum had called me to inform me that, 'We fancy a trip.' She said that Dad and Lyndsay were away at the TT races on the Isle of Man.

I was surprised: 'I didn't know that Lyndsay was interested in racing.'

'He's not,' she answered. 'Yet.'

'And where's Erin?'

I could hear her patience fracturing. 'She's *here*, of course.'

'But will she be all right?' Pregnant Erin.

'She's seventeen,' Mum groaned. 'She has lived here for seventeen years. She knows where everything is; she knows how to lock the door: what else is there to know?'

So they came, on the coach. Mum came down the few narrow steps with a collection of straw bags, plastic carrier bags, and soft cloth shoulder-bags: all hand luggage, or, rather, leg-room luggage. Lauren had a huge new suitcase in the locker, extracted with difficulty by the driver. 'What do you have in there?' he complained in a tobacco-scented wheeze.

'All my earthly possessions,' she said sweetly and very sadly, 'so please don't begrudge me.'

'Lauren . . .' admonished Mum, whirling around too late.

The suitcase seemed strange to me. Were people still buying suitcases, proper suitcases, and not merely finding them in the cupboard under the stairs? Even the name seemed strange: a case for suits. Surely most people were buying haversacks or holdalls? Stranger, then, was the fact that Lauren's suitcase was a birthday present, a specific request.

'Don't ask me,' wailed Mum whilst Lauren displayed the suitcase to me, coaxing it up onto its tiny back wheels.

Later, back at the flat, I glanced through the doorway into the spare bedroom, vacated temporarily by holiday-making Coralie, and saw some of the contents of Lauren's suitcase arranged meticulously on the mantelpiece: a green purse; a small black address book or diary; half a packet of polos, topped with a tough twist of silver; a bottle of perfume; a teddy bear wearing a tiny tartan scarf; an awesome hairbrush and a pair of electric curling tongs for straightening her hair.

They stayed for three nights, two days. On the first day, in the morning, they wanted to go shopping. We met for lunch in the Modern Art Gallery.

'Scenic route, eh?' chirped Mum, arriving with Lauren after following my directions through Dean Village. Lauren was crackling with carrier bags.

'This place is fabulous for brownies,' I said.

'Brownies are American,' puzzled Mum, 'not Scottish.'

'Not any more.'

They wrote postcards after their brownies, pressing the words painstakingly against the pine tabletop. Glancing at one of Mum's postcards I saw *Last night we had a nice vegetarian meal*. Vegetarian meal? Baked potato?

I cooked on the second evening. Friends came to the flat throughout the evening with poorly suppressed curiosity, ostensibly to return books or borrow pyrex and toilet roll: Maddy, Jordan, Neil. Neil stayed for the meal.

Alex was there, too: our temporary replacement in the flat for Amanda, who was on an ecological expedition to Africa for six months. Neil sat chatting, asking Lauren about English schools and exams, and attempting to answer Mum's questions about Holyrood

Palace and Mary Queen of Scots. Later, at Mum's request, he listed his sisters: four of them, finishing with Maria.

'Continental,' concluded Mum excitably, meaning Catholic.

Throughout the evening, Alex wandered unasked around the kitchen, uncorking the wine, dressing the salad, whipping the cream.

I watched Alex and Neil with a Waltham-squint, trying to see what Mum was seeing: scruffy? Were they scruffy-young-men? Perhaps not so young, in a sense: mid-twenties without proper homes, proper jobs, proper clothes, and cars, wives, babies. And not so young for Lauren, of course. How old were they, for Lauren? For Lauren, did they look as old as fathers, teachers, shopkeepers, newsreaders? How much did Mum and Lauren share a view of them? Mum-and-Lauren, who had always seemed so distinct, were suddenly aligned on one side of the table, with identical sceptical Blaney-blue gazes and tidy blonde Blaney-waves. And where was I? I was knocked back and forth across the table all evening between the tired, too-bright Blaney smiles and the blank but busy eyes of the boys.

A few months later Mum phoned me to tell me that Lauren, who is in a local Amateur Dramatics Society, had the title role in the play.

'Eggy . . . Eggy . . .' she struggled with her memory.

'Eggy?'

'. . . Joe Eggy?'

'Joe Egg.'

She was surprised. 'You know it? About brain damage? It's well-known?'

I shrugged. 'Well, yes, it's quite well-known.'

'Have I seen it?'

Rather than saying I-don't-know and risking a conversation full of With-Burt-Lancaster? I said, 'No.'

'Oh.'

'How did she get the part?' I was enthralled.

'Well,' Mum settled into the story, 'she practised every evening

238

for a week before the audition, in a trolley outside the supermarket, taking her best friend to push. I'm surprised that there were no complaints.' She paused. 'Lauren favours method acting, you see. I know about method acting because I read an article about that man who put on a lot of weight to play a boxer.'

I murmur wordlessly to prompt the story onwards.

'Which seems rather unnecessary: twelve stone, thirteen stone, fourteen, who can tell the difference?'

'Yes,' I said ambiguously; then, 'has she told you that she has no lines?'

'Yes, no lines to learn; and what a relief after you going around the house muttering, *Out, out* . . .' Then she paused sharply to confide, 'I was worried about Lauren playing a boy, but she reminded me about those principals, girls playing young boys.'

So, *Equus*, next, for Lauren?

Lauren rang me a few days later, saying, 'Hi Lalie, it's Lauren, I want to talk to you about brain damage.'

'Not again,' I joked.

'Ha Ha,' she said acidly, 'seriously. I need to know everything about epilepsy.'

I was unable to take leave from work to see the play, but Mum told me about the rave reviews and encouraged Lauren to come from the telly to the phone.

'So you're going to be an actress now?' I patronized hopefully.

'No way,' she drawled. 'Who told you that? Acting is a mug's game. Speaking someone else's words.' Then she added, 'I'll act only if I can't do anything else.'

So now I ask Mum, 'What are Lauren's plans, currently?'

Mum seems furious with Lauren's scuffed shoes. 'You mean today, tomorrow, for the wedding?'

'No, I mean for life.'

'Oh, life.' She slackens and glances mildly upwards from the thickening darkening leather. 'Harvard.'

'Harvard?'

'But I've told her that we might have some trouble raising the fares and fees, so please can she consider somewhere nearer home, follow in the footsteps of her dear old sister.' She places Lauren's shoes side by side. 'Now, do your shoes need polishing?'

'No,' I reply, perhaps too frantically. I have decided not to break the news that my shoes are not the type that need polishing. If she says, tomorrow, *But they're ballet shoes*, I shall say something like, *And – to think! – you bought me my very first pair all those years ago*.

'Lauren is a saint, though,' she says, 'compared to Lyndsay, at the moment.'

I am baffled, so I shrug speculatively. 'He's three years older.'

She fixes on me. 'Do you really think so?' she asks fervently.

What does she mean? 'Well . . . he's thirteen, and she's ten . . .'

'You think she'll be the same when she's thirteen? You think Lyndsay's problem is his age?' She has been pausing on all fours on the newspaper, but now she retreats, covering her tracks, clearing the crackling debris. 'I can't remember any of you others having been so awful at thirteen.'

'You always say that. You forget, every time.'

She smirks, pushing the container full of cleaning materials into a non-existent space in the cupboard. 'Erin was no trouble,' she says.

'No. Excepting Erin, then.'

'Which leaves you and Jane.' She stares meaningfully at me, so I busy myself by replacing Roz's pink baby in the envelope, and putting the envelope in the pocket on the side of my bag.

Mum is washing her hands around a palmful of washing up liquid. 'All those old dears at the supermarket,' she begins again, jollily, 'whenever they see Erin with the buggy they think they're seeing the work of the devil.' She snorts a laugh. 'If only they knew!' The tea towel flies from the hook into her snatching hand. 'Erin's trouble-free adolescence is the world's best kept secret.'

'But what's wrong with Lynd?'

She slaps the tea towel back onto the hook and sighs hugely. 'Firstly, the Scouts.'

I frown in alarm.

'No, he stopped going to the Scouts because, he said, they were paramilitary.'

I can do nothing but nod, carefully.

'But you all went to Scouts,' she wails, 'without any complaint.'

'Mum,' I begin gently, 'that's a physical impossibility because we're all girls.'

'Scouts, Guides,' she whoops, 'what's the difference? It's all participation.' She takes the breadknife from the block and tentatively tests the blade on the tip of her forefinger. 'This is blunt,' she says resentfully. It clunks back into the block. 'Lyndsay won't do anything.'

Now Erin sweeps again from the doorway, thin soles flapping across the tiles. Dory, riding Erin's bouncing hip, is damp. Her wet hair is smeared across her scalp. Her crazed smile rotates, and she gnaws a tiny, sore finger.

'Lovely and clean!' Erin announces indiscriminately, slotting Dory into the highchair. 'Biscuit!'

Mum races Erin, turning swiftly and extracting a rusk from somewhere inside one of the cupboards. Flourishing it, she lunges melodramatically towards the highchair. Dory seems impressed, and bites circumspectly into the rusk.

Erin drifts away from Dory, and engages Mum's attention with a faint but close wave. 'I'm just off to make a quick phone call, OK?'

Mum nods. 'If Lyndsay's still on the phone, tell him that he has five seconds to get off.' She turns wearily to me as Erin leaves the echoes of her footsteps to crack against the walls. 'No one needs to speak to anyone for half an hour.'

I open my mouth to reply, but then close it again: where would I start?

'And he says that he won't come to the wedding.' She pads across the kitchen and stretches outwards from the doorway. Her mouth slackens and her eyes lose focus: she is listening. Suddenly she explodes with, '*Off, now!*' Then she returns. 'He says that it would be hypocritical because he is a non-believer.' She stares until she realizes that there will be no response from me. I remain cautious. 'So I said to him, *Lyndsay, I'm not asking for a conversion.* I said to him, *It's a registry office, it's civil, which is more than YOU are.*'

I feel an overwhelming urge to lock myself in the bathroom. So I fuss with my bag, extracting bottles of lotion. Mum is dabbing with the tea towel at the slops of rusk on Dory's chin. 'But he insists that the ceremony has God in it, somewhere. I told him that everything has God in it somewhere. Even *Goodbye.*' She towers above me, inspecting the tea towel: it fails the test; she bundles it into the hull of the washing machine through the open porthole. 'I told him that Goodbye means God-be-with-you . . .' Above my head, an opened drawer bounces back into the unit . . . 'That's right, isn't it?'

I say nothing, but the zip shrieks from the top of my bag.

'So I said to him, *You still say Bye, eh?*' She leans emphatically on a worksurface, watching me. I am wildly envious of Dory's rusky nonchalance in the corner of my field of Mum-filled vision.

'And do you know . . .?' These slow, relished words contain the promise of a little laugh. 'Do you know, ever since, he has been saying *Ciao?*'

I laugh upwards, and rise, but already she is frowning again. 'This bloody wedding,' she mutters.

'Mum,' I goad gently, 'aren't you pleased? One of your daughters is getting married.'

The frown sharpens into a scowl. 'I'd rather it wasn't to Duncan.'

Somehow I know that she is joking. As far as Mum is concerned, Duncan will do. For Jane. She snaps away and listens again in the doorway for Lyndsay, without success. 'Do you want some cheese?' she sighs, returning.

I am baffled.

'Or something. Aren't you hungry?'

'Oh. No. Thanks.'

'There's a lovely crusty loaf. Poppy seeds.' Still the deep frown.

'No, thanks. I'm fine. For the moment.' Throughout the journey, on the train, suspended somewhere, nowhere, on four hundred miles of electrified line, I was eating food that I do not normally eat: crisps, and biscuits bought in a pack of three from the buffet. Chocolate, too, bought with newspapers at both stations. Then throat pastilles to freshen my mouth. I will eat properly later; I will hunt in the back of the garage among the tall mummies of ex-carpet for the freezer, and then hunt in the freezer for vegetables. I suspect that I can look forward to a meal of spongy cauliflower florets glittering with sweetcorn.

With both hands, Mum is hauling the loaf from the breadbin. The legendary crust creaks inside the starchy swaddling of the white paper bag. A black scurf of poppy seeds falls onto the formica surface. 'I'm starving,' she mutters. 'I'm late with the tea today. I'll do pizzas in a while.' She pronounces *pizza* as *Pisa*. This reminds me that *Nazi* has always been *Nazzy*, seemingly a hybrid of *gnat* and *mozzy*. How can she have spent her whole life hearing these words, but continue to mispronounce them? Perhaps it is conscious. Perhaps she is ridiculing Nazis. Perhaps pizzas came from Pisa.

From the window I watch the faint flashing of falling rain on a puddle on the paving. It has been raining, on and off, North and South, for a week. There has been no sun at all. The woolly sky is thick and heavy with water. Here, on the ground, there is no residue of warmth. Today, when I was running for trains and buses, I was surprised not to be running through those spectacular white whispers of my own breath. My feet, in summer shoes, were – are – wet. Water is lying everywhere on the ground, filling flat surfaces, shading the hidden dips and furrows. Now the cold wind is shooting into the leaves of the trees in the neighbouring garden. Earlier, it was leaping around street corners, and I – running with my bag – was defenceless. Already I have forgotten how it feels to be warm. When I am cold, I cannot imagine warmth, and vice versa. My body has a poor memory.

I suspect that this is the end of the summer; it is too late in August for a revival. I am sceptical of Mum's *Indian summers*: a phenomenon which, suspiciously, has never occurred during my lifetime. I can sense winter now: the wearing of lumpy layers; the rushing from indoors to indoors, damp. I glance at my watch. Not so many weeks ago, I could have been sitting in the garden, enjoying an endless afternoon. Now this dim day will be dark in an hour or so. What is the point of a long dusk when the evening is so cold? Soon — in ten weeks time? — the days will be dark when I leave for work, and dark when I return. These last few long days, so cold and damp, are lost to the winter. As I hurry from indoors to indoors, the long dusk is a mere curiosity on the cold side of a window.

Mum's eyes follow mine skywards. She stares anxiously into the void for a moment, and then says, 'Poxy sodding weather.' The size of her slice of bread — and the slice of butter on top — is worthy of Lauren. But, unlike Lauren, so much older than Lauren, Mum will gain the equivalent weight in fat. She turns away from the window, chewing. I remember how odd it was for me, as a child, whenever Mum moaned about the weather. What did it matter? But for Mum it was a subject for moans, amongst friends, all the time, along with prices and husbands. It was odd for me, too, that they took every opportunity to sit and talk. Their talking seemed so boring. But, now, I cannot remember what I would have been doing. Playing, presumably.

Suddenly Mum whoops in ecstasy: 'Oh! You little treasure!'

The cat is the object of this adulation. It is smarming into the kitchen, tail cocked, languid after a hard day in an armchair. It sits neatly in the middle of the floor.

'You saucy whatnot!' Mum continues merrily, rustling the white paper bag around the loaf.

The cat rises and swanks across the floor to its food bowl, hinting heavily. Then it sits, watching Mum, as expressionless as ever.

'You'd do anything to please your poor old mum, wouldn't you,' she croons to the cat.

I doubt this.

'Oh yes you would,' sings Mum. She takes a tin of cat food from a cupboard and the cat launches into the usual frenzy. 'Oh yes you would,' she continues, as the ragged little teeth of the tin-opener crunch through the tin.

Lyndsay appears in the doorway, shocking me with his height and his hair. He is very tall, and his hair is long in the front and very short at the back. I can make no sense of his baggy clothes: are they trendy?

'He is in trouble at school for his hair,' Mum says in a rather different tone of voice. She nods knowingly towards him. 'Too long and too short.'

'Hey, wildcat!' Lyndsay yells joyfully to the cat.

Mum slots the saucer of diced horsemeat onto the floor and the cat swoops in pursuit.

'Hey, fabulous!' He runs his hand down the length of the crouched body. 'Hard day at the office?' he asks it.

'Hello Lyndsay,' I interrupt dryly.

He looks up from his tête-à-tête with the feasting cat, stares at me with blank blue eyes and nods very slowly, several times, as if he is trying to follow a complicated line of argument.

Mum says, 'And stop using that bloody phone all day every day, Lyndsay. I'll have your calls traced.'

He transfers the solemn stare to Mum and replies, 'Great,' sonorous with sarcasm.

'Don't Great me.' She begins washing her hands with another palmful of washing up liquid. 'And did you put that dirty washing in the pile upstairs, like I asked? And leave that cat alone, it's trying to eat.'

He remains crouched with the animal.

'I might as well talk to myself,' she announces to me. Then she turns again to Lyndsay. 'When you've finished fondling the cat while it tries to eat in peace, perhaps you can do what I asked you to do earlier, twenty times, and put your filthy clothes on the pile upstairs.'

He does not reply. Eventually he says, 'What's for tea?'

'Never you mind,' Mum mutters petulantly.

Lyndsay rises slowly and then staggers inside his baggy clothing into the hallway.

Mum turns to stare at his absence in the doorway. 'I'd like to move and not take any of them with me.'

Even Dory? Unperturbed, Dory is beating the tray of her highchair with a soft, damp, rusky fist.

'Maybe if me and your Dad had more time alone together . . .' She adds no conclusion to this grumble, and once again I am left to wonder about this mysterious marital malaise. Is the marriage worse, worse than usual, worse than in the olden days? And if so, how?

'We've looked at a few nice places over near Bridget-and-Derek; very nice little villages.'

'You're really thinking of moving? From here?' For me, if they leave, this place will disappear, or become a blip on a map of suburbia. I will have no reason to return.

'Well . . .' she frowns, but not unhappily, 'I like to look around. It keeps me busy.'

'And you won't be sad to leave?' Or do I mean, incredibly, that I will be sad?

'Oh no,' she says briskly, hurrying around Dory with a damp cloth. 'I've never liked this place.' She wrinkles her nose, dabbing at Dory. 'Poky hole.'

A possible place-name: Poky Hole. But this Poky Hole place is my home. *Was* my home. *Is* my *ex*-home. Mum is fluttering back and forth in the small space between Dory's towering chair of chrome and the big steel sink, frowning faintly at her handful of grimy wet cloth. I never knew that she did not like it here. But, then, of course, I never asked; I assumed. I assumed that she liked it because she had been here for so long. But, then, I was here for a long time too.

'Jenny has a place in Hertford,' she is continuing. But suddenly she stops, cloth aloft, and asks, 'Did you know that Jenny had left?' Left Graham, she means.

'No,' I reply.

'A little one-bed place,' she resumes, 'but it's OK, better than most.' The cloth spews runny rusk into the sink, under a torrent of tap water. 'And I know, because I looked at a few with her. And she has a little job, now, too. In a solicitor's office, mornings.' She dries her hands on her skirt. 'And your Dad is giving her some office work, too, whenever possible.'

'Dad? Office work?' *Invoices* and *the books*, presumably: years ago, those words would seep upwards in weary voices through the floor into the darkness of my bedroom.

The hands stay low, the back bent, and she confides, 'We feel that it's the least we can do.' The eyebrows rise. 'Graham is giving her nothing.' Snapping upright, she sighs, 'Twenty-seven years. A whole lifetime.'

She says nothing more, so I ponder this for a suitably respectable time before I suggest, 'I might ring Lucy.' Home for one night, I had not been intending to contact Lucy. But I have heard nothing from her for a long time, so I am curious; and, anyway, what else will I do, this evening? I wait for Mum to shout: *Must you? This evening, of all evenings? When we're all so busy. Can't you find anything useful to do? I wish I could find the time to go off to ring all MY friends.*

Instead, she flips her eyebrows to indicate reluctant approval. 'Lucy.'

'Lucy Evans?' barks Jane, walking briskly through the doorway, looking at no one. She sweeps a new box of tissues from the top shelf of the cupboard. 'She's working in the Bella Brasserie in New Compton Street.'

I wonder what this is supposed to mean.

Jane stops, turns to face me, slapping the unpunctured box of tissues nonchalantly against her hip. 'We go there quite a lot.' And now a nasty little wrinkle of the nasty little nose. 'It's okay for a quick drink.'

So this is what it means: *We* (who? Jane 'n' Dunc? or friends?), a sense of exclusive membership; We *go to Soho*, of course; We go there *quite a lot*, carefully casual.

I glance at Mum, and Mum responds with a pop-eyed Miss-La-Di-Da expression; an expression which I loathed whenever it was her wordless comment about me, but which in this case, Jane's case, seems wonderfully appropriate and utterly hilarious. We titter, and Jane leaves for the stairs. 'Oy!' calls Mum after the disappearing family-size box of tissues, but to no avail. It strikes me that it is my misfortune that Jane, of all the Blaneys, is the closest to me in age, and also the most unkind. My past is available to her for brutal scrutiny. Erin is incapable of malice. Lyndsay favours brooding silence. Even Lauren, with her sharp, sceptical nonchalance, is not unkind.

Lyndsay shuffles into the doorway, and pauses.

'Have you done what I asked you to do? With that stinking washing of yours?'

'Yes.'

I watch him, pausing in the doorway, and I recognize his sullen reluctance. It is the same as my own teenage terror, yet different; scrambled or revised, perhaps.

'What *is* for tea?' he asks.

Mum's face is tight and swollen with a pout. 'Nothing, if I had my way.'

Lyndsay lurches towards the breadbin.

'Stop it, Lyndsay; don't touch the bread. Stop eating us out of house and home. Just wait.'

He opens his mouth to protest, but she reaches across him and slams shut the roll-top lid of the breadbin beneath his hand. 'I *said*.'

His attention turns to Dory. 'I'm going to take Dory to the park.'

'No-you-are-not.' She is standing between them, facing him, hands on hips. 'It's nearly Dory's bedtime.'

'The garden, then,' he snaps, and reaches somehow over or around Mum to Dory, to lift her cleanly from the complicated chrome contraption.

I tell Mum, 'I'm going to ring Lucy and then fight for the bathroom.'

She nods, preoccupied. As I haul the bag from the floor and leave the room, my attention is drawn by the smell of rainsoaked soil to the newly open doorway. I can see Lyndsay and Dory on the boundary of the patio and the wet lawn, facing outwards. Lyndsay is bearing Dory high in his arms. His shoulders, neck, and head are shaking and swaying and swooping with conversation. Dory turns and turns again between his face and the garden. She is bobbing and babbling, eager to please.

Coincidentally, the phone at Lucy's bungalow was answered by a Scottish voice. I asked for Lucy. 'Sorry, dear,' said the mysterious voice, 'but they've moved.' Tentatively, apologetically, I asked for the new number, expecting no help, but she obliged immediately. The new code was local. I dialled and was answered by Lucy's mum. 'Oh, she *will* be pleased!' she gasped as soon as she found out that it was me, and passed me immediately into silence to wait for Lucy. When Lucy came, she said only, 'Where are you?' and, 'I'm coming over.'

And now, from the bathroom, I hear another silence spring from beneath the murmur of a car engine outside.

My bouncing bare feet beat the specific rhythm of our stairs into the stairwell. From the bottom of the stairs, I can see that Lucy is kneeling on the driveway behind the car. Her hair is longer, touching her shoulders. As I skip over the doorstep, she glances towards me. 'What's wrong with this fucking car?' she shrieks in despair. Crossing the paving, I frown urgently and gesticulate towards the house: Mum.

'All the fucking way over here: Judder, judder . . .'

I stand over her.

'It *can't* be the exhaust,' she bellows. 'It's new, nearly.'

Playfully, I tap her bottom with my toes. 'So why are you on the ground, staring at it?'

'Well, it *must be* the exhaust.'

I squat beside her. But instead of looking at the exhaust, I look into her fretful, unfocused, flickering eyes. 'Judder-judder?'

The gaze slows, and finally, reluctantly, becomes still, linked to mine.

'Everyone was looking,' she says crossly. 'It was backfiring.'

'Misfiring, perhaps.' I rise. 'Open the bonnet for me.'

Behind me, her feet scratch onto the paving. I wait by the bonnet until it pops free. Then I push it upwards – blocking my view of long-haired Lucy, sprawled in the driver's seat – and prod around the distributor cap. Nothing seems amiss. 'It might be cracked,' I muse, but necessarily in a shout.

'What?'

I close the bonnet and press downwards. 'Okay, let's call the breakdown people.'

'Where's Jane?' asks Lucy, fascinated by the notion of a bride-to-be inside our house.

'Terrorizing everyone from the bathroom.' I point out the phone in the distance in the living room, and then continue along the hallway into the kitchen.

'Where's Lucy?' frowns Mum, who is attending to a row of small puffy pizzas under the grill.

'Broken down.'

Her frown deepens. Behind her, under the grill, a svelte black genie of smoke pirouettes on the ragged rim of one of the pizzas. She sniffs and turns in alarm. 'Do you want one of these? I'm going to do a second batch.'

'No. Thanks.'

'Suit yourself.'

Lucy startles us both. 'Hello Mrs Blaney,' she twinkles in the doorway.

'Lucy,' says Mum, warming. 'Do you want one of these pizzas?'

She shakes the new floppy hair. 'No thanks, I don't eat cheese.'

I hear Mum echoing in disbelief, 'Don't eat cheese?' as I shove Lucy back into the cool calm of the living room. Lucy saunters in front of me and drops into an armchair. 'I can't smoke in here, can I?' she confirms, gazing up at me, wide-eyed.

I sit down opposite, on the settee. 'No.' I notice that she is chunky. Last year, she was larger than in the old days; this year, she is more solid, the new flesh has settled. She is attractive nonetheless. I remind myself that Marilyn Monroe was chunky. And Madonna.

'Jane says that you're working in . . .'

'Oh, yes,' she rushes brightly, 'and it's OK, actually.' She shifts and sweeps both legs into the armchair, settles into a comfortable fold. Her pastel cotton dress is short, plain, thick: 'fifties. 'They're a laugh, there,' she says approvingly. 'They're all out-of-work actors, or artists or designers or whatever. All waiting for something else to happen.'

She sounds like a beatnik.

'So, it's interesting. People are coming and going all the time.' She shrugs happily, vacantly. Then she grimaces playfully. 'I mean, yes, it's tedious to wait on people, and it's hectic, and, yes, we're overworked-and-underpaid . . .' another fluffy shrug, ' . . . but they're a good crowd.'

I have a horror of bar work and waitressing. I have a poor memory, poor maths, poor tolerance of smoke, poor co-ordination, poor circulation in my legs. But I suppose there is worse work. I could have been born poor in Bangkok; sometimes I can hardly believe that I was not born poor in Bangkok, I can hardly believe my luck. I have not been sold into prostitution. And what would I have done? And what will I do, if I ever become a refugee? I am sure that I am not a survivor. I could have been born anywhere, any time. How would I have survived the nineteenth century, slums and mills? Would I have chosen to be born here and now?

I ask Lucy, 'How long have you been there?'

'Six months. I'm Shift Leader now.'

Of course she is Shift Leader now, after six months; everyone else has gone to act, paint, or design.

She laughs. 'I have my eye on the Assistant Manager's job.'

'Do you? Really?'

Momentarily she parodies careful consideration. 'Well, yes.'

'And is it likely?' Secretly I shudder at the thought of the endless succession of late, smoky, sweaty, booming, food-filled nights.

'Quite likely,' she replies in the same fey tone, but with a hint of mystery.

'And what about you?' she asks pleasantly, with interest. Wait until she hears the answer. My work is neither pleasant nor interesting. So, should I lie? . . . I-work-in-a-travel-agency: easy to understand, and a cue for pleasant chats about the availability of late bookings for Crete or the pros and cons of Fly-Drive. Instead, I say, 'I work in a Centre . . .' And I stop. Bad start. A *Centre*? Somehow the word suggests service-for-customers, a sham of plant displays and puce industrial carpets. Centres are to be mistrusted, avoided; except, I suppose, modern health centres, because I am old enough to remember the alternative, the prefab surgery on the side of the home of the lone Dr Gaylor, who was known locally as Whisky Galore.

'. . . for women with learning difficulties.'

'What?' yelps Lucy gracelessly.

'Mental handicaps.' At least I tried.

'Oh.' She looks at her knees for a moment. 'Doing what?'

Good question. I try to sound casual. 'Reading and writing, and . . .' I shrug to imply infinite possibilities, '. . . other things to increase their independence.' Or so I was told when I took the job. But this is untrue on both counts. Firstly, I teach reading and writing, Basic Skills, the three Rs, but I am one of four tutors. The others teach Social Skills, Domestic Skills, and Personal Hygiene – titles which smack less of independence in the modern world than the 1930s, a Women's League of Health and Beauty. Secondly, the Centre is an Adult Training Centre, so the aim is merely to train. The aim of the training is preparation for a job; in the hospital laundry, perhaps. But the local Centres are graded and this Centre is the lowest. The women who come to this Centre cannot travel alone, cannot count, some cannot feed themselves, some are incontinent, and some have fits. Yet still the women come to train. The policy of the Social Work Department is for independence, integration, care-in-the-community. Which sounded good to me. This seemed to be the job that I had always wanted.

But the women come from their homes, or from residential institutions or units, in minibuses bearing the logo of the Social Work Department. They come down the lane in the little buses for their nine-to-five. And some of them have been coming for ten years or more. And there is another untruth: my casual tone, to Lucy. I do not feel casual about any of this, about collaborating with this.

I do not feel casual about walking into the building, an ex-convent, at half past eight each morning, into the Staff Room and up the narrow aisle between the two tight rows of newspaper-shielded armchairs. Behind the newspapers, the staff sit in their specific chairs. The chair which is now my chair was the spare chair. At the end of the newspaper-noisy aisle is the shelf holding the kettle, coffee, milk. Above the shelf is the year-planner, a mosaic of holidays. I am a temporary worker, employed month by month, so there is no long streak of felt-tip pen for me across the planner. For each month that I work, I collect slightly more than one and a half days – slightly less than two days – of holiday. I have worked for a month or more so that I can attend Jane's wedding.

I do not feel casual when I hear the women arrive in the cloakroom. The arguments rattle the Staff Room door: Janet-took-my-purse, Clare-pinched-me, Ann-is-eating-my-apple, Eileen-started-everything. In the distance, thin metal doors clatter against toilet cubicles and there is the siren of indignant protest from the majority when someone less able, or more confused, wanders back into the corridor with her knickers down. I am protected for those first few minutes by the Staff Room door. The Staff Room is out of bounds to the women. I do not feel casual when I leave the Staff Room and go to my room. My room has flock wallpaper, endless crests of tomato-red fur. Officially, the women come to me in groups of eight; but one of the other groups is usually cancelled because the tutor is away – Personal Hygiene has bronchitis, Social Skills is pregnant and sick, Domestic Skills is a single parent of three small children – so the groups grow to ten or twelve. I am a locum covering long-term sick leave, and no more locums can be funded.

253

One group comes for the morning, another for the afternoon. I do not know what to do with them. Some of the women have little square books with soft fawn covers. Inside, they practise writing their names. Behind my desk, on the wall, is a chart: TODAY IS ; and, in the drawer of my desk, pieces of cardboard written with names of the days of the week. At the back of the room there is a cupboard full of games: peg boards, picture cards, jigsaws, and a battery operated board which produces an indistinct electronic animal noise whenever someone presses the cartoon pig, cow, goat or hen. I have been learning what the thirty-two women can do. Some of them can write. Caroline writes a diary: *I went to the shops with my mum, I went on the bus, I went to the pool.* Sarah decided to sit for several months with the pile of women's magazines, *Sizzling Summer Treats* and *The Day I Nearly Died*, before showing me that she can find anything and everything in the telephone directory; but her numeracy is poor, limited to single figures. Most of the women can copy their names and addresses, but have been doing so for years. Even more of the women can draw, stick-figures beneath blue strips of sky, but not Doreen, Sandy, Lesley, Kim, Chloe or Jane, who lose interest within seconds in their inky squiggles, and not Mary, Anne, Liz or Susan, who cannot hold a pencil.

Diana shouts my name all the time. Jenny wanders for hours around the room. Without warning, Eileen will throw chairs and overturn tables whilst the others run screaming and crying into the cupboard. Sabrina has severe fits.

I want to know what they think they are doing at the Centre. Most of them have parents and siblings who drive or commute to work. All of them watch television, and no one on television works in an Adult Training Centre. Do they wonder why they do not have jobs, cars, children? I have begun asking them why they come to the Centre. And the faces, usually so animated, become blank. Oddly, the most able of the women seem the most confused by my question. Chatty Mona, resplendent with perspex Maths Set, stopped and stared at me, speechless. She is working very hard to move on to the next grade of Centre. It was Alison, old and blind, who told me proudly, 'I'm handicapped. My Dad says.'

Sometimes Alison refuses tasks with the same answer: 'I'm handicapped!' To me, this seems a sensible response to everything in the Centre. A similar tactic is reserved by Jane, who is usually mute, for Keep Fit on Monday mornings: 'I'm a cripple!' Perfectly formed, perfectly functional, she sits beside me on the radiator in the Hall and we watch the others with their balls and hoops and scarves. I love Keep Fit: for half an hour each week I can abdicate responsibility to the two Keep Fit Ladies. One of the Ladies plays the piano and the other one organizes the women into lines and demonstrates the exercises. The balls and hoops and scarves flung by the women flop against the windows, roll beneath the piano, or loop over the low-strung strip-lighting. *Concentrate, Girls!* chides the Keep Fit Lady; and *Manners, Doreen!* and *Behave, Chloe!*

Apart from Keep Fit, there are no other breaks in the daily routine. No one can leave the convent during the day without the permission of the manager. Social Skills are supposed to incorporate Road Sense, but if the tutor takes the maximum three women out into town, onto the roads, there are fewer of us left for the others. So she goes rarely. And the less often she goes, the more time she takes. I watch with envy whenever she returns with the breeze entangled in her hair, and a fresh newspaper under her arm. Domestic Skills requires shopping trips, planned on a rota: four women, every Friday. Basic Skills is deemed to require nothing but the classroom with soft notebooks and electronic animal noises.

Mine is the sole classroom on the ground floor. (Lesley takes twenty minutes to crawl up the nuns' steep staircase to Cookery). It is opposite the Staff Toilet. I spend my days planning the next trip across the corridor to the silence and privacy there: I give myself a little break, every half hour or so. I do not have permission to leave my room but I delegate responsibility to someone reliable like Mona.

Between trips to the Staff Toilet I sit at the back of my room on the radiator. I look through the old french windows (locked, no key) onto the field. In springtime, drifts of pink blossom came across the field from the row of small trees lining the distant stone wall. I sit amid the shouting and fighting and wait for the official breaks: ten minutes before each break, I give the order to pack away the books and games. Then we sit and wait. All breaks take place in the dining room, which is Thelma's territory. Thelma arrives mid-morning, buttons a nylon blue housecoat over her own clothes and pushes a pair of haircombs into her swirl of gritty grey hair. From my room I hear her patent court shoes slamming on the disinfected dining room floor as she carries the trays of cups to the urn.

During the break I sit in the dining room, joined usually by one or more of the other tutors. Thelma supervises, and becomes the centre of attention: *Thay-el-ma, Kim wants the toilet; Thay-el-ma, Janet says you're having a baby, Oooo!* Thelma mutters and yells replies. Diana continues to call her name: *Thay-el-ma! Thay-el-ma!* Whenever Thelma passes me, on her merry-go-round of broken teacups, she glances grimly at me and growls, *This attention-seeking from Diana, it MUST stop, we MUST ignore it.* But I never do anything else.

Lunch arrives early in the morning, before Thelma, from a central kitchen somewhere. The food stays warm inside aluminium containers inside the huge ovens in the kitchen. There is a starter, always soup, often vegetable or lentil but nevertheless made from meaty broth. I discovered the suspicious background broth, the telltale flecks of salty pink fibres, on a close inspection. On Fridays the main course is fish: *Brown fish*, says Caroline, meaning breaded. Puddings are chopped bananas stuck like erasers in chunky ladlefuls of cold custard; trifle, the colours of traffic lights; chocolate mousse, or mess, pale and runny; or gaudy, fake fruit salad. Nevertheless the food is popular with the women. Thelma supervises distribution, but there are rotas for the clearing of crockery and waste from each long table. I do not enforce the rota on my table. I dread the reluctance and chaos of Sandy or Chloe; I trust in officious, capable Caroline. My table finishes quickly, and we leave for the Hall for recreation. As I leave, I pass the manager, sitting at one of the tables with Anne. The manager stays there until the beginning of the afternoon, intent that Anne should eat the food rather than sit in a smiling trance fractured by an occasional attempt to lob the plate across the room at Thelma.

The Staff Room is out of bounds to the staff during the day, except for brief visits to the kettle. After lunch, I take a cup of tea with me on duty into the Hall, and a soft semi-circle of women collects around me: Mona, reading a magazine, perhaps; Clare, Janet and Caroline, chatting about their boyfriends; Sarah, leaning against me, staring into the distance, turning her keyring in her fingers. A group surrounds the record player: Slade's *Merry Christmas* is first choice, regardless of the season. There are three other records, all by Shakin' Stevens. Other women sit on the chairs lining the room, knitting; or tackling jigsaws on the big table in the corner.

Often, the Personal Hygiene tutor arrives in the doorway with a pair of clean knickers for Sandy. Sandy is nineteen years old, an orphan, living in the old family home with her beloved twenty-year-old brother. An extended family is scattered around them on the estate: countless siblings with countless children and little spare time for Sandy. Sandy boasts to me of living on chips and sleeping in front of the telly. She is on a waiting list for a place in a hostel. The waiting list is two years long. When the Personal Hygiene tutor calls across the Hall for her, she responds happily, wiggling across the makeshift dance floor. Her idol is Madonna. Blonde and petite, Sandy imitates Madonna very well, despite the Down's Syndrome.

And now, here, Lucy is sitting opposite me, and she is resigned, carefree, plucky, optimistic, substantial, gloriously hardened by work, a real-life version of a chunky, cheery worker on a Soviet poster. I do not know what to say to her. I leave my bed every morning and I go to work; then I leave work at the end of the day, return home, and eventually return to bed. I long for an illness, a long illness, a long absence from work; or preferably an incapacitating injury. How do I tell Lucy this? On each journey to and from work I contemplate the impact of a car or lorry, the possibility of a broken leg. I favour a broken leg, a lengthy convalescence without illness or undue disfigurement. How do I ensure a nice clean snap?

A few times I have been out into the daytime world. It bustles beneath the stone of the nine-to-five. The streets tick slowly, lorries rolling to and from the kerb with deliveries, bakeries simmering with pies until lunch time. But between five o'clock and six, in these same streets, on my route home, the sound of hundreds of stiletto heels rips into the air like rotating rattles at a football match.

In the daytime, if I am away from work, I watch the clock, checking the time every ten minutes to administer the rush of freedom: twenty-five to nine . . .? I'd be in the Staff Room, standing over the gurgling kettle, gazing into the grimy net curtain, blinking back my sleep; twenty to eleven . . .? Thelma sweeps away breaktime; lunch time . . .? today, brown fish, a dry brown shoal stuck to the dull silvery tray.

I shrug and admit to Lucy, 'It's a job.'

More importantly, it is a job which will lead to another job, a better job, a job that I will enjoy. It is not for long, not much longer. But for now, work never leaves me. Evenings are shadowed by mornings. I live for weekends, but weekends mean weeks. In September my contract expires and I shall refuse renewal. Until then, I will crawl through the weeks with the help of bank holidays, hoping for a royal wedding. Until then, Monday lunch time is the first achievement of the week, Tuesday means Wednesday and the middle of the week, Wednesday means Thursday and Friday and the end of the week, Thursday is hopeful and Friday is too long. In September, I will go, but, of course, all the women will remain.

Reclining coyly in the armchair, Lucy cocks a sly smile. 'You remember Simon Steiner?' Her voice is hot with intrigue.

Has my face changed colour? 'Simon Steiner?' I repeat, to give myself more time. And it feels strange to say his full name. I want the extra time to prepare myself for whatever she will tell me. Yet

I want to know now. Or, no, I want to have known a moment ago: over-and-done. Because I suspect that whatever Lucy can tell me about Simon is bad news. Bad news for me.

'Well,' she luxuriates in this opening word, taking my *Simon-Steiner* as confirmation and permission to continue, 'I had a fling with him.'

'When?' When Lucy was spindly and spiky and shorn, in the Sixth Form? A Sixth Form secret? Did Lucy have secrets in those days? But if it was a Sixth Form secret, why tell me now?

'When? Oh, I don't know.'

Don't know?

'About a year ago, I suppose.'

A year? Suppose? 'A year?' Think, Lucy, *think*. For once.

'A year or so, yes, why?' The smile is dropping down her face, followed by a frown. She is tightening to attention. Now she shrugs: 'Where are we . . .?'

'July. Was it after I saw you last summer?'

'Yes,' she says, definitely, happier.

I curl myself into my chair, collect myself. Because I must let Lucy continue. Because I need to know the details. I smile. 'For how long?'

'Oh, I don't know,' she says, becoming nervous. 'Not long. A month or two.' Now she is wringing with curiosity. 'Why?'

'Nothing.'

Nothing preoccupies me but Lucy's big soft face. Which is saying nothing, telling me nothing. So I smile again, to prompt her.

Lucy reflects the smile, rather unsurely, and starts, 'My car broke down around the corner from the Steiners . . .'

I yell, 'You went to the Steiners because your car broke down?' I have not seen Mr and Mrs Steiner since Deborah's memorial service; Lucy has not seen them since *before* the memorial service, sometime when Deborah was alive. So, Lucy went to the Steiners, to use their phone, as if nothing had ever happened?

Lucy flares, 'Yes? Why? What else was I supposed to do?' She flaps a hand towards the window, 'You've seen . . .' She stops suddenly to insist, 'Life goes on, Lalie.' She sighs emphatically. 'Unlike my car.'

I am nodding loosely, conceding, deflating in my chair, hurrying her onwards.

'So,' she begins again, crossly, 'I went to their house, and Mr-and-Mrs were out, but *he* was there. He was home for the weekend, painting one of the rooms.' This last comment was a verbal flourish, *Painting-one-of-the-rooms*: because this is a story, and painting-the-room is an incidental detail, a scene-setter. She continues, 'So he answers the door and says, *I remember you*; and I say, *Yes, I'm Ali Mortimer.*' She laughs. 'And, by the way, to this day, he thinks I'm Ali.'

Which rips me from my musings. '*What?*'

'Or, at least, I *think* he does,' she backtracks.

'*Why?*' I shriek. 'I mean, why did you tell him that you were Ali?'

She argues, '*I* don't know,' as if this is an unfair question.

Why am I horrified by the prospect of Lucy being mistaken for Ali?

She is saying, reassuring me, 'I would never try to do that to *you*.'

In this case, she would not have succeeded. 'He knows me,' I tell her.

'Oh,' she says, happily.

I want to ask why, if she would never do so to me, did she do so to Ali. But I resist, because I so badly want the rest of the story.

She obliges: 'So I went in, rang, had some coffee whilst I was waiting. Had a laugh about old times.'

A laugh? 'Old times?'

She explains impatiently, 'Well, I knew Deborah, and he knew Deborah.'

'A laugh?'

Matter-of-fact, she says, 'Lalie, I'm going to ask you a question to which you should know the answer: how many sides are there to every story?'

I shrug, reluctant, sceptical. 'Two.'

'Actually,' her face glitters with a quick smile, 'no. At least two.

Anyway, to me, *Deborah* doesn't mean *misery*. To me, *Deborah* doesn't mean *accident*. You're not doing Deborah, nor yourself, any favours by remembering everything in terms of the accident.'

Is this how I am seen? I have always been sure that I have solely good memories of Deborah. I can only manage, 'Well, you certainly do have all the answers today, don't you.'

Very briefly, with the same smile, she adds, 'Another piece of advice: be careful whom you patronize because not everyone is as easy-going as me.'

Which surprises me even more, and shuts me up.

'Anyway,' she continues with the story, 'when I was leaving, he asked me if I wanted to meet later for a drink.'

'*He* asked *you?*' I check, immediately. *Are you absolutely sure?*

'Yes.' She prickles, affronted. 'People do, you know.'

'So you went for a drink?'

'Yes.'

'And?' Now I want the details. I think longingly of the expression Spare-me-the-details. Unfortunately, in this case, so long as there are details, then *spare* is over-optimistic.

'And what?' Momentarily, her blue gaze is flat, wide, expressionless. Now she says, 'Oh.' And now, 'We had nowhere to go but the back of the car, can you believe that?' She smiles indulgently at me. 'You, who live away, in a place of your own.'

I want to tell her that she is wrong, that having a-place-of-your-own means nothing if it is four hundred miles away, but she is explaining, '*My* car. Because he didn't have one.'

Now that we have reached the back of the car, I am surprised to find that I am much less interested in the details, in *those* details. Realistically, I cannot ask *How many times?* It is more important to know what he said to her, whether or not this was ever supposed to have been serious, and how serious.

'It fizzled out,' she says. 'It was nothing much, and it fizzled out.' She shrugs. 'I don't know why, exactly.'

But I do. And I'll tell you.

But she is saying, 'He doesn't seem to know what he wants.'

Another shrug, hopeless. 'I can tell you what he *doesn't* want.' Now she is talking to herself rather than to me, but I can do nothing except listen. 'What he *doesn't* want is a girl from around here. He wants a lawyer-type, like himself. He wants a clever girl.'

Who says lawyers are clever? And *he* is from-around-here. And his beloved sister Deborah was a girl-from-around-here, and her friends – me.

Lucy looks very directly at me, tweeks her face with a smile, and says mildly, conclusively, 'He's on another planet.'

I say, 'A girl on every planet.'

She is murmuring in agreement, gazing untroubled towards the window.

'And I'm one of them.'

She switches blankly to me. 'No,' she breathes.

'Yes.'

'When?' Now her face is sharper, her tone higher: but in surprise, rather than pique. She is poised to spring onto the details.

I shift in my chair, and settle newly folded. 'Well, *now*. I mean, *still*.' I laugh feebly. 'So it seems to me that *When?* is the question that I should be asking you.'

'You did,' she says carefully. 'And I told you. It's over.'

'Yes,' I say politely, apparently gratefully; but, in fact, I am confused by Lucy's vague details. 'Well, it started about a year ago.' Started? How has it progressed, since, strung across four hundred miles, threaded through two working lives? 'It was after the memorial service . . .'

'The memorial service was more than a year ago,' Lucy interrupts doubtfully.

'A lot more.'

She says quickly, 'That's what I meant: a lot more.'

More like eighteen months ago.

'Lucy. Let me finish.' Let me *start*. 'I don't mean that this was straight after the service; but simply after the service. Sometime. Sometime a year ago or so. I rang him up.' I laugh, almost. 'Actually, it was you, it was your fault: the last time I saw you, here, you told me to make an effort, to liven up my life.'

'I did?' She is amused and fascinated.

I nod.

'Yes,' she says, 'an *effort*, but it didn't have to be *him*.'

I laugh knowingly. 'Oh yes it did.'

'My God,' she is laughing, too, now, 'what must he think, all Deborah's friends calling on him and ringing him?'

'He doesn't seem to mind, does he,' I manage dryly, having chosen to ignore *all*-Deborah's-friends. 'Anyway, I rang the Steiners for his number, then rang him, told him that I was going to be in London for a few days, asked him if he wanted to meet for a drink.'

'And were you?' The big blue eyes are open wide and steady to receive an answer.

'Was I what?'

'Going to be in London?'

This snatches my breath away. Because, no, I was not going to be in London, not unless he said yes; but how did Lucy know? How could anyone know that I was so devious and desperate and determined? I ignore her question, say instead, 'He said yes, and so that's when everything started.' Started? In a sense, I have no more to tell than Lucy. Probably less. I have probably spent less time with Simon in a year than Lucy spent with him in the back of her car in a month or two. Until now I had persuaded myself that time did not matter, not ultimately; I had told myself that, for now, quality was more important than quantity. Suddenly I am less sure.

She is protesting gently, 'Why didn't you tell me?'

'I *am* telling you.'

'Why didn't you tell me before I made such a fool of myself?' Now she is laughing.

'You're not the fool, I'm the fool.' I look very closely at her. 'I should have known about you.'

She is not looking at me, not really, because she is still laughing, her eyes are busy with laughter. 'I wouldn't have gone on like that, just now, if I'd known.' She stops laughing and asks, 'Why did you let me go on?'

'I was thinking.'

'Oh, *thinking*,' she repeats sarcastically, but good-naturedly. 'Didn't your mother ever tell you that too much thinking means trouble?'

Yes, often, if not in so many words. 'I needed to know,' I tell her. I needed to lie low, to listen.

'Well, you certainly know now,' she chirps.

'Lucy,' I stress, 'it's not funny.'

'Oh yes it is,' she replies spiritedly, happily. 'It's a lot of other things, too, but it *is* funny.' Accompanying a bubble of laughter, her hands clasp each other so that there is a solitary stunned clap. 'We weren't called The Terrible Twins, all those years ago, for nothing,' she concludes.

'We *weren't* called The Terrible Twins.'

'Oh yes we were.'

Were we? By whom? *Twins*, Lucy and me? I scrutinize Lucy, linen-pale, lines of snail-trail-silver around her eyes, lit top-to-toe with laughter as she relishes our misfortune: an angel gone wrong. 'Besides,' I close my eyes, 'Simon and I have told no one.' Because everything seems too uncertain, still, as if a single word could break the spell. Whenever Simon and I meet, he comes to me in Edinburgh or I come to him in London, by-passing home. A-wing-and-a-prayer. If I look down, everything will fall away. I open my eyes to find that Lucy has stopped laughing, even stopped smiling. Worry delves into her brow. I am worried too; more so, surely. I still have my decision to make: do I leave my life to come to London, to him? What life? But now I suspect that I will never be able to think further than this: 'He lied to me.' I meant this to be a complaint, but it came as a threat, sliding low.

Lucy tries to calm me: 'He didn't *lie* . . .'

'As good as. As bad as.' I did not mean to raise my voice, not so drastically. Not that I will disturb anyone except Lucy because, as ever, I can hear shouting elsewhere in the house; on this occasion, above me, the ceiling humming with Blaney belligerence.

Lucy bursts back, 'But what does it matter?'

'*What?*'

Shaking her head so that the air is full of blonde scribbles, she starts again: 'What I mean is . . .' her hands and eyes dabble for words . . . 'Perhaps it matters too much. Perhaps he was afraid of losing you. What would you do if you'd made a mistake? You might try to cover your tracks, right?' She is straining towards me from the armchair, eyes huge, willing me onwards, begging me to agree momentarily, hypothetically.

'Wrong.'

The eyes flare further, a pair of fizzy sparklers. 'You *might.*'

'I would *never.*'

She deflates into the armchair. '*You* might never, but we're not talking about *you.*'

Apparently not. She is making excuses for him.

She is persisting; but grumpily, now, rather than enthusiastically: '*He* might.'

I would love to say What-would-you-know? But, of course, I cannot. Because she *does* know. She knows all sorts of things about Simon, the consistency of his eyes and the tone of his voice in the most intimate moments. She is turned away from me, into the armchair, into herself. I watch her for a moment, but nothing moves, not even an eyebrow or a finger. Drawing my gaze back over her soapy skin, I concede, 'It's a nice thought.'

Without moving, she snaps, 'I don't deal in nice thoughts.' Now she turns slightly towards me and I see the spark of a smile in her eyes. 'I speak the truth.'

'Well,' I laugh sorely, 'that's true.' Now I feel that I can manage, 'You should have told me.'

She is decidedly breezy: 'It wasn't important, Lalie. And, anyway, I did tell you, just now. How could I have told you before? I never see you.'

I cannot resist, 'You could have written.'

'Suddenly I could have started writing to you about my love life?' she counters cheerfully, dismissively. She has never written more than a postcard to me. Now she warms the air between us with intrigue, laughing, 'Are you certain that we overlapped?'

I am tense, to quell physical recoil. But should I be Lucy's friend, if I feel like this? Am I Lucy's friend? Or did I summon her into this armchair because there is no one else for me to call when I am home? And did she come over for the same reason? I cannot stop myself insisting again, much more forcefully, 'You should have told me.'

Shifting, composing herself anew in the chair, she says, 'Correct me if I'm wrong . . .' and she reflects momentarily on this with a silver smile . . . 'Not that you ever fail to do so, but if anyone is cross, then it should be me, because it's likely that you took him from me.' She finishes calmly, 'Not that I care.'

'Lucy,' I say far too loudly, for no particular reason that I know.

She continues, even more calmly, 'You're angry with him, not me.'

No, I am angry with you. Lump-like Lucy, forever stuck into armchairs, caring about nothing.

'Don't blame me,' she is saying, sing-song.

'Well, who else?' I challenge. And now, grudgingly, I admit, 'I can't blame him, he's such a mess.'

Lucy leans forward, large smooth white forearms covering the soft cotton lap: 'Home Truths time, Lalie,' she says steadily, unflinchingly. 'If he tries to keep you hidden, then you can be sure that you're not all that he has to hide.'

Often I wonder if I would have told Deborah, if she was still alive. If she had been alive when Simon and I came together, which is so very hard for me to imagine, although I do not know why. I cannot imagine what I would say to Deborah, or what she would say to me. About anything at all. In the beginning, my imaginary conversations with Deborah, boundless conversations, felt endless, timeless; so that, in a sense, it did not seem to matter that she was not there. But eventually there was an end, and I suppose that it came a year or so after the accident.

Lucy says lightly, 'Go on, then.'

'What?'

'Tell me how wonderful it is: you and Simon.' She is sitting back, arms folded, smiling faintly but indulgently.

Reluctantly I turn my thoughts to Simon, and to the past year. I have no words ready because I have never talked to anyone about Simon and me. Perhaps I have not very often talked to Simon about Simon-and-me, because I do not often see him. I talk to him all the time in my head but concerning the details of all my days, days without him; I take him back with me into my days, I paint the details with the colours of his eyes. Whenever I see him, I forget everything, I forget myself; and whenever we are together we are too busy living to bother to talk.

I accuse Lucy, 'You're so cynical.'

Which knocks her eyes wide open. 'What have I said?'

' "Wonderful." '

She remains incredulous. 'So it's *not* wonderful?'

And now he is coming back to me, and I shrug helplessly. 'Oh I don't know,' although I do: 'He understands me.' I stare hard onto the distant net curtains.

The reply, the correction, is very quiet: 'He understands about Deborah.'

I ignore this, ignore Lucy. Instead I chase a particular, peculiar feeling, only to shrug again when I find something: 'I want to get inside his mind.' I am even less convinced when I hear this aloud. But I know that I am on the right track. Somehow Simon is where I belong.

Lucy comments, 'We're past all that.'

I snap her into focus. 'Past what?'

'Being inside someone else's mind.' She splashes her fingers through her hair and settles deeper into the chair. 'What you want now is the opposite: space.'

Don't tell me what I want. 'And you'd know, I suppose?'

Do I imagine that she rises again, slightly, in her chair? She is definitely, instantly, on her guard.

'What would you know about it?' I goad, surprising myself. 'You, who couldn't care less.'

Dismayed, she pipes, 'I didn't say that it wasn't important at the time.'

'Whenever has anyone been important to you?'

'Lalie,' she says quickly, if only to stop me. And is she counting to ten, now, to keep her temper? Why do we *keep* and *lose* tempers? Is there anything less like losing, mislaying, than the hurling of a temper? She says, 'This isn't about me.'

Oh yes it is, partly. You, here. You and here. Which reminds me, with considerable force: 'He's different from everyone else, Simon is different from everyone else around here.'

'Which isn't saying much,' she replies, equally forcefully.

Rightly.

And now she is imploring me, 'Forget about here, Lalie. You need to do some forgetting.'

Does she mean Deborah?

'You move hundreds of miles away . . .' she halts and blinks thoroughly, wearily, implying, *But-it's-not-the-answer*. 'You need to get away from here,' she concludes.

'You can talk.'

She shrugs, unconcerned. 'I don't think I'm as unhappy as you.'

'I *was* fine. I *will be* fine when I come back to London.' Back to London? I have never lived in London. I have spent what feels like a lifetime sleeping on floors in London. And would this time feel any different?

'You're coming back to London for him?' Lucy's question peeks nervously.

I nod. But it has been worrying me for some time that he wants me to move down to try, no, not to try but to *try-it-out*; which is different, which is the opposite of try, which is simply try-for-size. He wants me to move somewhere near to him to find out how we feel. But I know how I feel. How can I be so sure and yet unsure? Sure of myself, unsure of him.

Lucy is asking, 'Where is he living now?'

The question brings me round. Easy to answer. 'Docklands.'

'Figures.' She smiles briefly, for emphasis.

I find myself smiling in reply, a different type of smile; which triggers another, kinder, smile from her, for me. 'No, it's not like that,' I tell her, 'it's a shared flat.' Very. I wrinkle my nose. 'It's small, cheap. Cardboard walls. The owner is a friend of Simon's, he owns several around there, he's going to sell.'

'Do you want to move down?'

I shrug airily.

'Why not?' she asks pleasantly.

Involuntarily I shrug again, but gently, a ripple.

'Because he's a creep,' she corrects good-naturedly.

'*Lucy*.'

'*Lalie*,' she is forward in her chair before I realize, swilling me into those huge blue eyes, those ridiculous blue eyes, too-good-to-be-true blue eyes. 'Will you listen to me?' Not a question but an order. 'He's normal, human, nothing special. He's no different from any of the other boys around here who I've had in the back of my car.' I try to catch my breath but she is unrelenting, urging, 'Believe me, I've met some creeps, so I know one when I see one.' For a moment we stay stuck together, face to face. 'He's not Deborah,' she says finally.

'Deborah liked him,' I sulk, in his defence, in my defence.

'Deborah didn't know any better,' Lucy dismisses instantly. More thoughtfully she adds, 'Ali doesn't like him.'

'I don't care what Ali thinks.'

'Yes you do,' she says flatly.

Which is true. Or *is* it? It *was* true, certainly. How do I know, now, with Ali gone? And when, and why, did, or do, Ali and Lucy talk about Simon? (When did, do, Ali and Lucy talk?) And what did Ali say? More pinpricks burning my brain.

Lucy is insisting, 'Ali has good judgement.'

'The problem is,' I blurt, to confront Lucy, 'I do love him.' My heart, lungs, the whole of the middle of me pulls hard, holds hard, refusing to relinquish anything, not even one breath. I am conscious, suddenly, that I am made of threads, bound together inside by threads so strong, and yet whenever is any thread strong enough?

She exhales gently for me, dropping everything: her prattle about Ali, her snipes at Simon, her irritation with me. 'I'm not saying that you don't love him.' Her eyes, on me, have retreated somehow so that she is – what? – looking *at* me rather than *to* me? I can see that she is thinking about me. 'What I'm saying, I suppose, is that love is made of so many things, but never all of them, and not often most of them.' She shrugs expansively, to open up the idea, but insufficiently to allow me to squeeze inside. 'Attraction, yes,' she continues briskly. 'Sexual attraction, or other attraction,' she smiles inwardly, pleased with this initial distinction. 'Admiration, empathy, perhaps pity. Shared temperaments, or tastes, sense of humour, shared lives.' She shuts her eyes. 'Aspiration, ambition, identification.' Now the eyes open and focus firmly on me. 'There are as many types of love in the world as there are people, but I'm not sure that Simon Steiner's the one for you to *marry*.'

Indignant, I protest, 'Who said anything about *marry*?'

'You know what I mean.'

The door booms open and shoots Mum into the room. She stops unsteadily in front of us, over us, and focuses on me after a dismissive glance at Lucy. 'It's off,' she says.

'Mum,' I snap, 'I've told you, I don't want pizza.'

'Not the Pisa,' she shrieks. 'The wedding. Jane says. The wedding's off.'

1988

....

I do not recognize the boy on the doorstep until he says, 'Hello, Lalie.' And suddenly I know that this is Lyndsay, pinned onto a khaki background of looming rucksack. He has no hair; or, rather, he has a scalp of blond bristle.

'Lyndsay, what are you doing here?'

He steps forward, rattling with rucksack. 'Can I come in?'

I step back, step around him, behind him, and shove my full weight against the warped door. When I turn back into the hall, the huge rucksack is shifting from the shoulders below the prickly yellow head and slipping in front of me to the floor. What do I do with him? I walk around to face him, and ask encouragingly, 'Do you want something to eat?'

Bending and bouncing the rucksack into a corner, he makes a politely enthusiastic noise.

But *what* to eat? There is some bread. 'Cup of tea?' I try cheerfully, setting off for the kettle.

'I don't drink tea,' he calls behind me.

'Coffee?'

'Nope. I don't drink coffee.'

No tea or coffee? A Blaney without tea or coffee? And what else is there to drink? 'What, then?'

'Milk, please.'

The usual problem: 'I don't have milk, I don't drink milk,' I can't *keep* milk. I contemplate the closing times of the nearest shops.

'Water, then, please.'

'Water?' I turn to find him towering behind me. *Towering?* Surely there is some natural law against this: I am oldest, so I am tallest, surely? I turn away, quickly, and hurry through to my kitchen.

271

'Yes, water, please.'

I realize that the words I want to say are Mum's words: *Water? You can't have JUST WATER!* And we, the Blaney babies, were mystified, and irritated, because water seemed so suitable: quick and easy, and an unsurpassed thirst-quencher. But now, I am wondering whether it is possible to sit and chat over a glass of water.

'How did you get here?' I am avoiding a return to What-are-you-doing-here?

'Hitched.' He slides onto a chair at the table.

'Hitched?' Scanning the shelves of the fridge, I grab a pot of hummus and a jar of pickle. 'How?' I turn to the cupboard for more jars. 'Do you want some cereal?' I wave the two packets in his direction.

He looks at them with interest, but says, 'Not without milk.'

I do not tell him that I eat them with water: I have learned that people recoil with squeals of horror. Instead, I put a jar of honey with the hummus and pickle on the table; and add butter, and the bread from the breadbin, and knives and a plate from the draining board.

'How do people *usually* hitch?' This tone could belong to Mum.

'But how did you know the way?' I remember the glass of water, and return to the sink.

'Ever heard of a map?' The same dry tone. His big blue eyes bounce towards me, but blankly, the focus elsewhere, probably inwards on an immense mouthful of bread.

Yes, but when I was Lyndsay's age, fourteen or fifteen, I had heard of maps, and I had seen them in Geography classes, but I am not sure that I could read them. I could read the tube map, which is not a map but a diagram.

'Does anyone know that you're here?' The crux question, subtly re-worded.

'No.'

Oh. So, what now? 'Do you want to stay?'

'If possible. For a couple of days.' His jaw grinds, his cheek swells.

What can I do with him? 'Don't you want some of these?' I tap the jars.

Munching, he swings his head from side to side.

Why are adolescents constitutionally unable to eat anything provided for them? I am merely trying to help.

'And then where will you go?' I ask calmly.

He finishes the jawful, and swallows graphically. 'I don't know.' He shrugs, reaching for more bread. 'Perhaps the Highlands, for a while. I just need to get away.'

The central admission, tossed nonchalantly across the table: *I just need to get away.* Immediately he blocks his mouth with another mass of bread.

'Why?' I ask him casually. 'Why do you need to get away?'

Busily chewing, he replies evenly, 'Because I'm sick of them all going on at me.'

I leave the table to make myself a cup of tea. 'Who?' Carefully I follow his conversational tone.

He leans backwards in the small wooden chair, suddenly expansive, flicking his hands upwards and outwards. 'Mum, Dad, Mr Carnegie, Mr Dalton . . .'

Mr Carnegie and Mr Dalton? Teachers, no doubt, to judge from the tone of familiarity and contempt.

'Why are they going on at you?'

'Oh, I don't know!' If this was an attempt to portray mere exasperation, then it failed to conceal the underlying anger. His eyes follow me very closely across the room. Unshaded by hair, below the balded head, the eyes are huge. 'Because they like to ruin people's lives for them, that's why.' He shrugs himself back into sulky silence, and spins the lid on the jar of pickle.

'Well, yes . . .' I start sceptically.

'Listen, Lalie,' he bursts, threatens, 'you don't know what it's like . . .'

No? I know exactly, but, six years on, I have no solution. I resign myself to hearing Lyndsay's catalogue of complaints; but the telephone chirps in the hallway. 'One moment,' I tell him. In the

273

hallway I lift the handset, but before I can speak the telephoned voice says, 'Lyndsay is missing.'

'Mum,' I reply irritably, 'he's here.' Only when I have said this do I wonder whether I should have done so: presumably yes, because how long would a lie survive?

'What do you mean, he's there?' Now she is cross.

'I mean, he's here, in my kitchen.' Can he hear? Why is all this so complicated? Why is all this in my own home? In my own home, more than four hundred miles away.

'Why didn't you say?'

'I did say. He has been here for two minutes.'

'How did he get there?' she wails in dismay.

'He hitched.'

'Hitched? Hitch-hiked?'

I wait.

'And did he tell you that he took two tenners from my purse?'

'Mum, he has been here for two minutes, he has told me nothing.'

'And did he tell you that we are going to a meeting tomorrow with his Head Teacher and his Form Teacher?' She continues hotly, 'About his behaviour?'

'Mum . . .'

'What would happen if we *all* ran away?' she puffs.

Again, I wait.

'Well,' she begins again, deflated, 'are you going to send him back?'

Am I going to send him back? 'Shall I call you later?' I ask carefully, meaning I'll-call-you-later.

'I'll call you in an hour,' she rattles officiously.

'No, *I'll* call *you*. Later.'

The echo of a gale of irritation and impatience blasts into my ear. 'Well, I'll have to call the police.'

'What?'

'Lyndsay has been reported to the police as missing; I'll have to

274

let them know that he has been found. So, you can expect a visit from your local Bobbies.'

Wonderful. And I bet they come during *Neighbours*.

'And, in the meantime, Lyndsay can tell you all about the toilet wall at school.'

I am supposed to say, What about the toilet wall? Instead, I say, 'Yes, I'm sure. I'll call you later. Bye for now.' I go back into the kitchen, where Lyndsay drains the glass of water with one big swig.

'Was that Her?' he asks, apparently unconcerned.

'Yes,' I snap. 'And she has told the police.'

'What?'

I shrug and return to the kettle. 'You were missing.' And now I frown at him. 'So, Lyndsay, you're responsible for bringing The Law into my home.'

'Not me,' he replies.

'And what is all this about school, and toilet walls?'

'It's nothing,' he scowls predictably.

'Nothing or not,' I counter, 'what is it?'

He blows a condescending sigh, and rubs his blond bristles with the palms of his big hands. 'I wrote a poem on the wall. That's all.'

I sit down slowly with my cup of reassuringly warm tea. 'What sort of poem?' There-was-a-young-lady-from . . .?

Head in hands, he flashes those blue beacons: this upward, wide-eyed gaze has the physical attributes of a plea. 'Quite a long poem. I wrote it during double Maths.'

'But what was it about?'

Lyndsay explodes with irritation, hurling the gaze to the ceiling. 'Life, love, what else is poetry about?' He pauses to savour a deep, steadying breath. 'Anyway, that's not the point; the point, for them, is that it's on the wall.'

Wearily, he examines his empty glass for beams of light.

I never expected Lyndsay to cause trouble. At home, *I* was the one who was trouble, who was different. Or was I? Because what about Jane? How was Jane anything but trouble? And Erin had a baby; which, popularly, counts as trouble, *big* trouble. Perhaps all adolescents are trouble, but different types of trouble. Perhaps Lyndsay is my type, continuing a tradition, my tradition, now that I am no longer home. Perhaps everyone is trouble, but less obviously so than adolescents, who have nowhere to hide, who are cornered in their parents' homes. Lyndsay looks well on his trouble. Larger than life.

I ask calmly, 'Do you often write poetry?'

'Of course,' he snarls immediately, without raising his eyes from the glass.

Of course. Another gentle probe: 'Could you have written your long poem on a piece of paper?'

'Lalie,' he lectures, discarding the glass, 'you are missing the point. Walls are perfect for poetry. The point is that it's on the wall. Paper is . . .' he shrugs hugely, '. . . is scrap.'

Rapidly, to save us both, I change tack: 'But how did they know that it was you? Why were you caught?'

He subsides, slips back to the glass. 'They just knew.'

So, if he is to be believed, Lyndsay has a reputation: notoriety or ridicule?

'Why did you shave your head?' I ask lightly.

'I don't need hair.'

Well, no, not unless you want to look nice.

He looks at me. 'Why haven't you been home this year?'

I never expected Lyndsay to be the one to complain about my absence. I do not know what to do with his question: there is an assumption that I should go home; and an assumption that I will have noticed that I have not done so. And of course I have noticed. 'No reason,' I reply vaguely. In Lyndsay's words, *I just need to get away*. To stay away. But for how long can I stay away? For how long will home be too-close-to-home?

'Well, I kept hoping that you'd come home,' he grumps, 'because They're as bad as ever, if not worse.'

Would I have been his saviour, his ally, or a mere witness?

'But there is the new house,' I say, pathetically.

'Yes,' he agrees flatly, 'there is the new house.' He scowls.

'New packaging,' he spits bitterly, 'for the same old contents.'

'What is it like, the new house?' I continue cheerfully.

'*The-New-House*,' he quotes vehemently. 'And don't I know it!' His face twists for mimicry: '*Not-in-my-new-house* and *Now-that-I'm-in-my-new-house*.' He is mimicking Mum, of course.

I ignore this and ask, 'But what is it like?'

'It's all right, I suppose.' He shrugs faintly and peels a strip of crust from the loaf. 'It would fine without the endlessly expanding collection of garden furniture, toppling all over the patio.'

What happened to our old beanbag cushions, and the beached Lilo? And is Mum spending weekends at the local Garden Centre rather than in the garden? Perhaps, after almost thirty years, she is expanding her furnishing empire from the house to the garden. So everyone will spend the winter looking out over scattered white drift-plastic, dripping and gleaming.

'It would be fine if I didn't have the smallest room,' he says gloomily, dabbing a patch of crust into the open jar of pickle.

Six-foot Lyndsay in the smallest room? 'How come?'

He nibbles at the smeary piece of bread, fixing me with a knowing stare: 'Lauren says that she is disturbed by Erin-and-Dory, so she has been given the room at the other end of the hallway, coincidentally the next biggest room, and I am next to Erin-and-Dory, in the smallest room.'

I return a knowing glance, and pause respectfully. Then I venture, 'What is Lauren doing, these days, generally?' She sends cards to me, Christmas and birthday, with the message *I WILL WRITE*.

'She is learning the saxophone.'

The loudest, most raucous instrument in the world.

'At least you're rid of Jane,' I try.

He explodes again, tipping backwards on my frail wooden chair. 'We should be so lucky!'

I raise my eyebrows: physical question marks.

'She and Bill-The-Bore are having a conservatory built onto the back of their house, so she needs storage space, she keeps dumping garden furniture on us, and yuccas.'

I smirk. And I imagine the Sunday Supplement conservatory, a giant jam jar, strapped with creosote-coloured timber.

'And their bathroom is being renovated, so she comes around constantly for baths.'

'Lyndsay,' I contradict, 'Mum told me that Jane's house is new. So how can the bathroom need renovation?'

He halts me with a dismissive wave of his giant hands. 'Jacuzzi.'

It is more than a year, now, since Jane called off the wedding to Duncan. Whilst I was sitting with Lucy in the living room, Jane was upstairs in her bedroom, hauling the boxes of lingerie across the floor and feeling with her fingertips on the carpet for an earring which had fallen from her ear. The earring, a pearl, had been lent for the wedding by Gran Blaney: Something Borrowed. One of the boxes was particularly heavy, and Jane explored inside, beneath the deep fluff of black and scarlet nylon. And she found Something Blue. Duncan had been importing videos. Skimpy underwear had been the perfect cover.

Mum came to tell Lucy and me, and then we followed her upstairs. She returned to the doorway of Jane's room, shrieking in horror, 'In my house! In my own house!'

Jane turned in fury from the splayed box, which had spewed a tangle of shiny thongs down its sides. She had built a stack of the videos on the floor. 'Sod your house!' she screamed at Mum, brandishing the most recent video to have been extracted from the box. 'We're talking about my husband! My husband-to-be, my ex-husband-to-be!'

No one heard the content of the conversation between Jane and Duncan, because Jane slammed as many doors as possible before ringing him on the cordless phone from the bathroom. Only Mum remained upstairs for a while, twittering about the danger of electrical equipment near the bath. But everyone in the house heard the *tone* of the conversation, or, at least, of Jane's half of the conversation, which, progressing without pause, seemed to be the whole of the conversation. Jane was still reeling from the neat stack of packets, each one a fixed eye on a parade of wan women, on a coral of orifices.

I wanted the phone for my own confrontation with Simon, but I had to form a queue. There is always a queue for trauma, in the Blaney household. Lauren, returning from a short walk with the cat, came into the kitchen in dismay, through Jane's screams.

'It's off,' Mum told her, in a daze. 'So you can scuff those shoes of yours to High Heaven.'

No doubt Duncan denied all knowledge of the videos, but Jane refused to believe or forgive him. So, as instructed by Jane, he came to the house, an hour or so later, to remove them. Mum had gone to the supermarket, taking Lauren. Jane had gone somewhere else, perhaps to the Gym. Lyndsay had refused to go with Mum and Lauren, causing an enormous row. I could not leave because I was instructed to provide the minimal necessary supervision for Duncan's visit – to open the door – and Lucy stayed with me. Duncan took the box to his car to the strains of *That's Entertainment*, whistled by Lyndsay from his bedroom window. Ten months later, Jane married Bill-The-Bore. I made vague excuses to Mum about the difficulty of taking leave from work, and the expense of train fares; and this time, she did not dare to try to persuade me to go.

'I don't care what happens to me, as long as I don't end up like Jane and Bill-The-Bore,' says Lyndsay caustically, picking suddenly at the label on the jar of honey.

'What, married?'

He scowls at me. 'No.' Then he reconsiders. 'Well, yes, or not to someone like them.' He flaps away this aside. 'No, I mean, living in a little house in suburbia.'

I feel weary when he looks across the table to me for support. I am surprised to find that I am longing for the police to arrive. Anything to avoid Adolescent-Onslaught-On-Suburbia.

'Their neighbours breed giant Japanese goldfish,' he says.

'*Do* they?'

He scowls me into silence. I pick at the label on the jar of pickle. Eventually I ask, 'So where would you like to live, Lynd?' Accentuate-The-Positive.

He muses pleasantly for a moment. 'Possibly the Highlands. I'd like a big old stone house on the shores of a loch.'

Oh, yes, I remember my own big house, although it was nowhere near a loch. There was a suite or two for my guests, for their privacy and mine; an office or two, for personal mess and phone calls; a balcony from my bedroom; a block of stables across a yard of warm cobbles. How do people afford a big house? How do people afford any house? I wish I could afford this flat, which is for sale.

'And what would you do, up there?'

He smiles bashfully. 'Write poetry.'

'Oh, yes,' I laugh, but quietly, 'of course.'

He sweeps happily to his feet. 'Well, someone has to do it.' Stalking across the room, he glances in surprise through the window towards the castle in the distance. 'Is that the castle?'

I nod.

He leans across the sink to stare. From the window, the castle is a small rough mound at the far end of a corrugated mile of high grey roofs. Buried beneath the view, invisible to him, are The Meadows, criss-crossed by lines of thin trees, with a sparse traffic of footballers and cyclists, overlooked by the brooding insomniac Infirmary.

'Do you have any juice?' he asks after a while, turning to the fridge.

'Grapefruit.'

He wrinkles his nose, and then dribbles an inch of juice from the carton into his glass before returning to the sink to mix it with water. 'O levels will turn me out like Jane,' he states flatly.

'I'm not sure that Jane *has* any O levels,' I offer in reply.

Is his darkening expression due to the first mouthful of juice?

'Do you have any sugar?'

'No.' I do, but where? I am too drained to search, or to direct Lyndsay's search. I suspect that the bag of sugar is an old brown sticky lump, and I cannot face Lyndsay's whines and complaints.

'I don't need O levels.'

'For poetry?'

He nods slowly, between sips. He seems acclimatized to the juice. 'You need Mr MacKenzie,' I tell him.

He frowns, questioning.

And I flap away the question: forgive-the-foibles-of-an-old-lady, Mr MacKenzie belongs to the past, to *my* past. Presumably little Lyndsay cannot remember Mr MacKenzie, or never knew much about him. And now, in a new school, Lyndsay will never know. He will grow up Mr-MacKenzie-less.

He is peering at me. 'Isn't that a kids' programme, *Mr MacKenzie?*'

'No.'

'Captain Brainwash,' he mumbles. And now, with more urgency: 'Who says that Their idea of education is the right idea?'

'*They* do.' I indicate the mess of bread-and-spreads: 'Do you want any more of this?'

A *No* registers briefly on his bared, bright-eyed face. 'But why should I listen?' he demands excitedly. 'Perhaps They don't even exist, except in my imagination. Perhaps They are *literally* a nightmare.'

'Idealism,' I comment, sweeping the jars across the table.

He crosses the kitchen towards me in two easy strides. 'And what's so wrong with having ideals?' he breathes, behind me, as I grapple with the jars.

'No, *idealism*: nothing-exists-outside-your-head, or something.' Philosophy, Module One?

He steps back to let me deal with the table, and lounges against the wall. 'Nothing exists *inside* most people's heads,' he says eventually, desolately.

I peek at him from the wheezy, icy fridge. 'Nothing exists *on* your head.'

He gazes mildly into the murky uric juice.

'Berkeley,' I conclude, slamming the fridge door.

He rises against the wall. 'What did you call me?' The tone is incredulous, and smudged with laughter.

'Lyndsay,' I protest, 'you're getting as bad as Mum. I didn't call you anything. I said Berkeley. Because it was Berkeley, I think, who came up with Idealism. Centuries ago.'

He shrugs and discards the glass on the table. 'And I thought it was all my own work,' he says, resignedly, sweetly.

'Well,' I manage, 'that's one of life's little tricks, isn't it; to make us feel that it's all our own work.'

I know that his blue searchlight is on me as I turn away to busy myself nonsensically with the breadbin. And why not? Why am I so ungiving to him? I was always so sure that I would know what to do with Adolescence Part One. So why do I feel helpless, hopeless? I do not seem to know what to do about anything any more. I finish trawling the breadbin for crumbs, and wish very hard that Lyndsay would go and have a bath or something, anything to leave me alone for a while.

'Sis,' he says uneasily, behind me, 'could I have a shower?'

I am tugged around to face him by a handful of smarting heart. 'Oh yes, Lynd, of course you can have a shower.' I smile helplessly. 'Have two.'

Lyndsay leaves in search of the bathroom, and I can return to my thoughts. And my thoughts are of Simon. Last summer, when Lucy told me about Simon, I did not go immediately to confront him: Duncan did not come and go with the videos, nor did Lucy leave me, until mid-evening. I wanted to *see* Simon, not simply to speak to him. If I had gone to him as soon as I was left alone, I would not have reached him in London until late. Too late to travel home, and I did not want an opportunity to stay the night with him. But although I did not want to speak to Simon immediately, I wanted to speak to someone; I wanted to speak to someone who really knew me, who knew the real me, from the old days. The real me? The old days? Were all those days The Old Days? Even the streaming black Saturday afternoon when we Blaneys went sightseeing in Leamington Spa after a trip to the castle, Erin bubbling in the pushchair with bronchitis? Or the thick silt of Sunday afternoon visits to indistinguishable aunties and uncles, Beryl, or Doris, or Joan and Ted, or Eric, or Bob? On the way there, in the car, Mum would flick her scrutiny from the pavement to our backseat Blaney belligerence, and, full of her own resentment, snap at us: *I don't ask much of you, and it has to be done, and it's not for long, so make an effort, try to look like a proper little family, and behave nicely.*

We would look out of the windows, ignore her. Luckily, when we arrived there was no chance to behave in any way at all. We did not have to perform. We would sit and wait for Mum and Dad to finish with the aunties and uncles; sit inside the wadding of those living rooms, facing the telly, the Sunday afternoon quiz shows, with droning buzzers and yapping comperes on sets decorated like daleks. In the living rooms, all the surfaces were matted with a faint bile of cigarette smoke and dog hair. Often there was a saucer of water on the floor to pacify the gas fire. At the window, pastel porcelain figurines posed coyly in the blinding drifts of net curtain, alongside a small vase, empty, lacking even the dry brown autumn left in the bottom by long-gone flowers. The only light relief was provided by the leatherette pouffe.

During the visits, Jane would claim the pouffe and sit cross-legged, frowning at the telly. Was this nice behaviour, or the opposite? I was never sure. Erin was afraid of dogs, so the adults' conversation bore a descant of Don't-be-silly-he-won't-hurt-you. Lyndsay usually had a physical need requiring attention from Mum – trouser buttons, or a scratch – and Mum would deal deftly but carefully with this without faltering from the conversation, her hands tidying Lyndsay as if he were a piece of knitting. Where was Lauren? Was she not yet born?

When I was Lyndsay's age, it was Ali who was going to be there for me in the future. Not Roz, who was going to go, to leave me for a man and a family of her own. Nor Lucy, who was never with me, with any of us, in a sense. And, when I was Lyndsay's age, Deborah did not exist, for me. She had not yet come to our school. And now she was gone. And Ali was almost gone, but not quite. I was alone for the evening, waiting for the morning; I decided that if I was now the real me, then I wanted to be real friends with

283

Ali rather than school friends, classmates, near-neighbours. I felt that Ali would know what I should do.

I craved Ali's flat black stare. No-nonsense Ali. Throughout my childhood Mum told me that dark eyes are beautiful but not to be trusted. She claimed that the element of foreignness was coincidental: the problem was that *You can't see what they're thinking*. I should have argued with her; I cannot believe that I did not argue, that I did not defend my own dark eyes. Why did I argue so much about the cut of my bras and the volume of my Genesis and Pink Floyd records and not about the colour of my eyes? Perhaps arguments about half-cups and bass balance were about behaviour (Oh-no-you-can't, Oh-yes-I-can) rather than opinion. Because Mum's opinion, in my early days, when I knew nothing and she knew everything, was fact. Other voices, in those days, were strange and distant. And I suspect that Mum's comments about dark eyes came first during those very early days, as soon as my own soft, baby, blueberry muddles were hardening to black pips.

I could have argued that dark eyes are not beautiful, but are trustworthy. In contrast, blue eyes, green eyes, eyes which are light-coloured will sparkle and attract the eyes of others, and, aware that they are being watched, become self-conscious, defensive and quick-moving eyes. Roz's extraordinary eyes were the colour of the three baubles of thick green glass which hung for years in our kitchen in a loose net of string, after being brought back by Mum from Majorca for reasons best known to herself. Lucy's eyes have no colour of their own – the blue is an illusion, like the blue of the sky. I could no longer remember Deborah's eyes, not with any certainty. I craved Ali's brown eyes, clogged with pigment, which could watch without being seen, and see so much more.

So I rang Ali. In France. For a few moments the electronic space between us, the ocean of air, fizzled with exclamations and news, until, partly in response to yet another So-how-are-you? I enquired, 'Has Lucy said anything to you?' *About me.*

'Lucy?' A return to the echoey tone of surprise. 'But how?'

'Well I don't know, does she ring you?' And suddenly I was curious: '*Does* she ring you?'

'*Lucy*? Does she ring *you*?'

'Well, no.' I had not intended a conversation about Lucy's habits. Nevertheless, I added, 'She writes postcards.'

I flinched from the bleat of Ali's short laugh. 'Not to me, and I'm the one who's abroad.'

Since Ali went to France she has written letters to me, regularly, several times each year, remembering what she has told me and then telling me more, about a new flat, work, or a holiday, and plans, perhaps a purchase, a car or a cat. Lucy prefers postcards, so much shorter, but no more frequent, addressed to *Miss Demeanour* and scribbled with a few unconnected observations, *I saw Killit in the Co-op buying French Fancies*: a horrible perversion of Mum's instinct to dispense local chit-chat to me. There are no plans, no purchases, no changes of address.

I told Ali, lightly, 'I've just seen Lucy and she gave me a lecture.'

The line sang back Ali's disbelief: 'Noooo. Not Lucy.'

I slipped my murmur of agreement beneath these words before she stopped to ask, 'About what?'

Which, of course, I had been expecting her to do. Yet still I was not ready. 'The lecture? Oh . . .' my lungs spooned the air, '. . . Simon Steiner, actually.'

'Oh no,' the line tingled with her deep, low sigh. 'What have you done now?'

Now? 'It has been going on for a year or so, actually.' But I have to add, to explain, 'Sort of.' Explain?

'Oh.' In surprise, rather than disdain.

I said, 'You don't like him, do you?'

Her tone continued, careful, and perhaps puzzled. 'I never said that.'

I smiled to myself, but hoping that the smile would trickle down into my words. 'You said that you wouldn't trust him with your chihuahua.'

I did not know if she was joking when she said, in the same careful tone, 'I don't have a chihuahua.'

'But you don't trust him.' Trust? Trust him to *what*? Trust him *not* to what?

Then she said very quickly, too quickly for me, 'Surely it's not important that *I* trust him,' before emphasizing, 'I don't know him, Lalie.'

I wondered what she would say if I explained that he was under the impression that she knew him very well indeed?

Ali continued, 'I only knew whatever Deborah told me.'

'Deborah didn't trust him?' I stayed tense, braced.

Her tone dropped, dismissive, 'Deborah didn't say much about him.'

I was sifting these words, wondering how to draw a conclusion from them, when she added dismissively, 'I've not seen him for years.'

So Ali had known him; he had known Ali. So he had known that Lucy was not Ali. 'You never said.'

'Said what?'

'Said that you knew him.'

'Well of course I knew him,' she began to explain, pointedly patient, 'I saw him whenever I went to Deborah's house.'

I checked, 'And *since*?' Which was a reference to Deborah's accident. Deborah's *death*. Why do I not say the word even now, even to myself? We never say *Deborah's death* to each other. None of us, not even Lucy.

'Well of course not *since*,' she replied irritably, over a hard pip of puzzlement, before, more surely, qualifying this with, 'not unless you count the memorial service.'

It was then that I came to my point, asking her, 'What should I do about him? About Simon?'

She did not seem surprised; gently, she challenged, 'And I know better than you?'

I do not remember replying; but I do remember that she followed with another jaunty question: 'What's the problem?'

I sighed, and started, 'It's a long story,' fully intending to continue, to try to tell.

But she said happily, 'I'll have to trust Lucy to put you right, then.'

I stopped her: '*Please*, Ali, *not* Lucy.'

My objection was swept away on her sigh of exasperation.

I tried to explain, 'It's okay for you; you don't have to see her, to have her drifting around you . . .' I knew that I was failing to explain. 'Lucy's hopeless.' In more senses than one.

'You two,' Ali murmured indulgently.

Us *two*? *Who* two?

'You'd be lost without Lucy,' she was saying fondly. Fond of whom?

'No I would not.'

'Yes you would.'

She seemed to find this amusing, but it was then that I felt that she was trying to dump me on Lucy. I asked her, 'Do you think that you'll ever come home?'

'Home?' Suddenly she was confused. 'You mean back to our town?'

'Well, no.' Of course not. I wanted to say London, which should sound plausible – because surely London is where people live? – although I knew that I did not mean London. In the end, I said it tentatively anyway: 'London?'

The laugh was tinny. 'Whereabouts in London? Edmonton? Leytonstone?'

And she was right: because for us, this was what living in London would mean. Hardly Highgate. 'Anyway,' she argued, '*you* don't live in London. You probably live as far away from London as I do.'

As far away from London, but in the opposite direction. Twice as far from Ali.

I complained, 'I never see you.'

'Well, no,' she said defensively. 'Of course not.'

Embarrassingly, I did not stop. 'Nothing's the same, any more.'

She said simply, 'Of course not.'

Pointlessly I provoked her, by repeating, 'Do you think you'll ever come home?'

'I can't come home, Lalie,' she despaired; despaired of me. 'My whole life . . .' And she sighed, declining the effort to finish.

So, I was on my own. Ali had become someone with priorities: Oh! the beauty, the simplicity, of priorities, excuseless excuses. But people who need to invoke priorities are weary, wary people: was there something which Ali was not telling me? Instead, she was trying to imply that the distance between us was inevitable. All my life I have been struggling against the inevitable, trying to live slightly differently, to keep alive the possibility of difference. And suddenly, connected to Ali yet unable to connect with her at all, slowly pressing an impression of the receiver onto my ear, I began to doubt that I could continue to struggle alone.

I did not want Ali to prove Mum right: *Family Is Blood*, family sticks around and friends drift away. My Mum, the Sicilian? And a strange sentiment, too, for someone who professes to hate the bulk of her own family, the Blaneys. But *for better, for worse*, perhaps? Blood sticks, stains, ceaselessly seeps: for Mum, blood means inevitability. For Mum, I was simply one more Blaney baby (but bigger than the others, so a bigger problem). So much for family, then. Was family the best that I could expect from life, was family the ultimate in human relations? But whoever said that we choose our friends? Not true of old friends, surely; not school friends, especially. Once upon a time, I lived in a house with the Blaneys and I went to a school with Roz, Lucy, Deborah, Ali: what was the difference, where was the choice? Away from Waltham-way, though, I was choosing, and I had chosen Ali. But the phone call left me afraid: was she proving Mum right, would she render me an ex-school friend, ex-school, ex-friend, an irritation on a Christmas card list?

Early the next morning, I rang Simon, told him that Jane's wedding was off, told him to stay at home because I was coming to see him. When I reached his flat, I was let in by one of the flatmates. Seeing Simon in his room at the end of the hallway,

I went immediately to him, slamming his thin door behind me. Which, in one fell swoop, excluded the others and made clear to him that I wanted his full attention. Perhaps for the first time ever. I said to him, 'You were seeing my friend Lucy.' *When you were seeing me; or, no, more accurately, whenever you were not seeing me.*

He had been feeling vaguely behind him, along the window sill, for his cigarettes, but now he froze. 'How do you know?'

So it was true. I was surprised to realize that I had been hoping, even until this moment, that it was a story. And I was shocked that his immediate concern was to return the situation to his control: How did I *know*? I stayed leaning back onto the door, my hands pressed behind me. Keeping him in the room? Keeping myself in the room? Keeping myself in touch with the outside, everyday world. We stood looking across the room at each other. We looked more, in those few seconds, than ever before. I saw the glints in his eyes as impurities in stone. And I saw that he was afraid. Of me. And I was pleased. Which frightened me. I wanted him to feel what I had felt when Lucy told me, when everything became bigger than I had thought, when I became smaller.

I started, 'How *could* you?'

And he started with my name, 'Lalie,' to implore me. 'It was nothing. It was a mistake.'

So it was nothing, and yet it was something, a mistake. A mistake, *one* mistake?

He was whining, 'It was over, almost immediately.'

Almost.

'So it didn't seem worth telling you.'

But thanks for agonizing. 'I found out, Simon.' *Which is what happens.*

'From Lucy?' This was said angrily, to shift the anger to Lucy.

I shouted, 'Lucy didn't know that we had anything to do with each other. Whereas – correct me if I'm wrong – you *did* know.'

His eyes switched emphatically to the wall adjoining the living room.

Typical Steiner, keeping up appearances. 'Sod them,' I shouted louder. Which, of course, meant, *Sod you*.

He shouted back, 'Lucy shouldn't have told you.'

'No, you're right, *you* should have told me.'

And for a moment, this would have been enough, would have been a start; so, for a moment, he had won, and the problem became the telling, not the doing. My anger was coming in bite-sized pieces. I felt that if he had told me, everything would have been fine, everything could have been simple. Because what is the odd friend, between friends? 'Why didn't you tell me?'

Encouraged, newly conciliatory, he said, 'I would have done.'

Which is when my hope unravelled, spectacularly. 'When?' I shouted. 'When, Simon?' Behind me, my hot hands were stuck to the door. Stuck *fast*? Going-nowhere-fast.

He was stuck, too, in front of the window, full of frozen movement. 'It was nothing,' he backtracked.

'What a pity that we seem to disagree,' I managed caustically.

He surprised me by flaring, '*Listen* to you! *This* is why I didn't tell you.'

My words came down hard on him: 'Don't blame this on me.'

'It was nothing,' he wrung the words from his suddenly softened face, 'I promise you.'

Promise? Promises from Simon? 'How many times was it nothing?' I taunted. Then, more pertinently, 'If it was nothing, you could have told me.' And was it really nothing? If so, my worst fears about Simon were confirmed: 'Nothing much is anything to you, is it?'

'That's not true,' he countered indignantly, petulantly.

I began to ring silently, body and brain, with weariness; because now I was going to have to endure him telling me how he was suffering, how he was misunderstood.

Instead, he tried again, 'I would have told you.'

I stressed, 'But I found out.' The problem with secrets is that they have a tendency to stop being secrets. And then what are they?

'And presumably I'm nothing, too, because you keep me secret.'

His eyes widened but the pupils remained small. And of course they remained small, but of course they seemed even smaller, like the narrow windows to the lime-green soul of a cat. 'That was your decision as much as mine,' he said sharply.

I widened my own eyes strenuously in reply: a look which challenged, *Are-you-sure?*

He climbed down, his eyelids came down: 'Well, I don't want my parents prying into my private life.'

The Steiners, prying? *Try having the Blaneys for a family.* The all-shrieking Blaneys. But what harm can parents do? What harm can anyone's parents do, particularly the Steiners?

But none of this was coming close to what was important. I demanded, 'Why did you do it?'

He sat down on his desk, tipped back his head, drank the air into his huge sigh. Without looking at me, he said, 'Because you weren't there.' He reached for his cigarettes.

'So it's my fault,' I goaded sarcastically.

He horrified me by seeming to take this seriously, returning his gaze slowly to me, refusing to reply. Sunbeams twitched on the surfaces of his eyes.

'Well that's a shame,' I continued, my tone worsening, 'because I won't always be around, will I?' And then I said, 'In fact, I won't be around at all, from now on, so you can do whatever you like with whoever you like.' As the words came, they felt absolutely right.

His hands rose, to nowhere in particular. 'Don't be silly, Lalie,' he began to appeal.

'*Silly?*'

'You brought this up.'

'No, *you* brought it up, by *doing* it.' How could he not see? I despaired, 'Is it me?' Meaning, *is it me who has the problem?* Meaning, *it is NOT me who has the problem.* And then I said, 'Right, I'm going.'

As I turned for the door handle, he was agreeing, complaining, 'Well, you're certainly in no fit state to discuss this now.'

I turned briefly back, glancing towards him. He had spoken around a cigarette which was held unlit, absurdly clean and long, between his lips. He was feeling, behind, on the desk, for a box of matches, clumsily rattling paperclips and pens. *No-fit-state* is never a statement intended to endear.

I informed him, 'I never will be in a fit state to discuss this.' And when had he ever discussed anything with me?

He asked, as I opened the door, 'Where are you going?'

'Home.'

'Which home?' Blaney-home, or my own home? He had taken the cigarette, still unlit, from his mouth.

'Does it matter?'

Well, yes, because, 'Are you coming back? Later?'

'I've told you: no.'

'Don't go.' A sudden irresistible cross between a plea and an order.

And I was stunned by a realization of the misery that I lived with for so long, for the previous year. Which is not so long, though, in a lifetime.

He pleaded, 'I'll tell you whatever you want to know.'

But, of course, I wanted him to tell me because he wanted to tell me and not because I was holding the future to ransom. I turned again, struck that what had been so important to me was our equality: it could always have been Us-against-the-world, but Deborah, losing Deborah, had made this even more so, so that we were identically imperfect, uniquely blighted. But now, and recently, instead of Us-against-the-world, it was becoming Us-against-each-other. Because, of course, there was more to life than the memory of Deborah. I closed the door, but reiterated sadly, 'This will never work.'

He chided gently, 'Don't say that.'

Simon's answer to everything. As if not saying will solve the problem.

He reached to open the window. He was going to smoke. I had never known, would never know, if he opened windows solely for my benefit. I leaned back on the door again, and watched him. I could not stop myself thinking that if I did not sleep with him now, once more, then the last time would already have been and gone. The world, recently, had seemed painfully short on goodbyes. I ran my gaze along his outstretched arm, the skin, like white sand, rough, hot, dry, yet cool silky smooth. I could not stop myself doing this, thinking this, despite what I was saying. I was saying, 'You know it won't work.' I had said the same words before, to other lovers, hoping to provoke a denial, a declaration. But this time it was the truth. And I wanted him to agree. The-minimum-of-fuss: *It won't work* is easier to say than *I'm leaving*. No, there was something more that I wanted, I wanted him to be sad, as sad as I was. And it is easier to be sad over *It won't work* than over *I'm leaving*.

He conceded, or I felt that he conceded, with a huge, gloomy, smoky exhalation.

I sighed too, relaxing muscles I had not known were tense. I was becoming somehow both heavier and lighter, and the world was becoming more and less real. This was the new me, in my new world, without.

Simon pleaded, 'I'm sorry.' He was holding the cigarette very low, out of the way. 'I mean, I'm sorry for me, too, very, if it's any consolation.'

'Don't,' I winced. I had thought that this was what I wanted – him, sad – but it was not. It was too sad. Two lots of sadness was suddenly too much.

His eyes flashed despair skyward. 'I know, I know,' *I know it's no excuse*, 'but I've been bad company for *years* because of Deborah.'

For no particular reason – a mere reflex? – I said, 'The accident was a year and a half ago.'

He responded loudly, 'I *know* when she *died*.'

I was frozen in his stare. I had never heard the word *died* said about Deborah so loudly, so angrily, so desperately. Perhaps I had never heard it said at all. He seemed to be so very still, but I could see that he was shaking, I could see from the edges of him that he was shaking. I felt that I could still him with a single steady touch of my finger. But I did not dare. And he was so far away from me.

His voice was very low, below the shaking, very firm. 'When did you last see Deborah?'

I was surprised to find that I had no answer, that there were no immediate memories. The best I could manage was, 'I saw her in Spain.'

Suddenly, momentarily, everything changed, and he relented. 'Oh. Yes.' He lowered his eyes and smiled thoughtfully. 'Spain.' Then he raised his eyes, without the smile, to check eagerly, 'Did you? Did you see her in Spain? I didn't know.'

I humoured him. 'Yes, I did, just before she came back.'

'She enjoyed Spain, did she?'

'Yes, she did.'

'Seemed to have done her a lot of good.' This was said appreciatively. 'She was so relaxed, when she came home.' Sharply disappointed, he asked, 'You never saw her after Spain?

'She wrote – every six weeks or so, I suppose – after she came home.'

I regret, now, that she did not hear so frequently from me.

He exhaled noisily; was he sighing? 'That's not what I asked.' Then he repeated, evenly, clearly, 'You never saw her after Spain?' 'No.'

'How much do you weigh?' The same flat, uncomplicated tone.

'*Simon!*' How could such a question be relevant?

'How *much* do you *weigh*?' He was desperate for my answer.

Immediately, resentfully, I replied, 'Eight.' Untruthfully, too, because I am eight-two or three. I tend to round down.

He took another mouthful of smoke, a controlled breath, and then said, 'When Deborah died, she weighed a little less than six stone.'

Quickly, I tried to visualize six stone, a little less than six stone, five-stone-something. As thin as Lauren? But is Lauren thin, or simply small, simply young? Who is thinner than Lauren but not simply smaller? What about Aunty Mo? When she died, how much did she weigh? But was Aunty Mo thin, or dying? What do ballerinas, gymnasts, weigh? How low can a grown-up go? When is it impossible to walk? Do bones show, below six stone? If so, which bones? All of them? 'Was she ill?'

'Yes.'

'How ill?'

He was lifting the cigarette blindly to his lips.

So I urged, 'How ill, Simon? What was wrong?' I was prickling with panic. 'Was she going to die?'

He by-passed his lips, pushed the palm of his hand onto his forehead to signal exasperation. '*Was she going to die?*' he mimicked cruelly, meaning *She DID die*.

In a surge of panic I insisted, 'She died in an accident.' Car, brow of the hill: I knew the details. Or did I? I had been told. I could not remember who had told me.

'God,' he shouted, 'I know how she died. I saw, I went to identify her.'

He went to identify her. My words came out despite my deep inward breath. 'I didn't know.'

'Well, who else do you think went along?' he continued shouting. 'My parents? Oh, yes, they would have loved a trip to the morgue, they were in the mood for a trip to the morgue, they would have loved to have seen her – '

'*Stop it, Simon.*'

And it worked. We looked at each other in this new, sudden, spectacular silence. He continued to smoke to control his breathing: regular, blunt puffs. His gaze was hard in mine. Because, as usual, this was a challenge. Any cries and confidences and intimacies had to come from him as challenges.

I managed an expressionless, 'You never said.'

His reply burned. 'You never asked.'

He had seen her. He had been the last to see her. He had seen her afterwards. When everything was over. When, in a sense, she did not exist. There had been so many questions that I had wanted to ask the person who had last seen Deborah. I had wanted so badly to find the person. And in the meantime I had gone there, myself, in my imagination, so often, to the morgue, to the graveside, wherever. Why? Now I had found the person with the answers but I could not remember my questions, doubts, fears. I could not remember my imaginary visits to the morgue, the morgue's visits to my imagination. All I could remember was Simon in his suit in the church at the memorial service. So neat, so clean, so new.

He said, 'She had anorexia.'

I snapped to attention. 'All of a sudden?'

His laugh was a bitter, knowing sigh, a private joke which was not a joke. 'No,' he replied quietly, knowingly, 'not all of a sudden.'

'See?' I protested: *more lies*. 'There was nothing wrong with Deborah.'

'There was a lot wrong with Deborah.' Nothing moved except the hand with the cigarette, which was moving reassuringly regularly but soupy-slow. Deliberate. Maintaining his balance. His eyes still did not move; the gaze, in mine, was simultaneously close and distant. Detached.

'But I'd have known,' I gabbled. 'Don't you see? How could I not have known?'

He said, 'Well, you *didn't* know.'

'But I *would've* known.' I stopped, giddied, to steady my thoughts, to start again. 'I'd known Deborah for *years*.'

Blinking his gaze ceiling-ward, he countered sceptically, 'You'd known her for – what? – four, five years?'

'Which is long enough.' Long enough to know.

'She was mostly fine for those four or five years,' he said, barely, wearily, before flapping a hand towards his bed. 'Sit down, for God's sake,' he said, not unkindly.

It felt odd to be invited, to have to be invited. No, it felt right. So I did: I slid quickly across the room to the bed, and sat down. I knew exactly the movement of the slim still-single bed beneath me. *Give*: the word, strangely, is *give*, I knew the particular give of the bed beneath me. I knew, too, that Simon was telling me the truth. There was a new give in his voice. And in his eyes, too, which were singed in the thin smoke. His face showed nothing but the dull shine of eggshell, both tough and frail. So I sat, which signalled that I was willing to listen.

He sighed, to announce the start of the story. And then the words came quickly. 'It had all happened before, when she was young; thirteen or fourteen, I suppose. She got better, and we moved.' He raised his eyebrows knowingly, meaning *Moved to the place you call home*, meaning *This is where you come in*. 'I don't think that she was the only reason for the move, but she was one of the reasons. Maybe the main one, I don't know. My parents were very keen on a Fresh Start.' These last two words – *Fresh, Start* – were said unusually clearly, to indicate that they were not his own.

'Was Deborah?'

He considered this for a second, his gaze running unfocused along the window sill, over the white-gold cufflinks, the soft wipe-clean cover of the English-French pocket dictionary, the hot purple velvet petals of the African violet. 'Yes,' he decided, 'she was keen. Because, if people have seen you when you're five stone, then they've seen all of you.'

'Were you?'

He blinked me into focus. 'Was I what?'

'Were you keen to move?'

He smiled patiently down on me. 'It wasn't up to me.'

'But were you keen?'

Very precisely, he forced all the cinders of the cigarette down onto his cold slippery silver ashtray, the upturned lid of a jam jar. 'I suppose not.'

'You *suppose* not?' I complained, mildly outraged. *On his behalf?*

He shrugged loosely, perhaps to imply that he could not remember, perhaps to imply that he did not care. Neither of which could be true, surely?

But he was continuing, 'Things started to go wrong again when she came back from Spain.'

Immediately, I sat forward to protest, 'She would have told me.'

He merely replied, cruelly, 'Well, she didn't.' Then, slightly more reasonably, 'Anyway, what could she have said?'

I did not answer, there was no answer. Instead, only a sceptical question: '*Why* did things start to go wrong when she came back from Spain?'

'Oh, you know,' he replied miserably, 'work, love, life.'

Yes, I did know. But I did not know this about Deborah. Simon could have been talking about me, but surely not about Deborah. Deborah had everything under control.

'Oh, I don't know,' he continued to speculate: 'There were a lot of decisions. There was a lot of pressure from Mum and Dad to find a job, the right job, the Career, the right rest-of-your-life.'

Pressure from his, her, Mum and Dad? Incredulous, I tried, 'But they'd be happy with whatever you choose to do.' The Steiners, of all parents.

He laughed dryly, bitterly. 'No, what *they require* is for *us* to be happy with whatever we do. Which is a very tall order.'

I could not stop myself. 'You *are* happy, aren't you?' It was impossible for me to concentrate on Deborah, dead Deborah, dear dead Deborah, when faced with this real live Steiner, *my* real-live-Steiner, the Steiner whom I was supposed to know. '*Aren't* you?'

He shrugged.

Which meant *No*. If he was happy, the answer would have been a simple *Yes*.

Shocked that I had not known, and now not knowing what to say, I found that I was switching hurriedly to Deborah. 'But Deborah was so good at everything, she could have done anything.'

Nonplussed, he suggested, 'Perhaps that was the problem.'

I was unconvinced. 'It's not enough, it's not enough to explain . . .' Why Deborah but not Simon nor I? Why anorexia?

He shrugged again, inconclusive, non-committal: *Sorry-but-that's-your-lot.*

I insisted: 'Simon.'

His gaze sparked on mine.

'I don't believe you,' I said calmly, by now utterly lacking animosity. 'Not *Deborah*. And not *that*. Deborah was so . . .' I stopped, to choose the word.

'Sane.'

'Yes, sane.'

'*That's* why she didn't tell you,' he said hotly.

Which told me nothing. 'Why?'

'Because you would have thought that she was mad.' He had begun to tap the desktop with the packet of cigarettes: a new, different, way of shaking?

I protested, 'I didn't say . . .' And then I did not say, I would not say. I would not incriminate myself by using a word which was not mine.

Something in his eyes stirred knowingly for a second. 'Which words *do* spring to mind, then?'

I said nothing. I sensed a trap.

'*Manipulative*? Maybe *vain*?' Questions, but masking an accusation.

Still I said nothing. *Your words, not mine.* I could not say a bad word about Deborah.

'Lalie,' he said passionately, 'Deborah was trying to control *herself*. She had no interest in manipulating anyone else.' Then he relented, swayed backwards, allowing, 'Okay, she didn't *listen* to us, but lots of people don't listen to other people. And, *okay*, we were *worried* about her but she didn't *want* us to worry.' He sighed hugely, adding, 'Nor did she care how she looked, because, believe me, if she had cared about how she had looked, she wouldn't have been so thin.'

I felt uncomfortable, sitting and listening to those words from him. I felt self-conscious. What did he think of me, of the size of me?

Now a contradiction was flickering on his face. 'Well, no,' he muttered, 'she *did* care, she knew she looked bad.'

I cringed from the unimaginable: Deborah looking bad.

He said reluctantly, 'It's a very visible illness.'

I bit into my lip.

'Anyway,' he concluded listlessly, 'I presume that's why she didn't tell you. With you, she could be normal. With us, she was six stone.'

Us: The Steiners.

'But how were you' – you Steiners – 'any more likely to know than anyone else?' Deborah had been living away from home.

Simon said coolly, 'You know the Steiners.'

Well, yes and no.

'They know *everything*.'

I wondered, more to myself than to Simon, 'They don't know about me.'

He smiled slowly, sadly, as close to tenderly as he had ever smiled at me, and agreed, 'No, they don't know about you.'

I burned with a feeling which I could not recognize, which I could not place. So I dragged my gaze away, asked, 'Did you ever tell anyone? About Deborah?' Which meant, *Did you NEVER tell anyone?*

His tone snapped to attention. 'My parents were very much in favour of saying nothing to anyone.' These words, in some sense not his own, slid on top of his disdain, bitterness, anger. Then his own words burst through: 'And, yes, I said nothing, but I think, I *think*, I *hope*, I did it for *her*, not for *them*.'

So the Steiners had slipped from *Us* to *Them*.

And now I knew. Because he had told me. So where were *we*, in this Us-and-Them? Yet still I could not quite believe him. Again I tried to visualize Deborah. As far as I could remember, she had not been particularly skinny. Not like Lucy had been: bony, loose Lucy. Nor like the slim silky chrysalis of Roz. Nor me, with my hard edges. No: Deborah had had the perfect figure. 'So,' I questioned Simon sceptically, 'when things started going wrong, she stopped eating?'

'Not stopped. Started controlling.'

Not good enough. 'Over-controlling?'

He conceded, 'Because she couldn't stop; because it was . . .' Momentarily lost, he tried to trace his thoughts with an arcing shrug.

'A compulsion.' I had read my books. My magazine articles.

'No,' he decided, 'an addiction. Harder and harder to stop.' Suddenly he coaxed, 'Think about it: the lower the weight, the more difficult to keep it there, the more likely that any food will mean a gain.' His gaze settled unnervingly heavily on me. 'Once you start, how can you stop, without the worst happening?'

I hurried with, 'But why her *weight*? There was nothing *wrong* with her *weight*.' I was surprised by the sting of my words in the air.

He said, 'You and I won't know anything about trying to lose weight.'

I decided not to contradict him. The world is so much simpler for boys. I looked down at the floor between us.

'But it's *so* hard to do.'

I glanced up; an involuntary twitch of my attention.

'It was hard work for Deborah. Do you know that muscles hurt when they waste away? Yes, they ache. Apparently it's a particular kind of ache.' Somehow these increasingly soft words were becoming slippery with threat. 'And she was cold all the time. And tired, so tired that her brain was numb.'

'Simon, please.' *Waste away, numb, cold.*

He snapped forward, almost excitedly, 'But don't you see? Don't you see that she succeeded? She lost weight almost every single day. She could do what no one else is able to do.'

Neat, disciplined, high-achieving. Perhaps not so very mad after all.

'On the other hand,' he said, dropping into despondency, 'she felt that every day was a failed day.' He folded his arms, high, drawing his shoulders upwards and inwards. 'Too many calories.' His arms stayed firmly folded; neat swellings of muscle, tough strips along each bone.

It seemed to me that he knew so much. He had been even closer to her than I had realized.

His shoulders lifted further still: a tiny, tense shrug. He finished faintly, 'It was one way to keep the world at bay, I suppose.'

'But did it?' I whispered doubtfully, rhetorically.

'Well, no. Because she's not here now, is she.' His eyes were steamy.

Briskly, I asked, 'Was she having any treatment?'

He barely managed an angry, 'There *is* no treatment.' Then, immediately, worse: 'Do you mean, Was-she-visiting-someone-who-was-telling-her-to-eat-and-threatening-to-force-feed-her? If so, then your answer is yes.'

My answer. I knew that I was supposed to say, *Don't take it out on me*. But why not, why not take it out on me? Because I could take it; for this one particular moment, I could take it. I stood up. To take it better. I went across the room and threaded my arms over his slim hard shoulders, around his neck, threaded myself to him, breathed in his dry hair. And his unique smell, bitter, familiar but still unfamiliar. Soon to become unfamiliar. In my arms he was hard all over but soft too, because how could I have held him so hard unless he was soft?

He said hotly into my hair, 'She hated doctors and hospitals.'

I could feel through my skin that he was not angry with me. So it was me and him against the world, again, briefly, finally. Stroking his hair, probably for the last time, stroking goodbye, I soothed, 'I bet she did.'

He turned free, slightly, in my arms; so that his eyes, grey marbles, could knock mine. 'No, really,' he urged anxiously, urging me to understand.

'I know.' I slipped my hand from the back of his head to the side of his face so that his chin lay in my palm, a warm smooth stone.

'Waste of time, in her opinion.' His head grew heavier and his lips turned on the base of my little finger.

Gently, hoping that he would not notice, I took my hand away, took hold of his shoulder.

He said sadly, dismayed, 'She had early morning appointments so that she wouldn't miss lectures; can you believe that?'

I smiled, murmured sympathetically, 'Of a Steiner? Yes.'

'That was where she was going,' he said. 'To an eight o'clock appointment.' He meant, *That was where she was going when she died.*

When I left Simon's flat, I left alone, having declined his offer to accompany me to the station. Outside, it was late afternoon, early evening; which in winter would have been twilight but, because it was summer, was indistinct from the morning when I had arrived. I wanted to be alone, to think. I did not want to be in anyone's home: his, mine, or the Blaneys'. If there was any place where I could think, then it was in that huge hushed area, built up but deserted. The new, smoothly finished, red-brick blocks of flats seemed to be empty: huge Marie Celestes, moored on the banks. The old blocks were different, their stone balconies busy with Bangladeshi children and patchy banners of laundry. But there were few cars around the old blocks so they were quiet, too. The dark honeycomb of stairwells hummed with foreign voices and shook occasionally with the slappy footfalls of children's play. The route through the blocks, old and new, to the tube station was long and meandering; no main roads, simply small sandy paths. At some point, I abandoned it and went to the river.

Why do we go to rivers, or the sea, when we feel lost and hopeless? As if there is something so fundamental about a shore, a bank, that everything will become clear. *Down* to the river. I wound around the new blocks of flats, across the empty car parks, through the maze of low, red walls inlaid with floodlights, giant pearls. When I reached the final wall, I leaned over and stole their view. The river, slopping the bank below me, was colourless, depthless, lifeless. But wide. No doubt it is tiny in comparison to other rivers in the world, but on its own, in London, in front of me, it was wide. It was wider than a road, quieter than a road, immune from roads. Roads are required to follow. And, usually, roads follow nothing, everything follows roads, which are everywhere, going nowhere, lying on the ground between one place and another. Rivers are rare and they go to the sea. I leaned on the wall and, as far as I could see, this river did not widen, did not promise a sea, an end. So I listened, instead, to the gentle washing of the bank by the dirty water, and I started to sift the feelings which had formed a lump inside me.

I began to work loose a strange feeling: six feet under, under six stone, Deborah was less than I had known; one quarter or perhaps one third less, to be precise. But why precise? Suddenly I realized how I had been piecing her together, holding her together, exactly, carefully. And I had nothing but pieces, accessories: Deborah's boxy suede jacket, her second skin; the precarious dynamics of the brittle tortoiseshell Alice band, arcing from temple to temple, the tiny teeth biting into her fudge of hair; the sleepers threaded into her earlobes while the rest of us owned studs, gold cysts. Sometimes I sparked with a feeling of Deborah, a Deborah-feeling, often when I recalled the way that she said my name. (How can a name – knowing a name, saying a name – be such an indicator of intimacy when it is also the most public aspect of a person?) But now I knew that I was wrong to try to hold Deborah together. My Deborah was not the real Deborah. The *real* Deborah? There was no longer a real Deborah.

If I had not known her, if there were things about her which I had not known, then she was not *less*, she was *more*. The voice that I had given her, in my conversations with her, had been a quiet voice full of answers. But if she had been able to speak to me, her voice would not have been quiet, not nice-and-quiet, would have given anything and everything but answers. I had been so afraid that she had suffered, and she had, but differently, and even more than I had feared.

Leaning over the river water, I wanted to talk to someone who had known her. But not to Simon, nor to any Steiner: I wanted to talk to someone who had known her yet not known her, someone like me. Roz, or Ali, or Lucy. I did not want to ring Roz, not simply because we were out of touch, not even because she probably did not know that Deborah had died, but because she would not care. Not really, not for Deborah. I was sure that her response to the news would include the chime, *Only-the-good-die-young*. Chicken-or-egg? Have the good who die young had enough time to become bad?

Did I want to ring Ali? I had rung Ali the day before. And she had been cold towards me. Incredulous, I had realized that, for Ali, I was a reminder of home. *Me, home?* And it had been obvious that, for her own mysterious reasons, Ali wanted to avoid reminders of home. If I rang and told her about Deborah – no, even worse, told her that *Simon* had told *me* – then there was a possibility, or a probability, that for the same reasons she would choose to disbelieve me. Even more unfair, even more unkind. I looked down into, onto, the brown water and wondered whether Ali had been right to say that I should talk more, listen more, to Lucy. Did I want to talk to Lucy about Deborah? Lucy had not been a particular friend of Deborah's. But, then, Lucy had not been a particular friend of anyone. Except me.

Lucy: Lucy was *my* friend. Not ungrudgingly, I realized that she had always Been There for me. Literally. She had always spoken her mind, but she had never inflicted her problems on anyone. Which was a balance that the rest of us had failed, were failing, to achieve. And perhaps Ali had been right, too, in her belief that Lucy – what? – *has a feel for things?* Turning from the water, I decided to quell my inexplicable irritation with Lucy and go back to talk to her; but in the same instance I realized that I did not need to do so, did not need to break Simon's confidence. Because Lucy would add nothing, say nothing, she would make no difference. Which was her strength. If I told her about Deborah she would say, *No one's perfect.* I have been wrong, over the years, in taking Lucy's lack of surprise as a lack of care. It is simply that nothing surprises Lucy; she has learned never to be taken by surprise.

Last year Lucy told me that I needed to do some forgetting. Lately I have been realizing that she is right, that I could never do anything as dramatic as actively rid myself of Simon. Ridding would be too much effort, too conscious, I would tie myself in knots. If this is going to end, I have to forget him. He has to become less important to me, eventually unimportant. And it will happen, I know that it will happen. Given time. Sometimes I

305

wonder if I have already done all the missing of him that there is to do. Other times I feel the missing beneath every breath, like seasickness, which seeps from the sea to dry land. But I have begun to realize that when I miss Simon I am missing something which, in the other sense of the word, I will not miss at all, something unsettling. Simon unsettles me. I have begun to realize that the good-old-fashioned word for the effect Simon has on me is *swoon*.

Last summer, when I came back here, after Jane's cancelled wedding, I left Simon. As soon as I was back, we manoeuvred ourselves into a proper separation mainly by phone – tapping out the message in sharp grudging phrases, short breathy pauses and clicks of the tongue. There were several of these calls each week, for several weeks, the words distorted initially by recrimination but gradually quietening. In this sense, it is over, we both know that it is over. At the end of the summer I did not leave my job to move south. I left my job for another: research assistant, the type of job that I have always wanted. It is temporary, one year, like almost all research jobs now. The project concerns Siblings Of Children With Special Education Needs. Known to the project workers as *Sibs*. I love this job: I love sitting in the busy university library with my pile of journals; I love our tatty, musty office with the unassembled jigsaw of in/out-trays and the colony of seal-grey telephones. Unfortunately my year is very nearly ended and there was never any prospect of renewal.

I see Simon whenever I go down to London, or am passing through. But it is different. Even to the extent that I hear him differently now when he falls asleep beside me: previously I did not often hear his breathing, but if I did, I could not sleep; now I listen for his breathing and I fall asleep listening to him. As far as I know, there is no one else, for him. No one *else*? *I* do not count. *No one*, then. Not so far. But of course this is simply a matter of time; we are biding time. Often I ponder how someone else will make a difference, another difference. All the difference because, practically, I could no longer lie there next to Simon, stunned by his sudden sleep-silence. Almost no difference because there are ways and means and no one could stop me. No one except Simon, who will not stop me because he lacks will power. I will have to stop myself.

And I will. I last saw him a few weeks ago. Travelling back, the train flew for hours through uninhabited or barely habited farmland, the thick bleached countryside of early summer. I did not know where I was, except that I was in the middle of England. For hours I saw no buildings except distant churches, rooted among trees: one church every few miles, linking invisibly across the landscape like ancient pylons. In the days when the churches were built, Edinburgh would have been weeks away from London. Simon would have been weeks away. I stared at the shifting fields: meticulously tended, but without obvious products; just bales waiting, huge and perfect, and perfectly placed like monuments. I saw a swan stretching into the sky from a solid silver river: *Look, Simon, a swan in flight!* And I turned again towards a field of some precious fruit or veg: *See, Simon, how I mistook the plastic sheets for snow, snow in the middle of the summer!* But Simon is weeks away, years away, worlds away.

I can hear Alex screwing his key into the lock and shoving with his shoulders against the front door. There is the familiar whinny from the hinges. I snap to attention and steel myself to break the bad news: *there is a runaway in the bath and the cops are coming.* Poor Alex; I suspect that the flat is miserable enough for him these days – with me, miserable me – without the prospect of performance poetry and a police presence. Once, after passing on a message in person, a non-message, *Simon called, no message*, he said very quietly, 'You're very sad these days, aren't you.' It was a statement, not a question. I was surprised because I had been thinking of myself as angry, not sad. Sad was a little word, for other people. But, 'Yes,' I said, 'I am.'

Alex and I are going on holiday together. It was his suggestion, but I had not failed to notice the lack of suitable trips for the single traveller. Alex refers to the holiday as Our Very Own 18–30. Likewise he organizes the other, more mundane aspects of my life:

307

my laundry accompanies his own to the launderette; my shopping arrives with him from the Supercentre. How does he manage, find time? He is an architect: whenever he arrives home from work with bags full of laundry or shopping, I ask him, *Hard day at the cardboard models, dear?*

He calls me The Walking Unorganized.

He says that he cooks for me because he likes cooking. He likes to go out for meals, too, and says that he is taking me along. Often there are other trips: last week he suggested a trip to the zoo.

'Alex,' I tried gently, 'I'm not entirely happy with zoos.'

Now I stand in the kitchen doorway and tell him, 'My brother is here.'

Staring at me, he slides his key into his pocket. 'Where?'

'In the bathroom. Having a shower.' I nod towards the closed bathroom door.

'Your brother?' He shrugs his jacket off. 'The one with the girl's name? Louisa or something?'

I sag in the doorway with a big sigh of impatience. 'Keep your voice down,' I hiss, and nod again at the prim bathroom door. 'And his name is Lyndsay.' Then I add, 'OK, Alexandra?'

He strolls across the hall with a smile and ruffles my hair as he passes into the kitchen.

I turn and follow. 'He has run away from home,' I stress urgently, 'he wants to stay.'

Alex is inspecting the interior of the fridge. 'Good,' he says enthusiastically. 'Someone to try my spam fritters. I've been looking *everywhere* for a recipe, an *authentic* . . .'

'How can you think of spam at a time like this?' I protest. 'My *brother* has *run away* from *home*.'

Extracting the carton of grapefruit juice, he looks up at me. 'Fritters,' he says, 'spam fritters. Like we used to have at school, remember?' He swigs from the carton.

'I wasn't *at* school with you,' I object crossly, although I do remember the fritters.

'We've all run away at one time or another,' he says kindly, dropping the carton back into the fridge. As he turns in front of the window, I notice that he has a tan. How does he have time to catch the sun?

'I was seven,' I tell him, 'the first time. I don't remember why I was running away, but I do remember packing my new little vanity case.'

'What did you pack?' he asks. On the bridge of his nose there are *sun kisses*; or *sun slavers*, in his case.

'My nightie, of course.' And his hair is lighter, too; sunbeams seem to have slammed into his soft tufty hair.

'Where did you go?'

'Oh, you know,' I shrug, 'the end of the road.'

'Oh, yes,' he laughs, 'the end of the road, I know it well.'

And for a moment we both contemplate the ends of our respective roads.

'I'd better ring Mum,' I sigh. In the hall, picking up the receiver, I call back to Alex, 'And he's my brother, so I'll cook tonight.'

'And *what* will you cook?' A melodramatic whoop of panic.

'A big juicy lentil. If you're lucky.'

I dial the number and wait in electronic space for connection, then realize that I am humming along with the ringing tone.

'Hello?' The voice, cracking across the line, is strange.

Presumably I have been shunted the wrong way across the electronic space. 'Oh, sorry, wrong number.'

'Lalie, is that *you?*' Now the voice is animated and familiar.

'Ali, is that you? What are you doing in my Mum's house?'

'I'm not in *your* Mum's house, I'm in *my* Mum's house.'

Alex is crossing the hallway in front of me, slapping the newspaper onto his thigh in a precise but private rhythm.

I shriek into the mouthpiece, 'Did I dial the wrong number, then?' Did my fingers do-their-own-thing?

In passing, Alex frowns at me over the flappy display.

'Depends what you mean by wrong. I was just about to call you.'

'In fact, Ali,' I continue excitedly, 'what are you doing in your mum's house?'

'I'm home for the weekend for my sister's baby's christening.'

'Grace has a baby?'

'Well,' drawls Ali guardedly, 'you know Grace: she decided that she ought to have one; she was worried that she would miss out on something.'

'So now she'll miss out on a lifetime of peace and quiet.'

Ali sniffs a little laugh. 'You can hear?' She pauses, and her phone shifts somewhere with a squeak. Suddenly there is an angry sighing in my earpiece, like the sea despairing inside a seashell.

Ali squeaks back into aural focus. 'Did you hear him? Did you hear Silas?'

'Yes, thanks, Ali, that was lovely.' I add sarcastically: 'Home for long, are you?'

She laughs happily. (Is she drunk?)

'*Are* you home for long?'

'No. The weekend. Back tomorrow. Back to work on Monday.'

The bathroom door booms open, releasing a hot clean cloud. Lyndsay appears in the doorway, boiled soft and sticky, with a towel tucked around his waist. He mimes confusion for me, which resembles panic. I point at the spare room. Going to collect his rucksack, he points at the phone and mouths: *Mum?* I shake my head.

'So, are you OK?' I ask Ali.

'Yes, I'm fine,' she chirps. Then, more quietly, 'I'm fine . . .'

'Yes?' Successfully, I will Lyndsay across the hallway, into the spare room, and behind the closed door.

Ali whispers into the phone: 'Can you hear me?' Testing how low the voice can go: a telephonic strategy familiar from the past; from the era of Mum flouncing past me, shouting, *Good God, you see her all day long at school, do you have to spend all evening on the phone?*

'Yes.'

Her sigh is surprisingly loud. 'I've arrived here,' odd vowels and consonants ticking in the whisper, 'to find chaos.'

I wait.

'It seems,' she continues very carefully, 'that my Dad has been having an affair with a woman at work.'

'Your dad?' I whisper in return, meaning, *Not your Dad, surely?* Not nice Mr Mortimer, wearer of gentle jumpers.

'Yes,' she hisses evenly.

'No,' I say, 'not your dad.' Which trick of the light gives everyone under twenty-five the impression that everyone over twenty-five is beyond all this? And is there *any* point at which we become grown-ups? Vanishing point?

'Yes,' she says again. 'We think that it has been going on for a couple of years.' She sounds like a scientist, carbon-dating.

'You think? You don't know?'

'Apparently, questioning him is like trying to force blood out of a stone.'

Alex swoops in front of me from the kitchen doorway, requesting permission to speak by raising his eyebrows, flapping a hand, opening his mouth. Frantically I wave him away. He stares in surprise at me, trying to read my face for further information, before swooping away again.

'How did you find out, then?' I puzzle into the phone.

'He told my Mum,' she replies faintly, fazed.

'Told her?' Lovely Mrs Mortimer, perfect Mrs Mortimer, her skin and eyes and hair cut from priceless cloth. 'So what does he want?'

'He doesn't seem to know,' she wails very quietly. Suddenly there is an indistinct blare in her background. 'I'm going to have to go,' she says loudly, brightly but regretfully: 'Christening party in full swing. Not a good time, I'm afraid, for a chat.'

For me, neither. 'Can I call you later?'

'Yes, do.' I can hear that she has other listeners: her voice has become a fog horn warning of others nearby.

'I'll call you later,' I tell her.

Alex appears in the doorway, jolts me. He does not look at me but wanders out across the hallway towards his room. He is carrying a slice of bread, folded: a makeshift sandwich, a snack. Suddenly he turns towards me. 'Simon?' he asks, shunting my gaze momentarily with his own to the phone. His frozen wide-eyed face flickers with worry, like a face beneath a wobble of water.

'No.' My breathing is stoked with panic: I feel its new rhythm, strenuous and ungainly. Alex has broken the unspoken rule: no mention, from him, of Simon, or questions. I tell him what I want to tell him, when I want to tell him.

He shrugs and bites into the wad of bread. I watch the mouthful rotating inside the lower half of his face. Is it true that, for women, food is never simply fuel? That hunger is always a problem? I remember how, in my schooldays, in the younger years, the days before Deborah, there was a time when we felt that we had found the answer to the problem of hunger: water. The chief advocate of this strategy, Tilda Penny, claimed that a couple of pints would fill our stomachs. Of course our plan was forever failing because the answer to hunger is food. Now I want to ask Alex's opinion: *Why Deborah?* Was it a matter of degree? Or was Deborah different? Alex knows about Deborah; or, he knows as much as I have told him.

Suddenly Lyndsay steps from the spare room and Alex turns away from me. He calls to Lyndsay, 'Hi!' with the calculated non-judgemental enthusiasm of a youth worker.

I do a hurried, perfunctory introduction: 'Lyndsay, Alex.'
Lyndsay's drooping head jerks. 'Hi,' he mumbles reluctantly.

Why do adolescents, nowadays, shun everyone as if there is a threat of contamination? I am sure that I was rude solely to Mum and Dad. (And Jane, of course). I remember that there seemed to be no point in being polite to family; because they would think no differently of me, and they would stay around, regardless.

'Do you fancy fish and chips?' Alex asks Lyndsay.

This startles Lyndsay; I watch him groping for the hitch, as self-conscious as if the offer was a million pounds. 'Sure,' he replies eventually, more pleasantly.

'Good.' Alex pulls the car keys from his pocket. 'Dinner is served,' he says, throwing the keys in a spangling arc across the hallway to me.

Momentarily, in pique, I consider letting the keys fall to the floor, but somehow they clatter into my palm. 'I don't want to drive,' I warn Alex. I do not want another driving lesson now.

He comes towards me, to usher me.

'I'm not in the mood for driving, Alex,' I whine. 'I can't.'

'There's-no-such-word-as-can't,' he says behind me, cheerfully, munching. 'As your Gran would say.'

How does he know what Gran says? Is he bluffing, does everyone's Gran say There's-no-such-word-as-can't? Or have I told him more about myself than I realize?

1989

....

Mum's big new kitchen is empty of everything except sheer white walls of cupboard, and the discreet sparkle of appliances. *Brand, spanking*: I can appreciate the origin of *brand* new, but why *spanking*?

'Lovely, isn't it,' she comments lightly. I remember that she told me, last year, on the phone, in a tone of hushed horror, that 'The price of fitted kitchens these days is ludicrous.' So ludicrous that she bought one.

'New house, new kitchen,' she emphasized in a later phone call: 'I've told him that I'm sick of being stuck in some poky muddle at the back of the house.'

Dad bought one. *For* Mum. I remember that there was a boiler in the corner of the old kitchen, in the old house, warm throughout the winter. I liked to sit there, and so did the cat.

I cannot imagine buying a fitted kitchen. I crave the personal touch, an accumulation of personal touches: in Mum's words, *a mess*. This kitchen has nothing, not even a sleepy clock on the wall. Why solely fitted *kitchens* and *bathrooms*? Fitted wardrobes, too, I suppose; so, in a sense, fitted bedrooms. These rooms, full of necessities, are reduced to blank wipe-clean surfaces. Mum favours fitted rooms: a strange choice for someone so keen on exerting her own personality within her household. Perhaps not so keen? Perhaps she lacks confidence: I remember that whenever she was faced with evidence of the homemaking skills of others – cakes at the Christmas Fayre, crochet on babies – she would sigh and say *I'm not one of these clever women*.

Mum is fussing over frozen mini sausage rolls in rows on a baking tray: featureless, colourless embryos. 'Just in time,' she says.

314

As I come closer, I see that she is brushing them with milk. Just in time? Me? For sausage rolls?

'Mum,' I say wearily, 'there is meat in sausage rolls.' I lack the energy to draw her attention to the further possibility of animal fats in the pastry.

'Meat in these?' She flicks a smile towards me. 'Are you quite sure?'

And I smile in return, because she is learning.

'How is Lauren?' I ask.

Mum looks sharply upwards and beyond me. 'Why don't you ask her yourself?'

I turn to see Lauren thumping and swinging on her crutches towards me. 'Hi, Sis,' she purrs. Her left leg is a trunk of grubby white plaster.

'Lauren, how are you?'

She clatters into a chair, and collapses further, crossing her skinny forearms over her stomach. 'I need a hysterectomy,' she groans.

'Oh really, Lauren,' Mum interjects, horrified, treating the comment as blasphemy.

Lauren releases a long thin arm, and flails. 'I know, I know, it's my natural function to have kids.' She sighs. 'Which makes it sound like going to the toilet.' She clamps the arm back over the stomach. 'So, better luck next month, eh? And I hope it's a girl.'

Mum stands rigid with the tray. 'Lauren . . .'

'Well?' goads Lauren in reply. 'It's my natural function, or so you say. So why is it my natural function *in ten years time*, but not *now*? I'm fit and fertile now.'

I am smirking at Lauren's fearlessness, when Mum turns to me. 'A chip off the old block,' she mutters, turning away again to slide the tray into the oven.

'I'm no chip,' objects Lauren calmly. 'I'm Lauren Blaney, utterly, uniquely, supremely.' She smiles. 'You might have wanted clones, Mum, but DNA got the better of you.'

'Thank you, Lauren,' says Mum wearily, slamming the high-tech self-cleansing door of the oven, 'for the biology lesson.'

Lauren's words imply that DNA was injected like pigment into each tiny egg to give each of us our own unique colour. But we *are* DNA.

In the chair, Lauren groans.

'Do you want some aspirin, Lauren?' I ask quickly.

'No, thanks. I rattle.' She frowns irritably at Mum. 'But, Mum, you can fulfil your natural function, please, and make me a cup of tea.'

Mum flounces petulantly to the kettle. 'When I lived at home, I took my mum and dad a pot of tea every morning, *every* morning, at twenty past seven.'

Lauren sighs. 'Thank God that the Dark Ages have passed.'

I am hopeful that I will never have to worry about Lauren.

I sit down next to her. Her clothes baffle me, although I recognize elements. Far more serious is my suspicion that she dismisses me, in my clothes, as a nonentity, a non-person, clueless. An adult. When I was Lauren's age, I vowed that I would never stumble into clothes in the careless manner of teachers and parents. Worse than those in drab clothes were those who tried but failed: Roz's pejorative term for them was *modern*. I wonder what Roz looks like now. As an adult. No one who is twenty-six can dress like Lauren, so how does Roz cope? How has she become Adult-MOR?

'Everything is ready,' Mum is twittering, 'more or less. But remind me to start defrosting the cheesecake in a minute. And perhaps you could do one of those dips, one of your nice yoghurty dips, for us?' She glances expectantly at me.

'Yes, of course.'

'And where's Lyndsay?' she asks Lauren, rather less happily.

Lauren is surprised. 'He said that he was going to Southend with some friends for the day; didn't you know?'

'Oh my God,' bellows Mum, as if she has been told that he is dead.

Lauren stares at her. 'Alive when last seen, Mum.'

'You let him go to Southend with his mates?'

Lauren huffs, and reiterates, 'I didn't *let* him . . . I thought you knew.'

'You think I'd let him go out for the day, today? On the day of Gran's send-off?' She rubs her floury hands over her face and then backwards through her hair. 'When is he coming back?' she demands sharply from Lauren.

'Well *I* don't know. This afternoon sometime, I suppose.'

'But it's four o'clock now,' she wails. Then she pauses to take a deep breath. 'Don't tell your father,' she adds quietly. 'I don't want to be blamed for this.'

Lauren leans conspiratorially towards me. 'It's Lyndsay's *natural function* to roam Southend in a pack,' she says in a voice lower than Mum's plea. 'And it's our natural function to mix the dips.'

Mum pauses melodramatically with a fork over a bowlful of swelling cream, and looks knowingly at us. 'So far, Lyndsay is the only one of my children, in fact, who shows any interest at all in producing my grandchildren for me.'

'Except Erin,' I remind her.

Mum prickles with embarrassment. 'Well, yes, of course, except Erin.' She thrashes the cream with the fork. 'But, then,' she adds more lightheartedly, 'Erin won't necessarily produce any more children. And I want five grandchildren each from the five of you.'

'Twenty-five,' says Lauren in awe.

'Isn't Dory good enough for you, then?'

'Well, yes, of course,' more embarrassment.

'But if you're lucky, the next grandchild will be legitimate?'

Mum chucks the fork into the bowl and reels around. 'Do you really think that Dory is somehow *less* because of her parentage?'

'No,' I reply passionately, 'I think she's *more*, because she isn't part of anyone's Ideal Home, double-glazing and three-piece-suite and two-point-four . . .'

'Stop it, Eulalia, you've gone too far.' Mum plants her hands firmly on her hips. 'In case you've forgotten, I didn't have two-point-four kids. I had five. There has never been anything normal or cosy about *my* life.'

'But what about over-population?' interrupts Lauren. 'Twenty-five is a lot.'

Mum glances briefly at her, distracted; and then returns to her, more carefully. 'Well, yes,' she concedes sadly, 'these days, yes. But it's a Third World problem, isn't it. Those poor people can't feed themselves.'

'But, over here,' Lauren protests, 'we all consume far more than . . .'

'Lauren, please, I have a headache.' Mum squeezes her eyes shut and presses the palm of one hand onto her forehead.

When I was a child, history was full of Poor People: storybooks and school textbooks, films and television, were full of a specific history, of ragamuffins, orphans, and tiny workers sleeping in mills beneath the savage sweep of looms. It baffled me that people could have lived Upstairs on the backs of those who worked Downstairs, who were only free for a few hours on Sunday afternoons. And downstairs in the kitchens, they were the lucky ones. Because, in those days, Poor People were hungry. It baffled me that rich people could pass starving people every day in the streets. If I had been rich, I would have fed the poor. But now I pass starving people every day on the television in my own living room and I do nothing. Often I do not even look. There are so many of them. And I am not rich enough to make a difference.

'A headache? Now?' Lauren peers across the kitchen at Mum.

'Yes, a headache now. Is that all right with you?'

'Do you want some aspirin?' I ask.

Mum smiles unhappily with a shallow sigh. 'If I said Yes, you wouldn't know where to find them.'

Not in this spanking kitchen, perhaps; but I have my own packet, somewhere inside my journey-mangled bag.

But she is shaking the ruff of curls. 'No, a cup of tea will do the trick.' Suddenly she slaps a little squeak back into her mouth with two tight rows of fingertips: 'Lauren! Your tea! I clean forgot . . .'

Lauren straightens slowly and spectacularly in her chair, becoming as tall as me, simultaneously shaking loose a Rapunzelesque escape route down her back. 'I'm the least of your worries, Mum: Erin and Dory are here.'

We all turn together towards the distant front door which is suddenly alive with little noises. It shrinks into darkness under a wedge of sunlight containing two figures: one big, slow, and careful with the key; the other, tiny and twitchy. The twitchy figure bolts towards us.

'Dory!' Mum reaches down to sample the blonde curls of the child who halts in front of her. 'Are you hot? Do you want a drink?'

The child nods vigorously.

I am relieved that she does not resemble Sky from *Neighbours*, the only toddler with whom I am acquainted. Suddenly she turns and stares at me. It seems to me that this stare is some type of challenge. 'Hello Dory,' I say uneasily.

Erin sweeps among us, wielding a shoulder-bag full of babyware. Her short sleek bob is strapped to her head by a bandana. The bag thuds onto the table and she drops to the floor, to Dory. They look up at me together, one pair of eyes muzzy with a smile and the other suspicious but gloating with fascination. I feel very big and conspicuous.

'This is Lalie,' breathes Erin into Dory's ear. 'You don't remember her, do you? Lalie is the biggest of mummy's sisters.'

'Gee, thanks, Erin.'

Erin sniffs a laugh, and rises.

'Jane's taller than me,' I tell no one in particular.

Erin is rummaging in the bag. 'Like toes, I suppose,' she replies. 'Sometimes the second one is the longest.' She turns to Mum with a plastic beaker, to find that Mum is swooping upon Dory with her own.

'Do you want tea, Erin?' Mum enquires, her attention fastened firmly on Dory.

Erin replaces the beaker in the bag. 'Yes, OK, thanks.'

'How do you travel here?' I ask.

Erin transfers the smile to me. 'Train. Easy. Two stops.' She rounds on dwarfish Dory. 'You love the train, don't you, Dory. The choo-choo.'

'Choo-choo,' Dory calls back in approval.

But trains do not go choo-choo anymore, and have not done so for years.

'When you've finished that drink,' Erin continues to Dory, 'we can go out into the garden to find that naughty old pussy cat.'

Erin and Dory live in a flat, gardenless and catless.

With grim satisfaction, Mum announces, 'Everything is going according to plan.'

There is no indication that anyone is listening.

'But I must defrost the cheesecake.' She catches my eye. 'Do you like my microwave?' she asks me, patting it.

'Very nice.'

'Very *useful*.' Then she sighs loudly, louder than the busy kettle. 'It's a shame that Gran Blaney didn't manage one-hundred. It would have been nice to get a telegram from the Queen.'

'Mum,' I remind, 'you're a Republican.'

'Yes,' she muses, crossing the kitchen with a claw of mugs, 'but if we must have royalty, then they might as well send us telegrams.'

Lauren cranes over Erin's sagging bag. 'Can't Gran still have a telegram? Can't the Queen send it to her in Canada?'

'Perhaps Gran should send a change-of-address card to Buck House,' I scowl at Lauren.

Lauren looks serenely across the table at me. 'Canada is still part of the Commonwealth, isn't it? It still belongs to the Queen.'

In the steaming distance, Mum puffs derision and scepticism into the waiting tea pot. 'I don't think *belong* is quite the right word, Lauren.'

'Same difference,' says Lauren dismissively. And now more urgently: 'But I don't understand why Gran is choosing Canada. There are millions of places better than Canada.'

'Where?' I ask, interested.

'Australia.'

'That's one place, Lauren; not millions.'

Mum turns, exhibiting an alarming disregard for the boiling water rushing from the kettle in her hands to the tea pot. 'I've told you, Lauren: Gran wants to return to die in the place where she was born.'

Erin and Dory are performing their intricate dance of whispers, confidences and promises across to the door and out into the garden.

'I was born in Barnet,' Lauren announces dolefully.

I titter. 'You drew the short straw,' I tell her. I was born in the City of London, during the days of Mum's resistance to exile in Blaneyland.

Mum is lit by the beacon of a bottle of milk. 'I did my best,' she flares. 'Barnet had a good Maternity Unit.'

'So good,' I remind her, 'that the heating system was operating throughout a heatwave and the windows were stuck.' I was fourteen when Lauren was born, so I remember the grisly details from start to finish.

With a jab of her thumb, Mum punctures the tough silver membrane at the mouth of the bottle. 'A good Maternity Unit in terms of staff,' she specifies, 'not architecture.'

'No doubt the architect was a man,' I comment sourly.

'No doubt,' mutters Mum, sniffing the milk.

Lauren shifts her crutches. Crosses her crutches. 'But Gran isn't dying,' she objects.

'But she is very old,' replies Mum. Then she focuses joyfully on me: 'Did I tell you, Lalie, that she tried to con a free flight on Concorde? She told them that she was a Great-Grandmother and had never flown before.'

Doubts prick my memories: all those trips to Ireland? 'Is it true?' I ask. 'That she has never flown before?'

Mum shrieks playfully. 'Not unless you count the broomstick.' She composes herself. 'I don't know whether it's true,' she says, unconcerned. But then, more thoughtfully: 'There was a rumour that she went after Brenda, your Dad's mother.'

'Our grandmother,' says Lauren solemnly.

'God knows what she would have done to her, if she had found her,' Mum adds darkly.

'Tried to bring her back?' I suggest reasonably, weary of Mum's insinuations.

Mum is shaking her golden, chaotic head very slowly. 'No,' she says, 'she would never have allowed her to come back.

'Anyway,' Mum continues, with forced gaiety, 'it was No Go with Concorde. Apparently they are as busy as the Queen with geriatrics. So there was a change of plan for Gran. Originally she wanted to fly on Concorde to New York, and take the train to Canada.'

Dissenting noises come loudly from Lauren. 'There are no trains in America. Or not many. Not proper trains.'

'I thought she was born in Wexford,' I hazard. I have been troubled by this notion since I was told of the plans.

Before she can form the words, Mum shakes her curls and her hands to hurry away the misconception. 'We all thought that she was born in Wexford. But now it seems that she was not born Philomena MacNamee in Wexford, but Kathleen O'Farrell in Nova Scotia. When she was three years old she came back to Wexford with her mother, because her father died. And, a few years later, her mother married a Mr MacNamee.'

I remember Gran's gold signet ring, the largest of all the rings on her fingers, and so solid in contrast to the shifting glitz of her charm bracelet. It was engraved with the initials K M. 'The ring,' I muse aloud, 'the initials, K M. I presumed that K M was a relative or perhaps a long-lost lover.'

Mum hoots. 'That woman loves no one but herself.' She extracts a tea-strainer smoothly and swiftly from a momentarily visible drawer. 'Her real name is Kathleen. Philomena, which she prefers, is her Catholic name,' she says, without explanation. 'And although she was an O'Farrell by birth, she was brought up as a MacNamee.'

'Simple,' pronounces Lauren dryly.

I am stunned that the facts of someone's past can be given such a thorough gloss; someone who is not a spy or a dissident, someone ordinary.

'As the years go by, there are fewer and fewer people to remember the truth,' concludes Mum, reading my thoughts. 'Fewer witnesses,' she reiterates ominously.

But NostraMadamus worked as a future-maker. And perhaps a name is not a fact, or perhaps it is a different species of fact. It occurs to me that my initials are often written for me as L B: Lalie Blaney; the Eulalia discarded or forgotten, or, nowadays, in my second life, away from Mum and Miss Killit, never known.

'And she was cross,' Mum is continuing, 'that your Dad didn't know all of this, about Nova Scotia et cetera. She would not accept that she had never told him. I said to her, *Look, Gran, my husband's hobby is stock car racing, not genealogy.*'

Mum brings two mugs of tea to the table, and shudders noisily as she places one of them in front of Lauren. 'Plain black tea! I don't know how you can stand it, Lauren.'

Lauren watches Mum turn away for her own cup. 'It's easy when you have diabetes,' she says calmly, to Mum's back.

Mum's slim shoulders flinch and she glances fearfully around, but Lauren's unperturbed blue gaze glides sideways to me. 'My cross to bear,' she enunciates very clearly.

We all know that this is Mum's expression.

Mum's face stiffens. 'Don't mock, Lauren,' she manages. 'It's a serious matter.'

'You're telling *me*,' mutters Lauren, before braving the tea.

Suitably subdued, we sip in silence for a moment. During the silence it occurs to me that there is another mystery, for me, about Gran. There are many mysteries about Gran but, this afternoon, one in particular has begun to bubble in my brain. 'How did Gran manage to have only one baby?' I wonder aloud, eventually.

Mum thumps her mug enthusiastically onto the Formica surface. 'I'd love to know.'

'What?' asks Lauren.

'Pardon,' jerks Mum.

'That's what I said.'

'No, it wasn't.'

'Lauren,' I interrupt quickly, to explain, 'baby clinics were not allowed by the government to give birth control advice to women until 1937, and then only if the women or the babies were likely to die.'

'*What?*'

'It's true,' I stress. 'I read it in a book.'

'But why?' Lauren persists. 'Why no birth control? Why was the government interested in people's sex lives?'

'Why indeed?' I echo, in disgust.

'Because,' says Mum, irritably, in her pretend-patient voice, 'birth control was . . .' she becomes stuck, and her face sinks into a frown '. . . immoral.'

'But not now?' Lauren's nose twitches, detecting illogicality.

'Not now.'

Mum is tapping her lips with her forefinger. 'Except, of course,' she adds after a moment of this contemplation, 'for certain religions.'

'Oh, they *all* do it,' I insist, giving Mum the benefit of my knowlege of Catholics at college. 'They find their own justifications.'

Mum stares at me with alarm.

Lauren places her elbows on the table and brackets her face with her long, pale, unnervingly physical hands. 'Perhaps Gran didn't have sex,' she suggests thoughtfully.

Mum's mouth opens, closes, and opens again. 'Rather far-fetched, Lauren, surely,' she says unsurely. 'No sex at all, for all those years?'

'No penetrative sex,' Lauren elaborates.

'Do you mind?' utters Mum. 'We're talking about your grandmother.'

Lauren's face shifts inside the pair of hands towards Mum. 'Seriously,' she says expressionlessly. 'There's more to sex than penetration.'

I smirk. 'I don't think they had aromatherapy in those days, Lauren.'

Mum whirls from Lauren to me. 'Have you put her up to this?'
'No!'
'Kissing,' Lauren muses, 'cuddling, touching, licking . . .'
Mum sags casually against the dashboard of the dishwasher. 'You can't shock me,' she states coolly.
Lauren rearranges her forearms on the table. 'I'm not trying to shock you,' she replies pleasantly, 'I'm trying to educate you.'
'Safe sex,' I call knowingly to Mum.
'Don't encourage her,' she snaps back at me.
Jane stalks into the room. This is my first sighting of Jane for a long time − two years? − and despite my reflex revulsion I am curious. She is partially obscured by a ferociously fuzzy, long perm, but nevertheless I can see that her dress resembles a toga. Sound is provided by two huge golden bracelets which crash up and down her forearm as she pushes ineffectually at the mass of hair. This is post-model Jane, who works as a receptionist at a video production company.
'Don't encourage who to what?' Jane continues across the kitchen to the window, and peers outside, presumably at Erin and Dory.
'Don't ask,' mutters Mum.
'Yes, Hi, Jane, and yes, thanks, my journey was fine,' I growl.
Jane turns and stares blankly at me. 'Oh. Hello.' The voice is hollow. Then she flicks to Mum. 'Don't encourage who to what?' she asks again, with much less patience.
'Lauren,' Mum begins reluctantly, wearily, heavily, 'was speculating on aspects of your Gran's married life.'
'It had aspects?' snaps Jane. 'Lucky old Gran.'
Mum frowns through the soothing steam rising from her cup of tea. 'Perhaps you shouldn't generalize too much from your own recent misfortunes,' she suggests, apparently sincerely.
'I wasn't.' She pushes past Mum to the kettle. 'Marriage is a sodding sham.'
'Jane! That's not a very nice thing to say.'

325

'It's not a very nice thing to *be*.' Jane subjects the kettle, in the sink, to a torrent of water.

I turn to Lauren and say, 'Did you know that women weren't allowed the vote until 1918,' – when Gran was twentysomething – 'and then only if they were over thirty?'

Lauren's eyes flash their flawless sheen like two new nickel coins. 'I still don't have the vote.'

'1918?' bellows Mum, frantic to escape further conversation with Jane. 'Is that true?'

'Why?' objects Lauren. 'What was so wrong with women that they weren't allowed to vote?'

I wonder where to start. But Mum is puzzling aloud and saying, 'I suppose that it was felt that women didn't need the vote. They weren't property owners, for a start . . .'

I hurry with, 'But they *were* by then: Married Women's Property Act, eighteen-something.'

'And surely,' Lauren begins spiritedly, 'they weren't property owners because they weren't *allowed* to be property owners, and they couldn't change their situation because they couldn't vote.' She shrugs conclusively: 'They couldn't vote for birth control, either.'

Jane seems to be slamming boxes of teabags, bottles of milk, and bags of sugar all over the worksurface in a spectacular display of tea-making. 'It's pathetic,' she spits over this hoard. 'Why are men so pathetic?'

I shrug. 'Small willies?'

She glances up with a glimmer of interest. 'All of them?'

Mum is chuckling uneasily. 'Not in front of the children,' she jokes, meaning Lauren.

I remember my own childhood full of the more serious *Not For You*: Mum planted firmly with one or two of her girlfriends on sunloungers or around a kitchen table, contributing to the ceaseless drone of conversation, yet, triggered by my lightest distant step, defending this territory with a sudden high-pitched *Not For You*. Separate spheres, adults and children; yet Mum was forever inviting herself across the line.

Lauren has turned her stunning eyes on Mum. 'I am not a child,' she lectures. 'I have a bank account . . . I leave this house at ten past eight in the morning, every day of the working week . . .' Rather than choosing the common denominators, she is selecting the factors which distinguish herself from Mum. The implication is clear: Lauren is part of the world, but Mum, at home, is no more than a child. I cringe in anticipation of Mum's anguished, wounded, outraged response. But Mum flaps a hand in surrender.

'I suppose that women didn't go out to work,' she continues blithely. 'Except during wartime, of course.'

'They *did* go out to work,' I correct strenuously. 'Even Gran Blaney went out to work.'

'Well, yes, as a shop girl.' Mum is deeply sceptical.

'And all men were lawyers and doctors?'

Her nose tilts. 'Miners, actually, mostly,' she counters stiffly, 'dangerous work.'

'Mum, the mills were full of women.' And I halt, exasperated beyond words.

She digs aimlessly in her muddle of hair. 'I don't see that it has made much difference,' she says eventually, faintly. 'The vote, I mean.'

Silently, watching the tick of her stubby fingers against her loopy curls, I sympathize.

'But it's the principle,' Lauren insists quietly.

The principle. And the campaign for the vote became the principal campaign. And history, in my classrooms and picture books, changed feminists into suffragettes; all of them good missionaries, slightly giddy from a bit of window-smashing, but respectable nevertheless in their long dresses. Suffragette: and who remembers, nowadays, that it was originally a term of mockery? And who knows that those long dresses were torn by mobs of men and policemen? Or that those men stubbed out their cigarettes on the women's arms? And how, and why, do we not know this any more? How did *I* not know?

'Well, yes,' I join Mum, reluctantly. 'It's all about the attitudes of men.'

'Yes,' says Mum sadly.

Lauren leans back grandly in her chair and surveys us. 'You mean, doing the washing up?'

'Well . . .'

'Yes,' says Mum.

Lauren barks a laugh. 'Whenever Lyndsay did the washing up, he left a worse mess than before.'

'Precisely,' says Mum. 'Because he doesn't *care*.'

Lauren leans forward again. 'But we have a dishwasher, now.'

It is my turn to laugh. 'And who loads it?'

Lauren's eyebrows rise into question marks: 'Who afforded it?'

Mum yawns, stretches, and turns with her empty mug to tackle the bouncy basketful of crockery inside the dishwasher. 'Yes, but your Dad wouldn't have been able to go out and about affording it if I wasn't here to look after all of you.'

'Mum,' says Lauren loudly to compete with Jane, who is blowing vigorously onto her cup of hot tea, 'if you weren't here, there wouldn't be all-of-us. We were for you, remember?'

Booby prize; Blaney booby prize.

'In my day,' Mum sings, starting to assemble ingredients which are probably for the yoghurt dip, 'children weren't luxuries, Lauren; they were expected to contribute to the household economy.' She slaps a pot of yoghurt onto the worksurface. 'I understand now that your Dad was right, after all: you're all spoilt rotten.'

It is uncomfortable to be insulted by proxy; uncomfortable and frustrating because there is no opportunity to reply.

Lauren is apparently unconcerned: 'It's different, these days,' she informs Mum, matter-of-fact.

'The M.E. Generation.' Jane is smirking. Confronted by three expressions of disbelief, her smirk sinks without trace. 'I read it in a magazine,' she pouts.

'See?' crows Mum. 'You spend a fortune on rubbishy magazines, and yet you moan about the speck which I ask from you for your board and lodging.'

'I don't moan,' Jane's voice blasts like a siren. 'And, anyway, it isn't a speck. And,' she seethes, 'don't worry, because I'll be going as soon as I can, as soon as I can get my rightful share of my house from my ex-husband.' She humps her folded arms across her chest. 'And they're not rubbishy magazines. You wanted me to keep that article on pension plans for you, remember?'

'*We're* Mum's pension plan, apparently,' I tell Jane.

Mum stares meaningfully at me and taps the top of the yoghurt pot with her fingertip.

'Mum,' Lauren begins reasonably, 'what did you want to do with your life?'

'Have a lovely little family of my own,' she replies immediately, confidently.

'Why?' asks Lauren evenly.

'Because I grew up wanting sisters.' The same sunny tone.

Jane shakes her giant sponge of hair. 'I grew up wanting brothers who would bring home friends.'

'So that you could divorce them?' snipes Mum.

Jane rolls her eyes to the ceiling, where they stay, in protest: eyes rolled upwards, mouth turned downwards.

'No, why?' Lauren urges. 'What was the point of having a family?'

'The point,' answers Mum, becoming impatient, 'is to raise the next generation.'

'Why?'

'So that the next generation can raise the next generation.'

'But why? What's the point?'

Regardless of the point, an unfortunate side effect of this cycle is the perpetual swell of teenagers burbling such questions.

Mum snaps, her tongue twanging inside her mouth. 'Well I don't know, Lauren. I'm not God.'

'So God knows?' Lauren sits rigid, staring at Mum.

'No, of course God doesn't know. There is no God.' In a spasm of restlessness, Mum strides across the kitchen with the pot of yoghurt, a bowl, and a whisk, and places them on the table in front of me.

I peer at this pathetic offering. 'Anyone fancy whisked yoghurt?'

'Well, what else do you need?' she demands in the same tone that she is using for Lauren.

'What else is there?' Browsing is difficult in a very fitted kitchen. Anxiety tweaks Mum's hardened expression, and she begins frantically to examine my face for clues.

'Avocado?' I suggest. 'Or blue cheese? Or sour cream, or lemon juice and a fresh herb or something?'

'Avocado,' she says, very definitely, and springs back across the room to yet another cunningly concealed cupboard. From inside she shouts, 'What's the point of tinkering with someone's engine?'

'What?' we shout back in unison.

She reappears, with the green grenade. 'What's the point of spending your whole life tinkering with engines?' she asks us all, rhetorically. 'Why is there any more point to your Dad's life than to mine?'

Lauren shrugs happily. 'There isn't.'

'All I ever wanted,' emphasizes Mum, laying the avocado on the table in front of me with surprising solemnity, 'was some lovely little girls.' She retreats. 'Not you harridans.'

'What's a harridan?' sighs Lauren.

'Nothing,' I comment, rising from the table to go in search of some serious cutlery, 'ignore her.'

And I bump into Erin, who was suddenly gliding across the tiles. She drifts away from me, the flames of a translucent smile licking her face. 'Mum,' she says lightly, 'didn't anyone ever tell you that if you call a child names, it tends to grow up to believe them?' She turns to a row of drawers and, from somewhere, extracts a pair of tweezers.

'But, of course,' says Lauren, 'I am not a child.'

Mum blows a wild sigh. 'Lauren would never believe anything

from me.' Then she frowns spectacularly: 'Anyway, what if the names are true?'

Erin glides back towards the door. 'Names are never true,' she says in parting, 'they're just names.'

Lauren fixes on Mum again. 'Anyway, you never-had-it-so-good, when you were young: we did it in History.'

Mum looks queasily from Erin to Lauren. 'History?' The expression deepens into alarm, and then loosens again. 'Well, yes, but that was a Tory speaking. You'd never-had-it-so-good if you liked cars and Blackpool and council houses.'

Lauren turns quickly to me and says, 'I've always wanted to go to Blackpool.'

Mum sighs. 'Oh, Lauren,' she says disappointedly.

'But I've never been!' Lauren protests.

I remember that Mum liked to complain *And what would happen if we all wanted a council house?*

What did the future mean when I was growing up? Curing cancer, and shopping from home by computer. But what would Saturdays have been, for us, without the trip to the supermarket? And the future was Concorde; everyone was going to travel everywhere on the new invention, Concorde. No one mentioned the expense.

Mum advances and snatches our empty mugs from the table like a sullen waitress. She returns to the dishwasher and contemplates the jigsaw puzzle of crockery. Where I work, there is a dishwasher. All mod cons, as Mum would say. I work in a home; not a *Home*, an institution, but a *real* home, a *house*; or, in fact, a bungalow. A bungalow in a Crescent of bungalows. The Crescent has a chain of small square lawns on both sides of the road: two rows of green teeth in a smile. The front gardens teem with stalagmite hollyhocks and blunt blocks of hedge, and shake occasionally with the thunder of open-and-over garage doors. When the bungalow was chosen, it was vital that the area was as normal as possible.

My job, inside the bungalow, requires competence with the new dishwasher, microwave, washing machine and dryer, aquavac, electric shower, and video recorder.

'How much is this house costing?' Mum asked, quietly aghast, when I told her.

'A lot,' I replied, 'like all the best things.' And then I suggested that she think of it as compensation for the householder, Sally, who spent twenty-five years, since the age of six, in two institutions, in derelict wards, often tied by her bedclothes to the bedstead, lying in her own mess. Her crime was brain damage, acquired sometime during birth or babyhood. Six months ago, when she came out of hospital, came to live in the community, in the Crescent, she weighed four and a half stone. And chronic malnutrition results in chronic diarrhoea. She had had TB and hepatitis, too. Caught in hospital, I stressed to Mum. In this country. In Surrey, in fact.

If the bungalow, complete with dishwasher and tumble dryer, is compensation for Sally, then surely it is cheap at the price? She shares with three others: two women and a man, who are capable of making their own toast in the mornings and then walking through town without staff supervision to their Training Centre. The staff tend to concentrate on Sally: there are ten of us on a rota, working in groups of two or three during the day, one sleeping in the house at night.

'Think of the cost of the *staff*,' said Mum, in awe.

'It keeps me off the streets,' I reminded her; because, before this job, I was on the dole again.

But, then, Mum's faint unease was a feature of the last days before Lauren began to cost the health service – in Mum's proud, grim words – *a tidy sum*.

'Is there nowhere else for this Sally-Person to go?' Mum wondered, troubled, at the time. 'What about her family?'

'She's a stranger,' I protested. 'She was taken away from home twenty-five years ago.' Her parents were told that she would benefit from care in a specialist institution. They visited every Sunday but after two years they were asked by staff to stop because their departures were upsetting for Sally. For a while, they came occasionally, even after they had moved a hundred and fifty miles away. On one occasion, Sally had been moved without notice to

332

another institution. At some point, the parents separated; at some point, the visits ceased. Her father died years ago. Her mother was recently swiped by a stroke and is still reeling, living alone with difficulty in a tiny flat above a shop in Crawley. Sally's younger sister, who knew nothing of Sally, lives somewhere in Wales and is now plucking up courage to visit.

Two or three of us are needed on each shift because Sally struggles ceaselessly, attacks us, and rips into everything in the house: food, fabric, appliances. Always angry, and always hungry. Once, a whole cake, left carelessly on a rack to cool, was gulped by Sally in a few uncontrollable fistfuls. In the larder, the soft pads of jelly, ruby and amber, are firm favourites during her raids, despite the mouthfuls of plastic wrapping. Sending Sally to her room presents problems: the tatters of curtain remaining at the window have now been replaced with a tough vinyl blind. She is fastened very firmly into jeans, day and night, because otherwise she reaches down into her plastic padded pants and spread the contents all over herself, her room, and then over us. Never have I been so thankful for my straight dull hair, which does not seem to attract Sally's attention as much as the bright bouncy hair of less fortunate members of staff.

Her strength is stunning because she is so small. The labels inside her clothes claim *7–8 yrs*. Presumably, when she went into hospital, she stopped growing. *Rip Van Winkle*, we call her, with the emphasis on *Rip*. There are rumours that she was able to speak before she went into hospital. But there are so many rumours among the staff about Sally, more rumours than those about the Royal Family in the tabloids. There are rumours among us that, once upon a time, when she was a child, she was toilet-trained, and that she was able to feed herself with a fork; that she went on a holiday with her parents to Spain; and that she was a favourite for a while with one of the doctors and his family, spending weekends with them in their home, until they left for a new life in Australia.

Last week three of us spent three quarters of an hour in the bathroom whilst Sally flailed around on the floor, naked, groaning and growling, refusing a clean pad. Arms loose, she slipped through our grasps; or, legs contracting, she hung on us, dragged and then dropped from us. The most recent directive from Management had been for one member of staff to work alone with Sally for each half hour; the other members of staff should concentrate on housework or the other residents. But in the house, day by day, we do not follow directives or tick timesheets; sometimes because we are too relaxed, and, other times, because we are too busy.

Management wants *normalization* for Sally. It has been decided that it is normal to vacuum bedrooms for a few minutes each day, so we are required by the timesheet to take Sally into her room, to hold one of her hands firmly around the stem of the Hoover, and begin. Sally does not like to go to her room during the daytime, and reveals less than no interest in the cleanliness of the carpet: she violently resists our efforts. Management also wants Sally, after meals, to place her plate in a sinkful of hot soapy water, and to use the washing-up cloth. (Despite the dishwasher). So, from behind, a member of staff manoeuvres Sally across the kitchen: a human straitjacket, arms extended to clamp hands over Sally's own wriggling slop-sodden fingers.

Management insists that we behave towards Sally as we would towards any other adult. So, of course, we fail. Yesterday, coming onto the driveway, I glimpsed another member of staff, Melissa, alone with Sally in the kitchen. Pursued by Sally, Melissa was stepping backwards, sipping hurriedly from a cup. It requires skill and speed to eat or drink in the presence of Sally. Melissa swooped with the cup towards the dishwasher, but then paused. She turned, and Sally buzzed around the cup, nosing the rim. Slowly, Melissa tilted the cup towards Sally. Sally stood still, laid her hand on it, and drank the dregs.

Later I sat on the edge of the bath, Sally splashing freely below me, and stared at the list of instructions under Cellophane on the wall. The rationale for the list, all five pages of the list entitled *Bath*, is that if we follow a certain specific procedure with Sally, and use certain specific prompts for her, some verbal, some physical, then eventually she will recognize the pattern and learn how to wash herself. But Sally understands our words: it is obvious that she understands *Come here*, and *Take your coat off*, and *Bring your cup*; so, why not *Wash your face*? And she is capable of quite complex chains of action: she slaps bolts through their brackets, turns door handles, forages through piles of packets for the slippery wads of jelly; so, why not manage a sponge? Yesterday, sitting on the edge of the bath, it was clear to me that Sally did not *want* to wash herself. Fierce Sally wanted to pat her palms very gently onto the warm surface of the water. Sally loves baths. She loves solitude, too. I wanted very much to pour bubble-bath all around her and leave her alone for twenty minutes, so I did.

Management wants Sally to be normal; but she is not normal, she is special. She has been damaged, and she needs some belated bubble-bath in her life. Talk of *normal* skids over the icy past as well as this desperately difficult present. No doubt the goal of independence is good for the other three residents, but surely it is inappropriate – cruel – for Sally? As for me: yesterday I realized that I cannot take orders, nor give them. And for a long time I have known that I am exhausted by the filth which seeps all over the house in thick swathes and sly smears. When I took the job I was pleased at the prospect of working in a house rather than an institution. But now I am breathless at the smell of this house, this house under siege. I am weary, too, of the long shifts of wrist-wrenching struggle. I am wrung out. And, of course, I am not interested in day after day of washing-and-ironing: never one of my strengths. Yes, someone-has-to-do-it, but not me, not now.

Whenever I come home at the end of a shift in the bungalow, all I can contemplate is sex. Or not sex, but bed, and Alex. I want to lie down inside the untidy bouquet of bedlinen, smelling our unique, faint, clean scent; I want to turn on to his hot body, and steam clean with him. The bedroom is the sunniest room in the flat, sealed by sunshine, soft with the down of sunshine-dust. The two of us are alone in there together, with nothing but ourselves.

Everything else, the rest of the world, is a waste of time, or a biding of time until bed. And, yes, sex: suddenly those strong, free, rolling movements after a day of cringing and struggling; a long low laugh lapping through the two of us.

I remember Mum's whine: *All-these-handicapped-children-but-what-about-your-own-family?* She was wrong in those days, but now her words fit my life, the advice fits my life; now that I have my own family, not the Blaneys; well, not my own family but my own private life. All my working life, so far, I have been a carer, and now I need to turn inwards for a while. The secret to success is knowing when to stop, if only for a short while; to allow a balance to return. I will resign from my job.

Now, sitting here in this strange new kitchen, I am craving Alex and our own home. I have been ripped away, ripped awake. Mum flickers in front of me towards the edge of the bleached scene, and sinks through the doorway into the darkness of the hallway. Jane follows, drawn slowly into the same plughole. Then my forearm pings: a light touch from Lauren.

'You had a friend who died,' she begins nonchalantly; then, hesitantly, briefly, 'In an accident? a car?'

'Yes.' I lift and spin gently somewhere: giddy.

'A car accident?'

'Yes.' But why this, why now?

'Was she buried or cremated?' The tone is spiked with interest.

'Buried.'

I listen very carefully to the silence, try to fathom the deep pause from Lauren.

'I'd be dead now,' she says eventually in the same rushed, breezy tone, 'if it wasn't for the-miracle-of-modern-medicine.'

'Yes, I know.'

'But I probably won't live to be as old as Gran Blaney.'

I smile slowly. 'No one lives to be as old as Gran Blaney.'

Tentatively she follows my smile with her own. 'But,' she continues more firmly, 'everyone assumes that insulin is a cure. Insulin *copes*; but my diabetes will never go away, and eventually

336

it will ruin everything, my eyes, my kidneys, my circulation.'

I nod, but more in contemplation than agreement. 'A high blood sugar ruins everything,' I muse, having done my reading on the subject, 'so, surely, if you use your insulin, to keep the level down, then you'll be okay?'

She wrinkles her nose: *Too simple*. 'Oh, I'll *cope*,' she says despondently, 'but in the end I'll die of my diabetes. I know how I'm going to die, in the end.'

Too simple, surely? None of us know how we are going to die: *One false move* . . . And, surely, to cope is the best for which anyone can hope.

'Unless,' Lauren says abruptly, 'they start to do transplants.' She flicks the Blaney blue beam into my eyes. 'My Islets of Langerhans don't work,' she explains with relish.

'I know; I remember, from Biology.'

Full beam: 'You did Biology?'

'Yes?' Why the surprise?

'You were at a different school,' she mumbles, confused.

'Same system, Lauren,' I complain. 'Or did you think that I spent my time on Latin and Greek?'

'But,' she says, jaunty after a pause, '*until* the transplant, I suppose that I shall have to live very carefully.'

I laugh: '*After* the transplant, too, I imagine.'

'Counting the calories,' she continues. Her eyes sidle the length of another, cheekier smile: 'Do you know that it is important to have extra calories for sex?'

My response muddles into nothing.

'Do you realize that *Mum* will *know*? She'll be watching me for telltale extra pieces of toast.'

'You can lie, you can tell her that you used some energy running for a bus,' I suggest.

Now Lauren laughs dryly. 'Does Mum ever believe anything? Given two possible explanations, does she ever choose the innocent one?'

'No.' And wisely, in Lauren's case. 'But just think how healthy you'll be with all this carefulness.' Surely there is a case for issuing everyone at birth with a copy of the poster from the swimming pool: *No smoking, no running, no petting, no acrobatics*. I have faith in Lauren. If anyone can survive, sane, such a consciously careful life, then it will be Lauren.

'I'll be thin, too,' says Lauren, pleasantly, 'because I can always use an over-generous portion of insulin to shift those extra pounds.'

'. . . And take along your brain, for good measure.'

'How come you know so much about this?'

I mutter, 'From work,' where I have witnessed sugarless swoons, and sensed the brain cells dropping away like dried petals. But of course I do not only know from work. 'And take along your life, too,' I brave, in a rush, 'because, you know my friend, the friend who died? She died because her blood sugar was so low.'

Lauren strains wide-eyed to protest, 'I thought it was a car accident.'

'It was early morning, she hadn't eaten, she lost control.'

Mum barges back into the room. 'And remember,' she bellows, 'no sneaky sips of wine, tonight.' Presumably this bulletin was intended for Lauren; or perhaps not, or not entirely, perhaps it was also an instruction for me to watch Lauren.

Lauren looks soulfully into my face and says, 'Whose life is it anyway?'

'Not yours,' says Mum, clipped, officious, 'because you're under sixteen. It's my duty to take care of you.'

'Stop,' murmurs Lauren darkly, 'before your kindness overwhelms me.'

I frown at Mum: *Leave her alone*. If Lauren is to survive, then this carefulness must become second nature; and if it is to become second nature, then Lauren must start young.

'Who does the injections?' I ask.

'I do.' Lauren hauls the plaster cast from beneath the table into view, and knocks on the chalky surface. 'Fewer injection sites, lately, though.'

Mum saunters towards us, but halts in horror at the sight of the untouched ingredients in front of me on the table. 'Haven't you done the dip yet?'

'Apparently not.'

Lauren smiles, picking up the avocado and the pot of yoghurt. 'It's rather lumpy. Two big lumps, to be precise.'

'I'll do it in a minute,' I reassure Mum. 'It'll only take a minute, I promise.'

Reluctantly, she resigns herself, her mouth dimpling in disgust. Then she continues towards us, presses down onto the table on slack splayed hands, and says brightly to the top of my head, 'Lauren is very good, though.'

Lauren frowns fiercely at me, a clear statement of suspicion.

'I mean,' chatters Mum, 'there are all sorts up there at the hospital, in Lauren's clinic. Drinkers. People who make no effort to look after themselves.'

'I'm not convinced that it makes a difference,' says Lauren quietly to me. 'My best friend at the clinic, she takes as much care as I do, but it makes no difference. For her, it's one hypo after another.'

Above us, Mum swings her fluffy head from me to Lauren. 'But at least you try,' she urges, ecstatic. 'And that's the important thing, isn't it.'

Lauren scrapes to her feet. 'Is it?' She assembles the crutches. 'Watch me triumph over adversity,' she says to me, with a brittle fragment of a smile in her knowing eyes.

'Where are you going?' complains Mum, as Lauren bumps towards the doorway.

'Mum,' Lauren swivels angrily on the huge sticks, 'I'm a cripple and I'm going away to use all this spare time of mine on a worthy project; I'm going into the living room to write a letter to Gorbachov about world peace.'

Mum puffs like a wary cat. 'Are you?'

The crutches punch the floor again. 'No,' Lauren calls, impatiently, 'I'm going to write to my ski instructor.'

Mum ignites with outrage: 'Your ski instructor? The one who broke your leg for you?'

Lauren, in the doorway, turns her head very slightly in our direction. 'He didn't break my leg for me,' she barks. 'I broke my own leg.' She shuffles around to face Mum. 'And he came to see me in hospital. From thirty miles away. Twice.' The *twice* twangs in the distance between them.

'He as good as broke your leg,' Mum calls after Lauren. 'He was *in loco parentis.*'

I try to concentrate on the ingredients.

'What did I ever do,' Mum whines, 'to deserve a daughter like that?'

'Give her time, Mum.' *You don't know how lucky you are.* I return to the ingredients, realize that I need pepper. I want proper pepper, smoky black grits, not Mum's usual sneeze-powder. Hopelessly I scan the kitchen. From the living room, Lauren shouts: 'Lalie, your friend is here, the weird one.'

I look up, into the hallway, towards the front door. Jane, cantering down the stairs, pauses to peep through the tiny window on the landing. She turns away with a wrinkle of her nose. 'God. Lucy Evans.'

I lay down the avocado. 'Lucy.'

'Oh, no, Eulalia,' Mum whoops in warning, 'this is a *family* day.'

I turn to complain that it is not my fault if Lucy decides to call, but I lose the energy. Instead, I go towards the door, colliding with a cloud of Jane's hair. The doorbell screams, oblivious. I open the door.

'Lalie!' One of the few enthusiastic welcomes that I have had since I arrived home. Lucy is a silvery blur, surrounding me in a hug, subsiding again onto the doorstep; she is one huge undulating smile with limbs. Her hair has been snatched into a rubber band on the top of her head so that it spills in all directions and tickles the tops of her ears. She is wearing no make-up. Her lack of make-up shocks me, or, rather, I am shocked to realize that she must have always worn make-up, mascara or pencil, undetectable but crucial to the Lucy Look, a miracle medicine for pale eyes. Without make-up, the eyes are opals.

'I heard that you were home,' she coos.

'How?' I am home for one day. I did not tell her because there is no time for visits.

'I saw Hopalong at the supermarket last week, in the car park, in a trolley. And she told me.'

'In a trolley?'

Lucy laughs lightly. 'Yes, young people, eh? But, anyway,' the words gathering momentum, 'guess who I've brought along with me . . .' And she gestures grandly across the garden.

Ali is coming slowly from the car to the path. The small distant face is tense but yanked by a smile. *Ali*: Lucy has brought Ali to see me.

'I thought I'd try,' Lucy is chattering, 'on the off-chance: and there she was! Home until Tuesday!'

'Coincidence,' I call to Ali, approvingly.

The smile spasms. She seems to be holding her breath, and quickening her pace.

'French plait:' I point to Ali's hair, in amusement. 'Eurodolly,' I goad, when she reaches us.

Stopping in front of us, Ali dabs her hand against the surface of her hair, self-conscious and vaguely defensive. 'I think you're reading too much into my hair, Lalie,' she says with a short laugh.

'Did you ever,' Lucy shrieks excitedly, 'have your hair in a plait like this?' She loops a fingertip from ear to ear, miming a lobotomy. 'Heidi-style?'

'No,' we reply together.

'No, me neither,' she says hurriedly, subdued.

Ali and I cackle together at her.

Then Ali frowns. 'You're busy,' she says to me, definitely, fearfully. 'Your little sister said. Some party for your Gran?'

I wave away this worry. Looking at Ali, I remember that French children were so distinctive when I was a child, when they came en masse on trips to our school. Why? *Smart Casuals?* A contradiction in terms for the British, at the time. So, where have all the French children gone? Do I not have the same opportunities

341

to see them? Or have all children become indistinct, American-flavoured? And if so – if all our lives are filled with indistinct television shows, food, cars, words, heroes and heroines – will the landscape, the buildings, follow the trend? The style of architecture which means, to me, France and Spain – the walls of pale-painted plaster, baked lemon crusts, with the wooden fronds of shutters – will this eventually disappear? To be replaced by what? Red brick?

No one on the Blaney farm, apart from Gran, has ever been abroad. How does it feel, never to have been abroad? Never to have walked among those buildings, listening to the sound of abroad, and smelling the smell of abroad? The sound is mopeds, droning and bleating; but what is the smell? Food, presumably: coarse sweet sponge cake in Spain, perhaps, or steaming olive oil. Or possibly the soapy antiseptic slosh pushed across the pavements by the mops of householders and shopkeepers. Or perhaps it is simply smell, the smell of streets. In Britain, cold Britain, streets are gaps between houses, shops, bus stops. I cannot remember a time before I travelled abroad for holidays; but if I had never been, would I have known that there are places in the world which do not look and feel like Enfield?

'Come in, come in.' I usher them into the new hallway; and onto the thick new carpet, which is almost bouffant.

'Oh, look,' squeals Lucy.

'That's Dory,' I tell her. 'Erin's little girl.' Dory is standing in the middle of the hallway, sturdy legs wide, forefinger hooked over her lower teeth, staring at us. It amazes me that small children can continue to stare when the stare is returned, that they lack the reflex to look away.

Lucy is cooing, 'Hellooo,' and ruffling Dory's feathery hair. 'When I was small,' she muses loudly, as I shut the front door behind us, 'I thought I'd grow up to be someone special.' She breathes a light note of despair. 'And when I was not so small, actually.'

'Doesn't everyone?' I shift Dory gently by the shoulders, clearing a path for us.

'No,' she continues more forcefully. 'Look around at them, Lalie: happy with their jobs and their houses.'

'That's *now*, Lucy. I'm sure that, once upon a time, they thought they would grow up to be special.' Perhaps it is not possible to grow up otherwise.

'No,' Lucy says again. So, now she is special to have felt that she was special.

'Did you?' I ask Ali for confirmation.

Ali shrugs. 'Yes, I suppose so.'

'But I still feel it,' Lucy insists. 'I can't believe that this life is my life.'

It would be pointless to say I-know-the-feeling; so, instead, I say, 'It's not the *end* of your life.'

Lucy's serious face shines close to mine in the gloom of the hallway. 'Don't you feel special?'

I take a tip from Lauren: 'I *am* special!' And I soothe Lucy's shoulder. 'Everyone's special.' Unfortunately, this sounds like an advert.

'If everyone's special,' Lucy counters brightly, 'then surely it cancels out.'

We are progressing slowly through the hallway to the kitchen. 'No. No one is like you.' So true. 'Look, Lucy,' I try again, 'if you're famous, everyone thinks that they're like you, that you're like them, and where's the fun in that?'

As the refrigerated light of the kitchen begins to spark around us, Lucy grumbles, 'It's OK for you, *you're* special *to* someone.'

Alex. Lucy has known about Alex from the beginning, from before the beginning. Before the beginning, she taunted me during our annual Christmas phone call until I said, 'There's nothing going on between Alex and me.'

'Why not?' she asked. And then, later, she said leadingly, 'There's nothing going on *for you*, perhaps.' She knew nothing, though; and she had not met Alex.

'He's my *friend*,' I said crossly.

'And that's a very good start.'

343

'He's my friend,' I reiterated, despairing.

'Oh, for Christ's sake, Lalie,' she bellowed, 'don't make life more complicated than it already is.'

But the thought had occurred to me, of course; it was occurring to me every minute of every day, lacing all my other thoughts, humming inside me, seeping everywhere in my warm buttery blood. It was impossible for me to live with the nicest man in the world and not consider the possibility. Or the *inevitability*, for me? I was spending a lot of time pacing around Edinburgh inside the drawstring of this thought. Because, of course, I resent inevitabilities. Yet this inevitable love for Alex was humming over me like a blessing. And I had never had a blessing before. It shocked me. It lay all over my world, a real yet unreal covering like a fall of snow.

Yet the sole problem was Alex. I was busy divining for his feelings. Sometimes, *yes*; and then, suddenly, *no*. I was reading very carefully the chaotic script of his everyday movements, re-reading, reviewing. Yes and no. Usually yes, but I began to doubt my judgement. But when it was yes, I pondered how? How would it happen? During a drunken stupor? But we were never in a drunken stupor. During some other exceptional circumstance? But we lived together, we had been living together for so long that no circumstances were exceptional for us: power cuts, job interviews, late nights, bereavements, we went through the motions, the choreography already existed for us. So, how would it happen? I was living in dread of the unimaginable, impossible moment. And I was numb, all the time, with shock: he was my *friend*, how could he become my *lover*? He was, to me, almost a brother. Almost: Mum's words would have been that he was *Not Blood*. And it is blood, only blood, which is thicker-than-water, too thick to mix. But Alex was not water either. So what was he?

Sometimes I blew on the new surface of the world to try to find the old, familiar, sludgy world underneath, but without success. And the strange blood continued to beat inside my ears. The irony is that I would never have chosen Alex: he did not correspond at all to the identikit pictures which I had carried for so many years inside my head. There is no mystery for me about Alex. *WYSIWYG*, he says happily of himself: What-You-See-Is-What-You-Get. But, then, not every woman wants a baddie: even Scarlett O'Hara spent her life in pursuit of the goodie.

Mum looms from the sparkling centre of the kitchen. 'Lucy.' Then she halts. 'And look who else!' she announces, several tones higher. 'Ali Mortimer!'

Ali shuffles with a shy Hello.

'Hello Mrs Blaney,' sings Lucy.

'What a time you've picked for a visit!' Mum is persisting with the upbeat tone, but I know better. I can detect a threat from Mum at fifty paces. 'It's Gran's Grand Finale.'

Lucy swings into a chair. 'But we're almost family, Mrs Blaney,' she chirps.

Mum issues a trailing, 'Yes,' which means No.

'Tea?'

'No, thanks,' Ali says, apparently oddly shaken, as she sits down.

'No, no tea,' rejoins Lucy. 'I don't drink tea.'

'So, Ali,' begins Mum, blindly but accurately dumping the components of the aborted Operation Dip onto the table in front of me, 'what are you doing, these days? Are you still in France?'

'Yes,' she replies, settling her skirt onto her lap with the palms of her hands. 'I've just moved into a new flat. Much nicer. Much bigger.'

She is not coming back: the realization thumps in my chest.

'Oh, lovely,' coos Mum. 'On your own?'

How do I know that she is not coming back? A new flat means nothing.

'No. With my friend Elinor.'

But I just know. And I know that I know.

'That's handy. At least you're not on your own. I bet your mum's pleased that you're not out there on your own.'

I watch Ali smiling politely over her own incomprehension.

Mum is asking, 'Do you have French friends?'

'Oh yes,' replies Ali, gaining confidence.

'Really?' Not good enough: more details required. 'Where do you find these French friends?'

Lucy is bored. She turns to Dory, who is wandering watchfully in the open doorway, and twitters some baby-language. Dory pirouettes, ungainly, with a coy smile.

'Well . . .' Ali is thinking, 'I suppose I met some of them through work.' Her blank dark eyes stare into the distance as she tries harder: 'And both Elinor and I play a lot of tennis, so we meet people at the Club. And Elinor goes to a gym.' She relaxes, glances at Mum to assess her success. 'Neighbours, too,' she finishes.

Erin appears in the doorway, scoops Dory into her arms, and smiles over the baby blonde head at Lucy. 'I think we'll try the toilet,' she mutters pleasantly, turning away with floppy Dory.

'What work do you do?' Mum is asking Ali, watching the avocado slithering into my hands from its reptilian skin. Lucy reaches for the pot of yoghurt, and snaps through a portion of the seam of foil lid and plastic rim.

Ali laughs. 'Elinor has a job now with an advertising agency, managing the British accounts. She never imagined that she would be at all interested, but she loves the job. She has discovered that she has a head for business. She makes a lot of money, now; much more than I do.' The same embarrassed laugh. 'I'm still teaching. English. I don't mind. And I'm doing a post-grad. degree.'

I look up at her. 'Are you? I didn't know.'

She glints under my sharp gaze. 'Well, I've only just begun,' she says faintly. 'I don't know whether I'll finish.'

Lucy throws the contents of the yoghurt pot into the bowl.

Mum retreats marginally from the table. 'And what about you, Lucy?'

'Don't ask,' she blares. 'I'm working in a nursery.'

Deftly, I rescue the bowl from her busy hands. 'But you hate children!'

I detect Mum peering closer at this unnatural monster.

346

'It's not children,' Lucy complains, licking her splattered fingers. 'It's plants.'

Mum relaxes. 'Oh, a garden nursery, how nice.'

Lucy grunts a denial through a mouthful of finger. 'I hate it. It's a shitty job.'

Mum steps backwards.

'Boring. Hot in the summer, cold in the winter. Awful customers.' She pushes a fingertip along the inside of a curl of avocado skin. 'Awful owner.' She turns aside to me. 'What a wanker! He leaves me alone all day long. And he's a penny pincher.'

Mum sighs a small sigh. 'Sounds rather like my job, here.'

'And,' Lucy embellishes, 'I think he's having an affair.'

Silence. Eventually I say, pointlessly, 'What do you mean?'

Lucy flicks her cataractic eyes very briefly towards mine. 'An affair. You know. Sexual intercourse.' Then she grins at me, a finger dawdling in her mouth.

'How do you know?' Lauren speaks from the doorway, summoned magically by the mention of sex.

Lucy turns, unconcerned. 'Because he makes phone calls in a low voice.'

Lauren swings casually forward on the crutches. 'Everyone makes phone calls in low voices,' she says dismissively. 'I remember when Lalie used to make a lot of phone calls in a low voice.' She sends me a sure, superior smile.

Mum's arms nestle across her chest. 'Did you want something, Lauren?'

'Paracetamol.'

'*One*.'

Lauren thumps across the tiles. Ali frowns darkly at me and whispers, 'How did she do *that*?'

'Ski-ing.'

Lauren squeaks around. 'A temporary setback,' she announces to Ali. And then, to Lucy, 'Perhaps he's involved in smuggling. Plants.' She turns back, returns to her mission. 'Lynd says that drugs heighten perception.'

'*I'll* heighten *his* perception,' Mum mutters angrily.

Suddenly Lucy beams at me. 'And what are you doing with your life, Lalie?'

'The same.'

Mum's tongue rustles. 'Looking after the lame dogs of this world.'

Lucy rotates the beam to Mum. 'My mum has worked in the Oxfam Shop on Saturdays for ten years.'

'Really?' Mum's smile is rigid. 'Unfortunately I had so many children that I never had time for the rest of the world.'

Lucy stretches and runs both hands over her sweet mess of hair. 'Oh dear,' she says brightly, 'the old story: kids to keep us at home, the modern version of footbinding; kids to keep us quiet.'

Mum's mouth flinches with distaste, possibly because she does not consider Lucy as *Us*. 'You have a lot to say, then, do you, Lucy?' she asks with barely concealed scepticism.

Lucy sparks with surprise. 'Now?' She shrugs emptily. 'No. But I might, one day.'

'And you, Ali?' Mum smarms, warmly.

Ali becomes still, waiting for the answer to settle. 'I like the kids whom I teach,' she decides. 'But I don't know whether I'd want one of my own.'

Mum nods as if she is in a daze. 'I suppose they'd interfere with your travelling,' she says flatly, confusing a life abroad with travelling.

Ali muses seriously. 'Well, no.' Her face slips sideways into her cupped palm. 'Because I could travel *with* one; or I could *not* travel.'

'My dad didn't want kids,' Lucy announces, brightly. Notably she did not say *My dad didn't want me*. 'But my step-dad did, and I *know* why.'

The atmosphere twitches with dread.

'Because he wanted to stop stepping in for my dad, he wanted to place his own official stamp on us. Poor Elliott was his stamp.'

Mum comes forward again, and peers anxiously into the bowl in my hands. 'But your mum,' she says, 'didn't your mum want

Elliott?' Her face, still focused on the bowl, is misty with pity.

Lucy's face shrugs. 'Oh, yes. She wanted kids. She really liked having us.' As if they had been guests.

Mum's expression of pity rises, floats across the table, and fixes on Lucy. But I know that it is not *for* Lucy; it is for Elliott, born to be a stamp, and for Lucy's mum, whose treasured experience of mothering was, in Mum's opinion, wasted largely on Lucy.

'How is your dad?' I ask Lucy. The whisk is coughing now on the bottom of the bowl, beneath the green surf of the dip.

'Triple bypass.'

I pause. 'Heart?'

Mum utters a croak of horror.

'Yes,' answers Lucy quickly. 'I told my mum, and she said, *But he's so young.* I said, *Mum, he's a jazz musician.*' Her lower lip pokes forward, her eyebrows rise. 'And, anyway, he was so young, once, but not now. But she said, *He's forty-nine and that's no age.*'

'No,' says Mum quietly, 'it isn't.'

'It's nearly fifty,' Lauren corrects, dubious, across the room.

'Thank you, Lauren,' Mum whirls, 'but I think we can work that out for ourselves.'

Without looking, I sense one of Lauren's Don't-shoot-the-messenger shrugs. But more importantly, the front door is rupturing from the smooth lacquered lintel. It swings away into darkness and leaves a little round figure busy in the freshly siphoned sunlight. The figure is bending beneath a hovering UFO of a hat, bending inside an inky polka-dotted silky dress, picking up a bloated black handbag from the doorstep.

'Gran,' wails Mum.

The UFO lifts and Gran's pale patchy face floats upwards. 'What? Am I late?'

Mum reaches upwards to calm her quivering blonde curls. 'Not at all,' she says more normally. 'But where's John?'

Gran's leather-toughened trotters strike the soft carpet. (Will I have those dense fat feet when I am old?) 'He's parking,' she bustles. 'But there's a strange car in the way.'

Beside me, Lucy's chair jumps across the tiles. 'That's mine. I'll move it.'

Mum flaps a hand in our direction. 'Two of Eulalia's little friends have dropped by,' she explains.

Gran's gaze twitches through the dimness towards us. I take this opportunity to say, 'Hi, Gran.'

Lauren squeezes in with me: 'Hi, Gran.'

Gran laughs, which so often serves as her reply. (Strange, then, that Mum should refer to her as a Miserable Old Cow). 'How nice of Lady's friends,' she says.

Ali is simpering politely in her seat; Lucy is fidgeting, planning how to pass.

'They can't stay,' says Mum.

'And he wants to have a quick look around that big old car out there,' Gran continues, unhearing.

'That's mine,' I say, rising from the table. 'My biggest,' I add, joining Lucy and ushering her towards the door.

'That's yours?' squeaks Lucy, stepping onto the doorstep. 'Your biggest? How many do you have?'

'It's old,' I reassure her. 'It was cheap. It's my motorway car: safe and reliable.' Not cheap on fuel, though, unfortunately.

She inflates, to breathe into more questions and exclamations.

'Not the same as a run-around-town car,' I explain quickly, 'or a country-runs car. You don't have one pair of shoes – do you? – for hill-walking, and summer Saturdays at the shops, and nights out. So, if you have more than one pair of shoes, why not have more than one car?'

'Depends on the car, Lalie,' she says doubtfully. She means the price of the car.

Depends on the shoes: I am thinking of Ali's shoes, continentally luxurious. 'My cars are cheap,' I repeat reassuringly. My lovely cars, my own cosy cars. 'I have an eye for a bargain: it's in my blood, remember?'

I cannot see Dad, so I turn back on the doorstep. Then I turn

350

again: 'Oh, Lucy, by the way,' I whisper urgently, 'Ali's dad is having an affair. Or was.'

Lucy lights up with horror. 'After what I was saying about affairs?'

'Well, no, before.'

She rolls her eyes to dismiss this. 'Why didn't you tell me?' she continues in the savage tone.

'I *am* telling you. I couldn't *say*, in front of Ali.'

'But you could have kicked me, or something.'

But unspoken communication is not Lucy's forte. 'You know very well that if I'd have kicked you, you would've said *What?*'

I return to the kitchen to find everyone dispersed. Gran's voice is rattling in the distance, in the living room. Do voice boxes grow old, then, too? Dry and wrinkled? Mum's replies are faint and brief, mere dabs of words onto this new choppy surface of sound. I can detect nothing of Lauren, not her drawl nor the thud of her crutches. I can see Ali in the utility room, standing on the back doorstep, looking out into the garden. I slip beside her to find that she is watching the cat. It is ridiculously contorted, but casually, so that it can lick itself. She laughs briefly: 'And they get away with it. We still think they're cute.' Then she turns to me. 'We seem to make a habit of missing each other.'

'Well, yes. Near-misses.'

I know that I want to say *Stay with me*, but I do not know why. Or perhaps I do know. I feel, I have always felt, that Ali is the one of my old friends who was, is, most similar to me and yet she remains a mystery to me. I feel that I have barely begun to know her. It will take time. I tip back and forwards for a while on the thin silver lip of steel which is sunk into the concrete step, and ask, 'Are you happy with Elinor?' Immediately I am painfully aware that I sound like a life insurance salesperson.

She turns to me again, but this time with a smile. 'Yes. And thank you for asking.' She means this; perhaps people do not often ask.

I shrug away the attention; transfer it with my gaze to the cat, who remains awesomely self-absorbed.

'And you?' she asks. 'You and Alex?'

351

'Oh, yes, fine.'

Alex and I have moved south. Or, Alex moved south, for a job, and then there was nothing left for me in Edinburgh, or not so much, and I had no job, so I followed him. And Mum said to me, with grim satisfaction, 'So, you're back.' But I am a long way away from here, beyond London; London is between us. And she said, 'So, suddenly, England is not so bad.' But I am not living in Harpenden or Luton or Hoddesdon or any of those other places where we Blaneys went for shops and hospitals. Nor Doncaster, Reading, Crawley, all those places through which I have travelled in the past few years: my small crumbly city does not feel to me like England, *that* England. Mum said, 'You're a gypsy, just like the Blaneys.' I protested: 'Mum, the Blaneys have been on their farm for millions of years.' But she was emphatic: 'Gypsies nevertheless. The Irish are international gypsies, stopping still for a generation or two if they like the feel of a certain soil between their toes.'

Now Ali is saying very quietly, 'I'd die if I came back. There's nothing for me, here.' She looks at me. 'Elinor is right for me,' she confirms gently, 'for everything that I am, or want to be, or want to do. She's the right person for me to live with.' She shrugs against the sudden silence.

'I know.'

'She's the best person in the world,' she says flatly, almost bleakly. 'She's the kindest person . . . the cleverest person . . .' Ali stops. 'She's very beautiful,' she finishes.

'Yes,' I agree. 'She is.'

'So why should I want to live with anyone else?'

Beyond the flimsy fence, over the fields, a sooty smear is trailing into the sky, waving low over the horizon. Behind me, in the house, Lucy is yapping softly to someone. To whom? Gran? Mum?

'Look,' I show Ali, 'see? They're burning the fields.' Or, the fields are burning.

Beside me, she stiffens slightly to attention, and then steps down onto the patio. I follow her, and we cross the small lawn together.

Leaning on the fence, to frown over the fields, the black smoke. She mutters, 'It's illegal, isn't it?'

'I'm never sure.'

She dips her chin down onto her resting, folded, tipped-over, shadowshow butterfly of hands. 'The stupid thing is,' she says softly, 'that if I was living with the grossest man on earth, it would be more socially acceptable than living with Elinor.'

'Yes.'

'Can you *believe* that?'

I breathe a soothing non-specific sound out over my own hands towards the distant smoke. *Yes. I mean, No.* I stay still, and say nothing, because now she is talking to me and I want her to continue.

She flips around with sudden impatience, and leans back against the fence. 'When I fall in love with someone,' she says, 'I don't *check between their legs*, you know?'

I laugh carefully. 'Yes, I know.'

'It's not so very important,' she insists, more seriously.

How do I make her see? Without stopping her in her tracks. 'I *do know*.' No difference; and yet, the startling smoothness of a woman's body.

Her muddy gaze does not falter from its unhurried, apparently satisfying climb over the brown brick surface of the house. 'People have some funny ideas, don't they?' she says eventually, in a lighter tone. 'You know: *implements*, and all that.' The gaze springs down to me, with the quick incredulous cat-watching laugh.

I laugh too, with her; we are co-conspirators. 'Keep your voice down.'

But I am pondering: *best, kindest, cleverest*? 'Was Elinor after Deborah?' *After Deborah died.*

'Before,' Ali replies cheerfully. 'In Paris.'

I twitch with surprise. 'But you were so miserable. After Paris, in Spain.'

She smiles, slow and sure, in reply. 'Because I didn't want to come back.'

Which makes sense. 'People think that Simon, for me, was something to do with Deborah.' *After Deborah died*. I correct, 'Well, *Lucy* thinks so.'

We laugh a little: *Lucy*.

'But I've been thinking,' I tell her, 'and I'm not so sure. I suspect that it was much more simple, that it was good ol' Something Else.'

Ali is nodding contemplatively.

'I mean, in the very beginning.'

'I know,' she says, still nodding, 'I remember.' Now she stops nodding and smiles fondly, to mimic me, '*Simon-Steiner-this*, *Simon-Steiner-that*. All rubbish. You fancied him. No more, no less.'

I agree, 'The rest came later. It's easy to forget the beginning. People think that I was wrong about Simon, but the very first time that I ever saw him,' when he was sprawled on the sofa, 'I knew him. When I looked at him, I saw passion, Simon had passion.'

Ali's face flares with dismay and derision.

And I halt her: 'Oh, I know, I know that he didn't know what to do with his passion, I know that he was useless, that he was a fat lot of good in the end . . .' I shrug: full stop. Releasing her gaze from mine, I lean back on the fence, fold my arms, cross my ankles. 'But whenever we were together, whenever we were alone, I felt . . .' What? I search inside, find an old-fashioned word, '. . . cherished.' A less old-fashioned word: 'Relished.' Catching her eye with my sudden smile, I finish dryly, 'Which is what it's all about, isn't it?'

Her eyebrows skip skyward, airily sceptical, but there is no denial.

Now I remember that I had wanted to listen to Ali, not to have Ali listen to me. That I had felt that Ali was the mystery. Not me. But now I am telling her, 'Simon was the Steiner whom I understood.'

We glance into each other's eyes: *Deborah*.

'Simon told me something about Deborah.'

Ali looks away, shrugs: *How do you know that he was telling the truth?*

I realize that it is her duty to raise doubt. Her duty to Deborah. But I tell her, 'If I learned anything from my time with Simon, I learned to recognize the truth from him. Which was rare enough . . .'

She relents, turns with a sad smile, opens herself to my words. 'She was very low when she died.'

Ali says nothing for a moment, but now her reply seems very sudden: 'That doesn't surprise me.'

'No?' I say, idiotically. Does she know, or not? *What* does she know?

'No.' She looks into the distance, eyes narrow, so that she seems to be scrutinizing the wall of the house. 'Because it's so hard to come back. To real life.' These last two words were said without conviction.

'Oh. Yes. You said.'

She says nothing more.

So I say, 'But I wish I'd known.'

'Lalie . . .'

Turning on reflex, I am surprised to find that I had drifted; and surprised, even, to find Ali.

Her gaze mixes into mine, fixes, sets mine. Holding me still, she hushes, 'What could you have done?'

So everyone says. But since when have I believed what everyone says? Is it *true*? It would be nice if it were true. *Nice*? I stop, lost. Lost for words? Lost *in* words. Except for one sudden, different question: how can *everyone say*, when I've told no one?

Gran has waddled to the doorway. She stares short-sightedly into the garden. 'Where's Aaron and the baby?' she barks at someone; not us. Then she rotates unsteadily and we hear, 'Is she still living off the parish?'

Mum's voice bites through brick wall into the garden. 'Gran, it's not *the parish* anymore, it's *Social Security*. And I've told you, John has paid his stamps all his life and we've never claimed a penny until now, so it's about time.'

Ali and I laugh nervously. I can barely believe that Mum is

answering back to Gran. To her face. Ali says, 'We must go, Lucy and me. We shouldn't be here.'

I glance back at the doorway. Gran has gone, but Lucy is hurrying across the grass towards us. She arrives, breath jingling inside her lungs.

'Lucy,' Ali says quickly, lightly.

'Yes?' The word flutters out of her mouth.

'I think we should go, I think we should leave Lalie to it.'

I interrupt, 'The word is *abandon*.'

Pained, Lucy says to me, 'I was discussing divorces with your sister Jane.'

'Why? Who are you thinking of divorcing?'

She laughs but immediately compensates with a deep breath, tightening the rein on her respiratory chaos. 'Ali, you have the right idea,' she manages, the words shortened by lack of oxygen. Spinning around, she draws us behind her towards the house. 'Women are nicer than men.'

Ali turns to me, eyes sprung wide: *Who told her?*

I shrug, and call ahead to Lucy, 'Even Jane?'

'Well, women are *prettier* than men,' she muses, without turning. 'As Lauren says, we look better in dresses.'

Laughing, Lucy startles the cat, which darts, outraged, from the flowerbed. 'Men aren't worth the paper they're printed on, are they?'

I falter, to consider this.

And ahead of me, turning back to me, her small white face blinks cleanly against the looming brick wall. 'Figuratively speaking, or whatever.'

1990

....

'Please, Lucy.'

In front of me, she falls gently onto her arm which strikes the doorframe. Against the drapes of a domestic interior, the ruched coats on the cloakroom wall, she is the colour of willow bark.

'Please.'

She sighs the sigh of the good loser.

'Fabulous.' I step back into the communal hallway and bounce my car keys on the palm of my hand.

She slumps out of the flat, flicking the door shut behind her. 'Ten minutes,' she warns resentfully.

'Ten minutes,' I repeat jollily, untruthfully: not *Ten minutes*, but *Trust me*.

'I can't believe you're making me do this,' she shouts as we thump out onto the street.

I unlock the passenger door first, for her, and then dart into the road to the other side. 'You're a free agent, Luce.'

'Oh, yes,' she drawls in disgust, snatching at the door. 'I have chosen to submit to you.'

'It'll be fun,' I chirp, busy with my keys.

She is struggling with the seat-belt, whipping the hot air and then teasing the spool in search of the twist. 'Lalie, I thought I could rely on you never to use the word *fun*.'

Turning the wheel, I shrug with my eyebrows. 'Old age, no doubt.'

We are going to an Open Day at our old school. The Day is the school's twentieth anniversary celebration.

'No,' I had told Lucy on the phone, 'of course we're not

357

celebrating our school. Not unless we're celebrating having left. No, we're going to gawk at a horrible spectacle.'

Now I remark, 'You're wearing glasses.'

The radio is squawking under her twisting fingers. 'Well,' she says, glancing at me through the pair of thin glass pebbles, '*you* obviously don't need *your* eyes testing.'

I laugh to myself for a while, waiting until she settles on a station, before I ask, 'So, why the glasses?'

'I'm short-sighted.'

'All of a sudden?'

'No, but I hadn't bothered, before, with an eye test.'

I suspect that I should go to an optician; I suspect that I am marginally long-sighted.

'But then I was passing the new optician's shop, and I saw his son.' This is said uproariously. She winds down her window and smiles broadly into the stream of air.

'You're joking,' I try hopefully.

She gives me a shiny glance.

'Don't tell me, Lucy: he has lovely eyes.'

She turns back to the blaring draught and shouts, 'And, just think, I can have discounts on all those lenses as I become older and blinder.'

'Talking of which,' she says after a moment, turning back to me so that the air smashes through the spout of hair, 'have you seen your brother lately? Now *there's* a nice-looking lad.'

'Lucy.' No, I have not seen Lyndsay lately. He was out when I arrived yesterday; he stayed out; and he was in bed this morning. I cannot imagine how he looks; or cannot imagine that he is *nice-looking*. When I saw him last, at Gran's send-off, he was virtually bald and very tall: a mutant baby. Now I close my eyes, concentrate, but Lyndsay comes pedalling out of my memory inside his plastic car, and he is six or seven years old. 'He's *sixteen*,' I say.

'Old enough to marry,' she goads.

'Not old enough to marry *you*.'

The wind, squeezing through the narrow opening of the window, is beating on the smooth shield of her face. 'Oh, come on, Lalie,' she shouts above the commotion, out into the street, 'what's a brother between friends?'

'Don't you dare.'

We glide hopelessly to join a queue of cars. Lucy winds down the window until it disappears. Lounging with her elbow in the empty frame, she says, 'Wrong way around.'

'What?'

'Aren't *brothers* supposed to protect *sisters*?' She grins at me but then flicks her attention around to the occupants of the surrounding cars.

My own car is simmering beneath us. I run my gaze along the shelf of shops on either side of the road: this road, the road along which I travelled twice each day for – what? – seven years? The road to my old school. Some of the shops which have survived are unexpected: the small independent jewellers with a thin fur of blood-red velvet lining the sparse window display-case; and the electrical shop, which I was never sure was a real shop, or merely a place for repairs, despite the boxes of new kettles, irons, and radios piled in the window. But the pram shop – The Pram Centre – has gone.

The pram shop had two levels, two floors of prams exposed by the one huge window. It reminded me of my own dolls' house, the front wall swinging away to provide a cross-section of the dolls' stilted home lives. Where is that old dolls' house? How did it become lost? It was made for me, the first-born Blaney, by Grandad, Mum's Dad. It was evidence, for me, that he had existed. Because he died before I was old enough to have grown my own memory of him. The tiny house was hard evidence, from his own hands, plastered with his fingerprints.

Think of the hours and hours, Mum used to whisper in awe, over my shoulder, towards the little roof.

Grandad had had hours and hours because he was ill, very ill, he had nothing else to do. He had furnished my little rooms, patting antimacassars onto the backs of the chairs and pasting a scattered mosaic of mirrors around the scratchy flock walls. The four, square, outside walls bore paper printed with little bricks. Where had Grandad bought wrapping paper printed with little bricks? And where do people buy prams, now, without the pram shop? I have pushed the car back into gear and we are rolling slowly past the building, which is now Video Rentals. But there are no prams anywhere, any more. There are buggies, and life is easy. Mum spent my childhood threatening to save The Pram for me: me, the first-born Blaney. And did she? Is it in the loft, heavy over our heads, or perhaps bulky in the back of the garage? Erin became the first of us to give birth, third-born Erin, Mum's third-time lucky. And Erin is a buggy-mum. So, what happened to the pram? Is it lost; or is it still waiting, Mum's curse on me?

'Anyway,' Lucy pouts, 'I was only saying. I see your brother down the pub, and he's a nice-looking boy, but I'm not a heat-seeking missile. Credit me with some forethought, Lalie; some restraint, some subtlety, some *dignity*.'

I cluck derisively. 'If you have those qualities, Lucy, then the Queen has a huge collection of discount vouchers from biscuit boxes.'

She snaps open my glove compartment in revenge and stirs the deep silt of pens, barley sugars, emery boards and petrol receipts. 'Tests,' she muses aloud, noisily snubbing the glove compartment.

Tests? A glassy, sunny wink meets my curious glance. Eye tests?

'Well,' she starts, 'have you considered having an HIV test?'

HIV: the familiar warm flare of worry singes my stomach. 'No. Not *really*.' Not more than anyone else. 'Why?'

A pallid barley sugar spins invisibly quickly inside its cellophane chrysalis and flies on Lucy's fingers to her mouth. 'Do you think that I should?' she slurps.

'Well . . . *I* don't know.' Be careful, Lalie. 'Why? Do you need one?'

'Well, *I* don't know. That's what I'm asking *you*.' She ducks and hauls one foot into her lap, jeans creaking. What was the name of this position? Or is, for people who still do it. Half-lotus?

'Well . . .' I dance the car into a different lane, 'are you at risk?' Why is she making me do this, making me sit stuffed in the driving seat, talking like a form mistress?

She snorts a laugh and cracks open another barley sugar. 'Everyone's at risk, Lalie,' she says, utterly knowledgeably.

'Well, then,' I complain, rather pointlessly.

'Christ,' she rips, her attention snatched out of the open window, 'we're almost there.' Her frown falls back on me.

Twenty years: when I was a pupil, I felt that the school had been there forever. It existed over and above and beyond me, a black hole. But we both have a history now, and mine is the longer: the school was built in 1970; I realize now that it is younger than me.

I realize now that time is short. It was not so short when I was even shorter. When I was small, the six week school summer holiday was a strange airless independent world: day after day, the paddling pool leaking slowly into the hot crisp lawn; and those dusks, the hours and hours of steaming sunless sky which was never dark except in my broken dreams. September was a long way away. But nowadays I am forever bumping against Septembers. I am outgrowing time.

Mum had two children by the time that she was my age. The pictures of us, us three, form a slippery grey grime at the bottom of the bag of Blaney photos. In those old photos, all the colour of the sixties is blotted black-and-white; yet in the most recent photos, the black clothes worn by Jane and me are gaps in green grass and blue sky. In the old photos, we are all tubby: baby-fat on Jane and me, no doubt; but what about Mum? Was she Mumsy-tubby, barely between babies; or was she sixties-tubby, suddenly well-fed after a childhood of rations? I remember that she looks extremely happy, my young mum in those old photos. But was she looking at us with those smiles, or at Dad?

I always assumed that I would have children: it was natural; like being born, and dying. It was the middle of being born and dying. For Mum, childlessness makes a nonsense of life.

What will you call them? Mum liked to ask me: these new characters which I would be bringing into my life-story.

Until recently I assumed that I would have children, but *later*. And now I am not so sure. Mum must feel that I am unnatural; as unnatural as if I will never die. But for me, on the brink, childbearing does not seem natural but profoundly unnatural: from the growing of another body inside my own, to the smashing of my current cosy life. Or, *fragile* life? Perhaps it is something which will happen, like learning to drive and taking exams; something which everyone else manages to do and I will do too. But, for now, it is such a relief to live in the world of adults, at long last, that I am wary of children.

When-I-was-your-age is no longer simply a story told to me by Mum, sometimes a lullaby and sometimes a reprimand. I am old enough now to know the truth: that she was the same age as me, that she is the same as me, that we are the same. Yet now more than ever the smiler in the sixties' photos seems a very different creature from me. Mum feels that I am unnatural, but we both know that I have never been a manly woman, an unwomanly woman. I am not in between.

Lucy is winding up the window with surprising vigour. 'Do you think anyone else will be here?' she asks as we roll into the busy car park.

Deborah, no; Ali, no; Roz, probably not. 'Yes,' I answer, 'my mum.'

'Noooo,' she brays in disbelief.

I nod sadly. I sat in the kitchen this morning insisting to Mum that, 'You *can't* go,' as if her plans were contradicting some law of physics. I could not believe that she would choose to visit my old school.

'You forget,' Mum said in a superior way, 'that almost all of my children went to that school: my association with it is longer than yours.'

At lunch time she said, 'You go on ahead with Lucy. I must go to the supermarket. Then I'll come along, and meet you there.'

'But will you be all right,' I asked her, 'coming along on your own?'

She looked surprised and then scornful, and replied, 'I won't be coming along on my own; I'll bring one of the others.'

But who? There is no one else around at home, except the cat. Dad is working. Lauren left this morning before I was awake. When I came downstairs for breakfast, Mum told me that Lauren had gone with the saxophone to a friend's house, 'for a jamming session.'

'Sugar-free, I hope.'

Mum smiled wanly and said, 'She'll be there until this evening. She's . . . what does she say . . .?'

Banging kitchenware, I guessed, 'Triumphing over adversity?'

'Yes,' said Mum, satisfied. Then she added cheerfully, 'Minxville.'

Erin is busy: a vague, gentle, butterfly-busy in the different world where she has her home, two stops down the line. And Jane? Jane is in Watford.

It is six months or so, now, since Mum told me that, 'Jane wants to live in Watford, she thinks that Watford will be ideal.' And today, according to Mum, Jane is shopping in Watford for a three-piece suite: 'Because the old suite went to Bill, remember?'

Was I likely to have remembered this, if I ever knew?

'You're set up,' Mum continued, 'when you have a nice suite, aren't you.'

Are you? Alex and I have a mortgage, now, which is cheaper than rent, but we have no suite.

'But they cost so much; as much as a car.' Mum's sigh brushed the burnt air around my slice of toast.

'Less mobile than a car,' I complained.

'Well,' said Mum briskly, 'I hope so.'

Then I took the opportunity to ask Mum about Jane: why did she stop working as a model?

Mum swung down into a chair, sliced a crust cleanly from my toast, raised the sooty twig towards her mouth, and paused. Her bottom lip bloomed. Eventually she said, 'I think that she felt that there wouldn't be much work for her in modelling for much longer.'

I pulled apart the melting middle of my slice.

'Use a knife, Eulalia.'

'But there won't necessarily be much work for her in commercial video production for much longer,' I objected. Because of the recession. 'And it pays less.'

'Well, yes,' Mum agreed, frowning thoughtfully, dabbling two fingertips in the tiny pool of melted butter on my plate. 'It's odd that, for someone so nasty, she has so little business-sense.'

Mum was left with Lyndsay: 'Lyndsay will come along with me.'

'Mum,' I warned, 'Lynd will *not* come.'

He was still in bed. Apparently, the late nights and late days are convalescence after GCSEs.

'You never know,' Mum mused mysteriously. 'He might. It's just possible that the idea might appeal to him in some strange way. You never know, with Lyndsay.'

I asked Mum about Lyndsay's plans for the summer.

'He will only say,' she replied good-naturedly, removing the jar of Marmite from me to some sparse cavernous cupboard, 'that he is going to Tibet.'

'Presumably he has asked permission from China,' I remarked.

'He says that the sky is different, there,' she was continuing, faintly interested, in the sleek, fitted distance.

'It's thinner, isn't it? Thinner air?' I reached across the table for the tabloid, and ruffled the grey pages. 'He should do exercises.' To build up his blood; wheezy Blaney angel on the top of the world.

'In fact,' she said, swooping in front of me with a fistful of damp cloth, 'I think it's because he can't face his Maths result: he wants to be as far away as possible.'

And, apparently, Lyndsay will need Maths. Yesterday, Mum and I had been discussing Lyndsay's plans for the future.

'He'll do English, won't he, if he stays on to the Sixth Form,' I had presumed.

'Aha . . .!' Mum had exclaimed flamboyantly, '. . . that's where you're wrong.' Then she had settled under a frown of concentration: 'Because Lyndsay's latest conviction is that Science Is Art.'

This had jolted me from my almost aimless wandering towards the furniture catalogue on the table. I had turned to see the effort of Mum's concentration forcing channels around her mouth. 'Discovery Is Revolution.'

'Really?' I had uttered. 'I mean, does Lyndsay really say that?'

Then she had slackened with a shrug. 'Go up into his room and look at the wall.'

So I had gone upstairs and found Lyndsay's vacant room. The wall above the slim single bed is covered by an enormous poster. Peeking from the doorway, I had recognized it immediately: *Metabolic Pathways*, which had flown over my years and years of Biology classes. It is a map of the fizzling galaxy of intracellular orbits: oxygen and sugar seep into the system somewhere, into the cell, and, one whole wall later, one moment later, and every moment, there is life.

This morning, thinking of Lyndsay at the top of the world, I discarded the newspaper and complained to Mum, 'Why is the sky not big, here?' Why is it only big abroad?

Mum ducked to the window. 'Because it's broken up,' she replied. Then, shuffling in her slippers from the kitchen, she added, 'I fancy Florida.'

'But you've just been to Thailand,' I replied thoughtlessly. The story had been that Mum had a policy which matured so that she could afford to take Dad away on holiday. What do *policy* and *matured* mean? Will I ever have policies?

'So?' whooped Mum archly. 'Do you have a problem with that?'

'Well, no,' I said hurriedly. 'But who will look after the little ones?'

Mum shrugged, unconcerned. 'I'm not sure that they need looking after.'

I mused, 'It's nice for you to have some money now.'

She shook her head. 'I needed money when I was young.' Then she smiled wickedly. 'Anyway, I think that your Dad and I should call in on Canada, too, for a while; to check up on Gran, of course.'

So, no escape for Gran, not even in the New World. Because the Blaneys do not take no for an answer.

Now Lucy is frowning over the car park and protesting, 'But why would your mum want to come here?'

I shrug wearily. This morning, when Lucy was venting the same derision and despair at *my* decision to come, I told her that I wanted to find out what has happened to everyone. I would offer the same reason for Mum's fascination, *She's nosy*, but in most cases Mum seems to *know*: it was Mum who told me that Mr Allan has divorced, remarried, and had two small children.

'One of the increasing number of men who marry again in their forties and have another little family,' she said coldly. 'A second bite at the cherry,' she added venomously.

'But how do you know?' I wailed with excitement. 'About Mr Allan, I mean.'

Distracted, she fluttered in irritation. 'Everyone knows.'

'Two children?'

'A little boy called Thomas,' she said, much more interested, 'and a little girl . . .' she frowned, suddenly forgetful, '. . . it's some awful invented name . . . Catrin?' She wrinkled her nose. 'What's wrong with good old Catherine?'

'Nothing, unless you're Welsh,' I muttered. 'Catrin is the Welsh form of Catherine.' I knew a Welsh Catrin at college.

She sparked with surprise. 'Is it?' Then, darkening with scepticism: 'But Mr Allan isn't Welsh, so why not stick to the original?'

For Mum, there is a simple division among names between original and invented. I have noticed that original seems to mean biblical: so, bizarrely for an atheist, the Word of God reigns supreme, if only on this particular, limited issue.

'Mum,' I began wearily, 'all names are translations.' And derivations, and diminutions.

'But from what?' she breezed confidently.

My fuse was beginning to fizzle. 'And you can read the original, can you? In Hebrew? And what about before the Bible?' Anglo-Saxon? Greek? 'And outside the Bible?' Muslim? Japanese?

She shut down the argument with a huge huff.

We sat in hot, silty silence for a moment. Eventually I said quietly, 'Thomas and Catrin, eh? And it's the same for Mr MacKenzie.'

Mum was sucked spectacularly from her sulk. 'What?'

'Mr MacKenzie: new wife, new baby.'

'How do you know?' More of the thin high tone, the blazing Blaney gaze.

I shrugged off her avid scrutiny. 'We write sometimes. Christmas cards.'

'But you never told me.'

'You didn't ask.'

'I shouldn't have to ask,' she trumpeted.

I waited, and eventually she begged: 'Well? What's the story?'

So I relented, traded my gossip. I told her that Mr MacKenzie took early retirement years ago and went to live near Oxford with the new wife. I did not tell her that I had been surprised that it was early retirement, that I had been waiting to hear of his retirement ever since I left school. To me, Mr MacKenzie had always been middle-aged; but now, to my shame, I suspect that this was due solely to his loss of hair. Which, thankfully, is one problem that women do not usually have to face.

'Who?' Mum yapped. 'Who is the wife?'

I shrugged again. 'Some woman.'

'Oh, really?' she brayed in sarcasm. Then, calmer: 'And the baby's name?'

'Ambrose.'

'Oh,' she breathed, in wonder.

This morning, when I was trying to persuade Lucy to come to the Open Day with me, when I suggested that we would find out what has happened to everyone, she moaned, 'But we know what has happened to everyone: weddings and babies.'

367

I puffed incredulity into the phone. 'Weddings and babies haven't happened to us.' Nor to Deborah. Nor to Ali.

'But we're different.'

I was sitting slouched in the hallway, peering down at my cold, naked feet, the bony frets beneath the skin. 'Are we?'

'Yes.'

'*Are* we? *All* of us?'

'*Yes. Obviously.*'

The babies will be on display today. Why are babies such sources of parental pride? Perhaps I am missing the point, perhaps the answer is very simple: perhaps the source of pride is the *cleanliness* of the baby. Anyone can have a baby but not all babies are *clean*. I know that it is no mean feat to keep a baby clean. The proud parents, my ex-classmates, will be rotating around the buggies, showing on their faces the rapture of the saved. Because they believe that they have found unconditional love and secured their own immortality. How sad, then, that there is a such a fundamental drawback: parents cannot see their baby as anyone other than their baby; and the baby will never see my ex-classmate as anyone other than a parent. And *parent* has slightly negative connotations. If we have such a limited view of the people who are closest to us, then what hope is there for strangers? But, then, perhaps it is those who are closest who must be kept at arms' length.

Having twisted into a parking space, I settle the car and switch off the engine.

'This is it, then,' says Lucy flatly. She snatches into the glove compartment for another barley sugar, which she holds tightly.

This Open Day will be filled to the brim with indistinguishable babies and the endless echo of the one-and-only question, What-are-you-doing-these-days? I watch Lucy heaving herself disdainfully from the car. What will be Lucy's reply to the one-and-only question, never her favourite? Several months ago she was head-hunted by a rival nursery across the road to become their manageress. I suspect that she will answer that she works in horticulture, well aware of the possible confusion with Haute Couture.

I am teaching. Mum likes to say *Two teachers in the family!* because Jane is training to be an aerobics teacher. I hope that Mr Allan asks me what I am doing, because my answer – Adult Education – will seem to him to be a contradiction. For Mr Allan, education is for children. (And children are for education). No doubt he knows about evening classes, winter evenings of recreation and self-improvement, of Badminton and German, for jovially well-adjusted citizens, who, in less secular times, would have been going to church. All evening, in the Community Centre car park, cars tumble in and out of line, drenched in floodlight. Perhaps Mr Allan goes – or would like to go – to classes: Genealogy, Gemology, who knows? I teach in the evenings, four evenings each week, on three different sites, but the classes are in literacy. Mr Allan would judge any such class worthy of a discreet aversion of his clean glass-buttressed gaze; dyslexics excepted, of course, Susan Hampshire and Einstein or whoever.

He will assume that the people who come to work with me in abandoned classrooms in the evenings are very different from me. If not physically and mentally different, with small heads and tight eyelids and distressed tongues, then otherwise different: not merely *blue-collar* but *blue-overall*, young men draped from top-to-toe in tough blue cloth to protect against damage. And these young men will sound different from me, too; mumbling and stumbling, heads hung forwards over their words. I remember from my schooldays that Mr Allan's term was *Lad*, in the sense of He's-not-a-bad-lad with the suggestion of the contrary, and the hint of his own powers as saviour.

But no one comes to my classes in overalls; or no one except me, if jeans are overalls. One of the Tuesday women, Deanna, arrives each Tuesday deep inside a cashmere shawl. Throughout the week, many of the others – men and women – arrive from work in suits. Work was most often cited, in the beginning, as the reason for coming: promotion at work, promise or threat. *I'm not up to scratch.*

Scratch, so arbitrary but indelible.

The other main reason was children. My books had told me to expect these children, the hankering of their parents to be able to help them with their homework. But the books were wrong because these children need no help. Most of them are mooching through their A levels with finely tuned ambitions: doctor, banker, quantity surveyor.

One man, Josh, came originally to a class for a dare. Another man, one of the Johns, came with his wife, Susan. Two sisters-in-law, Delia and Joy, come together on Thursdays. Mary did not come at all to her first class but stood unseen in the corridor for half an hour, afraid, crying, before going home. Recently, when she told the story to the others, they whooped their disbelief: *No, not you, Mary; not you, Mary, surely.*

Several of them run their own businesses (*Fine with figures*, they tell me ruefully). So there have been perks for me, it has been a good year for me: discount plumbing and car repairs. One man, Jacky, told us that he blames his lack of schooling on his parents' business: 'It was a farm and there were cows to milk.' (And suddenly we all wanted to know about farms, all the shocking details, snowdrifts and awesomely early mornings). Everyone else agreed with each other that It-just-didn't-click-I-just-wasn't-interested-and-then-I-got-behind-and-then-more-and-more-behind. There was illness, too: David the plumber says that he was *delicate*. And Bridie discovered last year, when she failed a medical for the police, that she is partially deaf.

Sometimes we spend the evening filling in forms: a suggestion inside my kindly cheerful Resource Packs, which are eager for tasks to be relevant. And I have found that forms are often fun, nowadays: the routes marked in colour down the ladders of questions, the pages twinkling with logos and motifs. But I like to start the evening with a warm-up, surprising everyone with a few words which have been hanging unseen around us and daring them to attempt a sketch: *government*, perhaps, and *environment*, or *Europe* and *European*. The nib-noisy air wobbles with reticence, punctured in places by a few pleased-as-punch pen-slapping slouches; then comes a keen anticipation; and finally, when I reveal the spelling, a collective gasp and a vortex of congratulations and commiserations. Now they have begun to bring words of their own. And often the rest of the evening will turn around their suggestions, their difficulties brought back for me from their working week: perhaps *adding-words* (argument or arguement? and why not hopefull for full-of-hope?) or *shun-words*, ac*tion* and deci*sion*. And I like this, because how else can I know what they do and do not know?

And all the time I am learning how I make words; slowing ahead of my students, backtracking, tracing the steps before I can take them forward with me. Making the unconscious conscious, for their benefit. I arrive home breathless from working so hard so fast. I suspect that I spend my nights sleeping to the rhythm of the assurances which I spend my evenings repeating into pale posies of faces: *the rules are not rules but guides, and everything is changing all the time, and you know more than you think that you know, so trust your instincts*. Which sounds like something that Gran Blaney would say, but mixed with my own golden rule, *Always Answer Back*.

Because I am working in the evenings, Alex cooks dinner: I shop during the day, he cooks in the evenings. I arrive home from class to find the flat baking in a steam of seasoning and spice. No wonder the whole world wants a wife. Alex cooks my favourite foods because he insists that favourite foods are vital in the cold drifts of work-an-evening tiredness. When I arrive home so late there is nothing left to do but sit down together. So these short evenings are the most leisurely that I have ever known. But now, in the sickly Saturday sunshine, Lucy is tugging me across the scuffed school-grey asphalt. 'What's the hurry, Lucy?'

Bounding ahead of me, she groans miserably. 'Let's get this over as quickly as possible.'

I can see a group of Sixth Formers swirling slowly on the steps outside the main entrance. Am I correct to remember that we – the pupils – were banned from using the main entrance? that we, the main component of the school, the reason for the school, the workers and the product, were forbidden to stand in front of it?

I can tell that the teenagers on the steps are Sixth Formers because they are not wearing school uniform, I can tell from the suits on the boys and the careful grace of the girls: the sheen sealed onto them by the Sixth Form, the modern-day state-funded version of finishing school. They are uniform without uniforms. But, then again, perhaps not, because how would I know? How would anyone know? Now nearer, I can hear the molten confidence in their voices, they seem so *Full of themselves*: one of Mum's favourite expressions, but for Mum this serves as an insult, and I am not sure that I intend an insult, not for these Sixth Formers who are so briefly and terminally in full flight.

Beyond them, beyond the entrance hall, some of my ex-classmates will be answering Mr Allan's question with, 'I'm at home, now,' even though they are not at home but in the school's main hall. But *at home* means – what? housewife? no one is a housewife nowadays, not in my generation: *at home* means *mother*. *I'm at home now* implies a full circle. They have completed the circuit, they are complete.

They are sealed against the world, self-contained. I think of my evenings with Alex: I am at home too, very much at home, yet I manage to work.

I have spent my life trying to slip from circles. And if it is so difficult to step out of a circle which is someone else's invention, then I am beginning to sense that it will be much more difficult for me to escape my own, to turn away from my own life. If I should ever want to do so. I did warn Alex. I told him, in the beginning, that I was afraid that I would flounder. The exact words were probably *Let you down*. And *let down* means *drop*. He laughed kindly, dismayed, and coaxed, 'Don't say that.' He meant, *Don't damn yourself out of hand*. And, of course, he was right. Yet wrong because it was important for me to be able to say. Because there *is* such a word as *can't*, even if – worse – it is a disguise for *won't*. And I still doubt, sometimes, that I *will*.

I follow Lucy through the buzzing hush of the busy entrance hall to the double doors of the main hall. We halt and peer through the delicate steel veins in the reinforced glass. I was given a detention in the main hall, once, by Mr Williams, Senior Master, for talking. I remember that the post of Senior Master was relatively new, created especially for Mr Williams. What is a Senior Master when there is also a Head and a Deputy Head? Is Mr Williams still here, an employee in this building? At the time of my detention, the newly powerful Mr Williams' favoured punishment was an instruction to copy the entire list of stocks and shares from the newspaper. Why is so much of school life about punishment? I remember Mum telling me that, during her schooldays, transgressors were given the choice of belt or cane, and that this prompted endless anticipatory conversations among the schoolgirls concerning the pros and cons of both methods, and their own preferences: not an encouragement to healthy psychological development, surely?

My eyes have not yet adjusted to the crowd in the hall, I cannot distinguish the subtle shades of individual faces. If anyone brays at me that I have or have not changed, is either a compliment? Which would I prefer, changed or unchanged? I glance away from the floor to the walls. Above the shelves of trophies, the long broken line of dim golden urns and shields, the spoils of House competitions, is the huge board engraved with the names of Head Girls and Head Boys. Below, year by year, the bits of brass shuffle from shelf to shelf, often piling on one and washing away from another; but above, the names drop line by line from the crest of the board to the bottom.

'*Deborah*,' says Lucy, beside me; a thud of dread in her voice, the boom of a sudden remembrance that something has been forgotten, that something very important has been left somewhere irretrievable.

Deborah's name is still there, of course it is still there, half way down the board, held between all the others.

Lucy and I twist away from the door. Leaning back against the wall, we blindly watch the sedate dance of the nearby people around the display boards. I remember, with an ice-burn of surprise, that

I had wanted so much to visit the grave, the Manchester grave, once upon a time. But why? Because a lump of stone and a tiny plot of Manchester soil would mean nothing to me. If Deborah is anywhere, if my memories of Deborah are anywhere, then they are here. And seeing her name here, like this, in this list, provokes me to think differently for a moment. 'The statistics are right,' I say to Lucy, disappointedly. 'At least, I think so.' I saw some figures recently in a magazine article. 'There were a hundred of us, and two of us are dead.' Because, oddly, Deborah's name is balancing another memorial: our Head Boy died during his first year at university, from Hodgkin's disease. He was Mark Robertson, a bit of a physicist. Poor Mark. He was doubly unlucky because most people survive Hodgkin's. It occurs to me that the rest of us are survivors. But none of us look like survivors: the people who are leaping past me from the flapping double doors look very robust. We were first generation Welfare State. Laws were passed to prevent us dying for all the usual reasons. Death for young people became strange. I remember that, six or seven years ago, there was a local boy, a student at the local college, who went missing during a trip to the States, and was never found. At the time, at school, our rumours focused upon bears or the Moonies, as if these were the only ways to die or disappear in America.

One hundred people in our school year: one accident, one illness, one suicide? I am shaking very faintly; inexplicably, I try to cure this with a deep breath. My lungs harden but the fluttering continues in the rest of my body. I look at Lucy. She is chewing a thumbnail and looking at nothing.

With a snap of saliva, she turns to me. 'Car accidents, I suppose?' she says quietly. 'The most common cause of death, under fifty years old, or whatever?'

'Outside wartime, I suppose.' Statistics are easy. I know the figures. 'Take a thousand of us,' I whisper, 'and before we're twenty-five or thirty-five or something – I don't remember, but young – six of us will have died in cars.' This total might be for men, it might be different for women, but I do not want to complicate the issue. Lucy raises her eyebrows to indicate that she is impressed by the magnitude.

But I am thinking: there were roughly one thousand of us here at school at any one time; so, if we count Deborah, there was someone else.

'Annette Constantine,' says Lucy suddenly.

Annette Constantine, our Deputy House Captain when we were – what? – thirteen, fourteen? Annette Constantine, four years older than us, four inches shorter, four stone heavier. With a slow smile and a voice too small for her body, and for the job of Deputy Captain. Her arms were always slung into a fold, and she shuffled everywhere in a pair of Scholls. She died in a car crash shortly after leaving school. Such an exceptional death for such an unexceptional person. I remember that people said, at the time, that she *died instantly*. But isn't death always instant, in a sense? Surely every death has its instant. But, of course, I know what they meant, that she died at the instant of impact. It is supposed to be a comfort, *She died instantly*. But I am not sure that this is so, I am not sure that it is any comfort at all. Annette Constantine was especially unlucky because everyone else in the car survived. *Without a scratch*, people said. And she was sitting in the middle of the back seat. I have always assumed that the back seat is the safest; and the middle of the back seat, the safest of all. It is the place where I sat so often when I was a child. Annette Constantine fell forward and out through the windscreen; stretched out in an instant and flew.

'Do you miss her?' Lucy asks. Do I miss Deborah.

Miss? When Deborah died I felt that I had been stopped in the middle of something. Suddenly I knew the truth of took-my-breath-away. When she veered across the road and lost her life, I lost track of mine. I could not find my way back. But eventually I realized that there was no place to go back to. Life goes on now, but not from the same place, it is not the same life, not for me. And of course not. No, I do not miss Deborah. To miss is to ache for someone who is somewhere else, but Deborah is nowhere. Missing is a passion, and passions spark change on the surface of the world, there is always the possibility – if only a logical possibility – of bringing those changes to the world. But there are situations about which I can do something, and situations about which I can do nothing, and now I know the difference, I know when to stop, I know that I can do nothing about Deborah, the absence of Deborah.

I glance again at Lucy. 'I know that this'll sound funny,' I try, very quietly, 'but, no, I don't miss Deborah.' I am looking away again, away above the swell of the entrance hall, but I shrug my eyebrows for Lucy. 'Not *miss*. Because she's *gone*. But I do . . .' Do what? I try to squeeze the word from inside, but the inside is raw. But I do. I do. I do *something*. I cannot talk too much to Lucy about Deborah, because the story is not mine to tell. But secrets do not exist out of time: some burn out, some burn deeper, it is impossible to predict.

We stop together in silence for a moment. Then I say, 'I miss Ali.'

Lucy's enamelled fingernails strike her fluffy white hair. 'But you and Ali are very close,' she squeaks irritably.

'No, we're not.' *Not as close as you and me.*

'Yes, you are.' She snatches some device from her hair and it collapses around her face: the ruins of a perm.

'You look like Goldie Hawn,' I utter before I can stop myself. Is she cross with me or with the hair?

'I always think of you and Ali as very close,' she is protesting, trawling the hair. 'Although I know that she finds you rather remote.'

Remote? *Me? Ali?* And Lucy *knows* this? *How* does Lucy know?

'Look, Lalie,' Lucy is lecturing, the handful of hair tottering high on her head like a performing poodle's, 'she hasn't abandoned you, she just *happens* to be in France.' She laughs suddenly, briefly, apologetically. 'C'est la vie.'

'And I do miss Roz.' I did not realize how much, until a few moments ago, when I looked through the door into the place where I was given a detention for talking to her. Her life, however distant, should be running through mine. 'I'd like to see Roz,' I tell Lucy.

I would like to *see* Roz: just *see*. I would like to see her signature – that bold survivor's signature – on a Christmas card, even. Just a sign. We do not need to be friends again but I need to know that she exists. 'But I don't even know where she is.'

Lucy reaches out, hauls open the door, and suddenly I am passing through into the main hall. 'You can watch over someone without always knowing where they are,' she says to me, as the door closes behind us. 'But, then again, you do too much watching.'

The crowd is boiling in front of us and I can see Mum in the middle because she is shining blonde-Blaney-bright. Her mouth is open for simultaneous talking, laughing, and eating. I suspect that she is eating a piece of the dusty white shortbread which appears at the canteen hatch on special occasions, shortbread made by the cooks, without butter, made with margarine: shortbread without flavour, gratuitous shortbread. 'My mum's here,' I tell Lucy, incredulously. '*Already.*'

Lucy twitches to attention and then bounds happily ahead of me through the crowd towards Mum.

'Ah!' Mum calls to us, through an exploded mouthful of shortbread. 'Girls! Hello.' We sidle next to her and she swallows the pale paste before explaining with glee, 'I persuaded Lyndsay to accompany me.'

I glance around. 'So, where is he?'

Mum rattles with a sugary, dusty laugh. 'He's *here*,' she roars, slapping a small hand onto a big arm.

I follow the arm to the face. 'Lynd? Is that *you*?'

The eyes are the clue, the eyes are everything. 'Of course it's me,' he laughs down on me. His hair is black, and quite long.

'You're a Goth,' I utter, in shock.

I am not sure whether his mumbled reply is *No* or *Neo*.

Lucy's happy nudges are nestling on my elbow. 'It's Lyndsay, all right,' she says approvingly.

I turn to settle a frown on Lucy, with Mum's voice tapping away on the back of my head. 'And I was just talking, here,' Mum is saying, whilst Lucy is grinning mischievously into my face, 'just talking to a mother of one of your old schoolfriends – Tilda Penny? *Was* Penny,' the tapping drops a tone, '*now* Loveless, which is a shame, rather a sad name, especially after a jolly name like Penny, but that's life, isn't it.'

We both turn, belatedly, and confused. But Mum is veering away from us to a woman who is standing behind us, engaged in another conversation. 'This is my daughter,' Mum interrupts cheerfully.

The woman reels around, smiling, and settles on Lucy. 'Oh, yes,' she says enthusiastically, at Lucy, 'I can see. The resemblance is amazing.'

'No,' Mum is hit full-square by her own sudden intake of breath, '*this* is my daughter.'

'Oh!' The woman gazes at me in horror, and presses her hands momentarily to her mouth. 'Oh, I *am* sorry.'

And the small space between Mum, Lucy and me sparks with glances and then bursts into laughter, although I am not sure that we are all laughing for the same reason.

Suzannah Dunn

Quite Contrary

Elizabeth, a young, overworked hospital doctor gets a phone call from her father late on a Friday night telling her that her mother is dangerously ill. Over the weekend that follows, Elizabeth, on duty as ever and confronting the barely controlled chaos of a busy casualty ward, finds moments to reminisce about her childhood, its joys and its miseries. Past and present are interwoven into a series of vivid tableaux, drawing the reader into an intimate understanding of Elizabeth's life.

Suzannah Dunn was awarded a runner-up prize in the Betty Trask Awards with this, her first novel.

'In this vivid picture of "normal" life, Dunn's Elizabeth, the oldest of three sisters, is a witty, down-to-earth female whom you really care for. *Quite Contrary* isn't a weepy slice of bedtime reading, it's a well-observed chapter on growing up – and it proves a touching and remarkably unpredictable read.'   *Time Out*

flamingo

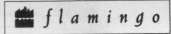

Flamingo is a quality imprint publishing both fiction and non-fiction. Below are some recent titles.

Fiction

- ☐ No Other Life *Brian Moore* £5.99
- ☐ The Kitchen God's Wife *Amy Tan* £4.99
- ☐ A Thousand Acres *Jane Smiley* £5.99
- ☐ Spidertown *Abraham Rodriguez* £5.99
- ☐ Tess *Emma Tennant* £5.99
- ☐ Pepper *Tristan Hawkins* £5.99
- ☐ Dreaming in Cuban *Cristina Garcia* £5.99
- ☐ Happenstance *Carol Shields* £5.99
- ☐ Quite Contrary *Suzannah Dunn* £5.99
- ☐ Postcards *E. Annie Proulx* £5.99

Non-fiction

- ☐ The Gates of Paradise *Alberto Manguel* £9.99
- ☐ Sentimental Journeys *Joan Didion* £5.99
- ☐ Epstein *Stephen Gardiner* £8.99
- ☐ Love, Love and Love *Sandra Bernhard* £5.99
- ☐ City of Djinns *William Dalrymple* £5.99
- ☐ Dame Edna Everage *John Lahr* £5.99
- ☐ Tolstoy's Diaries *R. F. Christian* £7.99
- ☐ Wild Swans *Jung Chang* £7.99

You can buy Flamingo paperbacks at your local bookshop or newsagent. Or you can order them from HarperCollins Mail Order, Dept. 8, HarperCollins*Publishers*, Westerhill Road, Bishopbriggs, Glasgow G64 2QT. Please enclose a cheque or postal order, to the order of the cover price plus add £1.00 for the first and 25p for additional books ordered within the UK.

NAME (Block letters)_____

ADDRESS_____

_____

_____